Goodricke's Time

A.C. Theokas

A C Theokas

Non est ad astra mollis e terris via.

A C Theokas

ISBN: 1546302964
ISBN-13: 978-1546302964

Cover artwork after Johannes Hevelius used with permission.

For deaf children, everywhere

A C Theokas

ACKNOWLEDGEMENTS

A historical novel requires research. Visits to archives and libraries to source original material remain necessary, despite the Internet. I am grateful for the professionalism and courtesies shown by The Royal Society, The Royal Astronomical Society, the British Library, the Houghton Library of Harvard University and the Beinecke Library of Yale University. I especially wish to thank Alex Stagg of the Royal National Institute of the Deaf, Anne Wheeler, Victoria Hoyle and Joy Cann of the City of York Archives, Martin Lunn of the Yorkshire Museum and Vikki Kerr of the City of Edinburgh Archives. Their assistance helped make this undertaking enjoyable and fruitful.

I thank Jim Kyle, Professor Emeritus of Deaf Education at the Centre for Deaf Studies (now sadly closed) at the University of Bristol who provided material assistance as well as point out inaccuracies in my recounting of the practice of deaf education in the eighteenth century.

Kay Coe's review of an early version led to improved pacing. Sandy Coates spotted inconsistencies in language and logic. John Moss' scalpel excised numerous errors and bloated sentences. Lewis, Marcie and Janice made numerous clarifications and patiently listened as I prattled on about the latest chapter.

Sarah Cheeseman proofread my grammatical and typographical errors. Any that remain are my responsibility alone.

Finally, I wish to acknowledge Zdeněk Kopal, late Professor of Astronomy of the University of Manchester. It was his impassioned lecture that first introduced me to young John Goodricke

A C Theokas

Prologue

Boston, USA Present Time

Cheerful children frolic on the broad expanse of a Persian carpet in the Henry Bayard Long Room of the Boston Athenæum Library. Its sombre portraits and classical statuary are not usually witness to such restive behaviour. Today, however, these restrained surroundings have been transformed into a temporary theatre for the performance of the ancient Greek myth *Perseus and Medusa*.

The sudden voice of an unseen narrator startles the children into silence.

'This is the story of the adventures of Perseus! Son of Danaë and Zeus himself!'

The youngest squirm in their parents' grasp to source the sound. Lights dim and eyes widen as marionettes as tall as the children themselves appear and step across the small stage with a typically jerky motion.

Perseus and Medusa is a curious choice for such a young audience. Greek mythology, replete with themes of violence, greed, lust and revenge, could be deemed unsuitable. Would this performance be faithful to the narrative and depict one marionette decapitating another? The dénouement of this myth is, after all, the beheading of the most feared Gorgon. But this is also the only Greek myth where magic plays a major part. A bottomless wallet, a helmet that makes its wearer invisible, and sandals that enable flight could be elements in any traditional fable. It

9

also demonstrates perseverance and courage prevailing over treachery and evil, a good moral tale.

The young audience is beguiled as Perseus commences his mission to slay the head Gorgon, Medusa. Soaring over scrolling seas on winged sandals he alights at the island home of the Graeae, the three blind Grey Sisters. He demands they reveal the location of the Gorgons' lair, lest he steal their shared single eye leaving them all sightless. Fearful and alarmed, they quickly disclose its whereabouts. The children are spellbound.

He comes to the Gorgons' cave and creeps inside. What is that horrible hissing sound? Medusa! Her hair is made of snakes! Should Perseus but glance at her hideous face he will turn to stone! Instead, he looks at her reflection in his polished shield and sidles ever closer. His little wooden sword strikes! Her puppet head pops off, snakes and all. Perseus slays Medusa and the children madly cheer.

The deep-voiced narrator returns.

'As a reward for his heroism, the gods, after his long and happy life, placed Perseus amongst the stars where he remains to this day.'

Thus was Perseus honoured. He yet holds Medusa's head in one hand, his sword held high in the other. But wait! Medusa is still alive! One of her eyes repeatedly dims and brightens.

This is the star Algol, named from the Arabic *Al Ra's al Ghul*, the Head of the Demon. Two thousand years later the true nature of this dimming would be brought to light through the work of a young Yorkshire astronomer.

1

Groningen, The Netherlands 1769

Henry Goodricke, Esquire, paced in his study. The sun had set and the feeble glow from the grate could not hold back the gathering shadows. A deadened voice drifting down from an upstairs bedroom and the interminable ticking of his long case clock the only sounds.

Recently established in Holland as a representative of His Majesty's government, his profession combined qualities expected of any diplomat or gentleman; restraint and acceptance of the inevitable in life. But he was not in an accepting mood.

He was the only son of Sir John Goodricke, the 5th Baronet of Ribston and His Britannic Majesty's Envoy to the Court at Stockholm. Sir John was, by common consent, the diplomatic corps' most quick-witted and keen-sighted. While a baronet may rank lowest in British nobility, it was a member of the order of honour nonetheless and hereditarily entailed. It was a title that Henry would eventually bequeath to his son who would one day be known as Sir John. If Henry did not quite match his father's distinguished career, he would see to it that his son did. Or so he had thought. Now he was about to learn whether he would only meet an early death.

He had married Levina Benjarmina Sessler, the daughter of a Dutch merchant, eight years earlier when he was but nineteen. Marriage into a prosperous family aided the exercise of diplomacy, but far from being simply an arranged union he did love Levina. He was enamoured by her spirit and intelligence, all the more when he saw these traits emerge in young John.

Life in Groningen had its advantages, but he now wondered whether, for the safety of his children, it had been right to remain. Anne, their first child, died in infancy. Mary and Harriet were well enough, as far as he knew, but *febris scarlatinosa*, scarlet fever, had bred within his son. Was it just last week when the physician was first summoned? He remembered asking for an honest prognosis, but winced at the ensuing clinical assessment. He was unsure whether the physician hid behind jargon or was only giving an honest opinion. It did not matter, he simply did not take to the man. He recalled his world being overturned by seemingly incessant argot.

'The malaise, dull headaches and slight fever your child has experienced, as I feared, indicate the incubation for something much worse. He has now moved to the, ah, primary stages of the affliction. There will be difficulty in swallowing, and the symptoms of a more severe fever will follow - thirst, nausea, vomiting, headache. This can be followed by the desquamate stage characterised by the detachment of the skin corresponding to the site of eruptions. Scarlatina with mixed eruptions often means either bronchitis or pneumonia will follow. If not, there remains a lifelong susceptibility to these. Of the several internal calamities delivered the more common one is a rather foetid purulent discharge from the nose due to, ah, to an ulcerative disease of the mucous membranes. I should add that a similar inflammation of the ears will result in permanent impairment of hearing and, quite possibly, its total loss.'

'Good God, sir! You are not reading a paper at some blasted academy!'

Goodricke regretted his unbecoming outburst. His son's illness was not this man's doing, but his gaunt features coupled with a cheerless deportment suggested he was allied with this disease, that he had brought it with him.

The physician had returned and was examining his son as Levina sat by. He instructed him to say nothing to her before first informing him. If the news was to be for the worse, he wished to at first bear it alone. A loss of composure was not something he wanted anyone to witness. He would prepare himself and then return to his son and waiting wife.

She spoke a bit louder.

'Bedankt voor het komen.' *Thank you for coming.*

The staircase creaked and Goodricke stopped pacing. The physician stood in the doorway, his medical bag in both hands. He spoke into the darkening room.

'May we have a little light, sir?'

Goodricke placed a taper in the coals and, in silence, lit a few candles. A small action, but it had a calming effect.

'You have your light, sir. Speak.'

'Thank you. Your son's condition is no longer dire. I believe the crisis has passed. He will live.'

A coal shifted in the grate, producing a small flare. Henry looked at it and then back at the physician, facial creases sharpened in shadow. His tone suggested this was the good news. He paused, took a breath, and continued.

'However, sir, I am sorry to tell you that I fear your son is now deaf and in all likelihood, shall remain so. I wish I were able to announce a complete recovery, but I cannot. I am sorry for it, but I must report otherwise.'

Goodricke heard the faint sound of Levina singing a familiar lullaby. The physician had apparently followed his instructions.

'You are certain there is to be no full recovery?'

He wanted to contend as he was used to doing, but knew it to be misplaced energy. Still, he continued.

'I realise that he has indeed suffered a serious affliction, but others have completely recovered, surely?'

'Not always,' the physician replied. 'The sepsis emanating from the ears is indicative of permanent damage within. The inflammation of the inner ear has grown to, ah,

13

to a suppuration resulting in a likely perforation of the membranes. At least he has not suffered a mandible abscess which can accompany this condition and is usually a sign that death will soon follow.'

'Of course. I am sure that you have done everything possible.'

He had the news he had been waiting for and wanted a moment before returning to his wife.

'Let me see you out.'

'I shall return in a day or two,' the physician said. 'Take heart, sir. He is now out of danger. So many others have not survived.'

'Yes, I thank you, you have been most …' he searched for a word. 'Clear'.

'Then I bid you good night, sir.'

Goodricke remained on the steps and watched the physician's carriage recede along the Noorderhaven canal. He heard the fading clip-clop, a woman's laughter from the canal side opposite, a dog's brief bark and then silence. He glanced up at the emerging stars as if to ask why, in all this creation, his son must endure what was surely to follow. He returned inside and climbed the stairs burdened not only with the thought of telling his wife but also how they would tell young John.

He approached the bedroom door and was confronted by the odour of the vinegar and hops applied to moisten the throat. Was it ever effective? The smell of stale sweat was added as he stepped further inside. Levina, sitting on the edge of the bed wiping her son's brow, looked up. Redness could be seen around her eyes, despite the dim candlelight. For a moment neither of them spoke. His hesitation was news enough. She looked at him and her expression turned to one of anger.

'Deze keer *niet*, Henry. Niet *dit* kind. Ik *verbied* het!' - *Not this time, Henry. Not this child. I forbid it!* she said, a fist pounding each syllable into her chest.

She calmed and sighed.

'What has the physician found? You may speak plainly. He sleeps,' she said, gesturing over their son with a clenched cloth.

We can speak plainly enough from now on, he thought.

Thankfully, scarlet fever had not afflicted his other children. Had the belladonna helped? It was children, mostly, it sought out. The sepsis the doctor had mentioned had been all too evident. John's eyes had been stuck shut by a brownish secretion while his ears discharged the same characteristic material. It was as if his small body could not contain all the putrefaction within. At least he did not suffer from desquamation of the skin, one of the more obscene symptoms. If the physician was right, the disease had burned out. The foetid discharge from the ears had ceased pulsing, but not before doing damage.

Levina, breathing heavily, impatiently awaited his reply. The only other sound was John's own ragged breathing, each exhalation ending with a thin little squeak like the cry of an expiring mouse.

The long case clock chimed sweetly and triggered a memory of when he first sensed just how unusual his son was.

'Father, how does it work?' asked John, his arm upraised, a forefinger protruding from a ruffled cuff pointing up at the clock.

Henry felt a surge of pride.

A fine clock was a possession subtly reflecting the traits of its owner, a gentleman of means who was reliable, steady, punctilious. The work of the well-known London clock-maker, Thomas Mudge, it had an oak case detailed with veneered burr walnut and roundels of satin-wood and ebony. The eight-day mechanism drove seconds on a dial plate and phases of the Moon. But John, he suspected, was not the least bit interested in cosmetics.

'Now, my boy, let us see what we can make of this, shall we?'

Henry carefully lifted the hood to expose the shiny brass clockwork. He then opened the doors in the clock's waist, revealing the weights and swinging pendulum.

'*Up, my boy, up!*'

Henry knelt down and lifted John to his shoulder, bringing him eye level with the clock's movement.

John was transfixed by the gleaming gears, this one hardly moving, that one a bit faster. It all seemed impossibly complex, gear upon gear, all rotating in rhythm with the syncopating beat of the pendulum.

'Now this little one here is the escape wheel. It turns once around every minute, so it drives the motion of the second hand. And this one is the centre wheel. It turns once around every hour. So, what do you suppose it controls?'

'The hour hand?'

'Excellent, well done! All these gears you see make up what the clockmaker calls the train.'

'But what makes the ticking noise?'

'Ah, this bit here. It is known as the deadbeat escapement.'

'What a silly name!'

'Yes, yes, a silly name, but it is important as it keeps the main gear here from jumping about as the pendulum completes its swing. This is what keeps time accurate to a second a day. It all connects to the hands, and chimes and the moon phase dial just here. Do you see?'

'And these, Father?'

'The weights? Well, this one keeps the escapement moving and the other powers the chime you hear when it strikes the hour.'

John thought for a moment and then asked, 'But if the weights keep the clock going, can it still go as you wind them up?'

This rather perceptive question took him by surprise.

'Yes. Well, this one does.'

'How?'

'Ah, well, I am afraid I do not know, but an excellent question. Well said!'

'Why must it be so tall?'

'Well, because the pendulum must be very long. The longer the pendulum, the more time it takes to swing from one side to the other. The shorter the pendulum, the faster it swings. So, there is one length where it takes exactly one second to swing from one side to the other and that is the length you see here.'

John Goodricke did not yet understand the physics of a pendulum's motion or its distillation to movement more refined, but he knew one day he surely would. It was as if the brass gears with their tiny teeth, the delicate springs and the pendulum's swing would carry him to some higher purpose.

He regarded the rolling gears a bit longer and looked at his father with his little smile.

The chiming ceased, ending Henry's reverie. He felt a sadness stirring within as he turned to face Levina.

'My dear…' he began.

2

Orange Fool

Day by day, Henry Goodricke watched his son's strength, what little there had been, return. It had been six months since his recovery and the pressing concern was now not health, but education. He arrived home after another round of diplomatic duties listlessly performed. He found Levina sitting in the parlour, head back, eyes closed.

'Levina?'

'Henry. I must have dozed for a moment.'

'Are you all right my dear?'

'Of course. Just a little tired.'

'And how does he this day?'

'Fine, but yet frail, even for him.'

He sat across from her and spoke as if he had come to some conclusion.

'I will not have it, Levina.'

'Will not have what, Henry?'

'He shall not be kept here, hidden away like some rare curio, some oddity.'

'Indeed, he shall not. Why ever say such a thing?'

'He is, despite his condition, exceptional. Of this I am certain.'

'Henry, of course he is. Why must you go on in such a manner? Has your day but failed?'

'Levina, I know a father will say such things, but I am right.'

'Papa!'

Harriet and Mary ran into the room.

He perched Harriet on his knee and held his arm around Mary.

'And how are my little muffins today? Eh? Did you miss your papa?'

Mary whispered to her sister, as if her father could not hear.

'Go on, tell him!'

'We are unhappy, papa,' said Harriet.

'Yes, papa, we *are*,' said a now emboldened Mary, blonde curls flouncing as she nodded vigorously.

'Unhappy? Nonsense. I shall not allow it,' said Henry.

He looked up at Levina. He suspected from her expression this had all been prepared.

'Well, now, what is all this to-do, eh? Why are you unhappy?'

'Our brother John,' said Harriet, looking down.

'Why? He has not been troubling you, has he?'

'Oh no, papa!' said Harriet.

'We love John,' added Mary.

Levina was close to tears.

'He will not play with us.'

'Yes, and he never talks to us.'

Henry realised he needed to do a better job of explaining his son's condition, but it was difficult enough explaining it to John. There was no preparation, no training on how best to tell a child they were to be deaf for life. It was grief unimaginable. The most he could think of, at the moment, was to write notes to communicate with his son. Eventually he seemed accepting and retreated into the pages of whatever book he could get his hands on. Could he read that well before he became ill? He could not recall. He wondered now whether he was spending too much time on the King's requirements and less on his own as a father.

'I'll have a word with John, and your mother will talk with you as well. She can explain things a bit better. But you mustn't be angry with your brother. He is not well.'

'Can you make him better, papa?' pleaded Harriet.

A long pause.

'Yes, my dear. I shall make him better.'

'You must promise, papa.'

'I promise. Now, run along and I will see you before bedtime.'

'Thank you, papa,' they said in weak unison.

He gave them both a little squeeze. Harriet slid off his knee and took her sister's hand. Henry stood and sighed as they departed.

'Where is John?'

'I believe he is in your study again. He went there after his supper.'

'I'll just go and see to him,' said Henry.

'And?'

'And what?'

'You just made a promise.'

'Well, I had best keep it then.'

Henry went to his study and slowly pushed open the door. John was sitting in a chair, feet dangling, engrossed in a book. He noticed his father's entrance, smiled briefly, and returned to his reading.

Henry held out his hand and John passed him the book, *The Mathematical Principles of Geography* by William Emerson. He read the preface to remind himself why he had purchased it.

> *This terrestrial globe on which we are seated, tho'*
> *it seem large to us that live upon it, yet when*
> *compared to the magnitude of the heavens, is only*
> *like a point in it, being in a manner lost in that*
> *vast fabric. All we can do is to remove from one*

> *place to another on this little ball, and pass from*
> *one region to another, and by this means we get*
> *acquaintance with our fellow creatures on*
> *different parts of the globe, with whom we can*
> *converse, carry on trade, or transact any business,*
> *by which we make a shift to get a living.*

A promising start, but when he turned to the page John had been reading he remembered why he had lost interest.

> PROB. IX. *To find what o'clock it is in any*
> *given place when it is noon, or any other hour at*
> *your place. First, rectify the globe…*

What appeared to be a useful text in descriptive geography was more mathematical than first thought, replete with problems such as his son was reading. Many of these, moreover, required the use of a globe, something he did not have. The book sat on his shelf unread until his son retrieved it, but was it not beyond him?

Henry handed the book back and raised a finger to secure his son's attention. He went to his desk and wrote out a note on one of the cards he kept at the ready.

Do you like this book?

A vigorous nod.

Do you understand it?

Another nod.

Henry had thought his son was bright, but this was different. He was six years old and reading this? Had he underestimated John's ability? Just how bright was he? This thought only compelled him all the more to take action.

You should prepare for bed now. I will look in on you later.

Henry did not like communicating in this manner. He could not inflect or emphasise. Words fell as flat as the paper upon which they were written.

He sighed and wrote again.

John, remember your sisters love you very much.

His spirit sagged as he hugged John's small, thin body. They walked together out of the study, John clutching his book. Levina was still standing outside. John looked up at his parents, gave a little wave and went upstairs.

'What are we to do Henry?' Levina asked.

'Well, first I am going to purchase a globe.'

'A what?'

'A globe, Levina. A little model of our planet that spins.'

'I know what a globe is, Henry.'

They were both silent for a while, lost in their own musings.

Finally, Levina spoke.

'So, he chose a book? We must provide others. I assume there is not much in your library for a child.'

'It would be more accurate to say there is not much in the library for *him*, but he did select something. A geography text of all things. It is the only one I believe I have with diagrams and that contains maths. Quite a bit on sundials as well, for that matter. And he seems to understand it, Levina. Incredible. Most incredible.'

Later that evening Henry looked in on his sleeping son, the copy of Emerson still in his grasp. Was John dreaming? Could he hear in his dreams? Henry Goodricke had a renewed resolve. Nothing could be done in Groningen. He would have to return to England.

*

A fortnight later he walked along Pall Mall, to his London club, the Savoir Vivre. Since returning he had no success in locating anything like a school for the deaf. He had the unsettling thought that he could not find one because there was none to be found. He was not one to give up easily, but had to admit to himself he was at an impasse.

The shops along his route held little interest until he spotted the sign *Tully's Head Books*. A small bell attached to the door announced his entry. The shop had the warming aroma of leather mixed with the sweet smell of old paper. He had the fleeting thought that the books here were purchased for tactile qualities as much as content.

An elderly bespectacled man emerged from a back room. Goodricke wondered whether he might be French because of his make-up and ribboned wig, but the accent was all London.

'Good day to you, sir. And how may we be of service?'

Goodricke had to get a hold of himself. He had entered because of a vague sense that there might be something here his son would wish to have. But what?

'I am looking for anything you might have, um, in geometry. Something that may be of interest and appropriate for a young lad who, ah… as I say, is young.'

'Oh indeed, sir, indeed, indeed. Perhaps we may recommend a copy of *Euclid's Elements*? We carry two splendid editions here.'

Euclid. Of course. Goodricke wondered why he had never thought of that. The clerk retrieved the two copies. After flipping through the pages in each he selected the one with more diagrams. Then, taking a chance, he asked whether there might be anything available on the education of the deaf.

'The deaf? Oh my, my, my. There is not much call for that sort of thing, but we may have something. Just give me a moment.'

That sort of thing, Goodricke thought as the clerk stepped into the back room.

He removed his hat and wiped his forehead, unsure of just how much he really wanted to know about deafness. The clerk emerged holding aloft a copy of Buchner's *An Easy and Very Practicable Method to Enable Deaf Persons to Hear.*

'Perhaps this may be of some interest?'

Goodricke opened it and read.

Anatomists commonly divide the parts of the ear into sorts, namely, those which belong to the external ear, and are situated without the temporal bones; and those that constitute the inner ear, comprising all the parts that lie within the said bones.

What am I going to do with this? he thought.

He wanted to find someone *else* who has read it, someone who might apply any knowledge therein to the education of his son. He nevertheless decided to purchase it for his own understanding.

'Please wrap this for me as well.'

'Of course, sir. Might there be anything else?'

He was about to say no when he noticed a massive tome on display and, out of sheer curiosity, asked about it.

The clerk came to life.

'Indeed, sir! This is an unabridged copy of Mr Samuel Johnson's *A Dictionary of the English Language*.'

The clerk placed both hands on it as if it were a holy relic.

'The owner of this very bookshop, Mr Dodsley, assisted in its publication, I am proud to say.'

'I had heard something of this work. It is the first dictionary ever written of the English language, is it not?'

'Oh, indeed it is, sir. A work of herculean effort, if I may so.'

'And the price?'

'Four pounds, ten shillings, sir.'

Goodricke considered its purchase, despite the exorbitant cost. But his goal was to locate the appropriate school for his son's education, not keep him at home reading a dictionary.

'A bit much to carry, but thank you all the same.'

'We can always send it on, sir.'

'No, no, that will be all. Thank you.'

＊

Goodricke sat alone at a table in his club absent-mindedly stirring his tea. Another member approached.

'My good fellow Henry Goodricke! Is this the maestro himself before me? I thought you were in Holland orchestrating the business of the Crown.'

'How are you, Harry,' said Henry, flatly.

Harry Newsome was a minister for the Crown and an old acquaintance.

'Will you join me?'

'Are you sure? You seem as if you might wish to be on your own.'

'It's fine Harry. Really,' said Henry.

'Excellent. So, what brings you back to London?'

'A personal matter.'

'I see. Perhaps I might be of some assistance?'

Henry at first hesitated, but then realised the more who knew what he sought, the better.

'Harry, I should warn you it has nothing to do with secrets of state.'

'I would not so assume, old fellow. Now, what are you having?' asked Newsome, trying to lighten the mood.

'I'm not all that hungry just now.'

'Are you just having tea? Perhaps you will join me in some light refreshment?'

Before waiting for a reply, he gestured and the head waiter smartly stepped over.

'Boodle, how is the Orange Fool this day?'

'Oh, very good, sir, very good indeed.'

'Then we shall have two of those. And a bottle of my usual,' he added.

'Very good, sir.'

'That should liven your appetite Henry. Now, might I enquire what brings you to London?'

Henry explained his son's condition and that he had returned to find some way to have him educated. Just as he finished Boodle returned with the claret as another waiter fussed with the Orange Fool. Newsome waited until they departed before replying in a more serious tone.

'Bad luck, Henry, but I believe it may be good luck you happen to be here on this day. Do you see the older gentleman sitting just there?'

Newsome discreetly nodded in the direction of another member engrossed in a book, the meal before him all untouched.

'You mean the fellow having thought for food?'

'Oh, very apt, Henry, but yes. Do you know him?'

'I do not believe we have met.'

They spoke in low whispers.

'Not surprising. He is rarely here, although he is a of course a member. David Hume. A Scotsman, mind you, but still not a bad fellow for all that.'

'The author of *A History of England*? I did find that rather useful.'

'The very same, but listen. I bet you a domino he shall know something of what you seek.'

'Why should he know?'

'Let us just say it is the sort of thing he would.'

'So, what happens next?'

'I shall go and speak with him, of course.'

'Harry…'

'There is nothing to lose, my good man, nothing to lose.'

Before Goodricke could reply Newsome was up, smartly approached Hume and introduced himself. Hume slowly nodded and gestured to the seat opposite. Goodricke watched the preliminary banter. Harry made a pleasantry, and Hume smiled. *You were always a charmer, Harry*, thought Henry. Harry leaned forward and adopted a more earnest manner. Hume was silent at first, then raised a forefinger and leaned towards Harry. The discussion had taken a serious turn. Hume spoke, and Harry nodded, thanked him, rose, shook his hand and returned wearing a grin. Hume looked his way, gave him a brief nod and returned to his reading.

'Well?'

'You are in luck, old fellow. Hume says the man you seek is to be found in his very own Edinburgh. That is why he knows of him, I shouldn't wonder. And do not worry, it was all in confidence.'

'In Scotland?'

'Yes, but why should that matter? He says this Braidwood fellow teaches the deaf to read, write, speak and understand others as well. It sounds worth at least a visit. Just my opinion, mind you.

'I am not sure, Harry. I have never heard of any such person or institution there.'

'Well, as I say, Hume believes him to have an excellent reputation. And, come to that, how would you know of him? How would anyone?'

'I was hoping for someone closer, here in London perhaps.'

'Well, of course you can keep looking, but he has not heard of anyone else. At least not this side of the Channel and I doubt you would leave your son to the mercy of some Frenchie.'

'What was the name again?'

'Braidwood. Thomas Braidwood.'

Henry Goodricke decided the Orange Fool looked tempting, after all.

3

Scotland, October 1773

'Declare it, sir. You were not expecting a landscape so beauteous,' said James Boswell as he picked at his meal of mackerel and gooseberries. He regretted the use of 'beauteous', but it was too late. He pressed on. 'Surely you will now put right any in your circle who pronounce Scotland's prospect as nothing more than nature's pudenda? Some even expect the inhabitants of the Highlands to come forth howling from caves.'

Another exaggeration, but he could never stop himself when it came to defending his homeland from all critics, real or imagined.

His dining companion, Samuel Johnson, looked up from his plate, but did not reply.

A group at a nearby table burst into raucous laughter. Had they overheard, or was it a coincidence? Boswell did not care so long as they recognised whom he was with.

The phlegmatic, Delphic Johnson and the ebullient, impetuous Boswell thirty-two years his junior were a study in contrasts. Johnson was tall and cumbersome with a plodding, stoic nature. Boswell, a foot shorter, wore an alert expression while Johnson often seemed elsewhere in his thoughts. Deafness in one ear and poor sight in one eye often required Johnson to cock his head, as if he looked askance at the world. His wily intellect patiently diverted every circumstance to its design. He was more truthful where Boswell was more tactful. He preferred depth while Boswell, given more to breadth, did not dwell or brood. Boswell's moods were as responsive as quicksilver, now expansive, now deferential, equable and irascible. He was constantly measuring himself against others, the trait of a keen watcher. While Johnson observed Scotland, he observed Johnson.

James Boswell knew Johnson's opinions before they set out - and few of them flattering. He was well aware that in his dictionary Johnson defined 'oats' as *A grain, which in England is generally given to horses but in Scotland supports the people*. What will he say of Scotland now that he has seen it? He was eager to learn something of the tone a published account would take.

Their three-month tour was nearly at its end. Beginning at Berwick, they had progressed along the coast north of Aberdeen, headed inland through Inverness, out across the Hebrides, inland again through Glasgow to stop at Hamilton for the evening before returning to Edinburgh. They had travelled with the rhythm of life in Scotland, by horseback, carriage and boat.

Johnson had been pressed for some time to make this journey. Now that it was concluding Boswell sought his judgement with an irritating frequency. He had discovered a Scotland not as wild as he supposed, but was that a good thing? True, there was a network of roads superior to anything he knew of in England, but he knew it to be the result of a policy of pacification by His Majesty's government. Johnson had long suspected Scotland would lose its ancient roots altogether as a result of the Jacobites' recent defeat. The clan culture too, was fading. It was important to experience its traditions before it vanished completely. He hoped for something positive, something he had not yet experienced. Perhaps he was merely peevish after a day's journey in a poorly sprung coach.

Boswell adopted a more even-tempered tone.

'Is the food in this modest establishment to your liking?'

This was something Johnson could readily speak to.

'It is not up to the standard of The Mitre and I shall hazard it does nothing for the lubricity of one's bowels,' he sniffed, his tone no more biting than usual.

A small cloud of tobacco smoke introduced itself between them. Johnson slowly turned with a scowl to stare at the guffawing group at the next table. A candle flared as one of their number lit his pipe. Boswell knew that Johnson had once declared smoking to be a 'shocking thing, blowing smoke out of your mouth into other people's mouths, eyes and noses and having the same thing done to us'. He waited for the eruption, but Johnson only sighed and returned his attention to Boswell and replied to his earlier question.

'As far as whether the Highlands are worthy of any discomfiture brought about by their remoteness and lack of civility, permit the following observation. All travel has its advantages. If the passenger visits better countries he may learn to improve his own, and if fortune carries him to worse, he may learn to enjoy it,' his knife poking the air in punctuation. He sat back with a creak of his chair and sipped port to erase the taste of greasy oatcakes.

'Well said, sir, but might you say anything about the inhabitants?'

Johnson glanced once again at the smoker before replying.

'I shall likely require more time to consider what I have observed, but I can tell you now that I have not seen anything to dislodge any previous conclusions.'

'About what?' asked Boswell.

'The poor, my dear sir, the poor.'

'Well, sir, poverty is an iniquity. Indeed, it is.'

'It is more than an iniquity, sir. Poverty removes the means of doing good, and produces an inability to resist evil, both natural and moral. The inability of a poor man to relieve the miseries of others is a loss to society just as the lack of money is a loss to a poor man's pocket. I have found little here to dispute that.'

Boswell shifted in his seat as he recalled visits to the estate of one laird after another, all through his own prompting.

'May I then presume those of means are agents for good?' asked Boswell.

'Not always, and more's the pity, but let it be remembered that he who has money to spare has it always in his power to benefit others - and of such power a good man must always be desirous.'

Johnson wondered whether his companion understood any analysis beyond conditions specific or peculiar to Scotland. He himself had undertaken this journey because he saw it as a chance to see, first-hand, what passed for a so-called uncivilised landscape in order to assess the relative merits of the language used to describe the natural world. It was also important for him to use the life of its inhabitants as a yardstick to measure how the population might benefit from advancing industrialisation. He suspected they would not. He was perennially sympathetic towards people at the margins of life, whether it was Negro slaves or maltreated factory workers. The measure of a society was how it treated its poor, its afflicted. Not many others, he accepted, were completely in correspondence with this qualification.

Boswell was relieved they would shortly reach Edinburgh, a centre of reform. Perhaps Johnson would find something in that richer pudding to bias his account towards the positive. He thought it might also help to head off any harsh conclusions were he to point out they hadn't really seen enough of the 'real' Scotland.

'Permit this analysis, sir. Whilst you have had the experience of an unfamiliar landscape, is it not one whose sparse population foregoes any complete understanding of a people possessing only meagre trantlements?'

Johnson thought for a moment. It was true they travelled through an uncultivated landscape largely inhabited by a poor populace, but no matter. He was concerned, even obsessed, with understanding an ebbing way of life. English culture was gradually overtaking Scotland's, and he doubted it was a change for the better. Johnson recalled those few inhabitants he did meet - the landlord's daughter who endeared him with her modesty and civility and so he presented her with his copy of Cocker's *Arithmetic*, or the old woman who had refused to show him where she slept. She had been afraid, he later learned, that he had wanted to bed her when in truth it was just one more attempt to note the living conditions of all he met. Thinly inhabited by a poor people? Yes, but there still swirled in his mind images of all those who befriended him, how they taught him as much about himself as the economics of life in their own landscape.

He came back to Boswell's question.

'Yes, that is a conclusion one may accept, but still, as I say, it has not been a landscape without its evidentiary components.'

Boswell decided it was best to let go of the subject.

'What are your plans for Edinburgh? Do you intend any final survey or study?'

Johnson pursed his lips and turned his head slightly to focus his good eye fully on Boswell.

'Arrangements have been made to call on an academy there administered by a Mr Thomas Braidwood.'

Johnson caught Boswell's raised eyebrow.

'I see you wonder at this, but I understand it to be most unusual. Indeed, sir, it is no ordinary academy at all.'

4

Edinburgh

Young Hannah Upton tried, and failed, to suppress a growing suspicion. Her parents, speaking with the stranger who had earlier greeted them, were about to depart. The mares were restless and the carriage driver at the ready, but her cases had been removed and her anxiety grew. Were they actually going to return to London without her?

The measles she had contracted years earlier caused a total loss of hearing. Sycophantic physicians claimed in succession it would eventually return. It did not. Her parents had finally accepted the condition as permanent and became desperate to have her educated.

Her father, Sir Thomas Upton, saw the world as a chess board and his daughter's move to Braidwood's Academy the end game. It was hard to entrust Hannah to the care of another, but it was the last option.

'You are doing the right thing, Sir Thomas,' said Braidwood who wore a perpetually patient expression. 'I understand it is difficult to leave your daughter behind, but she will be well cared for and, as promised, I shall provide you with updates as to her progress. One more thing, have you brought what I asked for?'

'My apologies. I do have it here. I had forgotten it in all the…,' said Sir Thomas, unable to find the right word.

'Understandable, sir,' said Braidwood, who had seen more than one parent upset at leaving a child behind.

Sir Thomas reached into the carriage to retrieve a large, rectangular parcel.

'Thank you indeed, sir,' said Braidwood. 'I promise you shall have it back when you next visit.'

'Of course, but I beg you take care, we have only the one. Might I ask as to its purpose? Her mother and I are most curious.'

Braidwood remained ever protective of his methods, despite the fairness of the question.

'I can only say that it will likely assist me in her first lesson.'

'I see. Then perhaps Hannah herself will tell me one day as to its use.'

'Of that, sir, I have little doubt.'

It was time to depart. Caroline embraced her daughter and said she looked forward to receiving her first letter, immediately realising Hannah had not understood. Sir Thomas touched his daughter's cheek, shook Braidwood's hand and assisted his weeping wife into the carriage. At the driver's 'walk on', the carriage began the long journey back to London.

Hannah froze in place. Any feelings of abandonment were only slightly assuaged by the two female students, selected by Braidwood, who held her hands. He knew she would understand soon enough why she was there.

*

The next day, Hannah Upton's anxiety remained. Why had her parents made this long journey? Why had they returned without her? She had been brought to what looked to be a man's study though it was much smaller than her father's. Wearing her new yellow frock with a blue bow in her blond hair she felt fresh and clean, but not at ease. With hands folded and eyes closed she summoned an image of her parents. Was it just yesterday? They were standing by the carriage saying their goodbyes. She imagined the whiteness of a father's wig, the tracks of a mother's tears, the glint of brass fittings on leather harnesses. But the remembered scent of horse and harness was replaced by another quite real, tobacco and a note of bergamot orange. She opened her eyes and gave a small start. The man who had greeted her parents was sitting across from her.

Probing blue eyes held her in their gaze. *Why does he stare so?* This did not help ease her anxiety. He slowly reached out to take her hand and she snapped it away, eyes widened, breathing sharpened.

Thomas Braidwood sighed, smiled and shook his head. She looked down with a slow nod.

She let him take her hand and he gently guided it to his throat.

What is this strange action?

Using both hands he carefully placed her fingers around the muscles under his chin and spoke slowly. She realised he was trying to get her to focus on the deliberate and exaggerated movements of his mouth through this positioning of her fingers.

What was the purpose of this absurd pantomime? She had never known an adult to behave in so foolish a manner and leaned away. He smiled and raised a forefinger. *Be patient.*

His facial expressions came in sequence. *Yes,* she thought — *he is repeating them.* They began with a smile, but not like a proper smile. The next was a bit more difficult to follow. He pointed at his mouth. He tilted his head back just slightly and she could see how he began with the tongue, first floating and then ending against the roof of the mouth. He drew a breath and let the air out with a puff, reminding her of a trout her father had caught, pulsing as it suffocated. Then the tongue at back of his teeth and that strange smile again.

An hour passed. Or was it more? She no longer felt quite so fresh and began to sweat. She could never understand the behaviour of strangers with their expressions of exaggerated sympathy or squirming discomfort when in her presence. She never understood fully why adults seemed not to know how to behave around her.

But not him. Not only did he ignore her difference, he seemed to square up to it and, in so doing, eventually helped her to feel a bit more at ease.

They stopped for a break and, after a lunch of soup and bread, began again. He smiled and clasped his hands together in a gesture of encouragement.

He began again with those strange facial contortions.

Again.

Again.

Hannah gradually realised the point of the exercise was not the expressions so much as the movement of the muscles under his chin that accompanied them. *Yes*, she thought, *they are different and they come in sequence, but what of it?*

He next positioned her fingers along her own throat, pointed at himself and then back at her, then back at himself. Her thoughts raced.

He began again, but she could only sit there with her hand on her throat. She was now desperate to please him, but unsure what it was he wanted. She fought back tears. Again, he pointed at himself and then back at her.

Ah! she thought with a slight nod and expulsion of a long-held breath followed by a tentative smile. She now understood that she was to feel *her* muscles move in way she had felt *his* move. When they were similar she would be more accurate in mimicking the same movements of the jaw, the mouth, the lips, the tongue. He began going through the sequence again, beginning a bit more slowly, now with his right hand bobbing up and down to indicate a cadence.

The repetitions quickened.

He took her hand away and with a slight nod of his head indicated that she begin again, but this time without touching her throat.

Braidwood, gestured for her to stop and smiled broadly. He reached over to the table, picked up a card and held it up for her to see. *Hannah Upton* was written on it in large bold script. He pointed at it and then at her.

She had no idea what this meant. Was she supposed to do something?

Braidwood then rose to retrieve the large oil painting he had put aside. She gave a start. It was the painting of herself with her parents that should have been in their London home. *Why was it here?*

Braidwood propped up the painting, held up the card on which *Caroline Upton* was written and then pointed at her mother.

She wrinkled her brow.

He held up a different card, *Sir Thomas Upton,* and placed it beside the image of her father.

Still nothing.

He then retrieved the original card that began the exercise and pointed at her own image in the painting.

Braidwood let this critical moment linger.

They again together repeated the facial expressions and breathing done earlier.

Again.

Again.

He pointed at the card with the script on it and then at her image in the oil painting.

Her eyes widened.

She looked at the card and then the painting.

The card. The painting.

She knew.

Hannah Upton, for the first time in her young life, had said aloud her own name.

She looked at him through grateful tears. Braidwood stood and placed his hands on her shuddering shoulders as she sobbed. The point of the exercise was not to learn to speak so much as to begin to understand the concept of *naming* things - a critical first step in her education.

'You have done very well today my dear, a beginning most promising.'

Braidwood called to have her returned for the evening meal, gave her a reassuring hug and closed the study door.

He knew of course that his new charges could never understand him fully at the outset. Nonetheless, they could still sense kindness and patience and this was what was important in order to gain their trust. Hannah would now understand why she was there. She would remain deaf, yes, but she could now walk through a once locked doorway.

The first meeting with a student was always important and Braidwood was relieved this one showed promise. He knew full well that if Hannah had been deaf from birth it could never have gone the way it did. She would never have been able to connect his machinations to graphics on paper. His path was easier if the children had some speech before deafness struck and Hannah had been on the cusp of conversing. On reflection, this was one of the least difficult beginnings he had ever had. Was he improving or was it her own native intelligence?

He walked around his desk a few times, rapping it with his knuckles before easing himself into his Windsor chair.

He had begun his academy thirteen years earlier, but with no thought of a career in deaf education. It was not *anyone's* career. He was not a scientist or a medical doctor. It was his reputation as a competent schoolmaster that brought him to this new calling.

He was well aware that he alone had inaugurated classroom instruction of the deaf and dumb in Britain. The conversion of his little mathematical academy began with a single student. Alexander Shirreff brought his son to Braidwood in the desperate hope he might be educated. Braidwood knew he could not cure deafness, but he knew he could teach. If there was some way he might establish communication with young Charles, given the lad had some native ability, he could learn. He never accepted the commonplace assumption that deafness meant dumbness.

That was too often an excuse to avoid trying anything at all. But how were they best taught? He first acquired literature on the subject. It did not take him long to discover that serious work on the education of the deaf went back a century. Copies of Wallis' *De Loquela,* Delgarno's *Art of Communication,* Holder's *Elements of Speech*, and similar texts, occupied the shelves in his little office.

He had discovered there was no widespread agreement on how best to instruct the young deaf. Moreover, these works were either too theoretical or expounded on work with only a very few subjects. No one had ever attempted to teach them in anything like a classroom setting. There was no one best approach, no definitive manual for deaf education. Was the point to teach articulation? Were reading and writing necessary to become proficient in 'hearing' with the eye? Was this more important than finger spelling? He had to find his own way.

It was sobering to learn that a resurgent interest in the potential of the deaf to learn did not originate from any charitable impulse. The meaning of language and its role in what, ultimately, distinguished man from beast was the subject of passionate debate. The deaf, accordingly, were brought into the debate on the universal nature of language and what it meant to be 'human'. It had become the focus of more secular, less esoteric, study. Philosophers were preoccupied with the simple but important question of whether language required speech. Any conclusion that it did not would inadvertently counter the centuries old belief that the deaf were incapable of reason or education.

Braidwood, however, was not the least bit interested in adding to this dialogue nor did he even understand all of it. He had no connections with any scientific society or the world of experimentation in general. He was a schoolmaster. What he did know was that he was the beneficiary of a growing conviction that the deaf child was as capable of learning as anyone. Formal education of the deaf was on the verge of becoming, quite apart from anything else, a business and Braidwood had always been more of an entrepreneur than a philosopher. There were those with means who were quite prepared to pay him well to educate an afflicted child. The status of Hannah's parents only added to his incentive. He was well aware that those in her father's social circle would learn of his success, or failure, with her.

A soft knock on the door interrupted his reflections.

'Uncle, some tea?' said John as he looked in.

'Thank you, but no. It is getting late. I shall return home.'

John sensed his distraction and suspected its cause.

'Very well, uncle. I shall close things up here. Everything is in order for tomorrow's visit I trust?'

'Blast it, sir, do you attempt to induce some disquiet?' asked Braidwood.

John was taken aback. He had hit a nerve.

'No indeed, uncle. I had only meant to enquire if all is in readiness and to learn if I may further assist. My apologies, and with your permission I shall proceed and see to the children before closing up for the evening.'

'Yes, yes, please see to it. And be sure to tell the students who will meet with Mr Johnson that I shall stop in to see them before leaving. Wait, perhaps I shan't. It may only make them anxious'

'Yes, of course uncle,' said John, slowly closing the door behind him.

His nephew meant well, but mention of the visit only heightened his own anxiety. Visitors were a double-edged sword. He wanted to demonstrate his achievements, but was always careful not to disclose too much of his technique lest others copy and compete.

Samuel Johnson, however, was different. He had been both surprised and pleased to receive his enquiry asking if he might visit. *'Inspect' might have been a better word,* thought Braidwood. How had Johnson learned of him? Did his reputation reach as far as London? Apparently, Johnson was to embark on a tour of Scotland and the Hebrides with someone named Boswell. Johnson had inquired if, while in Edinburgh, he might include the academy on his tour. Braidwood was effusive in his reply. '*You are indeed welcome…We shall be most honoured…*' This would be a visitor in a position to provide publicity that could either increase demand for his services or damn him to disgrace. Johnson, he suspected, had a nose for charlatans. He would want to know whether he performed a true service to his charges and was someone, he surmised, who would be on their side, not his.

He had selected and prepared his best students to meet with Johnson. Never having heard of him, they would not be intimidated. At least that was what he hoped. Well, there was no point in agonising over this any further. The arrangements had all been made. He blew out the candles and headed for home.

5

Johnson & Braidwood

Samuel Johnson sighed and splashed cold water over his face. It had been another night's version of sleep in a strange room, another morning away from London, where he often remained in bed until noon. He was eager to have this day end and finally return home.

The journey through Scotland with Boswell included castles and crude cottages. He burdened himself with a singular concern for the occupants of the latter, for people with no recourse but to press on. This day would bring yet more intimacy with society's sufferers, but with a difference. These children were alleged beneficiaries of specialist tutelage. He would be grievously disappointed to discover they were under the care of a quack. If, however, it was found to be otherwise, he could close out this journey on an uplifted note, a crumb of consolation.

The widespread adoption of coffee had gradually eliminated the inclusion of whisky with a London breakfast, but not yet in Edinburgh. Johnson preferred the small tipple meant to warm the belly and stir the appetite. After his *wee dram* with porridge, he stepped out of the White Hart Inn into the growing clamour of greetings and jibes as merchants set up their stalls in Grass Market Square.

Johnson held Edinburgh in a certain regard. True, it was more crowded and less sanitary than even London, but here social classes had more proximity and interaction. He put that down to architecture as much as anything. Tall, narrow tenement buildings ringing the square housed a small cross section of Scottish society, with tradesmen and professionals, ministers and merchants rubbing shoulders in the narrow common stairs. It was a place where one with an appetite for social inquiry, such as himself, could find much of interest.

A steep lane led from Grass Market up to Edinburgh Castle. There was practically no place in the city from where one could not see this fortress looming over all. He stood for a moment staring up at it before stepping away, his walking stick tapping cadence. He gripped his cloak about him with his free hand to ward off the morning chill and felt, at that moment, every one of his sixty-four years. Reaching the top of Cowgate he waved his stick at a passing cab. The half dozing driver caught its motion out of the corner of his eye and tugged on the reins. He looked down at Johnson to gauge the gratuity coming his way and was not optimistic.

'Thomas Braidwood's academy, if you please.'

'Aye, it's the Dumbie Hoos for thee, is it?'

Johnson scowled. So, this was how locals referred to Braidwood's academy? It did not help his mood. The carriage tilted and squeaked as he hefted himself aboard.

He sensed as they moved along Cowgate, their destination was not in the heart of the city. Eventually they came to King's Park at the end of Salisbury Street and beyond that, countryside. They stopped in front of a free-standing three-storey granite building. The sign above the door read *Thos. Braidwood's Academy for the Deaf and Dumb.*

Dumbie Hoos indeed, thought Johnson.

'That will be fivepence, if you please.'

Johnson paid the cabbie, stared at the waiting palm for a moment and drew his cloak around him.

'As you wish.' The driver departed, his suspicion confirmed.

Johnson considered the drab granite facade with two small dormers in a gabled roof. Two columns of windows flanked the front entrance with a single window above it. *The students likely live here as well*, he thought. He walked up the path to the entrance, ignored the knocker and struck the oak with the brass handle of his walking stick.

John Braidwood was tending to the fire grate in the classroom as the sound echoed down the hallway. Thomas Braidwood gave his nephew a knowing look.

'Will you see to him, John? I wish a final word with the students. Take him into my study and I shall attend directly.'

Some of his uncle's anxiety had seeped into him. He walked to the vestibule, tugged at his waistcoat, adjusted his wig and opened the door to reveal the odd-looking character before him.

'Good morning, sir. I am Samuel Johnson and…'

'Of course, of course. You are expected. I am Braidwood, John Braidwood, Mr Braidwood's nephew and assistant. You are most welcome. Most welcome. Please come through.'

Johnson followed nephew Braidwood's mincing gait to a room at the rear of the ground floor. He saw and heard no one else.

'Right this way, sir, this way. Just here. This is Mr Braidwood's study and office. He is just seeing to the students. I trust you have enjoyed a pleasant journey? No difficulties in locating us? Yes, just make yourself comfortable and uncle shall soon attend. I shall see to some tea, shall I? Everything is in order then,' said John as he fluttered out with a bow.

'*Obsequious fop*,' thought Johnson, with a tap of his cane. He hoped this *Thomas* Braidwood would prove worthier of his time.

He took stock of where he was. On one wall hung a large poster depicting sketches of fingers and palms in various configurations. The title, *Chirologia or The Art of Manual Rhetoric*, provided little information. The wall opposite was lined with books. He beamed his good eye over the spines and selected *An Easy and Very Practicable Method to Enable Deaf Persons to Hear*. Turning to a random page he read:

> *Sight and hearing are two of the principal external senses, as they supply us with the knowledge of a far greater number of external objects, than the other senses put together; which though indeed are considerable, are yet of a more limited usefulness, and their impairment or loss more tolerable; But blind or deaf, what melancholy objects! Both blind and deaf, what accumulated woe!*

He snapped the book shut and replaced it. *This Braidwood may well be no fool after all*, he thought. *He has deliberately left me alone to look over the contents of his little library.*

'Well, sir, the proof will be in the pudding,' he muttered aloud and looked around for a chair.

Thomas Braidwood entered and his heart sank. The figure now before him might well unsettle the students. Johnson was sitting on a chair altogether too small for his large frame. Both hands were perched on his walking stick, preventing him from pitching forward.

The prolonged silence became palpable. *He has caught sight of my scrofula*, thought Johnson, *and so much for Queen Anne's touch.* He slowly stood and towered over Braidwood who noticed facial scarring, an eye that did not appear to properly focus and, what was that? A twitch or tic?

Johnson was dressed in a sober suit of dark brown wool with wrinkled stockings, and shoes badly in need of a rub. An ill-fitting wig poked unceremoniously from beneath a wide-brimmed felt hat. And there was an odour. Braidwood wondered whether the person now before him might frighten a healthy child to muteness, let alone encourage his deaf students to speak.

'Welcome, sir. I am Thomas Braidwood. Apologies for not greeting you myself but I was tending to the students. Thank you for visiting our modest academy.'

Braidwood grabbed Johnson's outstretched hand and pumped it with both of his.

'I thought perhaps it best we become acquainted before meeting the students. Of course, I shall be only too happy to receive any queries.'

After his initial upset of Johnson's appearance Braidwood began to get more of the measure of the man. There *was* something compelling about him. He moved around to his desk and gestured to Johnson to retake his seat.

Johnson regarded Braidwood for a long few seconds. Unassuming and plain looking, he concluded he was not someone who would stand out while seated at The Mitre. Still, he had a determined look, his clasped hands giving him an earnest appearance.

'I trust your journey was uneventful? No difficulties?'

Finally, Johnson spoke.

'None at all, sir, but I was somewhat affronted by the cabbie's lack of civility.'

Braidwood, who had an ear for these things, noted Johnson's sharp Staffordshire accent.

'My dear sir! How so?'

Johnson hesitated, but was curious to learn of Braidwood's reaction.

'He referred to this academy as the Dummy House.'

Braidwood thought for a moment and then chuckled, his folded hands bobbing.

'Ah, I am sure what was said was *Dumbie* House. It is how the locals refer to our little academy and is more acceptance than insult. I would prefer something less pejorative, perhaps, but there you are. They mean us no real harm.'

Johnson was nonplussed and could only respond with a quick nod. Apparently, the expression was not pronounced with the degree of slight he had assumed and regretted not tipping the driver.

'Well, no need for concern. You have of course met my nephew John who assists?'

You mean the fellow with the supercilious civility? he thought, but kept his usual biting backchat at bay.

'Yes. Most courteous.'

'Might I enquire as to how you learned of us? London is at some distance, after all.'

'Indeed, it is, sir. It was a poem, of all things, by one of your students that led to my awareness of this academy's very existence. The young author, a Mr Shirreff, is apparently an admirer of the actor David Garrick and composed a poem in praise of him. Now this, in itself, is not quite so remarkable except Mr Shirreff could never have actually *heard* any performance by Mr Garrick. The poem was therefore invested with a revelation perhaps not altogether intended. *On Seeing Garrick Act* is, I believe, the title, with 'seeing' the pertinence. Mr Garrick is an intimate in my circle and it was he who brought this to my attention.'

Braidwood felt a surge of optimism. He had taught Charles Shirreff to read and to write, building faith in his own methods along the way. It was not lost on him that a poem written by someone who was deaf in praise of a stage actor said as much about *his* training as it did about Garrick. It was good advertising and Samuel Johnson was now here because of it. *Perhaps this day will not end up so bad after all,* he thought.

'Yes, of course,' said Braidwood. 'I remember Mr Shirreff's work quite well.' He looked off at some imaginary point and quoted a line.

'What needs of sounds when I plainly decry the expressive features and the speaking eye?'

He returned his attention to Johnson.

'Charles Shirreff was my first student and it pleases me no end that he is now matured and learned. He was not deaf from birth, but he had been left untreated for some time. As you might surmise, it is most difficult to treat those who are born in that wretched state. Such as these have no concept of language. Their thought is not driven by words, but by the functional aspects of movement. Most of my students have either lost their hearing from illness after they had at least acquired some of the concepts of language, or they are simply very hard of hearing. I will say that those few whose deafness is congenital benefit from the presence of others eager to assist, as they are keen to apply what they have learned. The full effect of this I have not yet been able to determine.'

'What illnesses have they suffered to bring them here?'

'Most you know of, I'm sure. We have just taken in a lass from London who had contracted measles. She, unfortunately, lost her hearing as a result.

The lexicographer in Johnson replied.

'The term comes from the old English *maselen* or *many little spots.*'

'Indeed, sir.'

'Yes. The poor child'

Johnson adjusted his train of thought and continued.

'Might I enquire, as young Mr Shirreff was your first, how you determined to proceed?'

Straight to the point, thought Braidwood.

'You may. It was, at first, a matter of trial and error. But first let me say a bit more of my own background.

Johnson decided to let the man speak. Any false claims would eventually be exposed.

'You have my interest.'

'I read mathematics here at Edinburgh University and then began my mathematical academy shortly thereafter. Its transformation could be said to have begun with the boy of whom you speak. He is the son of Alexander Shirreff, a local wine merchant. He brought his nine-year-old deaf and dumb son to me in some desperation and it was a challenge I could not refuse. I never really set out to establish myself as a teacher of the deaf. It was difficult at first, but soon enough I developed an approach that served me in good stead. I now have fifteen students under this roof, but the number changes as they come and go. Their ages have varied from five to twenty years. It is of course better to take them in hand when they are young, before the organs grow stiff and rigid, so that they may learn to speak most plainly and pleasantly.'

'They can learn to speak?' asked Johnson.

'But why not, sir? Young Mr Shirreff can do so. Or was that never made clear? Those who have lost their hearing after learning that ability can retain it, if treated in time. Those deaf from birth or shortly thereafter can also learn to speak slowly, *viva voce*. But they may not elect to do so, preferring instead to speak with their hands which of course they must learn in order to communicate with one another and those few hearing individuals who have learned how to sign.'

'May I ask *how* you teach them to speak?'

Braidwood thought for a moment. He had made a pact with himself to keep the particulars of his pedagogy a professional secret. Johnson, as he had suspected, did not appear to be the sort who would purloin them for any personal advantage.

'Well, sir, I have been described by some as an oralist, meaning that I teach speech to the exclusion of all else. But as you can see from the work of Mr Shirreff that is not all we endeavour to achieve here. I employ a combined system of communication. That is to say, finger spelling, signing, speech reading, reading and writing are all taught and, of course, literature and maths as well. But first I shall provide some understanding of my basic methodology, if I may.'

'You may.'

'I generally begin by showing them how the mouth is formed for the production of the vowels and then let them see the external effect that vocalised breath has upon the internal parts of the wind-pipe, whence they are caused to feel the vibration of the larynx with their thumbs and fingers, first in me and then in themselves. When they are able to repeat the vowels in the right sequence and cadence they are then shown the written form of what they have expressed, until they are perfected in their knowledge of the vowels or vocal sounds. In some harsh cases, especially where the child is deaf from birth, I may use this small round piece of silver.'

Braidwood then picked up the instrument that had been lying on his desk and held it up for inspection.

'As you can see it is but a few inches long about the size of a tobacco pipe, flattened at one end and with this ball about the size of a marble at the other. By means of this the tongue can be, gently mark you, placed at various positions respectively for forming the articulations of the different letters and syllables until they acquire, as we all do in learning speech, by habit, the proper method.'

Johnson resisted the image of its insertion into a child's mouth.

Braidwood paused and raised an eyebrow.

'Do I proceed too quickly?'

'No, no. Continue,' said Johnson, his underestimation leading to a desire for more understanding.

'Thank you. A more important point is that the deaf do not learn to write, nor to speak, in the same manner as those with the gift of hearing. I assume you understand what is meant by orthography?'

'That is simply the study of spelling and how letters combine to represent sounds.'

'Of course, of course,' said Braidwood, reminding himself with whom he was speaking.

'Traditional orthography is here complicated by imperfect notions of the relations between letters and their vocal utterance. Every character, every letter is, to the deaf, of *equal* importance. They have difficulty in distinguishing them. Beyond that they have no real way of understanding homonyms, such as weight as in what scales measure and wait as in 'wait for me'. And beyond *that* the same meaning can be easily comprehended in one context, but not in another. They can understand the meaning of 'clear' when it comes to the weather, but not so easily when applied to the mind as in 'do I make myself clear?'. To them words are not symbolic of names, but of *things*. Do you see? When they write they are not representing a sound but thinking of a physical form.'

Braidwood spoke as if was reading aloud something he had already written.

'I understand orthography,' said Johnson, 'as the study of spelling and how letters combine to represent sounds and form words. But here one cannot associate letters with sounds. Is that not so?'

'Indeed, sir, but it is not a limitation. It closes one door, but opens another. It does so because the relationship between ideas and language, spoken or written, is purely arbitrary. It is critical the deaf learn the meanings of words they articulate, otherwise they are no better than parrots. But whence these meanings? Words acquire meaning through mental images created by social tradition. Language consists of abstract sounds to which meaning is attached by mere convention. This is plain enough, but a deeper question is whether language is indispensable to thought. How does language aid it? Does it perform a service by means of properties inherent in the verbal medium itself or does it function indirectly by pointing to the referents of words? I take the latter view inasmuch as the deaf are well known to have, through signing, invented their own language and communicate quite well without words. So, they must be able to communicate via word-free imagery of some sort. Perhaps finger spelling might work in this way.'

'Finger spelling and signing? Are these not the same?'

'Indeed not, sir. Signing refers to ideas, whereas finger spelling relates more to the alphabet. Do you see this chart here? Each letter is clearly represented by the position of the fingers and thumb. So, when I introduce you I will demonstrate S-A-M-U-E-L like so,' said Braidwood, his fingers quickly morphing from one letter's representation to the next.

'Signing or gesturing, on the other hand is much more complex. Whole phrases or moods can be contained in one gesture. So, if I want to say *We are all very happy to welcome you here and show you what we have achieved* I would perform it thus.'

Braidwood then demonstrated broad, sharp movements designed to communicate inclusion, joy and display. Johnson was intrigued by how so much could be communicated by so few gestures.

'But perhaps we are getting a bit ahead of ourselves. Students begin here by following the formation of vowels and syllables followed by the meaning of common words and finally the construction of a sentence or sentences from which descriptions are composed. Of course, there is more, but may I surmise that you now understand the general nature of the process?'

'Somewhat, but is it not equally important they learn to listen? How is this need addressed?'

'Well, sir, to train those who have never heard a sound to convey their ideas both in speech and in written language, as you correctly anticipate, is only half of their education. The rest is completed by training them to hear with the eye. This means to become acquainted with the various positions of the organs of speech and be generally enabled to understand what is spoken by another. This is accomplished by looking steadily at the lips of the speaker. Unfortunately, it is easy to misinterpret what is said since many words are articulated with nearly the same action of the organs. Take for instance 'ship' and 'sheep'. You see? The occurrence also of equivocal words is very frequent in discourse, which, when unconnected with others, have a sense that cannot be determined absolutely even by those who *can* hear. So, it is left for the other words in a sentence

- to the context - to explain the meaning and application of equivocal words such as 'vein' as in blood, 'vane' as in weathervane or 'vain' as in vanity. And then there is 'right' as in correct, 'rite' as in ritual, or 'write' as in written. I could go on.'

'I am sure. I never thought on how assonance need be involved in their training,' said Johnson.

'Indeed, sir, and there are other similarities that can frustrate such as the labials or lip-consonants. For example, B, P and M can be somewhat difficult to discriminate, being formed with the same motion of the lips, with the only difference that M occasions a visible contraction of the muscles about the nose. But with practice one becomes able to distinguish even these subtleties by context. As difficult as it is for the deaf to attain pronunciation and speech, they have yet still more difficulty in acquiring a proper knowledge of written language. However, that it *can* be done is demonstrated by your presence. Nonetheless, as I hope I have made clear, the deaf do not learn to speak nor to write in quite the same way as the hearing.'

Braidwood paused, elbows on his desk, his blue eyes staring at Johnson over steepled fingers.

'If I may interject, sir,' said Johnson, who had been grappling for an intelligent question, 'it rather appears you have parallel projects. I assume you must ultimately perform as an ordinary academy endeavouring to teach literature and numeracy, but cannot do so in anything like the traditional manner. Does this not result in any limitations? Can students here attain the same level of learning they would otherwise achieve if they did not lack the power of hearing?'

Braidwood looked down for a moment as if Johnson's question had triggered something. He adopted a more serious tone.

'That of course depends on each student. I will confess that at first, I thought their ideas few and entirely confined to visible objects, to the passions and to the senses. But now, after some years working closely with them, I am wholly convinced of two things. First, the mind of a deaf child was wrongly assumed to be languid and not worthy of our mediation if ideas expressed in speech struck their ears in vain. But their minds are *not* languid, sir. They can learn. Persons who are deaf, even those who are born deaf are, in fact, neither depressed below, nor raised above, the general scale of human kind as regards their dispositions and powers, either of body or mind. They are human beings individually differing from their kind by an accidental defect. Give them language and, in great measure, you do away with their defect and bring them on a level with those of their age and station. Signing may be void of the symbology of speech, but it is no less a real language.'

Here Braidwood paused, his fingers now tightly clasped. He continued.

'And from this originates the second thing I have learned about them. I believe they may surpass us in the area of, of…'

He paused for the right words.

'Yes?'

'I believe them capable of a finer feeling.'

'I do not understand your meaning here, sir.'

'I shall explain exactly what I mean. What separates a deaf child from the rest of the world is not as marked or wide as one might suspect. They have thinner boundaries that separate them from the feelings of others and, nay, from the tragedies and cruelties of the world. They hear with the eye as I have said. They must closely observe facial expressions to understand what words are spoken. They perceive human behaviour whilst they remain all undistracted by babble and have a keener awareness of the emotions of others. The slightest of gestures or expressions do not escape observation. Now, they may not always communicate this understanding to us with some articulated conclusion. Nevertheless, I believe these subtle observations bring about feelings within them that, however deeply felt, they sometimes *cannot* communicate. It is as if they move amongst us as a silent conscience. Another way of saying this, and not without some irony, is that they are good listeners. A hearing person who is a bad listener has no advantage over the deaf. I beg you accept these most salient points. They can learn and they are most aware.'

Braidwood wondered whether he had gone too far. He wanted to appear professional and competent, but had he not strayed from discussing pure pedagogy? He decided to continue. Here, after all, was a man of some influence and things needed to be said.

'Might you agree that ours is not an age of sentiment?'

'Yes, but neither is it entirely uncharitable.'

'It is uncharitable, enough, sir,' said Braidwood, his tone now testy.

'Surely you must agree - surely you must be aware that those who profess to be high-minded routinely dispense humour at the expense of those with hunchbacks and harelips? Then of course we must not neglect those who stammer, have club feet or limbs missing altogether. But those who bring the loudest guffaws, besides the blind and the deaf, are the dwarfs. Is there nothing so humorous in our enlightened age as a dwarf? It is into this cruel culture I must discharge my students. They will become subjects, despite any achievement here, of the merciless tongue of drawing-room wags. Even though my students may become literate and educated they will, I am afraid, still suffer slights and ridicule. I say, sir!'

Braidwood let out a breath and lowered the uplifted forefinger that had jabbed home every word. He clasped his hands and stared down at his desk. He looked up and spoke again.

'Well, the less said about all that the better. You did not come here to suffer my blanket indictments.'

Johnson felt a sudden sense of shame. He could not now help but think of David Garrick's imitation of a fellow with a speech impediment who came to offer himself for the stage. He, along with everyone else, found it amusing.

He decided not to admit to this, but he did wonder how he would now react when he next experienced something similar. He had come here to learn about the academy and discovered a prejudice within himself.

Braidwood was waiting for some reaction. He thought it best to steer the conversation to a new line of thought.

'Sir, I would like to hear more about what is meant by hearing with the eye. It is rather an odd expression,' said Johnson, clearing his throat.

'What would you like to know?'

'If the deaf can accomplish all this as you say, and do so with some accuracy, then why must they also learn to sign as well? If you labour so to teach them to speak, why can they not understand each other's pronouncements by hearing with the eye as I believe you refer to it?'

'An excellent question, sir. The problem is that the deaf can display subtle but critical deviations from the universality of labial movement. They do not have explosive consonants. We have, you and I, different accents, but not so much to the deaf who see in our lip movements inconsequential differences. But a deaf person does not speak with an accent as such. It can be difficult for one who is deaf to hear with the eye the speech of another deaf individual, especially one deaf from birth. There are gradations of course but in general their pronunciation is too far off the mark to be heard by seeing.'

'I see. Pity,' said Johnson, glad he had not exposed David Garrick and, by default, himself.

Braidwood sensed it was time to move in a different direction.

'Let me say a bit about the students, which, of course, is why you are here in the first instance. It may well be that there is some bias in their presence here, in their selection. I suspect they are, in general, above average in native intelligence. I have noticed that they arrive with active, even aggressive, intellects. It was likely because of this that their struggles and frustrations within a world of silence were all the more amplified thus pressing their parents to seek a remedy. In any case, they are here and - like students anywhere - there will be different levels of success. We do have one very exceptional lad here who shall make his mark. Of that I have no doubt.'

'I understand, in a general sense, what it is you wish to achieve, but might you detail what is considered a successful outcome?' asked Johnson.

'Well, sir, you must keep in mind their education does not end here. The boys are prepared for their eventual relocation to an ordinary academy where they will continue their tutelage in a traditional circumstance. The young ladies will not continue in another institution, but shall likely receive private tutelage. The average stay here is about five years. It can be more or less, of course.'

Johnson returned to an earlier question he had.

'Mr Braidwood, there was no such training for *you*. How did you know where to begin? You have had no example to follow or improve upon. Or do I misunderstand?'

'There was something of a path to follow. Much research and experimentation has already been performed by the authors of these volumes you see here. Where I differ is that this school is the first of its kind on this island, but work had already taken place on the continent and we have been the beneficiary of some of the work done there. Let us return to my first student, Mr Shirreff. I had faith in the lad from the outset, but it is an association I would never have enjoyed had his father held the mistaken belief his son could not learn. He was, to the contrary, convinced that his son had an intelligence locked within. He came to me. I did not solicit. There was a time of course when such an unfortunate creature denied the power of utterance from the unhappy construction of his organs would have remained forever uneducated. But his arrival here might be considered the culmination of a long and slow improvement in the regard of the deaf and dumb, at least in some circles. I am only fortunate to have been in the right place at the right time.'

Johnson now believed Braidwood had indeed read all the books on the shelves behind him.

'Can you say more of this culmination to which you refer?'

'I can, sir. But first it may be useful, given that the work here may be likened to a maiden voyage, for you to understand something of the cultural seas we sail upon. If you will permit me.'

Johnson nodded.

'You must be aware those denied the power of speech have not always been regarded as capable of learning. The reasons for such a prejudice have been many, but the end result was the same - a separation from the community at large.'

Braidwood paused to collect himself. His teachings not only aided the deaf to learn and to communicate, but were also, he believed, a redress for centuries of insufferable treatment, an injustice he was now eager to recount.

'This intolerance has had a long and tortuous history. Aristotle, it could be argued, set the tone with the claim that knowledge was tied to speech and thus the deaf could not be educated and without education they could not be considered full citizens. I might add that the Greeks regarded anyone who could not speak the Greek language, let alone not speak at all, as a barbarian. In any case, Greek children who were deaf were included in this condemned group. The tragedy in all this of course was not that they could not learn, but that they were *kept* from learning. They were needlessly made bereft of the benefits of any discourse.'

'I had not so expected Aristotle to be part of this prejudice,' said Johnson. 'It is a pity as I now suspect his influence over a regard for the deaf lasted long after his death.'

'How so?'

'What of his conviction that our little planet sat at the centre of the heavens? The enduring dominance of this misconception was surely aided by the appropriation of his science to validate the church's geocentric dogma - to use his authority to sustain an incorrect astronomy for far too long. I presume his pronouncements on the deaf had no less of a legacy.'

'Yes, yes,' said Braidwood, now warming to the conversation. 'It is indeed lamentable that the church condemned the deaf by propagating the belief that a child's deafness was the result of God punishing sinful parents. The deaf were only a small part of God's complex world. They did not see it as right and proper they should change deaf people. It was not regarded as a problem to be solved by the church. There *was* no problem as far as they were concerned. Indeed, it was only one for the parents. And, as far as that goes, they were likely in some way sinful and not worthy of assistance or sympathy. How could a deaf child be saved if they could never understand the ritual of the mass? So, yes, Mr Johnson, the prejudice against the deaf and mute held a certain obstinacy. Each epoch sought out its justification for ill treatment much as water will conform to the shape of each new vessel that contains it. It was a prejudice perpetuated by changing beliefs or orthodoxies leading to the same result. Now, however, all this is changing and these students are the beneficiaries.'

Braidwood gestured as if they were standing behind him.

Johnson shifted in his seat for a comfortable position. He thought for a long moment and then spoke.

'It seems that what you are saying is that, whatever the nature of treatment now, there was always the assumption that if language and learning were linked to sound then the deaf were bereft of either education or salvation. Is that not a correct interpretation? There could be no language without speaking. Was that not a main point?'

Braidwood sat back and thought for a moment.

'To answer that sir, I might wish to first say a bit about how the deaf communicated *without* sound. May I say a bit more about signing inasmuch as you are about to witness some of it here?'

'Indeed, you may, sir,'

'Well,' Braidwood paused again to collect his thoughts. 'Historically, if I may generalise, all the policies or, ah, processes associated with the deaf were based upon an assumed inability to communicate. The central issue,' said Braidwood looking at Johnson past an upraised forefinger, 'as you have accurately seized upon, was one of language. If they could not speak they could not learn, they could not assimilate. From this viewpoint, the deaf as the disabled were more of a cultural construction and less one determined by some genuinely insurmountable condition of madness or insanity. They were defined because of a condition that ran counter to the physical expectations and demands of society. But gradually, over the last century, it seems clear this attitude has abated, but not because of some new benevolence, I hasten to add.'

'Do I sense some indignation on this point?'

'Forgive me. Sometimes my passions do get the better of me. But for too long the deaf were excommunicated in a literal as well as a figurative sense. This could only change when pedagogical techniques for the education of deaf mutes were perfected in the last few generations. Prior to that, they never matured and were unnecessarily subdued. Moreover, those deaf from birth are at more of a disadvantage than those blind from birth when left unattended.'

Johnson thought of his one good ear and one good eye and considered which of the two he would prefer not to lose.

Braidwood continued, his hands now tightly clasped.

'I suppose these episodes in society all have to run their natural course. Nonetheless, the motive for deaf education in the last century did not come from purely sympathetic inclinations. One might assume so, but this would be incorrect.'

'What was the motive?'

'Well, two things must be understood. First, as I mentioned earlier, there is the method of communication by the deaf known as finger spelling and then there is the development of the Royal Society in London, or rather of the drive for knowledge that led to its formation. The important connection between them is one of language. Would you like to hear anything about this?'

'Please,' said Johnson, now in rapt attention.

'There has been clear evidence in Britain that for the last two hundred years or so sign languages of various forms have been used by those who were deaf and between deaf and hearing people. John Bulwer was perhaps the first here in Britain who understood the significance of this. It was not just another method of communication - it also raised the question of whether for a language to *be* a language it had to be spoken aloud. If it must be spoken, it can be written. If it is written, then there must be meaning ascribed to each word. Whence these meanings? On this point, I am of course most impressed, as are others, by the prodigious achievement of your dictionary. We do not have a copy here, but I have seen it.

Johnson realised that he had never truly considered how language and thought were connected.

'Are you saying that if understanding can come without sound, then the connection between our ideas and a written language can be considered purely arbitrary?' he asked.

'Indeed so, sir, indeed so. It is therefore very difficult to give the deaf any notion of that mode of conversing when in the last instance, it is all mere hieroglyphs. And consider the reverse; in a deaf community, a hearing person who cannot sign is disabled. The disabled are not a natural construction, but a cultural one. Let me return to the earlier thinking of St Augustine for a moment. Although a strong Catholic, did you know that in the end he came to believe the deaf could be saved? And do you know why? Because it was in the monasteries that sign language was developed by different orders of monks to cope with periods of silence. Speaking was not allowed, but they communicated nonetheless!'

Monks, thought Johnson. *Of course.*

'And,' continued Braidwood, his voice now at a slightly higher pitch, '…once the idea that the deaf could communicate *without* speech took hold it caused a re-examination of the meaning of language. And not just the meaning of language, but what it means to be human. Nay, sir, of what it means to be *civilised*. If speech was considered to be civilisation itself then what did it mean that speech is not needed to communicate an idea, a thought, eh? And this takes me to my earlier point. The motive in the last century for a study of the deaf was not out of any compassion for the afflicted, no indeed, sir. It was to understand the nature of language and the search for the perfect or universal language that is the essence of humanity. Before this it had been believed that speaking was civilization itself. Now there was doubt. The focus was not to teach the deaf to speak. The focus was whether language depends on utterance.'

'And does it?' asked Johnson.

'Ah, you have me there, sir. I do know the deaf can be made to understand language, *our* language, and can be taught maths and literature. They can learn, as I have said. Now whether this means our words are only a superficial representation of something deeper and of universal import, I cannot say. The lingering question is if a person is born deaf, what language do they think in? I will say that the Royal Society is in no better a position to answer that than I.'

'And you, sir? You must have thought on this point.'

'Well, I do believe language is not a *direct* avenue for sensory contact with reality; it serves only to name what we have *already* seen, or heard, or thought. I do not say that it is unsuitable to our perceptual experience, but these experiences must be somehow coded before they can be named. For the deaf this coding is, perhaps, far richer than it is for us. That is about all I can say on the matter.'

'But is this not of any further interest? Would you not care to present a paper on your work here?'

'*I* present a paper? Surely not, sir. If you think that of me you are much mistaken.'

'But,' said Johnson, 'the rise of the Royal Society only reflects the rise of the rational mind and the rejection of superstition. Surely the increased dominance of the domain of reason must be relevant to your proceedings here?'

Braidwood stiffened.

'It is not a help. I will say that much. The rise of reason as you say has also meant that its antipode, madness, has become more of a threat. This only further penalises those deemed different due to some condition running counter to social norms. The rise of the role of experimentation in natural philosophy and of the domain of reason you refer to requires language, whatever that may be. So, you see sir, this 'rise of reason' is a double-edged sword. It brought attention to the deaf, yes. They became objects of fascination, but they were only seen as a subject of to study. All that is now changing, thank the Lord. The children here are able to read and to write. They are, sir, as capable of reason as anyone.'

Johnson enjoyed verbal sparring, but he had lost all desire to challenge Braidwood. Perhaps he might press a point or two, but he only found himself wanting to agree.

'You argue, then, that the deaf, once placed at our margins, now only enjoy new opportunities despite and not because of this rise in new philosophical thought?'

'Precisely so. This search for a secular and demystified rationality has only served to bias recent philosophical speculation. These so-called philosophers have sought the 'perfect language'. The attempt to glimpse its very nature brought a new engagement of the hearing world with that of the deaf. The manner in which communication was engaged in, by and with those who were deaf and mute, became of particular interest. Indeed, it became fascinating. This resulted in two important things. First, the deaf became a revised category of humans and second, it became clear that the deaf were *not* dumb and they *could* be educated. That is all I care for. I do not brood over a true meaning of language.'

Johnson thought for a moment and recalled an essay he had written in *The Adventurer* years earlier.

'It is observed by Bacon, sir, that, reading makes a full man, conversation a ready man, and writing an exact man. So, as Bacon attained a significant degree of knowledge, his observations make a claim to our regard. It would seem that you do not intend the students of this academy to forgo any of these approaches to a proper and fit education. Is this a correct conclusion?'

Braidwood was about to reply when there was a soft knock on the door.

'Ah, a fresh pot of tea and some cakes,' he said, clapping his hands. He thanked the departing house-keeper, who could not keep from staring at Johnson.

'Shall we have some refreshment before going to meet the children?'

'An excellent idea,' said Johnson.

What he really wanted, though, was time to collect his thoughts. He would have, if it had come to that, exposed Braidwood as a charlatan. Now, however, he dreaded finding these students incapable.

'Might you have any suggestions for me?' he asked.

Braidwood thought for a moment. He knew the students would be paying more attention than usual to their guest. Would Johnson assume they did so because of his rather less than appealing features?

'Yes,' said Braidwood, 'They all can hear with their eyes so please speak with clarity as is of course your usual manner. And, well, that is all really.'

He wanted to joke that, *'they will not be staring at you because you are an old brute,'* but thought better of it.

'Who are these students I shall meet?'

'Of course. Three lads and a lassie.'

'Do the young ladies here receive the same education as the boys? Sharing the same classroom as boys is not the usual circumstance.'

'Yes, and why not? Perhaps they will not proceed in their education entire in the same manner as young men but when it comes to *these* students it would be most lamentable to forgo educating one and all. That one who is illiterate because of this unfortunate condition be condemned to remain so because of their gender is not acceptable…I mean, well, sir. Surely a lass must be able to read and to write.'

'I should make it clear,' he continued, 'that not all students will be taking part in this little exercise. The newest student, Miss Upton, has only just arrived and of course is not yet ready to demonstrate what she can achieve, but she will be, I am sure. Now, as for the others, I have selected our most able students. You are free to ask of them what you wish. One thing I will say is to avoid the sesquipedalian, those long-winded, polysyllabic words little used in normal conversation. After all, it is only common speech and thought that is the test. Also, I ask you to bear in mind that they do not all speak with equal facility - they have begun from separate starting points, as it were. They have been provided with slates and will write answers to your questions on these. So, then, let us finish here and proceed, shall we?'

Johnson was relieved to discover that, whatever else he was, Braidwood was no quack. Nevertheless, the anxiety he awoke with remained.

6

Braidwood's Pupils

The students smartly stood as Braidwood and Johnson entered. Braidwood's nephew, off to one side, gave Johnson a smile and nod. Two of them began to sign. The one covered a laugh while the other's index finger of her prime hand alternated between straight and bent as it moved across her forehead. Johnson assumed it was about him and that it was not flattering.

'Children,' began Braidwood, 'this is our visitor, Mr Samuel Johnson,' gesturing broadly as he spoke. Immediately the secret signers faced forward while suppressing laughter. Braidwood pointedly looked for any other furtive fingers.

The students appeared enthusiastic and expectant. Johnson began to sense he had underestimated how important this visit was to them and felt a rare moment of intimidation. He had given too little thought to what his presence would mean to this young audience and had no desire to find fault. To do so meant he would have to embarrass them, something he simply did not have the heart to do now that he was confronted by their eager expressions.

Braidwood spoke and signed.

'He has come all the way from London. Our little academy is very well known and you should all be very proud!'

Johnson immediately wondered about the use of 'proud'. It was one thing to sign for 'apple', he thought, but this was something abstract. He would pay closer attention to how Braidwood interacted with them.

Braidwood motioned for the children to be seated, while four in the front remained standing.

'Mr Johnson, I wish to introduce those who have been asked to show what they have learned,' said Braidwood with a slight bow as he gestured to the students.

'The lass is Rose Ballantyne, from a local family.'

Johnson was moved by her curtsy and shy smile.

'The lads are Hugh Lansing from Harrogate, Richard Mulley from Glasgow and John Goodricke of the York Goodrickes. You may know of his grandfather, Sir John of the Diplomatic Service.'

Johnson directed a brief nod toward each as their name was mentioned. Goodricke's confident expression held him for a moment.

'Please greet Mr Johnson,' said Braidwood with a flourish directed at their guest.

They spoke in ragged unison.

'Good morning, sir.'

Johnson noticed how Braidwood had made deliberate eye contact with each student to alert them of their prominence at the point of introduction. This was how he ought to interact with them. It was now obvious how all this had all been planned for his benefit, more evidence of the significance the day held for them.

'You have my leave to press them as you will. Are you ready to proceed?'

Johnson looked at the students and managed a smile. They had all obviously been prepared and were dressed that little bit better than the others - hair combed and shoes polished. Rose wore what looked to be a new frock. Goodricke appeared to be the most poised and radiated a certain serenity. His scrubbed face bore the slightest trace of a confident smile. A neatly tied bow hung from his collar and he held his slate as if he were making a presentation.

Braidwood cleared his throat.

'Well, sir, perhaps we might begin with some word meanings. As you have written a dictionary, I imagine you have thousands from which to choose, eh?'

Johnson, relieved to have some direction, smiled and nodded.

'Fine, fine.' Braidwood then looked at each student in turn as he spoke.

'Mr Johnson shall write a word and you shall then write its meaning on your slates. Do you understand?'

They eagerly nodded, swapping knowing looks and smiles.

Braidwood handed Johnson a piece of chalk who then ceremoniously held it up as if he was about to make it disappear. Braidwood inwardly winced as Johnson dramatically turned to the board and wrote in a large florid hand, *mouse*, followed by a sharp half turn to the students. Braidwood wanted to say there was no need for histrionics, but it was too late for that.

Rose and John looked at each other. She gave a shrug and roll of her eyes and they wrote on their slates. Hugh and Richard soon followed.

'You can show your slates, show them,' said Braidwood, looking at each student in turn.

They turned their slates over and Johnson read *little beast, rodent, vermin,* and *food for cats.*

'Well done all,' said Braidwood. Mr Johnson, perhaps now something more of a challenge?'

Johnson nodded and thought of a word from his dictionary, *lamping.*

Each student quickly rubbed out the previous answer followed by scratchings of chalk. Braidwood stood by expectantly, clasped hands held at the waist.

The slates were presented. *Glowing, sparkly, shining* and *the stars.*

Unsure of just how far he should go with this Johnson looked at Braidwood.

'Another?'

'Yes, yes, but perhaps now something a little abstract?'

Without thinking why, Johnson wrote *melancholic*.

Braidwood pushed out his lower lip and gave a slight nod to the students. Johnson did not realise he was being led, since signing was much richer than the spoken language in expressing feeling and emotion. The students would likely have an answer whatever he wrote.

'Perhaps', said Braidwood looking slowly at each student in turn, 'you will now show Mr Johnson your answers one at a time, please.'

'Rose?'

How I once felt

'Hugh?'

Deep sadness

'Richard?'

Grieved

'John?'

Our visitor?

'Yes, yes, well done,' said Braidwood hastily.

Johnson remained impassive.

'Apologies, sir, they can be of a rather flexible mind, something we do not discourage. Take no notice,' said Braidwood.

Johnson was well nonplussed. He might have expected this from Boswell, someone who knew of his bouts with melancholia, but what had *this* lad seized upon? Was this an example of that 'thin boundary' Braidwood had spoken of?

Braidwood sensed his discomfort.

'May I make a suggestion, sir? Perhaps something that tests their knowledge of the rules of grammar?'

Johnson noticed how each student kept their eyes full on him. They were eager to demonstrate what they knew and were not intimidated. Why would they be? They did not know of his reputation as might some young pretender in his London club.

'Of course,' said Johnson. He looked over at Braidwood. *He must be aware he is being tested as well.* He turned to the blackboard, thought a moment and wrote *I toured the Hebrides in Scotland, stayed in Edinburgh, and Mr Boswell made arrangements for the return to London. - What is the grammatical form?*

The students all read his script and seemed to all be in thought at the same time. They then displayed their answers. Each one wrote *compound*. Other sentence structures followed - simple, complex and compound complex. Each correct answer by each student raised his opinion of Braidwood another notch.

'Well done,' said Johnson, making a point of saying this to each student directly. He was learning.

'Now, let us try this.' He pivoted towards the board, a little more relaxed and inspired. *A word I know, six letters it contains. Subtract just one, and twelve is what remains.*

Riddles were not quite what Braidwood had in mind and he was not sure how the students would react. Goodricke began writing almost immediately. After a moment Rose gave a little hop and wrote on her slate. Hugh and Ralph looked perplexed and amused.

'Perhaps that is enough time,' signed Braidwood and gestured for the students to show their answers.

Rose and John had written *dozens* and Hugh a question mark. Ralph, who had left his slate blank, spoke.

'You twicked us!' he said with a grin.

Braidwood felt Johnson might require a little guidance.

'If I may, sir, perhaps something from the *Book of Common Prayer*?'

'Just one more riddle, sir. Please?'

Rose had spoken.

Johnson looked at Braidwood, who returned a smile and nod.

Always in visible, yet never out of sight. What are they?

Braidwood, with folded arms looked at the board and then back at the students. He saw that they were straining, thinking.

When all the students had finished they turned over their slates. Each had written *I* and *S*.

Braidwood was taken aback not only because each student had thought of the correct answer, but because he could not. *Riddles may have a place here after all*, he thought.

'Now then, sir. You mentioned the *Book of Common Prayer*,' said Johnson. Let us try this. *We have left _____ those things which we ought to have _____; and we have _____ those things which we ought not to have _____.*

Each student wrote *undone, done, done, done.*

So, they are not kept from the word of God here, thought Johnson. He looked at Braidwood with nodding approval.

'You see, sir, this may be an academy for the deaf, but it is still an academy. Once they are able to read and write, then of course all subjects are open to them. And we also read from the *Book of Common Prayer*.'

He decided to move the proceedings along.

'Well, sir perhaps now you may wish to ask them some questions on arithmetic? May I suggest multiplication skills? Let them be challenged. And let us now test them one at a time going forward.'

Johnson remembered something from his donated copy of Cocker's Arithmetic.

'Might I try something other first, but for all of them?'

'Of course.'

Braidwood instructed the students that they should all attempt this next question.

Johnson slowly wrote, *If 4 yards of cloth cost 12 shillings, what will 6 yards cost at that rate?*

No sooner had he finished when they all began writing. They did not wait to be asked and held up their slates, almost all at the same time.

Each showed the correct answer, *18 shillings.*

'I am indeed most impressed, sir.'

'I do not mean to diminish their ability, but it is only the rule of three, after all."

'Of course,' said Johnson. 'Right, then, let us now take them one at time.'

'Rose?' said Johnson looking at her directly and then wrote *324 x 55=?*

She looked at the problem for a moment and then began, her little tongue exposed as the chalk dug into the slate. Finished, she boldly snapped the slate forward with a determined expression,

$$
\begin{array}{r}
324 \\
\underline{\times 55} \\
1620 \\
+\underline{16200} \\
\end{array}
$$
Answer 17,820.

Correct.

Hugh and Richard fared equally as well.

'Now, John. We come to you.'

Johnson wrote *79 x 65 =?*

Goodricke wrote only briefly and then stopped.

The poor lad is flummoxed.

'Show him, lad,' said Braidwood. 'Show him.'

Goodricke turned over his slate to reveal *5135*.

Nothing else was written.

Johnson gave Braidwood a questioning look.

'That *is* the answer, sir.'

Was it? He would have to perform the multiplication himself, but instead asked Goodricke to show him how it was done.

'It's all right, lad. Take the chalk and come to the board,' signed Braidwood.

Goodricke thought for a moment and then wrote:

79 or (80 - 1) x 65=

80 x65=4800 + 400 - 65 = 5135.

'Extraordinary,' said Johnson who did not completely understand the reasoning behind what was written.

'Might I test him with another?'

'As you wish.'

Johnson wrote *257 + 588=?*

Goodricke studied the numbers for a few seconds, wrote on his slate and turned it over, *845*.

'Sir,' said Johnson, 'I am at a loss.'

'Yes,' said Braidwood. 'He is an unusual lad.'

'He does you credit, sir.'

'He does *himself* credit. The lad carries an intelligence already within. I did not teach him this.'

'How old is he?' asked Johnson.

'You may ask him directly.'

Johnson looked at Goodricke.

'How old are you, lad?'

'Thirteen years, sir.'

Samuel Johnson had not expected any of this, least of all exposure to a budding genius. He could now return to London having at last found something to counter all the inequities witnessed on this journey.

The questions continued for another few minutes until both Johnson and Braidwood sensed it was time to end the exercise.

'Well done all!' said Braidwood while signing that he was genuinely proud.

The remaining students stood and Braidwood raised his hand as if to direct.

'Thank you for coming, sir,' they said, now in stronger unison.

Johnson returned their appreciation with a slight bow to each of those questioned. He then stepped forward and look a moment to look at all the students before speaking.

'It has been an honour and a pleasure to be here amongst you. I want to thank you and thank Mr Braidwood.' He wanted to continue, but, for once in his life, Samuel Johnson was at a loss for words.

Braidwood saw his slight loss of composure and intervened.

'We are all most grateful sir, most grateful. John has gone to fetch a carriage for you. I want to thank you again for your taking the time to be here with us. I must confess not having expected them all to enjoy it quite so much as they seemed to do.'

'As indeed have I. It has been most illustrative, sir. Most illustrative.'

Braidwood thought that answer rather noncommittal, but believed he need not be concerned about how Johnson might recount his visit.

Nephew John returned.

'I have secured a carriage for Mr Johnson and instructed the driver,' said John.

They all shook hands. Thomas and John watched as Johnson tapped his way down the walk and into the waiting cab.

'John,' said Thomas while waving at the departing carriage, 'please ask young Goodricke to come to my study. I think it may be near time he moved on.'

Johnson looked back as the door closed behind them. *So many currents in such a little pond*, he thought. He settled back into his seat, closed his eyes and made a mental note to send Braidwood's Academy a copy of his dictionary as soon as he returned to London. And he would tip the driver.

7

Warrington 1780

'Now lads, before you depart, I shall introduce the next topic so that you may spend your Saturday thinking on it.'

William Enfield, lecturer in mathematics at Warrington Academy, was met with moans and mumbled 'Yes sirs.'

Good Lord, he thought. *They took that seriously.*

He turned to the chalk board and drew a triangle and then another, as identical to the first as he could draw it.

Now this triangle,' the pointer sharply tapping the board, 'is congruent with this one.'

Blank stares.

'If two triangles are congruent as these are, then their corresponding angles are equal,' he said.

Tap, tap, tap.

'This you will already know.'

'Not me, sir!' one boy exclaimed.

Chuckles. He forged on.

'However, is the converse true? If the corresponding angles of two triangles are equal *must* they be congruent?'

'Yes John?'

Goodricke's hand had slowly risen. He shook his head and said, barely audibly, 'No, sir,' eliciting grunts and groans from the other boys.

'Well done, John. Now lads, the point of this is to introduce the concept of a theorem. A theorem is a mathematical statement which has been proven. It consists of two parts - a hypothesis and a conclusion. A distinction must be made between a theorem and its converse. This is of paramount importance. When a theorem and its converse are *both* true, they can be combined into one statement of the form 'if and only if'. So, two triangles are congruent if and only if…what? Be prepared to tell me on Monday. You are now free to leave!'

Enfield could always sense the mood of a class and it was well past time to end this one. He suspected he had made a meal of introducing theorems, but his mind had been elsewhere. He caught Goodricke's attention.

'John, would you remain for a moment?'

Two of the boys scrambling to depart sniggered and smirked.

The culprits, I'll wager, he thought.

Enfield walked around from behind his desk.

'Have any of the other lads been troubling you John? Are any of them still making sport with you?'

Goodricke looked at his notebook with *Mathematics, Trigonometry and Logarithms* written across the marbleised cover in his own bold script. He slid his finger down the handwritten table of contents to page twenty-five. Enfield tapped his shoulder.

'John, are some of the other lads still troubling you?'

Goodricke shook his head and turned to the selected page.

Enfield slid a bench over and sat next to him.

'Ah, the right-angled oblique triangle. You really do lose yourself in this work, do you not?'

No reply.

Perhaps it is not 'lose' so much as 'find', he thought.

'John, might I look at your exercise book?'

Goodricke nodded.

The handwritten table of contents contained chapters such as

The Solution of the several cases of right-angled and oblique angled triangles by calculation.

He went to the inside back cover and was surprised to find sketches of Orion, Taurus, Auriga, and Gemini along with the Moon, Milky Way and other constellations.

'I had no idea you were at all interested in astronomy.'

'Some, sir.'

He sighed and handed back the notebook. Goodricke was close to moving on from Warrington, but to what? He wondered what might be the best circumstance for someone so bright, but with a condition most employers preferred to avoid.

'John,' he said, gently resting his hand on his shoulder. Goodricke looked at him with the concentrated stare that always compelled care in his speech.

'Will you stop by tomorrow for afternoon tea?'

Goodricke nodded and returned to his triangles. Enfield stood, sighed and left to visit another Warrington tutor, Gilbert Wakefield.

He was in gloomy mood. There had been a few students pestering young John, but he could sort that out. His real concern was the lad's future. There had been disturbing rumblings about Warrington's closure and he wanted to set him on a propitious path well beforehand.

Warrington was one of a small number of dissenting academies established by those at variance with the Church of England. Emphasising maths and technological subjects, they were created to counter the stifling pedagogical orthodoxies of Oxford and Cambridge. Since its inception twenty-four years earlier only four hundred students had passed through it. A few of them had been part of the problem. Enfield found it hard to accept that some of those for whom the academy had been created would contribute to its closure, however inadvertently.

He arrived at Wakefield's lodgings and lifted the knocker. The door swung open to reveal his host holding a glass of sherry.

'Ah, Enfield, here for a bit of a grouse, are we? It is written all over your face. Well, come in for a glass and let us get stuck in.'

Enfield could usually abide his colleague's insufferably perky mood, but not at the moment.

They entered the study and Enfield was glad for the warmth the fireplace provided.

'Take a seat while I get you a glass.'

Enfield stared into the fire.

'What is on your mind, old fellow?'

'It seems that one or two of the lads have been troubling Goodricke.'

'Ah, that again.'

'Yes, well, not entirely. I fear the seeds of our ruination were sown in our own creation.'

'I am unable to take your meaning here, sir.'

Enfield was a bit ahead of himself and paused to collect his thoughts. His ultimate focus was not the academy, but Goodricke. Still, there were things that needed to be said.

'Wakefield, I needn't explain to you our founding philosophy. Because of it we have been the beneficiary of many philanthropists moved to support us as there is precious little in a Cambridge or Oxford education relevant to their industry.'

'And your point?' asked Wakefield sipping his sherry.

'My point?' said Enfield. 'My point is, what have *we* produced? The majority of our students have become either Unitarian ministers after dozing in Cairo Street Chapel or otherwise saw their idle time spent here as wholly adequate preparation for a calm future of happy uselessness.'

'Well,' replied Wakefield, 'I haven't actually done a count. Do you think it is as bad as all that? I mean surely…'

'Yes, I do,' said Enfield waving him off. He stared into his empty glass and continued.

'I am afraid there is a culture that sends the wrong type our way - students who do nothing for our reputation. We have acquired inflamed Irishmen and the snot-nosed scions of slaveholders who abuse the liberties granted them. And there's an irony for you,' said Enfield with an upraised glass.

Wakefield rose to fill it.

'And then we receive the profligate outcasts of our great public schools who have learned little and are sent hither as a last resort. And of course, we mustn't forget rejects from Oxford and Cambridge themselves - students whose indolence was too much even for them. We receive the pampered offspring of the wealthy who consider us as nothing more than a type of servant.'

He paused for a breath.

'Have you not heard of their latest perpetration?'

'I do not believe I have, no.' said a now subdued Wakefield.

'Just the other morning, several landlords here found their signboards had become signs of bewilderment! In a single night, the *Red Lion* became *The Roebuck*. The *George and Dragon* appears now as the *Eagle and Child*. It is not only bad advertising for them, it is also bad advertising for us.'

'But, surely, Enfield, a harmless prank...'

'No and no, sir! The students are too young and ill-educated when they arrive; there is not the sufficient power of enforcing discipline. Our academy is neither school nor university; it is without the supervision exercised in the one, and it lacks the influence and authority of the other. The students are treated as men, whilst they are but a set of reckless boys. We have even received a few letters from fathers complaining we have failed to transform the lead they send us into gold, the bloody cheek. I mean to say, sir, they should not be so surprised when their progeny returns as dead weight.'

Enfield wondered why Wakefield had not seen this side of the school's difficulties before now. He did not seem to realise the dissenting mind-set that gave rise to this academy should not extend into the classroom itself. The students, he had thought, do not seem to understand the meaning of personal accountability, of being mindful of their circumstance and privilege.

Wakefield again refilled their glasses.

'Enfield, what has brought all this on? Surely not this silly signboard episode alone?'

Enfield sighed. 'No, of course not. It is Goodricke that is of most concern.'

'Why him?'

'He is far and away our best student, Gilbert. No. He has been our best ever. I thought he was so in spite of his affliction. Now, however, I see it is just as likely *because* of it. He is not so consumed by distractions, by this swirl of anarchy about him. He does not take part in the high jinks of the other lads, but only gets on with his studies. So, they taunt him behind his back - and to his face as well. One would think they would tire of this, but he is a continual reminder of their own lacklustre performance, of time wasted. I am sure some of the others with a full complement of faculties might well wonder what they could achieve if the likes of him can so produce. Or perhaps I am mistaken in all this. I do not know.'

'It appears this has been on your mind for some time.'

'Yes, it has,' said Enfield. 'What if the majority of our compliment was like him? I would then not so dread our situation.'

'But really Enfield, what can we do? We have more or less an open-door policy here as you well know and therefore receive the leavings from every station. I do not see any way we might apply restrictions to our entrants. We may not even have taken in Goodricke, but that fellow - Braidwood? - did write a rather compelling letter.'

Enfield gave him a sharp look.

'No, no, of course not. Otherwise, we are no better than those Cambridge Conformists. We have taken in Goodricke whereas they would never have accepted him,' added Wakefield.

'Nor Oxford either. So, no restrictions,' said Enfield. 'But the truth is, I believe we are heading for our own dissolution. We cannot last much longer and I accept this. My concern is not for our academy's future, but Goodricke's. He will soon depart, but to what situation?'

'Well, he will not become a vicar!' said Wakefield with a chuckle. 'And in any case, his family is of some means and will sustain him. The lad will not be cast out.'

'Of course, of course, but it is not the circumstance of his habitation that is of concern. The lad has talent, Wakefield, real talent. It must not be wasted, but he will have obstructions others will not. It is one thing to have some acceptance for the deaf, to not be quite so dismissive, but to salary one is something else entirely. There are still those amongst us who would not give such as him a place under any circumstance. The lad just cannot go knocking on doors. There are yet many who shall unjustly regard his condition as a liability. I am convinced there is much he can achieve, but he requires a suitable circumstance.'

'You shall have no argument from me on that score,' said Wakefield.

'Yes, but the matter is pressing. We have been losing supporters. There can be no denying this. We are in a bad state, but you know all this, or at least you should.'

'Oh, I do, Enfield, I do,' said Wakefield who thought the whole school might as well now follow the smoke up the chimney.

'You have something planned, I'll wager,' he added and rose to stir the coals.

'Yes, yes I do. I meet with him on the morrow.'

'And your purpose in doing so?'

'How might you describe him?' asked Enfield who was glad he was finally getting around to what he really came to discuss.

'What do you mean? He is a quiet lad…' Immediately Wakefield said this he knew it wasn't quite what he meant. He now spoke through his frustration.

'Well, dash it all Enfield. I really do not know the lad all that well, if I must confess it. I will say he seems to lie between Scylla and Charybdis.'

'How so?'

'I cannot see him as a scrivener or something similar. Even if he were to prefer such drudgery I am afraid there are those who, once his condition is known, will shy away from any association. On the other hand, were he to attempt the predictable pursuits of an heir such as Parliament, philanthropy, hunting, indeed the whole ornate social life of the upper classes, I fear he would find that rather limiting as well. So, none of that. The signpost to his future points to what he might best accomplish in complete silence.'

Enfield paused, sipped his sherry, thought for a moment and replied.

'That is my sentiment as well. I am sure the best path for him is one where his impairment is not only irrelevant, it could also be an asset.'

'You do not ask for much, do you?' said Wakefield.

'No, I do not. He harbours a deep quiet but, oddly enough, I suspect *that* is the real Goodricke. It is not something *caused* by his deafness. I feel his condition only reinforces some deep-seated preference for depth over breadth, for keeping his enthusiasms private and so forth. Do you see?'

'Are you saying that his being deaf has made him become more of himself? If that makes any sense.'

'Something like that, yes.'

'Well, if that is the case, there's an end to it.'

'No, Wakefield, it is only the beginning. There is more. Do you not notice how he speaks?'

'Rather well, I would have thought.'

'This is all speculation, mind you, but his father informed me Goodricke lost his hearing after he could speak and read but little. His development of language after that must have drawn more on the written form than the spoken. That is why his speech is less colloquial, why it sounds like text on a page. His deafness has made him sound more intelligent than perhaps otherwise would have been the case.'

They were silent for a moment. Wakefield saw that his colleague was in some distress and thought of something else he might consider.

'How does he compare with other students?'

'You already know the answer. He is excellent at maths and…'

Wakefield raised his palm for Enfield to stop.

'Let me rephrase. Perhaps you might consider where his passions lie. What he is drawn to? That must narrow the question as to an occupation, surely. You have taught a fair number of our lads. Were not some of them more settled about the sort of man they expected to become? What subjects did they then pursue in aid of this? If you have any understanding of this then merely by knowing of Goodricke's own preferences you know him.'

'Well, there is his work in maths…'

'Enfield, again, that is not quite what I mean. I am saying to look at this from another remove. Look at the subjects *themselves*. What type of mind, what type of approach do they demand? Now, take Goodricke. He enjoys maths, correct? Another way of saying this is that he prefers to work in an established framework, in a discipline with accepted authority, where muddle and emotion are minimal. Do you see?'

Enfield shifted in his seat. Wakefield was right. Goodricke was drawn to work that demanded certainty, exactness, precision and order with an intolerance for ambiguity or vagueness. But there was still the problem of his deafness. He required a milieu where this was of no consequence, one where it might actually be an advantage.

And then it came to him.

*

The following day Enfield looked out at a darkening sky and hoped Goodricke would arrive before the rain. Was he doing the right thing? *Well, I'm not condemning him to be chained to an oar*, he thought. Still, this was more than simple counselling on a career path. He wanted him to leave with more of a sense of his capacity than when he arrived.

His housekeeper stood in the study doorway.

'A student has arrived for you, sir.'

'Send him in Mrs Dyson, send him in.'

'It's going to soon rain fierce, sir. I can smell it.'

'Yes, yes.'

Enfield rose and took a few steps to calm himself.

'Might we have some tea and cake?'

'I have already started preparing, sir, as per usual.'

'Thank you, Mrs Dyson.'

Goodricke entered, carrying his maths notebook.

'No, John. This is not a tutorial,' said Enfield pointing at the notebook and shaking his head.

Goodricke nodded.

Let's get right to the point, he thought.

'John, take a seat,' said Enfield, sitting opposite.

'Well, John, thank you for coming. I, ah, well…I have asked you here to discuss what you might wish to do after you leave Warrington. Have you given this any thought?'

Goodricke lowered his head. He looked up and spoke in his soft voice.

'Continue my studies?'

Enfield sat back in his chair and reflected.

'Yes, but what interests you the most, John? Is it maths? Geometry?'

'Must I choose?'

'No, John, of course not, no. You are good at these things. No, you are better than that. You are excellent. My question is whether you have given any thought on how you might wish to apply your skills?'

Enfield looked out as sheets of rain beat against the windows. Goodricke had followed his gaze and he waited for him to return his attention before continuing.

'Some lads here will find a suitable position clerking somewhere. And there are some who shall manage to continue their idle ways, more's the pity. But neither of these is you.'

Enfield paused. A low rumble of thunder seemed to underscore the occasion.

'On the other hand, there are not so many who have an application for your knowledge of triangles. Do you understand?'

Goodricke nodded.

'John, I wish to suggest something. Perhaps it is something you have already given thought to,' he said, hoping against hope.

He waited for a reply, but none came.

'Yes, you ought to continue your studies in natural philosophy with more a focus on the application of your skills. Do you see? Now, some pursuits do not require as much paraphernalia as might others. Chemistry, for example cannot be explored quite so easily without investing in special accommodation and material. Although, I will say it is a pity you have not had the benefit of Mr Joseph Priestley who was once on staff here. Do you know of him John? His studies on gases are most noteworthy, his discovery of oxygen in particular, although Monsieur Lavoisier may have another word on the matter.'

There was a soft knock on the door.

'Tea now, sir?'

'Yes, Mrs Dyson, just here. Thank you.'

She placed the tray on the small table between them, smiled at Goodricke and departed.

Enfield was grateful for this interruption to his rambling and poured out the tea. Goodricke became interested in the cake and selected a piece.

Enfield returned to the matter at hand.

'So, you see, John, your road will be easier in a field of study that does not require quite so much equipment. But there is more to it than that because of your... circumstance. Nature has denied you much, John, but not the gift of a splendid imagination.'

Goodricke's puzzled look had him wondering whether he had taken the right approach, but he pressed on.

'John, you cannot hear, it is true. But that is not a hindrance to the study of the natural world. The lack of hearing does not mean she cannot be studied. And where is this truer than the great repose of stars overhead? Do you like studying the stars, John?'

'I like looking at them. They are quite beautiful, but they are also a great puzzle.'

'Why do you say that?'

'Well, sir, they provoke many questions, yet I do not know how we are to ever answer them.'

'Well, John, would you not like to try? What I mean to ask is, have you ever thought to study the stars as a proper profession?'

'Not really, sir.'

'Never?'

'No, sir.'

'And why is that?'

He looked down before replying.

'Well, sir, it has to do with a passage in *Love's Labour's Lost*.'

'Shakespeare? I do not understand.'

Enfield had to strain to hear his reply over the wind and rain.

> *These earthly godfathers of Heaven's lights*
> *That give a name to every fixed star,*

Have no more profit of their shining nights
Than those that walk and know not what they are.

This was the opening that Enfield needed.

'A lovely passage, John, but Berowne, the character here, is only saying one need not study the stars to appreciate their beauty. It does not mean one should not try to understand the workings of the natural world all around. Do you understand?'

'I think so, sir.'

'You mustn't think yourself incapable John. You are most capable. May I tell you why?'

'Yes, sir.'

Enfield cleared his throat.

'John, astronomy is unique in all of natural philosophy. It cultivates nearly every faculty of the mind: memory, the power to reason and the imagination are all improved by its study. By the precise and mathematical character of many of its discussions it enforces exactness of thought and expression, and corrects that vague indefiniteness so characteristic of literary studies. Do you understand? I ask you to think on it. All you need is your mind and your eyes, both of which you employ in a manner better than most. It is the one subject in which human understanding appears in its whole magnitude, and through which man can best learn of this world he has been born into. Newton has given us the tools to understand the motions of the heavens. It is as if we are in a great clock, John. God is the Great Clockmaker and his creation a vast machinery of gears and wheels endlessly spinning in unceasing cycles.'

Goodricke remembered sitting on his father's shoulder, watching the goings of his clock.

'I have never thought of astronomy quite in that way, sir. I thought perhaps it beyond my reach.'

'No, John. It is well within your reach. You have the right qualities of mind and you are most fortunate to have the leisure and time necessary to its study. Let me say one more thing, the most important thing of all.'

Enfield paused for the final point he had been saving.

'Knowledge of the stars cannot be found in noise and restlessness. Only in silence can one learn of them. Look at how all things in nature grow in silence. The stars, the Moon and the Sun move in silence, they exist in silence. Their secrets, their hidden treasures are best found in silence. And in this way your own world of silence can be seen as a gift, John. Do you understand?'

No reply.

'John, are you all right?'

'Yes, sir. Sorry. It is just that I never thought my being deaf provided any real benefit,' said Goodricke as he quickly rubbed his eyes.

'It can, John. It truly can.'

8

Bath

William Enfield had little doubt that Goodricke could succeed at astronomy. He was less sure how he might be regarded by other practitioners of that science. *At least he is not a woman*, he thought, that would make it just about impossible to receive any acceptance by the fraternity of gentlemen astronomers.

He was not aware that one hundred and thirty miles to the south in the town of Bath, England's most productive and talented astronomer, William Herschel, benefited from the assistance provided by his sister Caroline. Through this close association she became as competent an observer as most of the members of that gentlemen's fraternity Enfield fretted over.

*

It was cold, yes, but that alone would never prevent William Herschel from observing. His sister Caroline was less hardy.

'Wilhelm, we must now to return to the inside, please.'

'Eh? You are mumbling, my dear,' said her brother.

Caroline Herschel brusquely peeled away the scarf wrapped around her head and spoke again, vapour rising with every exhalation.

'I say we cannot observe any more this night,' she said, one hand on a hip, the other gesturing.

'And why is that?' asked Herschel now finally lifting his head from the telescope's eyepiece.

'The ink Wilhelm, it is now like a - how you to say it - it is much thick now.'

'A paste.'

'Yah, yah. A paste. It is much cold to write to the notes or to draw any diagram. So, you must now please just to stop.'

'This is unfortunate. Still, just a bit longer, eh? Perhaps I can memorise this pattern here and sketch it out before a warming fire.'

Herschel returned to the eyepiece. They were observing from the road in front of their River Street home in Bath. There was not enough space in the small back garden to accommodate this new telescope.

They were an odd pairing. He was ten years her senior and over a foot taller. She was a tiny woman, heavy lidded and marked with smallpox scarring. Yet she had a confident bearing that belied her diminutive stature. Her brother, on the other hand, attracted attention the minute he walked into a room. Thin-lipped, with a broad forehead and an aquiline nose, he exuded an air of quiet resolve and patrician dignity.

Some would say Herschel was dedicated to astronomy, others that he nursed an obsession. He had arrived in Bath sixteen years earlier intending to work as a composer, performer and tutor. He came from a musical family in Hanover where he was an oboist in a regimental band. When marching began to overtake music, he emigrated to England. After establishing himself in England, he returned to rescue a grateful Caroline from days of domestic drudgery. She too had looked forward to a career in music, but it was now clear her performance as first principal in Handel's *Messiah* two years earlier may well have been its high-water mark. Since then she found her musical training slipping further down her brother's list of priorities. He did, at least, insist they converse in English to smooth her adaptation to English society. She remained loyal, but on occasion, like this night, she reflected on their divergent ambitions.

His reflecting telescope with a mahogany barrel and octagonal cross-section was of his own construction. He was especially proud of its hand-polished five-inch speculum mirror. No telescope could magnify stars enough to make them look like anything other than points of light, but a larger mirror did reveal more of them. He planned to survey the entire night sky in order to answer these questions. On some nights, such as this, Caroline suspected he strove to complete the survey in one go.

Herschel had divided the sky into several imaginary regions or 'tiles' to order his star counts. This night he searched the tiles that lay along the ecliptic. He was at Leo when he noticed that its bright star Regulus was drifting westward out of the field of view. The telescope had to be repositioned to offset the Earth's rotation, one of Caroline's duties.

'Caroline, it is time for a new bearing.'

'Ach,' said Caroline, stomping her feet whilst blowing on her fingertips protruding from fingerless gloves. She moved around to the rear of the telescope, lifted the wooden carriage and slowly swung it around into its new position.

'Ah. Just good.'

'*Danken sie Gott*,' said Caroline, reverting to her native German.

'Wilhelm, it is cold. I am cold.'

'Yes, yes, just a little longer. It will be dawn soon.'

Caroline was experienced enough to know that dawn was not going to be soon. She placed what few notes there were along with the ink and quills into a small basket and went inside, stepping past sundry tools, benches and unfinished telescopes in the ground floor workshop to return upstairs to the main quarters.

Regulus again reached the edge of the field of view.

'The telescope must be moved Caroline.'

'Caroline?'

He looked up to discover he was alone. Perhaps it was too cold after all. He was about to prepare the telescope for storage when he noticed a bright object just above the trees to the south.

Mars.

Planets, unlike stars, are resolvable as discs when magnified through a telescope. The Martian polar caps were just visible, but the southern cap appeared larger than he remembered. Had it grown? Did this indicate a seasonal change? He wanted to sketch it but had no ink. Well, there was always tomorrow.

He carefully wheeled the telescope inside, wiped it down and returned to the main quarters. Caroline, still bundled in a heavy cloak, sat at the spinet, absentmindedly playing random chords. He saw to the fire, lit a few more candles and sat across from her. She turned to face him with folded hands in her lap.

'Do not mind me, Wilhelm. I am just in a mood. It will pass.'

'So, this is more than the weather?'

'I know I am not a handsome woman, Wilhelm, tiny and scarred as I am. I know. But my singing was good. I worry that now it is no longer so good. I worry because one must both practice and rest and it is hard to do these when I am all the night awake. But my thoughts are restless. How you say it one time?'

'A curse?'

'Yes, a curse. I too now see a passion for the stars. Perhaps they pull me away from my music and I am sorry sometimes. Do not worry for me.' She gave a little shrug and added, 'And also it is cold.'

William Herschel cared deeply for his sister. He considered his thoughts and finally spoke.

'My dearest Caroline, you are an intelligent woman. Therein may lie part of the difficulty. You have had success with your music, but many attend only to be seen, not to listen. Perhaps I am wrong, but your mood is not from a lack of music, but lack of friendship. We both know there are many women in English society who struggle to compose a complete sentence, let alone sing an aria. They sense that you are not only able to do so, but that you engage in discourse on matters far removed from their grasp. They see you as they see me - someone not only possessed by the stars, but also on visitation from them.'

She gave a little laugh.

He continued. 'You are as familiar with the patterns and rhythms of the heavens as anyone I know. Better than Newton himself, I daresay, who spent his nights cloistered in the confines of his own brain and who did not know the difference between Perseus and a plum.'

She brushed away a tear.

'So, this being the case, I see your difficulties in making pleasantries with the ladies of the Pump Room who see no further than the hems of their farthingales whilst you skip about the stars. You discomfit them. I have heard you refer to more than one as a *dummkopf*. Never forget that the height of the stars is greater than that of the notes of any aria that strains and fails to reach them. Their contemplation requires a greater ascendance than one can ever reach singing Handel.'

She started to mention that Handel's *Ode for St Cecilia's Day*, the patron saint of music, may be an argument against this, but realised he was only making a point. She was not sure about Newton, but she knew her brother's insight into her relations with the ladies of Bath was true. There was no way she would broach the topic of astronomy over tea in the Pump Room, vacuous and vapid as they were. Their experiences and ideas tended to be common, but not deep, while those that were deep, were not common.

'And do not forget how our father would take you out on those clear and frosty nights into the road to make your acquaintance with the constellations and your delight in this. I remember your own fascination with our little globe upon which we drew the equator, the ecliptic and the stars of the zodiac.'

'I remember,' she said, looking off into the distance.

'I believe our shared passion has matured and we now march to a different beat than others.'

'Is that so true, Wilhelm?'

'I believe it to be so, Caroline. Most who regard God's great creation of stars only languish amongst them. But for you and me the silence of the night concentrates our restless yearnings which the busier day distracts in a thousand little ways. The day may afford groves and grottoes equally hidden and silent as the night itself, but it provides no mystery, no problems so worthy of the mind's attention. The stars move more silently than the Sun and calm the restive mind more easily. We may flatter ourselves that we are in some way connected to their mystery and are vain enough to give loose to a thousand thoughts about them that are extravagant and easing.'

'Wilhelm, I have not heard you speak such before now.'

'Perhaps, but I believe there to be little profit in voicing the more intimate aspects of our endeavour to all and sundry. To do so would only bring it to the level of gossip. But you, my dear, are not all and sundry.'

'Wilhelm, I…' She could not complete her sentence. She only knew the bond between them was stronger than ever.

'And do not forget that we do not work in isolation. We *have* been recognised by those that matter. You will recall William Watson of the Royal Society who solicited my membership in the Bath Society? And do not forget that

Nevil Maskelyne, the Astronomer Royal himself, has called upon us here and is someone with whom I regularly correspond. As for others who may laugh into their sleeves as we pass, such as these count for nothing.' He waved his hand as if swatting away a fly.

'Wilhelm, does this acceptance by other astronomers reach to a woman?'

He paused. This required a careful answer.

'I will say this much. A good result simply cannot be ignored. They could *not* dispute it merely on the basis of some difference on the part of its presenter.'

They sat in silence for a moment. The hint of a change in the light hung in the air.

'It shall be daybreak soon. I am sure we both need the benefit of sleep. I must rest before this evening's meeting of the Philosophical Society.'

He gently placed his hand on her shoulder and left. She walked to the window and watched the stars fade in the coming dawn.

*

William Herschel left for his weekly meeting at the Bath Philosophical Society. The Society had begun only a few years earlier 'for the purpose of discussing Scientific and Phylosophical subjects and making experiments to illustrate them', according to its founder, Thomas Curtis, governor of the Bath general hospital. Other such Societies had been formed throughout the country, largely to provide an opportunity for those scientifically minded, but isolated. Membership in the Bath Society was limited to twenty-five and Herschel was one of those first invited to join. He looked forward to an evening with those few who could appreciate his work in astronomy, or at least pretend to. It did not have the prestige or power of the Royal Society, founded in London over a century earlier, but it would do for now.

At the beginning of the century Bath still maintained its medieval form of tightly packed streets and alleys all squeezed within its walls. By Herschel's time, however, it had broken through to become a graceful sprawl with terraces and crescents elegantly draped over the surrounding hills.

The walk from River Street to the Society's meeting place passed through the Circus and gently descended to the town centre where an old Roman spa, built around naturally occurring hot springs, remained. This feature attracted tourists from the aristocracy and Herschel knew that although Bath was not London, neither was it a backwater.

He entered the Circus, a circular space three hundred feet in diameter bounded by honey-coloured Palladian triple terraces, and made for the southern exit leading to Gay Street. From there he moved on to Martha Bally's bookshop on Milsom Street. It was a natural enough choice for the Society's meeting place, as it was a circulating library where members might not only learn of books relevant to their field of study, but also borrow them for a time.

Other members who had already arrived were enjoying their pre-meeting sherries.

'Ah, Herschel.'

William Watson approached.

'And how has this day presented itself?'

'Sir, if you know me, you may well ask how the night has done,' said Herschel.

'Of course, Herschel, of course.'

'*Lord, you can be pompous at times*, thought Watson.

He knew full well Herschel was a dedicated observer, but sometimes it appeared he wanted everyone else to know. They had met in an odd circumstance. Watson had been heading home, spotted Herschel in the middle of the road looking through a telescope, and stopped his carriage to investigate. Herschel explained that, due to insufficient back garden space, he sometimes commandeered the road for his observations. Watson was astounded at the quality of the optics, all the more so when he learned that Herschel himself had made his own mirror. Moreover, he was not simply observing the Moon, but actually attempting to determine the height of lunar mountains by estimating shadow lengths. It was a true scientific study. He did not hesitate to invite Herschel to join the Bath Society.

'So, William, has the goddess of the heavens revealed any more of her secrets?'

Herschel thought for a moment about the possibility of seasonal changes on Mars, but was reluctant to divulge anything in so casual a circumstance.

'Nothing of note at the moment, but I suspect a paper or two to be forthcoming.'

'Of course. Pardon my curiosity, but we do not have many local observers of the garden variety to whom we might direct our enquiries.'

This play on words did not go unnoticed. Herschel asked, 'What might you know of garden varieties elsewhere?'

'I am sure you know of most. Ah, yes. there is this one gentleman in York, recently arrived - Nathaniel Pigott. I have heard he has built an exceedingly fine observatory. His son Edward is also keen, although I am told he is just as likely to be found in a Drury Lane circle seat than the one by his telescope.'

'Perhaps I shall make their acquaintance.'

'I am sure you shall. Ah, the meeting is being called to order. Shall we take our seats?'

9

The Treasurer's House, Spring 1781

Eleanor Dalrymple, manager of the Treasurer's House in York, knew the day ahead would be busier than usual. A new resident was scheduled to arrive.

Two maids and a cook saw to the domestic needs, while Cicero, a mute mulatto, maintained the grounds and ran small errands. At least she thought he was mute. He never spoke, but, strangely enough, could hear quite well; a curious condition. She had taken a liking to him all the same. He was a good lad and, more importantly, an excellent gardener and groundskeeper for someone so young.

Originally the site of an abbey treasury house built seven hundred years earlier, the current structure had undergone changes until nothing was left of its initial role or appearance but the name. After the Reformation, the 'treasure' was confiscated by the Crown and there was no longer any need of a treasurer's house as such. As it lay directly to the rear of York Minster, it was the home to a succession of bishops. Over the years marketplace trends reached even into the Minster Yard to convert it into a residence for solicitors, clerks and members of the rising mercantile class. Eleanor's brother-in-law had commercial interests that included this property and he took her on to manage it - a respectable position for a war-widow thirty-five years of age.

Visitors and residents alike never had any cause for complaint, but this newcomer made her more eager to please than was normally the case. A letter from his father had informed her that *he is deaf, speaks little, but understands quite well. He is most capable and we are sure you shall find him to be of a kind and conscientious nature.*

She was at the dining room table as Cicero rushed in.

'Yes, Cicero?' she said, looking up from the list of supplies to be ordered in.

Cicero pointed in the direction of the front entrance.

'What? Here now? This one is early - he doesn't give us half a chance.'

She noticed Cicero was still holding garden shears.

'And put away the blades Cicero. I suspect there will be some shifting for you in short order.'

She summoned one of the maids and they all walked out together into the sunlit forecourt. The carriage was rather magnificent with well-groomed horses and shining brass fitments. A rather tall distinguished-looking gentleman emerged who turned and spoke to someone remaining inside before approaching.

'Mrs Dalrymple?'

'I am, sir, and you must be Henry Goodricke. We welcome you to the Treasurer's House.'

He tapped his tri-corner and performed a short bow.

'Thank you. I have brought my son John to stay as arranged. You have received my correspondence, of course.'

'I have indeed, sir.'

'So, as I explained, John does not hear at all and speaks but little. However, he will understand your speech and is able to communicate.'

She gave a half turn towards Cicero to see if there was any reaction. There was none.

'I expect he will be happy here, sir.'

'I trust he shall be. It is important to his mother and I as this is his first residence since leaving Warrington, and…well, I am sure you understand.'

She did not, but nodded in agreement nonetheless. She looked past him towards the carriage.

'His mother is not here?'

'No, she preferred to say her goodbyes earlier.'

'Of course.'

He motioned for John to come and join them.

A slight young lad stepped from the carriage, looking over the grounds and building as he approached and Eleanor immediately sensed he was someone self-assured and purposeful.

His short, bespoke wig fitted his age and station. A blue velvet coat with red collar, cream coloured breeches and white stockings completed the image, but he looked slight for his age.

I'll have to fatten him, she thought.

He fixed her with gun-metal grey eyes, bowed and smiled slightly. He looked over at his father.

'John, this is Mrs Dalrymple who oversees the residence,' said Henry.

She noticed how he made sure John knew he was being addressed. She tried to follow suit.

'We welcome you to the Treasurer's House, Master Goodricke.'

'Thank you,' he said, barely above a whisper.

The silence lingered and Eleanor heard herself saying, 'This is Emeline, who will be attending to you. This is Master Goodricke, Emeline.'

Emeline dipped into her practised curtsy, blushing as she did so.

'And this is Cicero Samms, our groundskeeper,' she said gesturing to Cicero standing a step behind.

Goodricke smiled, stepped forward and extended his hand.

'A pleasure to meet you as well.'

Cicero did not react. No young gentleman ever offered his hand before. It was a first.

'Well, shake his hand Cicero, don't be daft,' said Eleanor.

Cicero reached out for a perfunctory handshake and then stepped back.

'Same,' he said.

It took Eleanor a second to realise who had just spoken. She wanted to halt the proceedings and ask him why *now*, but it was not the time.

'Allow me to lead you to your new quarters,' she said.

Henry Goodricke spoke to the driver. 'Harrison, fetch Master Goodricke's trunk and books, there's a good man.'

'Cicero will assist with those,' said Eleanor. 'This way, gentlemen.'

'Just one moment.' Henry returned to the carriage to collect a large wrapped parcel.

'Right then, John. Let us see your new home,' said Henry as he put his arm across his son's shoulders.

They climbed the stairs to the top floor, Eleanor puffing in the lead with Cicero bringing up the rear.

'Here we are then. These rooms are to be yours. One is of course the bedroom and the other the sitting room, study, what may you. There is also a passable view of the Minster, although some think Great Peter's peals can annoy at times.'

The second the words left her mouth she realised what she had said. She flushed a little and lowered her head.

'Oh, sir, I am sorry. I did not think…'

'It is quite all right, Mrs Dalrymple.' said Henry. 'We rather prefer to be regarded as if nothing is out of the ordinary.'

'Thank you, sir. Of course.'

Eleanor Dalrymple had the presence of mind to realise this was a milestone moment in the boy's life.

'Right then. We shall leave you to get settled. Emeline will return later to see to the wash-basin and light a fire in the grate. She will also carry any correspondence to the post-haste and Cicero can run small errands as well. The necessaries are at the rear of the garden, the morning meal is at half seven and the evening meal is at seven. Please let us know should you require anything further.'

'Thank you, Mrs Dalrymple, you have been most kind. Wait for us by the carriage Harrison, will you?'

'Very good, sir.'

'Right then, John, I think this accommodation to be quite suitable,' said Henry as the others departed.

John walked over to a window, placed his small compass on the sill, waited until the needle settled and gave his father a vigorous nod.

'It is perfect, Father.'

'This is for you, John.' Henry handed his son the large parcel.

John looked at him expectantly.

'Open it, then.'

He unwrapped it and gasped when he realised he was holding a copy of *Atlas Coelestis*, the star atlas astronomers either used or coveted. Based on observations made by the first Astronomer Royal, John Flamsteed, its cost was far beyond the reach of all but the wealthy. It was twenty by twenty-four inches of opulence and utility, and Goodricke knew at once how valuable this would be to his work. He could not speak, but his expression was all the thanks his father needed.

At that same moment Eleanor, Cicero and the coachman reached the ground floor.

'Would you care for some refreshment while waiting?' asked Eleanor.

'Thank you, ma'am, but the master doesn't dawdle. Perhaps some water?'

Eleanor saw this as an opportunity to learn something of her new tenant.

'May I ask you a question?' she said as she lifted the ewer. 'It is Harrison is it not? I do not wish you to be indiscreet, but as he will be in my care, more or less, I wish to ask you something if I may?'

'Ma'am?'

'Is he not well? He does not at all look the thing.'

'He is slight, I'll grant you, but is a lad of some exception and can look after himself well enough.'

'Yes, I do see that and, well, apparently he can speak.'

'He can right enough, but speaks little. He is the likes of those who choose their words most carefully. But he seems a quiet lad by nature and would likely not chat much any road. What's of more interest is not that he can speak, but that he can understand what you say, most times anyway. I do not know where the lad got his trainin', but all praise to the gentleman what did that I can say. It is a remarkable thing is that.'

All very interesting, she thought, *as well as reassuring*.

Henry Goodricke joined them and Eleanor tried not to notice his sentimental demeanour.

'Right then, we'll be off. I'm sure we shall be seeing you again. Thank you for your kind attention. We'll see ourselves out. Come along Harrison.'

Eleanor turned to Cicero, who had not yet returned to his clipping.

'Curious about the new resident as well?' she asked.

Cicero did not reply.

*

Eleanor dined with the residents at the evening meal. There were two others, William Guthrie, a young solicitor, and Richard Pomeroy, a clerk. She tried not to think of them simply as a pettifogger and stockjobber, but could not help it. Pomeroy loved to open his mouth to eat and Guthrie loved to open his mouth, period. She placed her hands on the back of Goodricke's empty chair and thought for a moment of what she should say to announce his arrival.

'Gentlemen, someone new has joined our little group here today.'

'Really?' said Guthrie.

Pomeroy wondered whether he should stop eating.

'There is one thing I must tell you. He is a young lad and, well, he is deaf. He cannot hear at all. But he does speak, if a bit softly and with rather measured speech.'

They looked at each other.

'Well, if I may enquire, Mrs Dalrymple. I mean to say; how should we regard him when he joins us at the table?' asked Pomeroy.

She wanted to say *like anyone else, you clot-poled mountebank*, but he instead heard, 'Like anyone else. The lad has the ability, if you do not speak with a mouth full of food, to understand what you are saying. And he has speech. So, yes, as any one of us.'

'Might he be in a particular employ? It would be easier to enter into some discussion,' asked Guthrie.

'Indeed,' added Pomeroy.

'Oh, I doubt you two will have much to discuss with him in that regard,' said Eleanor.

'And why is that then?' asked Guthrie.

'Apparently he is something of an astronomer. At least it appears that is to be his primary activity.'

Pomeroy lowered his fork to consider what that meant.

'An astronomer? What does one do as an astronomer? I mean to say, how is one an astronomer whilst sitting in one's rooms here? Or does he have a shop in the High Street? I do not recall any signboards announcing the business within to be astronomy,' said Guthrie.

'Yes,' said Pomeroy giggling. 'Astronomy done here - best prices in York.'

'You may ask him yourselves, gentlemen,' said an irritated Eleanor. 'I'll just check to see that he understands the evening meal is ready.'

'Right, then.' said Guthrie.

'Well, cheerio,' added Pomeroy.

Such dolts, she thought as she entered the stairwell. And where was he anyway? She climbed the stairs to his rooms, holding a candle in one hand, the folds of her dress in the other.

His door was slightly ajar. She waited until her breath returned and called out, but only got as far as 'Master Good...' She pushed the door open and peered inside. The fire in the grate had gone out and no candles were yet lit. She called out into the darkness, despite herself.

'Master Goodricke?'

She swung the candle around. The bed and wardrobe were in the outer room, but no Goodricke.

At least he has done some unpacking and settled in well enough. What on earth?

She could just see him in the inner room sitting by the open window. He was staring out at what? The Minster?

John Goodricke had been pleased to discover his windows faced southwest. Not perfect, because by the time any star appeared in his primary view it would have passed upper culmination, but no matter, this would still do. He was eager to learn his way around the night sky and identify every single star by name. At least those shown in his new star atlas. Betelgeuse was just moving behind one of the Minster towers. Above Orion was Taurus and to the right of that, Perseus. He felt he was about to step off on a grand tour.

Eleanor sensed she should just leave him be and backed out of the room.

10

The Pigotts & Others

'Sir? Post for you.'

'Thank you, Phillipa.'

'Will there be anything else?'

'More tea. I expect Edward will be down shortly. Or not. He was observing much of the night. Or should have been.'

'Yes, sir.'

Nathaniel Pigott picked at the red wax seal.

'Good morning, Father.'

Edward Pigott stood in the doorway.

'Ah, you have risen. Near a miracle as the second coming. Did you manage a successful night's viewing?'

Edward sat, yawned and reached for the empty teapot.

'Clouds. But I did manage to check the adjustment on the transit beforehand and set the clock. Everything seems to be in order. Is there any more tea?'

'Cook has been told. I trust you checked the clock's goings?'

'Of course.'

'Using what stars?'

'I made three measurements using Vega, Deneb and, um, alpha Cephei – sorry, can't remember the proper name.'

'Alderamin.'

'Right.'

Edward did not wear his light brown hair in the usual close-cropped style needed to accommodate a wig. He did not wear one. This distinction, along with his impish smile and hazel eyes, caught the attention of many a young lady. He easily managed to communicate that, whatever the situation, he was always poised to go his own way. Well, thought Nathaniel, *what I am about to tell him will put paid to that.*

The Pigott family had recently settled in York after living on the continent for over twenty years. Nathaniel saw to it that all his children were educated in France where opportunities were more plentiful for a Catholic family. Despite his maternal grandfather being the eighth Viscount Fairfax, he was considered the poor relation. He nonetheless acquired enough resources to outfit their newly built private observatory with instruments from London's finest makers. Earlier work on cartographic surveys of the principal towns in Flanders and elsewhere established his reputation as a skilled observer and mathematician. He was elected a Fellow of the Royal Society and awarded membership in the Imperial Academy at Brussels and the Academy of Sciences in France, but success came at a price. His work had required much travel, an itinerant lifestyle he had tired of. He hoped this latest move to York would settle Edward's own roving impulses that were at best unbecoming and, at worst, self-destructive.

The maid returned with a pot of tea with a plate of warm eggs and cold ham.

'Lovely,' said Edward as he clapped his hands.

'Thank you Phillipa,' said Nathaniel.

The letter caught Edward's eye as he poured his tea.

'What news have you there?'

'Ah. This has just arrived from Henry Goodricke, a distant relation actually - a sound fellow and gentleman. Do you know of him?'

'I am familiar with the family name,' said Edward while selecting an egg.

'Yes, well, it seems that his son John has moved here. In fact, he is now situated just down the road at the Treasurer's House.'

'Well, jolly for John, I say,' said Edward displaying his trademark charming, disarming and completely innocent smile.

'I'm glad you feel that way as I suspect that you shall be seeing rather a lot of the young lad.'

Edward sensed his father was composing the day's grumble.

'Apparently the boy is quite keen and wishes to pursue astronomical studies. As we are known to be accomplished in this field, Henry asks whether we might make his acquaintance.'

'That seems reasonable,' said Edward, who did not wish to hear anything more on the subject.

'I think we should do more than simply make his acquaintance. In fact, I think you should meet the lad and assist him in any way possible.'

'Um, how old is he?' asked Edward still holding his egg.

'Let us see, let us see,' said Nathaniel running his finger over the letter.

'Seventeen.'

'Seventeen? He is ten years my junior.'

'You were hoping for someone older? Someone you might rove about with?'

'I am not exactly sure what we are to do here.'

'Do? Do? We meet them of course! As requested! And you are going to teach this lad everything that you know!'

'Father...'

'What? Do you fear this shall curtail your dalliances and excursions? Your only saving grace is that what you lack in industry you make up for in intelligence. You can do more. And you shall.'

'But what am *I* to do with the lad? I am no tutor.'

'What you shall do is bring your arse to anchor. Answer his questions, make him feel welcome. Befriend him. Can you not do any of this?'

Edward stared at the egg now perched in its cup.

Nathaniel sighed, looked towards the window and spoke.

'There is one more thing you need to know about this lad.'

'And what is that, pray?'

Nathaniel turned to face his son.

'Young Goodricke is stone deaf.'

'He is what?'

'Are you now deaf as well? Sometimes I do fear you skirt that affliction. Yes, the boy cannot hear, but apparently can speak when 'so disposed' as it here states,' said Nathaniel, waving the letter.

'Now I am flummoxed. Is the lad dim-witted as well? They all seem to be in that lot. How am I ever to proceed? This has the makings of disaster written all over it.'

Nathaniel raised his palm.

'Save your breath to cool your porridge. John has attended Warrington Academy and received the highest marks in mathematical subjects no less. He is no idiot and you shall not speak of him in such terms.'

'Right, Father. If that is your wish.'

'It is my wish. For heaven's sake, man, Henry is a decent sort who has struggled mightily to see his son educated in spite of this disorder. We cannot, we *shall* not, refuse this request.'

'I suppose that could be considered discourteous,' said a now subdued Edward.

'Perhaps we shall have a supper party where we can make proper introductions, where the Goodricke's can meet us and perhaps others. It will have to wait of course until your mother and sister return from London. We shall make them feel welcome. I shall invite them in my reply and there's an end to it.'

Edward's egg had grown cold.

*

Eleanor was pleased to see that her new charge - as that was how she thought of him - had arrived for the evening meal.

'How are you getting on Master Goodricke? Is everything to your liking?'

'Yes. Thank you.'

'But you did not come down for your morning meal.'

'No. Sorry if you waited. I did not retire until dawn.'

'Are you not well? Shall I send for the physician?'

'No, no, I was up all the night observing. I am an astronomer, you see. Did my father not mention this?'

'Perhaps he did. But I did not realise this is something that will keep you awake all the night.'

'But that is when the stars are visible.'

'Of course, take no notice. I'll see to Cook and the meal,' said Eleanor, finally beginning to realise this new lodger was not typical.

Pomeroy and Guthrie entered. They looked at each other when they saw Goodricke and took their regular places. An awkward silence descended over the table.

Goodricke looked over at them, smiled and nodded.

Eleanor returned to see her full residential compliment had assembled for the first time. *How it will all unfold?*

'Gentlemen, this is John Goodricke. John, this is Mr Guthrie and Mr Pomeroy.'

'How do you do, sir? I am Guthrie, William Guthrie. And this is Mr Richard Pomeroy.'

'Yes,' said Pomeroy in confirmation.

'A pleasure,' said Goodricke.

They were taken aback by his youthful appearance. Expecting someone about their age, they sat across from someone ten years younger.

'Mrs Dalrymple tells us that you, um, you are an astronomer. Is this correct?' asked Guthrie.

No response.

Guthrie looked over at Pomeroy as if he might know what was happening. He looked at Goodricke and was about to repeat himself when Eleanor spoke.

'You do realise he must be looking at you whenever you speak?'

Guthrie waited until Goodricke looked over at him before he spoke again.

'Mrs Dalrymple says you are an astronomer,' he repeated.

'Yes.'

'Fascinating, I say, I find that most fascinating,' said Pomeroy.

'You needn't shout, Mr Pomeroy,' said Eleanor into her serviette.

Guthrie looked reproachfully at Pomeroy, despite having shouted himself.

'Do you have a shop in the town?' asked Guthrie as he helped himself to a potato.

'I believe Mrs Dalrymple wishes to speak,' said Goodricke.

Guthrie looked over at Eleanor who was in an attitude of prayer.

'Perhaps we might first say grace?'

'Of course,' said Guthrie

Eleanor touched Goodricke's sleeve.

'Will you say grace for us, Master Goodricke?'

Goodricke looked at each in turn and lowered his head.

'We give thee humble thanks for this thy special bounty; beseeching thee to continue thy loving kindness unto us, that our land may yield us her fruits of increase, to thy glory and our comfort; through Jesus Christ our Lord. Amen.'

'Amen,' said the others.

The *Book of Common Prayer* had been quoted, word for word.

'So, Mr Guthrie, you were saying?' asked Eleanor, while looking at Goodricke with renewed interest.

'Yes,' he said over the basket of bread passed his way. 'I was wondering what astronomers actually do? I mean, how does your consideration of the stars differ from that of others? What can one do beyond just look?'

'Well… Guthries is it?'

'Guthrie.'

'Apologies. As far as my own work is concerned I have only recently arrived and not yet established a proper observing programme. But I can explain the value of the study of the stars in more general terms, if that will suit.'

Guthrie looked over at Pomeroy, who shrugged.

'Is there that much to say?' asked Guthrie.

Goodricke sighed. It was best to avoid the arcane and answer in terms anyone ought to understand and appreciate. Well, almost anyone.

'I can say this much. First, there is the relation between astronomy, map-making and surveying. The extent and sway of the Empire depend upon this. We exert our global control because we know where we are. Ours is a maritime empire so the correct application of celestial navigation is of the utmost importance. I am not completely in sympathy with the ambitions that push the empire's boundaries, but the scientific exploration pursued by all those who sail upon its seas requires safe passage and safe passage requires empire. Astronomy improves the accuracy in determining one's position on the Earth, so it is right at the heart our imperial project. Do you not see the value in this?'

Guthrie was at a loss for words. Eleanor looked at Goodricke with a completely new regard.

He continued.

'And there is another, more important reason, to study the heavens. If we have the ability to understand something of the scale of our planetary system and hopefully that of the stars, then why should we not do so? A study of the stars encourages a pattern of thought leading beyond the distortions of our material existence to the pure harmony of the sublime. That is about all I can say at the moment on the matter.'

Eleanor was speechless. Pomeroy grinned and spoke.

'I would say that the lad has soundly answered, eh Guthrie?'

Guthrie had not expected such eloquence and was unsure how to respond. He asked a final, ill-thought question.

'But I mean to say, if you are…if one is up all the night looking at the stars, how does one acquit oneself during the day?'

Pomeroy thought that was indeed a good question and suspended eating while waiting for Goodricke's reply.

'Why, I sleep of course. And apparently scolded when I miss a meal,' sending a wry smile in Eleanor's direction.

Eleanor thought this last question of Guthrie's strayed into the personal and watched with no small pleasure at the implications of his reply sank in. Goodricke did not have to scratch for a living on the High Street, but held a gentleman's competency that was best not to mock.

Guthrie looked down at his yet untouched plate while Pomeroy smiled in mid-chew.

'Mrs Dalrymple, will you pass the bread, please?' asked Goodricke.

'Of course.'

Guthrie, for once, was unable to come up with a smart reply. Not today anyway.

11

York

Morning sunlight spilled through York, drying the last drops of dew.

'Are you going out, Master Goodricke?'

Eleanor had stopped him in the foyer.

'I thought I might look about the town, Mrs Dalrymple.'

'But you have not had your morning meal! You have missed it again and this will not do at all.'

John wanted to explain why he found shared mealtimes taxing; it was almost impossible for him to regulate the dialogue and even harder to determine changes in topic. Perhaps he would explain later, but not at the moment.

'No need, thank you. I have some rolls here in my haversack. I saved them from last night,' he said, lifting it in confirmation.

'So, you were up all the night again? And now you are going out? Honestly, Master Goodricke, you are but skin and bone. And why look at the stars anyway? They are the same one night to the next, are they not?'

'That is a good question,' Mrs Dalrymple.

'Well, it all sounds rather confusing.'

'The stars are possessed of a certain logic, it is people who are confusing.'

Eleanor did not know about stars, but thought he did have a point about people.

'And what of evening tea? You have missed more than one meal since you have arrived. All right, then. But do get yourself something in the town. I might suggest one or two places if you would like.'

'No, no. I shall be fine.'

'What do you plan to see? I'm afraid there isn't all that much really.'

'The Minster. See what the shops hold. A walk along the Ouse.'

'Right, off you go. I hope you will join us for the evening meal.'

'Yes, Mrs Dalrymple. Thank you.'

She sighed as he stepped out. He always paid close attention as she spoke. She knew the reason, but also thought it came as much from character as condition.

Goodricke crossed the forecourt, the Minster's Great East Window just ahead. He marvelled at the top tracery; God the Father presiding over ranks of saints and angels with biblical scenes from Genesis and Revelation depicted in panels below. He walked along the western side past the octagonal Chapter House and arrived at the main entrance, checking his compass along the way. It was as he suspected - the Minster's principal axis lay on an east-west line and surely not by chance. It meant the south-facing windows on one long side allowed for maximum interior illumination. *Perhaps all medieval cathedrals have a similar orientation*, he thought.

The front façade framed by twin bell towers held the Great West Window. He had to lean well back to take in its full extent. Massive oak doors were bordered by stone effigies of St. Peter and the Saints. He stepped inside and it felt as if he was crossing a symbolic, as well as physical, threshold. His eyes had to slowly adjust to the light before the archbishop's throne over four hundred feet away came into view.

He pulled a guide from his haversack.

The whole Length from East to West, is 524 feet,
The Height of the Lantern to the Top of the
Leads, 213 feet, Length of the Cross Aisle from
North to South 249 feet…The North-West tower
holds Great Peter which rings the hour
supplemented by the six clock bells whilst the
South-West tower holds 14 bells hung and rung to
announce Matins and other such.

Further reading revealed this to be the largest medieval cathedral in all of England, and second only to Chartres. Simple dimensions were interesting enough, but no guidebook could quite convey the atmosphere. Individual iconographic elements combined to communicate more than separate symbology. Was it not similar to the feeling he had when observing the stars?

The intersection of the choir and transepts was the heart of the cruciform floor plan. From there the view up into the Lantern Tower overcame him. He felt as if his soul was being tugged from his breast to float free. Coloured sunlight, filtered through the Rose Window in the south transept, spilled down columns and spread across the stone floor. But it was the central Lantern Tower high overhead that held his attention and he searched for a way aloft.

A little exploration revealed the entrance to a spiralling stone stairway. After a twisting and tiring ascent, he emerged into bright sunlight and beheld an unobstructed view in all directions. *If only I could view the stars from here!* He was startled to discover he was now looking *down* at the twin bell towers that seemed so high when viewed from street level. All of York lay below, a tiny tightly gathered town with a medieval scheme of alleys, ginnels and winding lanes, his new home.

The sweet air of the surrounding countryside encouraged flights of fancy. Great Peter struck the hour and he felt its low frequency vibrations as its deep sonorous swell washed over the rooftops below. He began to recall his path to that point. There was always someone there to help when needed. His father who was determined to find someone to educate him. Mr Braidwood, who did. And Mr Enfield, who helped him understand his deafness was no hindrance. *Is my next advocate here in York?*

After returning to the front of the Minster he sat on the entrance steps to decide where next to explore. His litttle guidebook contained an *Alphabetical Directory to the Merchants and Principal Tradesmen Resident in York*.

Harry Abbey, joiner in North Street.

No.

John Armytage, cordwainer at Ouse Gate.

No use for him.

William Hartley, clock maker at Stonegate.

Ah, a clockmaker. Yes.

The map was checked and a route decided on. Enlivened by this he dug a roll out of his bag and brushed away a fly. He was about to eat when he sensed someone standing over him.

'Have ye a crust for the likes of us?'

The beggar had spoken before Goodricke looked up.

'Are ye deaf? I say have ye a bit of crust for the likes of us? By the cut of your cloth ye can spare a bit.'

Goodricke stared into a soiled outstretched palm, the other hand gripping a crutch. One leg missing above the knee. He looked up into the weary, dirty face of someone not much older than himself.

'Yes, of course,' said Goodricke, surrendering his roll.

'Thankee,' said the beggar who stuffed it into his mouth, performed half a bow and hobbled away. As he did so a couple of street urchins laughed as another of their number hopped about on one foot. The beggar pretended not to notice. Goodricke's heart sank at this silent pantomime. He sat for a moment longer wondering whether he could have done more, but what? He was not used to encounters with the indigent. He got up, dusted himself off and headed for Stonegate, his mood now returned to street level where the air was not quite so sweet as it was atop the Lantern Tower.

York was layered in history. The names of the streets – *Petergate*, *Stonegate*, *Ousegate* – were named from the old Norse *gat*, for passage. The Romans had Latinised the local place name to Eboracum. The Saxons called it Evorwik. Later Vikings, unable to wrap their tongues around this, called it Jorvik. It was, however, signs of the Roman habitation that most endured. A wall still surrounded most of the town, but any enemy had long since vanished.

Goodricke ambled through narrow streets flanked by timbered frame buildings two storeys tall, each kept upright by its neighbour. Upper floors often projected out beyond the dimensions of the floor below, making it possible for someone in one over-sailing storey to reach out across the street and shake hands with someone on the side opposite. Heavy shop signs hung from iron bars. One swayed in the breeze so much the facade itself seemed to torque in rhythm. Wind-blown rubbish scuttled along, bypassing airless alleyways. He looked downward as he walked to avoid the numerous droppings from horse and dog. Responsibility for street cleaning lay with the property owners, but it was one inconsistently met.

Tired and tattered as York was, its citizenry seemed largely of good cheer. A knot of people standing on a corner laughed at something or other. A merchant inspecting his sign hanging from one hinge gestured with a 'what-can-you-do' shrug. Goodricke watched these silent tableaus assemble and dissolve against a backdrop of muddy lanes and half-timbered buildings.

He reached his destination. 'Wm. Hartley - Maker of Fine Clocks', but hesitated to enter when he realised he was not completely sure what to ask for. Astronomical clocks used something he knew to be 'sidereal time', but was that what he needed if he was not using a telescope? Besides, he had squashed a dog turd and thought it best not to carry the odour inside. He reluctantly decided to postpone his visit and continued on down Stonegate toward the Ouse where he would clean his shoe. Now dispirited, he walked through Thursday Market, St Helen's Square and came to King's Staith on the east bank below the Ouse Bridge, a landing stage for small cargo vessels. This was where dung was loaded with not all of it ending up in barges. Many of the city's drains also found their way here. The result was an almighty stink and Goodricke wondered whether his shoe would be the worse for washing it there.

*

That afternoon Eleanor sat alone in the kitchen clutching a cup of black tea mixed with hyson, a personal blend and her one indulgence. Cook was out shopping for the evening meal, while Pomeroy and Guthrie were out doing whatever it was they did. The only sound was the distant rhythmic snipping of garden shears - Cicero trimming back the privet. Cicero. What had happened in the forecourt? She had never heard him speak before or since. She continued speaking to him as if he might reply, but he had withdrawn into his silence once again. The garden was immaculate and there was no cause for complaint, but it was a mystery to ponder, nonetheless.

Women in her social class were rarely in employment, but this was an acceptable circumstance. The Treasurer's House no longer had any connection with the Minster. It was now privately held and well situated to accommodate the working professional gentleman. Someone was needed to manage it - like a manor's overseer who saw to it that what needed to be done was done.

Her thoughts floated well beyond the boundary of the back garden. She wondered, after so much time, why she still grieved over the loss of her husband, but there were no rules about such a thing were there? She became a widow the instant Major Thomas Dalrymple of the 5th Northumberland Regiment of Foot stopped a musket ball at the battle of Bunker Hill in Boston, a Pyrrhic victory for the British. A letter from a fellow officer explained it all. It was bad enough the British assault was poorly planned, but those Yankee marksmen actually had the audacity to aim at the officers. Thomas had been buried at some place in Boston called The Common. Was this like the common graves set aside for paupers in York? She nurtured a secret desire to travel there one day and find his grave. One day.

She looked at the letter from John's father that arrived earlier. Thoughts drifted. Perhaps if Thomas had not been shot dead, perhaps if the American Colonials had never had their insurrection, perhaps if the King had not been so belligerent, perhaps she would have had a son of her own.

John was standing in the kitchen doorway.

'Master Goodricke, did you wish to see me?'

'I just saw Emeline who mentioned you have some post for me?'

'Oh, yes, I have it for you here. And how did you find York?'

'The Minster is rather special, is it not? The town is not quite so compelling and a bit ragged in places. I did notice a beggar or two.'

'York does have its share.'

'One poor fellow did not seem all that old.'

'Was he a red-haired lad with a missing leg and the one crutch?'

'Yes. Not a very happy fellow.'

'That may well have been Richard Somerset who was wounded in the Colonies by something called chain shot. He has had a difficult time of it, I'm afraid.'

Goodricke sensed she too might be affected by the war in the Colonies, but thought it best not to ask.

'Mrs Dalrymple, I wonder if I might have a cup of tea?'

'Of course! And you have had nothing to eat I'll be bound. Some bread and jam as well, I should think. You really must look after yourself.

He read the letter while Eleanor left to prepare the tea. The encouraging news it carried brought back his Lantern Tower reflection on those who had helped him. Did this letter presage someone new with whom he might work?

Eleanor returned to the table with thick slices of bread and rhubarb jam.

'Good news I trust?' she asked, nodding towards the letter while pouring out the tea.

'Yes, Mrs Dalrymple. It is from Father. We have been invited to meet with the Pigotts here in York. It is for a supper invitation in a fortnight. He mentions that father and son are both astronomers and that they wish the pleasure of my company. I say, this is good news indeed.'

'I am happy for you, John. Does he mention where they live?'

John returned to the letter.

'Here in York on Bootham Road.'

'Oh, that is just nearby! You can walk from here.'

Goodricke nodded, smiling as he ate.

12

Goodricke & Pigott

'He is doing well, is he not?' asked Levina of Henry, more a statement than question. They were en route to collect their son for an evening with the Pigotts.

Henry thought for a moment before replying as they reached the Treasurer's House forecourt.

'Yes, yes he is. We expected him to have the same trials and concerns as any boy. You know, Levina, I do not worry over how well he manages the world of the hearing. I am more concerned that he develops a fruitful association with such as the Pigotts, who can aid his astronomical studies. That is the real purpose of this evening. My God, it was a lucky stroke sending him to Warrington. Enfield was only too right in seeing his potential.'

'But not your own father.'

Henry winced. It was true his father was cool towards John. He could never accept his deafness, or that he could in any way be accomplished. It was a side of his father he could not accept.

'True enough. But let us hope something can come of this evening, shall we?'

Henry looked up at his son's window, but no one appeared.

Eleanor answered his knock.

'A good evening to you, Mrs Dalrymple. We have come to collect John,' he said while touching his tri-corner with a forefinger.

'Good evening,' said Eleanor.

'But John is not here. He left some time ago.'

'Oh?'

'Why, yes. He mentioned you would be stopping, but preferred to leave earlier. Not to worry as it is just nearby.'

'Ah. I see. And how have you been keeping?'

'Well enough. Thank you.'

'And John, he has been settling in well I trust?'

'He has become a most welcome addition to our little community here, but he needs to eat and sleep more. His astronomical studies keep him up all hours.'

'Yes, well...'

'And, if I may, sir, he is an unusual boy. You have done very well, indeed.'

Henry did not know quite what to say. It was, for him, a level of familiarity not so quickly reached.

'Thank you. We shall be off then. Thank you again,' said Henry, pleased at learning of his son's initiative.

Eleanor gave a little wave to Levina. *An impressive man*, she thought, as Henry returned to the carriage.

'Where is John?' asked Levina.

'It would appear he is already there. Right Harrison, down Bootham Road, if you will.'

Neither Henry nor Levina spoke during the brief journey. Their son had become an able young man and they shared a quiet pride. They arrived at the Pigott residence and Harrison skilfully aligned the carriage step to a mounting block.

'Henry, I believe there is another carriage here,' said Levina as she pointed to one just ahead, the driver apparently dozing.

'It looks to be a hired cab.'

'I thought we were to be the only guests.'

They then felt the evening might be a bit awkward for their son. Henry simply wanted an introduction, but Nathaniel Pigott had insisted they make it a full-blown dinner party. True, the Pigotts may be distant cousins and Nathaniel had been recently elected as a Fellow of the Royal Society, but he was concerned that the topic of his son's interest in astronomy would become diluted with polite conversation. He lifted the shining brass knocker and only had to wait a moment before the door swung open.

'Welcome, Henry, and welcome to you Levina as well,' said Nathaniel as he ushered them through the front entrance with all formality.

'I do not believe you have met my wife Anna and our daughter Mathurina?'

The women simultaneously performed slight bows along with furtive glances at each other's frocks. Levina could not help but notice Anna's open gown, with its fourreau back, tight bodice and puffed-out bosom. This family was not entirely English.

Nathaniel turned to Henry.

'Your son arrived early, so I introduced him to our observatory and believe he is there still. Shall we have to carry his meal out to him?' he said with mock sarcasm. 'He seems quite the enthusiast, Henry, quite the enthusiast.'

Henry wanted to say he was more than an enthusiast, but held back.

'And Edward? I have heard much about him. He will be joining us, I trust?'

'Yes, he should be here shortly,' said Nathaniel.

He had, however, no idea where Edward was.

Nathaniel seemed distracted. His arms and legs were too short for his large round body and he nervously gestured about as he spoke, looking for all the world like an upturned turtle attempting to acquire some purchase. He was, in truth, annoyed over Edward's absence and could barely listen to himself natter on. And where was that giddybrained girl? He doubted their combined absence was a coincidence, but composed himself.

'Come along Henry, there is someone here I wish to introduce.'

Henry and Levina exchanged glances. They entered the sitting room where candelabras and mirrored sconces brought reasonable light. Levina detected an unknown fragrance. A heavy-set woman was perched on the edge of the settee, the man standing beside her smiled through plump cheeks and a permanent squint giving him an air of unwarranted jocularity.

'I would like you to meet Mr Godfrey Pennypacker and his wife Tabatha. Their daughter Penelope will also be joining us, but it appears she has, umm, just stepped away.'

Penny Pennypacker? thought Henry. *What were they thinking?*

Tabatha was holding a fan in one hand and a long, thin hook scratcher in the other - a tool used to dislodge itchy parasites on scalps covered by large coiffures. Levina hoped it would not be used during the meal.

Henry groaned inwardly and Levina looked at him with a raised eyebrow. All they really wanted was a meeting between their son and Nathaniel. Pigott might have meant well, but Goodricke did explain his son's condition in his letter. Perhaps Nathaniel was trying to say in his own way that it was no bother at all really. But Henry now suspected that he was also using this occasion as an opportunity to assist this Godfrey fellow in some way, *a quid pro quo*. It began to look as if it would be a long evening.

'Godfrey is a solicitor here in York and is interested in your work in the Diplomatic Service. So, I am sure you will have much to discuss,' said Nathaniel as he introduced his guest. Henry could not imagine why on earth they would.

'Most pleased to make your acquaintance,' gushed Godfrey, whose grin appeared to be perpetual.

'And I as well, I am sure,' said Tabatha with a high-pitched peep that matched her plump face.

Oh, this is going to go well, thought Henry.

'Anna,' said Levina to break the silence, 'there is a lovely scent here I cannot quite place.'

'Ah, you notice! *Merci*. It is the candles. They are from the American Colonies, something called the Bayberry. These are the last I have because of the rebellion there. I expect they will soon be free to send us more.' she continued, her deliberate *double entendre* revealing her political sympathies. Godfrey glanced at Tabatha, his grin slightly faded.

The parlour maid entered carrying a tray of glasses.

'Sherry anyone?' asked a relieved Nathaniel, clapping his hands and restoring Godfrey's grin.

*

'Ouch!'

'Keep to the path, it's just here.'

'You said that before.'

'Nearly there, now.'

'Honestly, Edward, I had better not have torn my stocking. And what is it again?'

'Our observatory - I want to show you my telescope.'

'Oh really?' huffed Penny, trying, and failing, to keep her hem off the ground. Edward carried a small lantern swinging and squeaking as he held it aloft. They came to a small building in a clearing illuminated by moonlight.

'Here we are,' said Edward.

The Pigotts had one of the best private observatories in England, an unusual octagonal-shaped two-storey structure. Charts and papers were stored on the ground floor, transit and telescope on the upper level. Edward was a little surprised to see that the door was already open as he ushered her inside.

'I can hardly see a thing in here.'

'It is an observatory,' said Edward.

There was no time to fuss. He attempted to supplant a kiss. She turned her head aside.

'You mustn't smudge me! The others.'

'Well, then, no need for preliminaries.'

Edward knew that beneath their gowns, petticoats, corsets and stockings most women wore crotchless pantaloons to allow for easier elimination. But this also brought another advantage. The thought only increased his ardour. He knew this was reckless behaviour, but that was who he was.

She suddenly dropped the gathering folds and shoved him away.

'There is someone else here!' she hissed.

'What? Nonsense.'

The floorboards above creaked.

He buttoned his trousers and lifted the lantern. The trap door to the upper level was open and he shouted up into the dark rectangle. No response.

'Edward, let us go back now, please.'

'No, we have a trespasser and there is valuable equipment here.'

He climbed the steep stairway, holding the lantern above him.

'I say! Who is there!'

Someone was at the telescope.

'Sir! I say! This is private property!'

Still no response. A woefully curtailed passion fuelled his impatience. He reached out and gave the intruder a sharp tap on the shoulder.

Goodricke snapped his head around. 'Oh! Edward? I hope you do not mind. I am John Goodricke.'

'Yes. No. I mean, of course not. How did you…? Never mind that now, we should all return,' said Edward as he instinctively looked along the telescope barrel to determine what Goodricke had been observing. He calmed a bit.

'It is a beautiful evening for this, even with a moon, but we should return to the house.'

After a pause, Goodricke spoke again. 'I am sorry, but I cannot quite see what you are saying.'

Edward almost asked whether there was some problem, but checked himself and merely shrugged. He backed down the stairs and motioned for Goodricke to follow.

'Oh, I know who this is,' said an annoyed Penny as Goodricke emerged. 'He's the dummy what lives at Treasury.'

Edward sighed. He held the lantern up to his face and looked over at John.

'Listen, you can return here anytime you wish, but now the others are waiting. This is Penny, by the way.' He surprised himself with his improved diction.

Goodricke nodded and smiled. 'Thank you. I came early. Your father brought me here as I asked to see it.'

Well, at least he is keen, thought Edward.

'Right then. Let us all now return, please.'

He led a frowning Penny and grinning Goodricke back to the house.

*

Nathaniel was stalling for time. Did the guests notice? There was no question of retiring to the dining table until all were present. The rules of etiquette might not match those observed at a duke's residence, but there were some to be followed nonetheless. After he and his wife were seated at either end of the table the others were free to choose their own places. He had hinted to Godfrey he should sit next to Henry and he had instructed Edward to sit next to John, but where were they? And where was that silly goose of a girl, for that matter? He was about to ask if anyone else wanted more sherry when the missing party entered. Desultory conversation ceased as they looked at Edward with John and Penelope in tow.

'Good evening all, sorry to have kept you. I…we… were at our observatory. It is a lovely evening, is it not?' said Edward in as innocent a voice as he could muster, which was considerable.

Young Goodricke surveyed the semicircle of onlookers. The grinning chubby fellow and woman looking like a large meringue were likely Penny's parents. The woman with her mouth open and hand on Nathaniel's arm must be Mrs Pigott. The young woman next to her stifling a giggle would be Edward's sister. Nathaniel Pigott looked as if he would shove Edward's head into a soup tureen, if one were available. His own parents, however, seemed as equable as ever.

Edward's explanation did nothing to convince Nathaniel and a panting Penny only confirmed his suspicions. It was not, however, the time to press the matter.

'Well, shall we adjourn to the dining room?' He said with a tone that carried the hint of a plea.

Nathaniel seated his wife and walked around to the other end of the table. Godfrey made it a point to sit next to Henry, while Edward chose to sit next to John. *Well, at least we got that right*, he thought. He tried to think of a topic to discuss that was as anodyne as possible. The news from the Colonies was not good. Friends in London told of dissension over the war's prosecution. It was a touchy subject here in his own house, especially so with his French wife. And then there was Godfrey whom he suspected might be naturally infelicitous. Best leave *that* topic out.

The soup course arrived. John looked at the overly wrought tureen and imagined a wriggling Edward's face in it. The lack of conversation made the slurping seem all the louder. Nathaniel finally concluded something discussed at a recent meeting of the Royal Society ought to be neutral enough. He was about to recount a paper about a new type of barometer when John spoke.

'I have a riddle. We love it more than life. We fear it more than death. The wealthy want for it. The poor have it in plenty. What is it?' he asked, his voice just that bit wobbly, but strong, nonetheless.

Soup spoons were suspended in mid-air. Everyone was too surprised to think of an answer except Edward. He turned to John and placed his hand gently on his shoulder.

'Nothing.'

'What?' asked Godfrey.

'Nothing. The answer is 'nothing'. Is that not the right answer?' asked Edward.

'Yes. Well done,' said John.

'Well this is, ah, that was excellent,' said Nathaniel.

Levina had been gripping Henry's hand under the table and now released it.

'As our guest has introduced riddles as a topic allow me one. Two people have apples. If the first gives the other two, they shall be equal. If the second gives the other two he shall have double. How many does each have?' said Edward with a smile.

Goodricke quickly wiped it off.

'Ten and fourteen of course.'

Everyone looked as if they were waiting for another of their party to confirm this.

'Well done, sir!' said Edward. *This young lad is no fool.* He had learned that much about him in this short time. Despite his inability to hear a single syllable, he was certainly no 'dummy what lives at Treasury'. Perhaps their association might become a true collaboration? If it were to help him do more work in astronomy it would improve him in his father's eyes, resulting in fewer repercussions to his London excursions. *Yes*, he thought, *this might work out rather well, after all.*

'Oh, I have one!' blurted Mathurina.

After a few more riddles and the meat course, another awkward silence settled over the table. Henry thought he might initiate conversation in a direction that could lead to astronomy and to his son.

'Nathaniel, I was wondering if you might comment on how the Royal Society compares with its continental counterparts. Or perhaps I place you in an uncomfortable position?'

Nathaniel considered the question and decided that he could be frank with this man. His opinion on that subject was not exactly a carefully guarded secret and Henry likely suspected what it was in any case.

'Not at all, Henry. The Royal Society, as I see it, suffers from two main problems. First, it is not particularly royal - it is more of a club. London is packed with them and sometimes I have the impression that is all London is for - clubs of exclusion, where we posture with kindred spirits. A club insulates its members from a hierarchical and competitive society and the Royal Society is no exception. It appears to be run by unwritten code that regards any genuinely interesting new theory or mathematical concept as suspect. And then there is the tendency to overlook shortcomings or a lack of industry on the part of its members. The Royal Society is reluctant to admit generalisers, theorists or, heaven forbid, anyone truly brilliant.'

'Present company excepted,' said Edward.

'Yes...well,' said Nathaniel as he assessed whether this was a true compliment or sarcasm. It was always hard to tell with Edward.

'I have never considered the Royal Society in such harsh terms,' said a concerned Henry. 'It appears from your description that one who posits some new theory in astronomy might experience some prejudice?'

'That depends, Henry. Astronomy's pragmatic side may have more of an endorsement. There are, as you may know, those who investigate it as such,' said Nathaniel.

'Present company included,' said Edward taking a sip of wine.

Nathaniel ignored him and continued.

'We had Newton, yes, but I believe his practical side may have received as much acknowledgement as the theoretical. He was, after all, an alchemist as much as anything else. We have had no real successor while the French celebrate Clairaut and Euler, two brilliant mathematicians. Also, if I may alliterate, they now have Lagrange, Laplace and Lavoisier. I mean to say, sir, how can we compare when the Royal Society accepts papers read by obscure country vicars on two-headed calves? Not to mention the dryness of reports by provincial industrialists. And if that were not bad enough this is all tolerated because it meets the general preference for utility over theory.'

'Yes. Newton,' said Godfrey. 'The very idea.'

It wasn't clear to anyone what Godfrey was objecting to, if that was what he was doing.

'And there is the location of the place,' added Nathaniel. 'I mean to say, sir. It is hardly royally situated, as the cramped quarters in Crane Court are closer to stockjobbers and grocers than to courtiers and state officials.'

'Nathaniel,' said Anna, 'I do believe our guests have heard enough about the Royal Society.'

Henry had one more question he wished to ask on the matter, but Godfrey took this as permission to change the subject.

'I suppose we are all aware of our struggles in the Colonies?'

'Not I! What about *you* mother?' said Edward.

Nathaniel gave him a sharp look. Anna spoke before he could say anything.

'*Certainement!* I Would love to hear what the gentleman has to say.'

Uh-oh, thought Nathaniel as he lowered his head and pinched the bridge of his nose. Edward grinned and passed the wine over to John after refilling his own glass.

Godfrey looked up and down the table as if he might require permission to continue and forged ahead.

'Why only yesterday I read an account in *The London Gazette* that these colonials have made rebellion not only against the Crown, but even against themselves. This

132

general Washington has suffered mutiny in the ranks and one might therefore wonder how these rebels persist.'

Henry wasn't sure how to reply to obvious propaganda, but it didn't matter.

'Godfrey, consider this. When either His Majesty or Lord Germain decides on a new tactic or policy it can take as much as six weeks for the vessel carrying these orders to beat its way across the Atlantic against prevailing winds. The circumstances upon which these new orders were predicated are quite likely, upon their arrival, to have changed, thus leaving them dead in the water, as it were. When news of this finally reaches our councils here a new set of orders is issued, but we then learn in due course these adjustments are also no longer appropriate. We are ill-suited to respond to events there in a timely manner. Do you follow?'

'I do indeed, sir, but what about our military in the West Indies, in India or the Gold Coast? We seem to administer their disposition at a large remove well enough.'

'A fair point,' said Henry, 'but these colonists have proven to be a rather strong and stubborn adversary. Certainly, there are gentlemen amongst them, but you must remember that the Americas have also performed as a penal colony. I am afraid there is now amongst them a goodly number with a profound hatred of all things British, any reference to unfair taxes aside. They have smouldered, burst into flame and are now a resourceful and vicious adversary.'

'Oh my,' said Tabatha, snapping open her fan.

'Perhaps I have said too much. My apologies, madam, if I have discomfited you,' said Henry turning to her.

'Well, our course is simple, is it not? The way forward is to send over more soldiers. Send enough and we shall quell this rabble once and for all,' offered Godfrey.

Before Henry could explain the reason for Hessian mercenaries fighting on England's behalf, Anna spoke.

'Why Monsieur Pennypacker, you run your thoughts with such celerity! I am all astonishment!'

It was all Levina could do to keep from spitting out a mouthful of wine.

Nathaniel prudently announced it was perhaps time for a move to the parlour and, hopefully, a change in topic.

With that everyone stood while Godfrey sat for a moment longer before realising the subject was now closed.

John considered what had just unfolded. The pudgy one looked as if something was at stake whenever he spoke. His father wore his patient yet patronising expression. It all had something to do with the government and the war in the Colonies. His thoughts drifted back to that moment on the Minster steps when he was confronted by that pathetic one-legged beggar. '*Chain shot*' Mrs Dalrymple had said. He imagined himself returning to the Pigott's back garden, into the observatory to travel through the barrel of the telescope all the way to stars, away from the vulgar and tawdry. The stars increasingly provided a certain truth and peacefulness. It was more than science. His tutor at Warrington had been right about that and right about him.

The hand on his shoulder brought him back to earth. Edward wanted to speak.

'I shall only be a moment, I have something for you.'

John nodded and decided to wait there while the others moved into the parlour.

Edward returned and handed over a leather-bound volume. 'This is for you. You can keep it for as long as you wish.'

Goodricke read the rambling title.

*An Introduction to the True Astronomy or
Astronomical Lectures Read in the
Astronomical School of the University of
Oxford by John Keill, M.D. Fellow of the Royal
Society and Professor of Astronomy at that
University.*

He read the chapter titles with increasing captivation. *Of Visible and Apparent motion, Of the System of the World, Of Solar Spots, Of Comets, Of the Equation of Time.* And more, over three hundred pages. Several fold-out maps, charts and diagrams fuelled a desire to begin reading. It was a treasure trove.

'Thank you, but why?'

Edward shrugged. 'I thought you were likely not to have this and, as we are going to work together, you should know as much as I do. More even. That is all, really. Anyway, I have read it through of course, and I have others.'

At that moment Nathaniel looked in on them. When he saw that Edward was engaged in discussing matters astronomical, he left them to it. *Perhaps Edward has taken my advice to heart,* he thought and returned to the parlour.

Mathurina and Penny were giggling over *Nouveau Jeu de la Chouette* - The New Owl Game that the Pigotts had brought back from France. Anna was laughing at something Henry had said in French and was now waving her finger at him in mock admonishment. Levina saw Tabatha's hook disappear into her coiffure and turned to Anna to avoid the sight.

'Please excuse, my husband. He is too often the tiresome humourist,' said Levina.

'Ah, the so-called English humour. I have never understood this. We value the *esprit* more in France,' replied Anna.

'The what?' asked Godfrey, who had been waiting for an opening.

'The *esprit*, the wit, monsieur. It is as two engaged in fencing, but with sharp words instead of the *epée*. It is our national pastime.'

'I believe there is an expression with regard to this, *l'esprit de l'escalier*, the spirit of the staircase. Is that not so, Madam Pigott?' asked Henry.

'Very good Monsieur Goodricke!' said Anna with a mock bow.

Henry did not wish to tell Anna that the English thought French acrobatic repartee as vulgar, their own culture of politeness having little tolerance for pretention.

'The stairs?' asked Godfrey.

'Ah, monsieur, allow me to explain. Suppose that someone says something you do not understand and you say that you are at your wit's end, as you English say. And they reply, Oh, but sir! Not to worry! It was but a short journey!' said Anna, ending with a mock English accent. 'So, what is to be your reply?'

Godfrey looked around for someone else to jump in.

'Ah, so you see? You do not think of the reply. You do not think of the, the…'

'Retort,' offered Henry.

'Yes, the retort does not come to you until later when you have left the apartment and are on the staircase, but then it is too late! *L'esprit de l'escalier.* Do you see?'

Henry refrained from adding that in Godfrey's case it was more likely *l'esprit de la rue* - the spirit of the street, or further.

Nathaniel noticed empty glasses.

'More claret, anyone? Henry?'

Edward and John entered. John held up the copy of Keill he had been given and grinned. Henry took that as his cue.

'Thank you, no. I think that we must be leaving. Our journey, you know.'

'Of course.'

Henry turned to Godfrey. 'Wonderful to have met you and your lovely wife. I shall write to a colleague, as I mentioned, to preface your visit.'

Godfrey mumbled something in reply that even John could not decipher.

The guests moved around one another signalling the end of the evening.

'I shall call in the afternoon tomorrow, John,' said Edward, making sure that Goodricke understood him.

'It was a pleasure to meet you and to meet your son,' said Anna. 'I am sure we shall be seeing more of him.'

'Thank you,' said Levina. 'I hope you are right.'

Nathaniel escorted the Goodrickes to their carriage.

'Sorry about that Henry. A favour for a friend.'

'Not a problem, Nathaniel. I believe it all worked out in the end. I had hoped that John would be working with you, but it seems your son has also taken an interest. As for your guest, while I did promise to foretell his visit in a letter, I did not mention what it may communicate.'

'I see.'

'I mean really, Nathaniel, the man has an excess of inconsequence.'

'Of course, just doing my due diligence.'

Godfrey and his lumpen wife would not be representing His Majesty's government in any capacity. *God knows we have enough buffoons doing that already,* thought Henry.

'In any case I can say from what I have seen here that our wishes have been met and we are most grateful.'

Levina was not so sure and held back her opinion. Edward seemed too much of a dandy for her taste.

The Goodrickes' driver had been sitting on the mounting block in amiable conversation with the other driver. He tapped out his pipe and moved to the Landau in sharp distinction with the hired cab, now occupied by the Pennypackers and their sullen daughter.

After waving off all his guests, Nathaniel spoke to Edward.

'Well done,' he said.

Edward simply shrugged and stepped back inside.

Later that evening Anna made certain all the Bayberry candles were out. After all, she was not sure when more would become available.

13

The Swan

A dull sky pressed against the casement as Goodricke idly watched raindrops join and track across the panes. There would be no observing that night, a depressing thought for someone who drew inspiration from the setting sun. He was not even sure where the Sun was. Was it past noon? That was reason enough to acquire a clock – to simply tell time. He was at least sure he had missed breakfast. Mrs Dalrymple would be none too pleased.

He had fallen asleep in the early hours while reading Keill's astronomy text. He picked it up from the floor where it had fallen, returned to bed and continued reading.

The book's thirty chapters seemed bit daunting. Only three dealt with stars. *It is they we know least of,* he thought, *and that in which I am most interested.* He turned to *Lecture VI, Of the Magnitude and Order of the fixed Stars, Of the Constellations. Catalogues of the Stars, and the Changes to which they are liable.*

One particular passage gave him pause.

> *HIPPARCHUS the Rhodian, about 120 years before the Birth of Christ, was the first among the Greeks who reduced the Stars into a Catalogue. Daring, according to Pliny, to*

> undertake a Thing, which seemed to surpass the
> Power of a Divinity; that is, to number the Stars
> for Posterity, and to reduce them to a Rule;
> having contrived Instruments by which he marked
> the Place and Magnitude of each Star. So that
> by this Means we can easily discover, not only
> whether any of the Stars perish, and others grow
> up; but also whether they move, and what is their
> Course, and also if they grow bigger or wax less;
> by which Means he has given them to Posterity
> the Possession of the Heavens, if any of them
> have Subtility enough to comprehend them.

Do I possess this 'Subtility enough'? He rose and began to restlessly pace. This early speculation that stars might be variable in both position and magnitude was an idea suppressed by later Christian doctrine declaring celestial regions to be immutable. It was a doctrine now well discredited. He did not know of any stars that grew brighter or shone less, but he knew he only had to look. If he were to determine which stars changed their brightness he needed only his eyes and time. That was one thing he had plenty of, yet also felt there was no time to lose. Observations must not be aimless or unsystematic, he knew that much. Beyond that what was he to do with his results? There had always been someone to help him along, to point the way when a new direction was most needed. He hoped that was now the case. He wished he had asked more of Edward the previous evening, but it was all a bit sudden and unfamiliar. He sensed there was more counting on this relationship than he had first thought. It was Edward's father he was expecting to work with, but now, whatever the reason, it was his son with whom he would collaborate.

The promise of a visit lifted his mood. He would not blame Edward if he decided not to venture out in such dismal weather, but he would be disappointed, nonetheless. If he could not observe the stars, the next best thing was to talk about them. He had not yet met anyone else in York with this same interest. Mrs Dalrymple seemed educated enough, but thought his stargazing a health hazard. He hoped that Edward might equal his enthusiasm for astronomy even though he clearly had other passions.

And there was his deafness. While reading or observing it did not matter. He knew, though, it made some ill at ease, one of the lessons learned at Warrington. How many others in York would disregard him as did fellow students? He sometimes felt pushed to the margins and a little lonely. His father had, in his own compassionate manner, helped by arranging last night's meeting and for that he was grateful. He had hoped it was the beginning of a little less time on his own. Still, whatever the days may bring, it would be the nights that would garner the greater joy.

*

'A visitor, ma'am,' said Emeline.

Eleanor looked up from the herb garden where she had been taking inventory, despite the drizzle.

'Who is it Emeline?'

'A Mr Edward Pigott.'

She found Pigott standing by the entrance, hat in hand.

'Ma'am, I am Edward Pigott and I have come for Mr Goodricke.'

'Oh?' said Eleanor. 'I have not seen him this day but I expect he is in. Top of these stairs and to the left. Please tell him that he has missed a prepared breakfast again. Sorry, no, that is not your place.'

'Not to worry. I plan on taking him for a meal at The Swan,' said Edward as he approached the stairs.

'Mr Pigott, there is one thing, your announcement.'

'Ma'am?'

'One cannot very well knock, can one?'

'Of course.'

This new association will take some getting used to, he thought.

'We have a simple arrangement. If his door is closed, he does not wish to be disturbed, but if open you have leave to enter.'

'I see. My thanks.'

'Not at all.'

Edward ran up the stairs. He was, as far as she knew, Master Goodricke's first visitor. She hoped he would have more and put the hood up on her cloak and returned to the kitchen garden.

Pigott reached the landing and saw the door was ajar. He slowly pushed it open and looked inside. Goodricke was standing at a far window with his arms folded and did not notice him at first. Pigott moved in further and gave a little wave.

'Edward! You have come!'

'Yes, I said I would,' said Edward who could not avoid looking around the sparsely furnished room. Flamsteed's huge star atlas caught his eye, its opulence contrasting with the room's sparseness. The copy in his own observatory was not the only one in Yorkshire, after all. He felt a damp chill and wondered why the grate was cold.

'There will be no observing this night, I shouldn't wonder,' said Goodricke.

Pigott stepped to the window for a closer look.

'Perhaps not, but when clear I see you enjoy a reasonable prospect. If tonight were free of cloud, what might you see from your little aerie?'

'Oh, about one hour past sunset there is a good view of Gemini, Taurus, and Fornax just setting.'

Edward spotted the small compass placed on the sill.

'Just so. But more astronomy later. I thought we might step out. There is a place nearby where we might have an ale or two and terrible food, if that suits. I imagine it cannot be much worse than whatever is served up here.'

'It's not so bad, whenever I do eat here anyway. Mrs Dalrymple is convinced I shall reduce to some emaciated creature who can but crawl to greet her.'

141

'I just met her. She seems to care for you.'

'She does that. I suppose in the end that is all that really matters.'

'Well, get your cloak, if you will. Don't let's dawdle.'

Edward took one last look around. *He is going to need a clock for what I have in mind for him*, he thought.

The rain had slowed, but not before the road was well muddied. They picked their way around puddles as they walked over to The Swan and stopped before the entrance. Edward turned to face Goodricke who was clutching his cloak and shivering.

'I hope this will suit,' he said. 'There are proper ale houses of course, but they do not have food.'

'And you want to be able to hear me. Fine,' said Goodricke, wondering just how soft-spoken he actually sounded.

'It's just that I thought we should have a proper chat.'

'This is fine.'

They entered and Pigott selected a table by a fire with a fresh pile of wood laid on. The only other customers were two others engrossed in a card game, each pulling on a clay pipe. *Perfect.* He looked around as if he was looking for someone. A short, rotund individual approached, wiped his hands on a dirty apron and spoke through his beard.

'Gentlemen, and what can I do for you? Oh, good day Edward. A bit early for you is it not?'

'Not too early for your fine fare, Thackeray,' said Pigott while still looking around.

'Is Cassie not about?'

'No, Edward. Off today. You'll have to settle for me, I'm afraid.'

'Two ales,' said Edward looking over at Goodricke who nodded. He looked up at the chalk board and squinted.

'Is that your script? Can't make hide nor hare of it. Cassie has more appealing lines.'

Pigott sensed impatience. Thackeray did not care much for back-chat, not a good quality in an inn keeper. Or in anyone, for that matter.

'The sign says soup, but what kind?'

''Tis soup, soup. I can always ask Cook.'

'Right, we shall pass on the soup. The doe venison and vegetables, then. And a loaf as well. There's a good fellow.'

Edward turned to face Goodricke.

'Not a bad sort is our Thackeray, but Cassie is much more pleasing to look at. I was hoping to introduce you.'

Goodricke just stared.

Pigott sighed.

'Right then. Well, last night was interesting, eh? I say, what was that you were about to observe when I interrupted? Venus, was it not?'

Goodricke shook his head.

'It was Saturn, but was it not I who was interrupting?'

'Yes, well, the less said about that the better,' said Edward who knew full well it was Saturn. The point was, did Goodricke? Just how much practical astronomy did he know? *Certainly not as much as I*, he thought, *but can he learn? Just how bright is he?* He did not, recalling his father's admonition, wish to associate with a dullard. He needed to find out more.

'Was that your young lady you were with last night?', asked Goodricke.

'Penelope? Merely an acquaintance.'

Pigott changed the subject.

'I understand your family is from Yorkshire?'

'Yes, Ribston. It's not far, but I was born in Groningen. My mother is Dutch.'

Their ales arrived. Pigott raised his tankard.

'Here is to continental mothers, then.'

Pigott was pleased to see that Goodricke at least did not shy from drink.

'Any other family?'

'A brother and two sisters. I had another brother and sister who died. I never knew them.'

'That does happen,' said Pigott. 'I understand you were at Warrington?'

'Yes.'

Goodricke noticed Pigott pause in thought.

'I know what you are thinking. It was an ordinary academy - not a special place for the likes of me.'

'Well, good for Warrington, I say.'

'But not for much longer, I fear. A correspondence from my old tutor there, Mr Enfield, tells me it shall soon cease instruction altogether.'

'Ah, bad luck.'

'Bad luck all right, especially for others who might have benefited as have I.'

Well, thought Pigott, *enough chat*.

'I say, that was a clever riddle you posed the company last night. I have another if you fancy them.'

Goodricke smiled and nodded. Edward took a sip and raised a forefinger.

'Right, then. What is the one spot on our globe where you can begin a journey by walking one mile due south, walk exactly one mile due east and then exactly one mile due north to end precisely at the spot whence you began?'

He looked at Goodricke with some anticipation.

Goodricke's tankard was poised in mid-air. He placed it down and looked at Edward.

'The North Pole of course.'

'Well done,' said Edward, *but it may have been too easy*.

'I have another,' said Pigott.

Goodricke raised his palm, lowered his head in thought for a moment, nodded to himself and then looked up.

'That was not quite correct.'

'Not correct? In what way not correct?'

'You asked what was this one spot. There is another. In fact, one might say there is an infinite number of such spots, but that would be a quibble.'

Edward thought for a moment, but no solution came to mind.

'Surely not.'

'Yes,' replied Goodricke. 'I am right.'

Edward became annoyed at this unexpected challenge, some play on words, some trick. There was no other such spot.

'All right, then. Where is this other spot, or spots if you must?'

Goodricke sensed his companion's unease. Working out problems in geometry was a genuine past-time for him. He did not want to embarrass Edward, but Braidwood, taught him to never hide what he knew. He would not begin now.

'Well,' began Goodricke, his hands positioned to shape an imaginary sphere, 'our globe is marked with lines of latitude. Now, each of these might be considered as a circle of some set circumference.'

Edward leaned forward looking hard at the table as he listened, clutching his tankard.

'Do you follow?'

'John. Please.'

'Right then. Let us imagine one of these circles, or lines of latitude, is at some distance from the South Pole such that when you walk one mile due south from any point on it you are now on another line of latitude whose own circumference is exactly one mile in length. Now, from that point, you walk one mile along it in either direction at the end of which you come to the same point whence you entered. Then you walk due north one mile and you are back where you began. I have not had the time here to work out the exact distance of this starting latitude from the Pole, but I am sure the maths involved to be trivial.'

Edward sat stunned and staring. Goodricke had a quick mind and his deafness, whatever he may have thought of it before, was suddenly irrelevant. He cleared his throat.

'Yes, that was, that is quite correct. You know your geometry.'

'My father provided me a text in geometry when I was quite young, and later Mr Braidwood did as well. Anyway, you said you had another for me?'

'Oh…not important.'

'I'd like to try.'

An embarrassed Pigott suspected Goodricke was well aware he was being tested.

'If you insist. A two-part question, actually. First, how long does it take the Earth to rotate once?'

'With respect to the stars or to the Sun?' asked Goodricke.

'Well, both,' said Pigott.

'Twenty fours with respect to the Sun and twenty-three hours, fifty-six minutes and four seconds with respect to the stars. Solar and sidereal times respectively.'

'What would be the relation to solar and sidereal time if the Earth rotated in a direction opposite to that in which it rotates at present?'

'Then the solar day would be shorter than the sidereal. Edward, are you testing me?'

'Sorry, yes.'

It was an awkward moment. They both knew what this was about.

Pigott finally spoke.

'Tell me about this Braidwood fellow you mentioned. Who is he?'

'An early teacher, much beloved, but please tell me more about yourself. I am most interested in your own work in astronomy.'

Edward sat back.

'If you would not mind, I should like to know something of your experience with this teacher of yours. He seems able to work wonders.'

Pigott wasn't sure if that was the best choice of words.

'I will say this. One of Mr Braidwood's objectives was to convince us we were not dumb. We only needed a different type of education. I did not know it at the time, but I have learned since he was the first to provide schooling for the deaf in all of Great Britain. I was indeed most fortunate to have his instruction.'

'How exactly did he teach you to understand what others are saying?' asked Pigott, now glad of the change in subject.

'With practice. Much practice. He was especially good at helping one to be – quickly sagacious.'

'That seems an odd choice of words.'

'It refers to those words that appear alike to one who hears with the eyes.'

'Such as?'

'Like *aisle* as in church and *isle* as in island. So, you must quickly decide what the speaker intends by the other words in the sentence. That sort of thing. Mr Braidwood explained how this was something to be prepared for.'

'I see.'

'Do you? Let me add one more thing about how not being able to hear might affect my work. The silence that has been imposed on me is no impediment. Silence can be thought of as a natural accompaniment to astronomy, to its practice, would you not agree?'

Edward thought about this for a moment. Goodricke had a point. Silence provided an atmosphere of repose and reflection. It enabled the concentration needed to locate an object and hold it in view, but there were also times he thought the experience unnerving. Should he admit to this? *Let us see where the conversation goes*, he thought.

'Of course,' replied Edward now feeling somewhat chastened. 'Now, about myself - where to begin? My involvement with astronomy is down to my father who, as you know, has recently been honoured with membership in the Royal Society.'

'Yes, Father mentioned it. I rather suspect he secretly wishes me to also acquire some recognition from them as well.'

Pigott was not sure how to respond. There was no point in discouraging someone whom you wanted to cultivate as a colleague.

'I was educated in France, in Caen where we lived for a time. Father's work in astronomy is quite good if conventional. But his work as a surveyor is superb. He is exceptionally skilled in the determination of geographical location and made his reputation performing a sound application of astronomy to determine the longitude and latitude of various and sundry places. I assisted him greatly in this work and in doing so learned practical astronomy.'

'So, now the inhabitants of these places have a better idea of where they actually are?'

Besides being bright, he can also display a bit of cheek, thought Edward. *Good.*

'Maybe some of them, if they ever thought on it, but it is more important than that. It is required in determining boundaries, distances and the production of accurate maps. It was for this work Father was elected as a Foreign Member of the Imperial Academy and of the Paris Académie des Sciences as well as the Royal Society. Developments in astronomy have been stimulated by the need for an accurate position, especially so in maritime applications. The work is not trivial I assure you.'

'Of course not,' said Goodricke. 'I did not think it was, but surely you have done more yourself have you not, or at least wish to do so?'

Why this question?

'Of course, and I do. Helping my father in this work was where I learned the minutiae of the profession. And you might be surprised how many so-called astronomers would not know how to calculate the exact latitude and longitude of a place, more's the pity. Well, the more it is done, the less it need be done. I wonder whether it will eventually become a lost art, but you are right - I have other observing interests. Recently, if I may be allowed to boast, I discovered a new nebula in the constellation Coma Berenices, something missed by Messier altogether.'

'I understand the term nebula, but who is Messier? Has he discovered what a nebula is?'

'It may be more correct to say he tells us what it is not. As for who he is, let me begin at the beginning, may I?'

'Fine.'

The beginning I speak of is Newton. He made it possible to truly understand the motion of celestial objects through the application of his mathematics. Take Halley, for example. He applied Newton's equations to the study of the orbits of comets and predicted the return of one in 1759 and return it did. What is now of interest are things that move - the planets of course, but especially comets. The problem is that there are many objects that deceive. They might look as comets, a patch of light, but they are not. One, however, could waste much observing time to determine this. Monsieur Messier has identified objects that masquerade as comets and his catalogue of these is a service to astronomy.'

'So, Messier is saying these objects are not comets and do not waste time to determine whether they be such?'

'I would not say they be ignored altogether. The point is not to mistake them for a comet. They might well be of more interest at some time in the future,' said Edward, taking a sip of ale.

'Anyway, it has become more and more the accepted view that everything is flying about, stars included, and now much of astronomy is directed at trying to understand these motions, but because of the immensity of distances we suspect some of them are imperceptible.'

'Perhaps I might acquire Messier's catalogue,' said Goodricke.

'Of course.'

Edward did not wish to add that without a telescope such a thing was not very useful, inasmuch as almost all of the Messier objects could not be seen without one. He did not wish to discourage Goodricke in any way.

'Tell me something of your observatory. You seem to have it well equipped.'

'Not much to tell. It consists of two levels as you know with an opening in the roof for the transit. There is the Bird quadrant of eighteen-inch radius, a Dollond three-foot achromatic telescope and the clock, of course. A sound timepiece is critical. The first order of business was to determine our exact longitude and latitude. I prefer the meridian Right Ascension of the moon's limb as the method of doing this. Once the location was set we could compare recorded times of upper transit of various objects with their known times recorded in the Ephemeris for Greenwich. Transit times, among other things, are used to set our clock.'

'Your clock is accurate?'

'Dead accurate.'

'And the positions of stars are of interest?'

'That and their proper motion.'

'I do not completely understand the term.'

'Well, my little Tyrol, we no longer believe the Earth to be sat stock still at the centre of all this business. So, as the Earth is in motion, why not the Sun as well? It too must be moving about in an orbit or path of greater immensity. We are then, as it were, going along for the ride, but to where? This should be revealed to us through the proper motion of stars. Some stars display motion that is reflective of the Sun's traverse through the heavens. Hence, we ought to be able to determine the direction we are heading. I understand Mr Herschel to be now working intently on this problem.'

'I do not know him.'

'William Herschel. He works in Bath, with his sister, no less.'

They drank and were silent for a time. Goodricke wanted to ask about Herschel, but Pigott spoke first

'John, how did you come by a pursuit of astronomy?'

Goodricke thought back to Warrington Academy and Enfield's heartfelt advice, but he was not sure Edward would appreciate it. He would have to know him better.

'I chose astronomy because I believe myself capable. That is the practical answer.'

'Is there a non-practical one?'

'Perhaps I follow the Greek astronomer Ptolemy, who wrote that he knew he was mortal, but when he scanned the circling stars he no longer touched the Earth with his feet, but stood at the side of Zeus and took his fill of ambrosia. Or something like that.'

'Uh, oh. Do I have before me a seeking mind coupled with a longing soul? Careful, for there be dragons,' said Edward.

'You do not feel the same? Are you not inspired in any way?'

Pigott stiffened.

'I have demonstrated my own abilities soundly enough. But your sentiment is not one I fully share.'

'Why is that?'

'You say when you scan the sky you stand at the side of Zeus. Well, jolly japes for you, but have you never thought on how this celestial spectacle can make us feel as mere trifles? Cannot this stellar display instil feelings of insignificance as well as inspirit?'

'It may be that way for some,' said Goodricke. 'But it has never made *me* feel small or trivial. Quite the opposite, in fact.'

He wondered if the source of Edward's feelings of diminishment were not much closer to home. He continued.

'Do you mean to say that the stars only serve to remind us of some irrelevance? For me the stars only serve to inspire. Any diminishment *I* feel is induced by some experience on the ground. What I see about me is not often inspirational. Surely you must understand this?'

Edward shifted in his seat. He decided that he would, after all, disclose more.

'Permit me to explain my thoughts. I maintain that reflecting on the heavens can cause one to slip into melancholy. It was simpler for those who came before Copernicus to have the comfort of believing we sat at the centre of all God's creation, but no longer. We have been displaced. What are we now? Even the Sun is not a special star, and she herself moves on her merry way across the heavens. To where? To what? I fear the more we learn, the less significant we become. And there is something else. The shining stars keep their distance. It is possible to become oppressed by their aloofness, by the awareness that nothing but emptiness stands between you and them. Sometimes, when I observe the stars, I feel as if I am taken to a place where there is no light nor sound, only an infinite nothingness. I believe that is what Pascal was referring to when he wrote *le silence éternal de ces espaces infinis m'effraie*,' said Pigott.

Goodricke looked puzzled.

'The eternal silence of these infinite spaces terrifies me.'

He thought for a moment and then continued.

'This 'infinite silence' does not terrify y*ou*, I'll wager.'

Goodricke had not expected this of Pigott. He wanted to discuss the practice of astronomy, not its philosophical implications. Edward was the 'seeking soul' here, not him. He suspected this detachment Pigott spoke of was his own, not that of all mankind.

'Edward, you do yourself an injustice. I am sorry, but I do not agree with you in saying the more we learn of the heavens, the more it leads to feelings of insignificance. For me it is the exact opposite. Take, for example, Mr Halley's prediction of the return of a comet.'

'What of it?'

'Did he not argue that three comets observed previous were actually one and the same and that it would return in a particular year?'

'Ah, you know about that.'

Goodricke ignored this and continued.

'It returned just as he predicted. A pity he did not live to see it. Still, he knew he was right. Does anyone yet regard comets as sublunar objects? Does their appearance foretell some catastrophe or herald the death of a monarch?'

'Of course not. None of that rubbish,' said Edward.

'And why is this no longer the case?'

Pigott was pressed to state something they both knew.

'It is there in Keill and elsewhere. We now understand their motion in purely mathematical terms. They have been stripped of all superstition.'

'And do you not think this an achievement?'

'I am not sure of your point,' said Pigott, his voice now tinged with impatience.

'The point is that we, here on this puny planet, dare to study the stars. We *dare* to uncover their secrets. Who are we to do so with our little brains, scuttling about like insects? Who are we to unlock any secrets the heavens hold? I say that to do this, to be *able* to do this, does not make us insignificant, only the opposite. It serves to elevate, not to diminish. On this point, I am certain.'

Goodricke thought he may have raised his voice, an unusual display of emotion.

Right, thought Pigott. *No more banter about the Meaning of it All.* He now hoped Goodricke would be better at practising astronomy than he was at pontificating about it. He had to be brought back down to earth. Goodricke now walked a fine line between seriousness and solemnity. Pigott could accept the former, but never the latter. That could make Goodricke uncomfortable company given his own natural inclination for the sardonic.

'Clearly you have passion for the subject, but are you also accepting of its drudgery?'

'What do you mean?'

'I mean to say that you will not be spending all your time imbibing with Zeus. The practice of astronomy is akin to that of the accountant who must fill his ledger with long, neat columns of figures. So, I must ask, do you possess the required temperament?'

'Are you saying that the test of a vocation is the love of the drudgery involved?'

'Something like that, although love may be too strong a term,' said Pigott.

'Well, I am quite accepting of this if these columns of figures, as you say, are astronomy's purpose.'

'Trust me, they are indeed.'

Goodricke decided it was time to steer the subject to something less contentious.

'Tell me more of the Royal Society.'

'What more would you like to know? Father gave a reasonable account last night.'

'But not flattering.'

'He thinks too many members are merely there to egg the pudding.'

'Egg? Ah, I see.'

'Yes, but perhaps I should add that, while it may be true that many of the papers presented are vapid lucubrations at best, the Society nonetheless provides the means for the introduction of all manner of new instruments. Where else might one learn of barometers, telescopes and transits, prisms, pumps, sextants and so on? But as far as *you* are concerned it is important you present a paper as soon as you can. Start your correspondence to make yourself known. I mean to say, suppose you deduce something remarkable, make some discovery. Then what is your course?'

'I am not sure of your question,' said Goodricke.

'What would you do with this new information?'

'I have not quite thought on that as yet.'

'Then you do yourself a disservice. You make your work known by presenting it in a paper to the Society. In this manner, you both share your knowledge and, most of all, receive credit. In such a manner, others will learn of your work and may build upon it. At this very moment, there are any number of letters flying about filled with ideas, questions and replies all serving to connect researchers for the advancement of science. It is a traffic you need step into.'

'Is this really so important?'

Pigott placed his tankard on the table and leaned forward.

'John, suppose you make some discovery, but it is not presented in a paper. Then someone else gets wind of it and, let us say, borrows your conclusion. If they then submit their own paper on the matter, you are pipped at the post.'

'Has such a thing ever happened?'

'How would we know without a complaint? All I can say is, no one had better try that on with me. But then there is a second point, your correspondence.'

'I had not really thought much on that either.'

'Well, you should. Anyone worth his salt will devote some time each day to their correspondence. It plays an important role in the practice of science. Certainly, in Father's, considering the time spent at his writing desk. You are part of a network of natural philosophers. We share information through our correspondence. It does no one any good to work in isolation. You won't get far that way, I can tell you.'

'Edward, it is not that I disagree, but I do not have much to communicate at the moment.'

'You will. Anyway, you can always ask questions. And, John, whatever Father might have said about the Society it is still the place where our work is judged and made legitimate. You would do well to start a correspondence with someone, anyone, and consider this as much a part of your duties as your observations. Understand?'

'Of course. So, the Royal Society *is* a scientific society, is it not?'

'Indeed, it is, why ever would you ask that? But not all its members are scientists, at least not in my opinion. Many do not practise science as I see it. The president, Joseph Banks, is a bit of a stiff rump. He is a botanist and a bit windy with it. He knows next to nothing about astronomy. On the other hand, we do have the likes of Alexander Aubert, a rich merchant who indulges an interest in astronomy. He is sound and has added to general knowledge on the subject. I put him above Banks as a scientist. I mean to say, is naming the sexual parts of a plant a science?'

'Have you presented any papers?'

'Only just recently, a letter I wrote to Nevil Maskelyne was read before the Society. It is an account of the Nebula in Coma Berenices. A bit brief, but still...'

'What is this nebula?'

'What indeed? It is neither a comet nor a star. It is something as yet unknown.'

'And Maskelyne - he is the Astronomer Royal, is he not?'

'You are full of questions. Yes, he is just that and clever, mark you, clever. Well, you would have to be to sit in that seat, unlike presidents of the Royal Society.'

'What work does he do in astronomy?'

'Ah, *that* is best answered by a visit to the Royal Observatory at Greenwich. It is a nice change from York, and you would learn more about its practice and a little of its history.'

'Might you arrange this?'

'John, there are advantages to having a father who is a Fellow, but Maskelyne would surely welcome you in any case. Just be careful he does not turn you into one of his computers.'

'What on earth does that mean?'

'You'll see, one day.'

'Well, what is he working on?'

'He likely spends most of his time on the production of the *Nautical Almanac*. It is vital to maritime navigation, but does not add one jot of new knowledge of the heavens. He might be considered the opposite of Mr Herschel, who attempts to map the heavens entire. He strives to move the boundaries of our knowledge whilst Maskelyne remains well behind the lines. But they both serve their purpose.'

He drained his tankard.

'I understand that Herschel does more than observe, does he not?'

'One might say this. He is rather unusual in that he constructs his own telescopes and by all accounts they compete with the quality of a Dollond. He then uses these to support a rather ambitious observing programme and if *that* were not enough, he then proceeds to speculate on the meaning of his observations. We have established a reasonable correspondence.'

'Any others?'

'Well, besides Father and myself there is Maskelyne of course, Winthrop, Mayer and Aubert, whom I have mentioned. Then there is Thomas Wright. There is a goodly number, but Herschel is the one who is by far the most avid, able and productive. He lives in Bath as I say and is often assisted by his sister Caroline, who also appears to know her way around the sky.'

'Edward, might I ask something?'

'If you must.'

Goodricke hesitated for a moment.

'You obviously are a skilled astronomer with many years of experience, but I sense you are not quite so eager to be more recognised. I only ask because we might work together and, well, I wish for someone to match my own interest. I feel I must ask this as it appears I shall be undergoing your tutelage, if that is the right word.'

Edward looked into his empty ale tankard. *The lad doesn't mess about, does he? He is quite right to think on that, but to ask it outright? And how has he reached this suspicion so quickly?*

'Perhaps you are right. Perhaps I am not so ambitious as some. It does not mean that I am not a keen observer, but I am not in this for fame and certainly not fortune. It is a passable profession.'

Goodricke suspected his reluctance for recognition might have something to do with his father, but decided it was best not ask.

Their food arrived.

'And two more ales if you please,' said Edward to a departing Thackeray.

'Edward, there was something more I wish to ask.'

'Yes?'

'Might you suggest an observing programme?'

'For you?'

'Yes, for me. Who else? I assume one does not observe willy-nilly. One must have a plan, mustn't one?'

'Perhaps we have talked enough for now. Let us enjoy our food, such as it is. There will be plenty of time for that,' said Edward with a flourish of his fork.

Pigott now had a better idea of how they might work together. It was clear that the young lad sitting before him was capable. He pushed aside the thought that he was clearly better at maths than he had been when he was that age. True, his knowledge of basic astronomy will need work, but how long would that take? Yes, he would spend time with Goodricke as his father desired, but he now knew the training would not be so onerous as he first suspected. Instead of being a tutor with a student, he would more likely have a colleague and that would be all to the good.

Goodricke detected the aroma of nutmeg, something often added to mask the distinctive odour of tainted meat. Still, he was famished and tucked in. He had decided he would enjoy Pigott's company after all, but he did have an intriguing mixture of irony and idealism, didn't he?

14

34 Tauri

While Goodricke and Pigott were dining, William Herschel prepared for another night's observing from the spacious back garden at New King Street. His recent relocation there meant no more observing from the road. Moreover, the property's principal axis had a near north-south alignment, permitting an excellent view of the southern sky. In addition, a ground-floor room leading straight into the garden was perfect for use as a workshop. Few others would select a property primarily in terms of how it functioned as an observatory. He could never imagine why not.

This night he used his largest reflecting telescope yet, with a six-inch aperture and focal length of seven feet. He carefully wiped it with a rag and a little polish to protect it from the damp. Constructed from the same West Indian cocuswood used to make oboes, he thought it a fitting merger of his knowledge of natural philosophy and music. He checked that his note-paper was at the ready, the ink pot full and his observing programme to hand. First one star appeared, then another and another, until the night sky was spangled, a sight that may inspire lines in literature, but he was after poetry of a different sort.

Astronomy provided him with intellectual challenges his musical career could not. Some, he knew, saw this as abandoning a promising profession for a frivolity. But the stars too had harmony and he would, by God, learn their rhythm. An early inspiration had been Ferguson's Astronomy, not only through the knowledge it contained, but also because Ferguson was self-taught. So why not him? It was also not lost on Herschel, that this text was typical in that the fewest chapters were devoted to 'The Fixed Stars'. There was, after all, next to nothing known about the nature of the energy that produced starlight. There had been a few well-documented instances of stars appearing where none had been seen before, or known stars displaying variability in brightness, but no one knew why. A more productive approach was to observe stellar motions. If the angular distances between them changed in a certain way, then this could lead to an understanding of the Sun's own motion. The examination of the positions of hundreds of stars was required to understand what this was, but he did not think this a problem in the least.

Caroline had remained at their former River Street residence 'to take care of some paperwork regarding our business matters,' she had said. She did not have quite his level of preoccupation with astronomy, but that would be difficult for anyone. It was one thing to observe the sky in a casual manner, to chance spotting a new comet or marvel at the motion of Jupiter's moons. He had, however, chosen to survey the stars one by one, including hundreds more invisible to the unaided eye. Some thought this unrealistic. Well, let them think that. Nightly observing was what it took. He secretly believed many of his colleagues in astronomy were but fops who would not know hard work if it bit them on the backside.

The commitment level of gentlemen astronomers did not concern him. But Caroline's? Aiding him in his astronomical endeavours began out of a sense of loyalty and gratitude after he returned to Germany to free her from a suffocating environment. Their mother saw to it that she acquired no employable skills. This and her lack of physical attraction made a marriage unlikely and he saved her from a life as an imprisoned domestic. She was grateful at first, but what began as casual requests to assist in his observations grew to the point where she hand-fed him while he polished a new speculum mirror. Still, she found sharing his work a welcome alternative to socialising with the women of Bath society with whom she felt no real affinity. He had saved her from a life of drudgery, but mused over her becoming more than his astronomical amanuensis. His solution was to train her so that she might perform her own observations.

His new telescope would allow him to observe well beyond the naked eye limit of fifth magnitude stars. Moreover, it was not enough to merely *look* at each star. Measurements of their relative positions had to be carefully made, a tedious, but necessary process.

The next target was 34 Tauri. He centred it in the field of view, a dim star in the constellation Taurus that, on a moonless night with perfect conditions, could *just* be seen by the naked eye. No one had ever observed 34 Tauri with as good a telescope coupled with a micrometre to measure the angular distance between stars.

This cannot be right, he thought, squinting through the eyepiece. He stepped away from the telescope and looked at Taurus to check his bearings. Was this the right object? He studied the surrounding pattern. There was no doubt. The telescope image revealed it as a disc. Whatever it was, it was *not* a star. His pulse began to race.

A micrometre check of its position further suggested it was not only not a star, but its position did not agree with that in Flamsteed. Not a star and moving? A new comet? Are comets seen as discs? He had never discovered one and was sorry Caroline was not there to share in this. He carefully recorded its position and continued on with his survey.

*

Four nights later he confirmed that 34 Tauri had, in fact, moved. Later that day he carefully composed a letter explaining his observations. He folded the sheet, pressed his signet ring into the wax seal and addressed it to 'Nevil Maskelyne, Astronomer Royal, Greenwich'. Herschel thought it was likely a new comet. After all, new objects found coursing through the solar system turned out to be comets. What else could it be? Since Ptolemy, the number of planets was fixed at six. The number of comets, on the other hand, grew. After centuries of myth-laden explanations they now belonged to the domain of natural philosophy. Some now surmised their purpose was to supply the Sun with perpetual power, others believed them a celestial analogy to known physical processes on Earth, a type of stellar eruption, perhaps. The discovery of a new comet only added fuel to this heated debate. Herschel would let others decide what 34 Tauri was. He would much rather return to the task of laying out the structure of the heavens. Compared to that, the discovery of just another comet seemed a minor matter.

15

Temple of the Four Winds, Summer

Two carriages headed for Castle Howard through the Vale of York on a sunny June morning. Henry, Levina, Nathaniel and Anna occupied the front carriage. John, Edward and their sisters Mathurina and Harriet followed. The weather was unusually warm and the open carriages offered a splendid view of the countryside.

'Henry, how do you come to know the Earl of Carlisle?' asked Nathaniel.

'Through the diplomatic corps. Not a bad fellow of course, but a bit unseasoned, at least for the task he was assigned.'

'And what was that?'

Henry wondered whether he ought to continue, but as it was common knowledge throughout London clubs, it could do no harm.

'The Earl, Frederick Howard, had a rather easy and pleasurable young life. Eton, Cambridge, the Grand Tour. But managing his estate's finances was not exactly a forte. He had need of a position and so entered the government. At the young age of thirty Lord North appointed him as Commissioner to the Colonies.'

'I have heard something along these lines. I take it this venture did not succeed all that well.'

'That should be obvious enough. Sir John - my father, and I briefly attempted to explain something of the tactics of diplomacy, but Howard had little opportunity to employ them. Due to a series of miscommunications and downright incompetency there was no way his so-called peace proposal could ever succeed. The colonials basically told him nothing would be accepted short of packing up our army and leaving.'

'It sounds as if the poor fellow was sent to milk a pigeon.'

'Indeed, sir. I shouldn't think we shall last another year there.'

Anna's fan hid her smile.

The carriages rolled through Flaxton and stopped at Barton Hill for a picnic luncheon. Edward and John fetched ales from a nearby inn and a spot on the village green was appropriated as blankets were spread. The ladies would have wine.

'How much further?' asked Edward to no one in particular, while helping himself to a slice of ham.

'A mile or so to the estate boundary. From there it will be another few miles to the house proper. The route is just there, northward to the main house. It is actually their road and goes nowhere else,' said Henry pointing across the green to a nearby turnoff from the main road.

'House, Father?' asked Harriet. 'Is not Castle Howard a castle?'

'It is the great house of an estate. Not a true castle. No crenellations or turrets, but it is rather large all the same. Some of great houses are called castles if one had formerly occupied the site. I do not believe that was the case here. Perhaps it was a bit of pomposity on the part of the original builder.'

'Henry,' said a reproachful Levina.

'But it is a bloody… a rather large country house,' he replied. 'And it was not our host who built it, but a predecessor.'

'It is larger than anything in York, except perhaps for the Minster. From what I understand you could fit the entire population of York inside it,' said Anna, making a sweeping gesture with her wine glass.

'Oh, surely not…maybe only half,' said Henry bringing laughter all around.

Mathurina and Harriet sat opposite chatting amiably, parasols in hand. Edward stood and stretched while John lay flat, hands behind his head, eyes closed to a sky devoid of stars. He then suddenly sat up and spoke to no one in particular.

'Does anyone know whether there is a proper observatory at this Castle Howard?'

Nathaniel gently touched his elbow. 'I do not believe there is one,' said Nathaniel.

'But there should be plenty of good food and wine,' added Edward when Goodricke seemed disappointed.

The moment arrived when everyone sensed it was time to leave. The party packed up and Edward fetched the carriage drivers from the ale house.

The journey continued along a road gently undulating through a rustic corridor of hardwoods followed by ordered columns of Beech.

They passed under a gateway, rubble built, topped with truncated pyramids and eventually came to another, much larger with a single complete pyramid. The main house could be glimpsed through serried rows of Lime. Nathaniel noticed they travelled off-axis to the main entrance of the estate, the opposite of the French chateau always approached straight-on, one design showcasing architecture, the other, authority.

An obelisk marked an intersection. John estimated its height at about one hundred feet as they made a sharp right onto the road running parallel with the north side of the main structure coming into full view. As they approached, he could see it was situated on a ridge - a perfect location for an observatory, if there was one.

The carriages turned into a broad forecourt framed by two massive wings either side of the central block crowned by a massive dome. Doric pilasters modulated a facade decorated with cherubs, urns and coronets. *The length of the house must be over five hundred feet*, he thought. The Fifth Earl of Carlisle and Lady Isabella were standing at the entrance, a retinue of support staff arrayed on the stairs behind.

'Henry, welcome!' said Frederic Howard as he approached with his hand extended.

Pleasantries and introductions were exchanged as the guests assembled at the foot of the grand entrance. The Earl announced that members of staff would escort them to their assigned rooms where they might rest and freshen before gathering for a tour of the interior.

'If I may, your lordship,' asked Edward, 'how does one have a tour, as you say? There are more than one-hundred rooms within, are there not?'

Nathaniel sighed.

'You know, I am not actually sure. About one hundred fifty my dear?' replied Howard with a nod to his wife. 'I have not been in all of them, of course. We shall only show the most significant architectural features my forebears had the vision to install.'

The guests were shown to their separate quarters. A maid led Goodricke to a room adjoining that of his parents.

'Will there be anything else, sir?'

'Is there an observatory anywhere on the grounds?'

'Beg pardon, sir?'

'An observatory, a place to observe the stars.'

'I shouldn't think so, sir. Not that I've heard, anyway.'

'What about a quill, ink and paper?'

'Just there, sir.'

'Right, thank you.'

No observatory? At least there was opulence. Still, he looked from the window. A distant structure caught his eye. Maybe not an observatory, but it *did* look as if it might be a good location to observe from.

The rest of the afternoon was spent on the tour beginning with the rich exuberance of the Great Hall. They all craned their necks to take in carved arches, niches, columns and capitals. Sculptures of the Four Elements, figures of the Zodiac, Apollo and the Nine Muses were arrayed around the base of the dome's interior depicting Phaeton falling from his chariot. From there they proceeded to the Garden Hall, Music Room, Tapestry Room, the Long Galleries North and South and the Chapel, working up an appetite along the way.

Later, after the formal dinner, Henry engaged in conversation with the Earl, and asked his thoughts on the situation in the Colonies. John examined the books in the substantial library while Edward sipped his claret. The Earl announced that he would lead them on a tour of the gardens and grounds before their return and jokingly admonished them to get a good night's rest. John Goodricke, however, had no intention of sleeping.

*

The next morning, Edward, after a few wrong turns, found the breakfast buffet. A long sideboard was laden with platters of grilled trout, cold ham, oatmeal with sweet cream, kidneys, bacon with a butter sauce, fresh kippers, veal pies, boiled eggs, breads with jams and marmalade, coffee, tea, Spanish brandy and fresh apple tarts. He was the first to arrive and, as protocol allowed, made his selections.

His mother and sister entered as he placed an overflowing plate on the table.

Good morning, Mother, Mathurina. Are the others still abed?'

'Your father, Henry and the Earl remained up quite late sorting affairs of state, I believe,' said Anna.

'And Harriet is just coming. Have you seen John?' asked Levina.

'He excused himself shortly after the men began their confabulations. I followed only when it seemed the affairs of state were in good hands,' said Edward

'Edward. Must you always play the apothecary?' said Mathurina.

He merely grinned.

'Apothecary?' asked Harriet, who had just arrived.

'He likes to mix it up. Don't you darling brother?'

'Has anyone seen John?' asked Harriet.

'He has not descended as yet,' said Edward.

'He never descends.'

'Harriet! You should not speak so of your brother.'

'Yes, mother. Sorry, but why would he not be asleep? There is no astronomy to be done from here, is there?'

'You do not know your brother,' said Edward.

Lady Isabella entered and Edward immediately stood.

'No, no do not be silly. Sit. I trust the breakfast is to your liking?'

'The kippers are very nice. Very tasty,' said Edward. 'A flavour to compliment the eggs.'

Lady Isabella wondered if he was making it up.

Edward decided he had had his fill and would leave the women to their gossip.

'If you ladies will permit me, it is a lovely morning and I wish to take a little stroll. Your ladyship.'

After bowing out he found his way to a south exit and stepped out into a sunlit manicured landscape. He chose to forego the heavy formality of the Walled Garden for the Temple of the Four Winds. The path, bordered by broad beds of daffodils, beckoned.

Its architectural style resolved as he approached. Cubic in form, there were four identical porticoes with a small dome above all. Two opposing sides were framed by statuary representing the wind deities of the Greeks, or was it the Romans? He did not know or care.

He ascended the steps and peered through the glass panes of a mullioned door. Columns of veined marble stood in a white and gold interior, but it was the bundle on the floor that caught his eye. Someone was lying there. Upon entering he saw that it was Goodricke, wrapped in a blanket and sound asleep next to a wax puddle and note paper. He gently kicked his foot, staring down, hands on hips.

'Rise and shine, sunshine.'

'Oh, Edward. It's you.'

'Well, it's not one of the winds. What the devil are you doing here?'

Goodricke sat up, stretched and yawned.

'Is it morning?'

'Decidedly so, and a generous breakfast awaits.'

'What o'clock?'

'Who knows? Late enough. So, what were you doing out here anyway? Did you have a little dalliance?'

'Yes, a dalliance with the stars, my friend. Do you have any idea what the night sky is like from here? Stars everywhere! Fantastic! I even spotted one that may be variable in Perseus. At least I think so. May have been the wine. Anyway, it is all recorded. I observed until the stars faded, then came in here to write a few notes. Must have dozed off.'

He stood and gathered his blanket and papers. As they walked back to the house Goodricke stopped and gestured back towards the 'temple'.

'I had been hoping this Howard's Castle...'

'Castle Howard, John.'

'Right. Anyway, I came out here hoping against hope that Castle Howard had an observatory, but does it? Not a bit of a one. Does it even have a sundial? Look at that – that pile of rubble! That bloody building should have been an observatory, not a, a...whatever it is.'

'Temple. Of the Four Winds.'

'A lot of damned hot air if you ask me.'

Pigott had never seen him display such emotion.

'John. Calm yourself. It will not do to have you return to the house all empurpled with a blanket trailing behind. Let's get you some breakfast.'

'Do they have oatmeal?'

169

Pigott sighed.

'Yes, John. They have oatmeal. And brandy.'

'Well. That's something then.'

They laughed as they walked.

A small safari of servants passed them walking in the opposite direction carrying baskets, chairs, tables and other paraphernalia suggestive of *al fresco* dining.

Later that morning, the Earl announced a special treat for his guests. Since it was such a lovely day they were to have a pre-departure afternoon luncheon in the Temple of the Four Winds.

'I understand it to have an unusual interior, m'Lord.' said Nathaniel.

'Indeed, it does! The temple was designed after Andrea Palladio's famous sixteenth century Villa Rotunda in Vicenza. And, as you shall see, the interior is finally decorated with scagliola by the stuccoist Francesco Vassalli,' said the beaming Earl.

It's not all that impressive, thought Goodricke.

'But, if I may your lordship, can it accommodate all the necessary *accoutrements* for a luncheon?' asked Anna.

The Earl eagerly replied.

'Well you should ask! Beneath the temple is a cellar where servants can prepare the food before serving it to our polite company. So, it can be used as a place for refreshment as well as for anything else. It really does command impressive views.'

Goodricke rolled his eyes and was nudged by Pigott, who hoped the servants would remove that wax puddle.

16

Cicero, Autumn

By September Edward Pigott was firmly convinced Goodricke would not be the burden he at first dreaded. A fast learner, he easily adapted to astronomy's all-night regimen. Pigott began as a tutor, but it wasn't long before he began to regard Goodricke as a true colleague. What he had not expected was that he was also becoming a friend.

Goodricke could not see well enough in a darkened observatory to decipher speech, making collaboration somewhat problematic. Pigott solved this by explaining the evening's programme in detail beforehand. He knew, however, that more might be accomplished if they observed separately with similar objectives, but how well could Goodricke work on his own? Could he properly record his observations? What could be accomplished observing from his Treasurer's House window?

*

The Sun's position suggested the evening meal was soon, but a clock would still help. Goodricke mulled over the acquisition of one and thought of how he might use it for knowing more than mealtimes.

The need to use the privy interrupted his musings. He noticed Cicero as he walked through the back garden. On his return, he thought to engage him in conversation, but how? The well-designed garden was as good a topic as any.

A series of interlocking spaces and paths were formed by raised beds with a variety of plants from the decorative to the herbal. A small vegetable plot supplied the evening table.

'The garden is looking very well, Cicero. Did you create all this?'

No response. He decided to try one more time.

'I say, you do good work here.'

Cicero returned a quick, shy smile.

'Plants. Me like plants. Me like to work with them.'

Goodricke steadied himself, but replied as if it were normal for Cicero to speak.

'It shows. The grounds here do you credit.'

'It small, but keep me busy still.'

'Cicero, why do you speak to me now? You know I have to ask.'

Cicero sat on a nearby bench. Goodricke hesitated and then sat next to him.

'Me accent, for one thing.'

'Your accent?'

'Yeah, mon.'

'Anything else?'

Cicero sighed.

'Wicked business. Wicked business in Jamaica.'

'I see,' said Goodricke, without really seeing. He pointed to the herb garden.

'What are these plants here?'

'Spearmint, lemon balm, aniseed, thyme, sorrel, feverfew, dill, and someting other I am forgetting. Them is called plant simples.'

'Where did you learn all this?'

'I begin in Jamaica.'

'Jamaica. Right. You have come a long way indeed. How long have you been here?'

'Three growin' season.'

'Three years?'

'Yeah, mon.'

'What brought you from dreary Jamaica to sunny England?'

'Me mother was housekeeper on a sugar plantation near to May Pen. I work in kitchen garden. She dead now.'

Goodricke's heart sank. He had been born a slave.

'I am most sorry to learn this, Cicero. What was her name?'

'What you say?'

'Her name, Cicero, I was asking your mother's name.'

No one had ever asked him that before.

'Myanna, her name was Myanna.'

'And your father?'

'Him de owner,' said Cicero, flatly.

'Ah.'

Goodricke thought it best not to ask *his* name.

'Again, I am sorry Cicero.'

'It all right. You never to know. Anyway, she die of fever, after I reach twelve years. Me father send me first to a relative of the owner of here. He know Mrs Dalrymple. So here I am. That all of it.'

'Your father sent you away?'

'He don't want me there. I hear him say me look too much like himself.'

'But this garden position, I mean…'

'You mean why they give this work to me?'

'Well, yes.'

'Because I good at it. And because of me father. He wan' me to have some work better than there.'

'But why do you choose not to speak when you can speak?'

'To say what?'

'I do not understand.'

'I not even sure. It just that me tongue seize up.'

'Cicero, you said it has something to do with the way you sound. Are you ashamed of it? You should not be, you know. What about me? I do not think I sound quite like everyone else when I speak.'

Cicero agreed. He could not explain it exactly, but Goodricke did sound that little bit off when he spoke.

'Is it more than that?'

'I angry. But me can do nothin' 'bout it.'

'Angry about what?'

'I don't wan' talk 'bout it.'

'All right, Cicero. Of course, you do not have to.'

Goodricke suspected it had everything to do with life in Jamaica, with his experience of plantation life. Mrs Dalrymple was only one link in a long chain of people he associated with it and he would rather not speak to her. Or anyone else who might have the remotest connection to slavery.

'Cicero, how did you come by your name?'

'I no know. What 'bout it?'

'Well, it is the name of someone very well known.'

'It is? I never know anyone else to have it.'

'Cicero was a famous Roman poet and writer.'

'I never know. What him say?'

''Well, he a wrote a great deal about friendship, for one thing?

'So, what him think 'bout it?'

'That it was a good thing, of course. He wrote that fire and water are not themselves of more universal value than friendship.'

'Hmm.'

Goodricke also recalled something else that Cicero had written, but kept it to himself; *a friend's estimate of himself is to be the measure of our estimate of him. It often happens that a man has too humble an idea of himself, or takes too despairing a view of his chance of bettering his fortune. In such a case, a friend ought not to take the view of him which he takes of himself. Rather he should do all he can to raise his drooping spirits, and lead him to more cheerful hopes and thoughts*. He was not sure how or when, but he wanted to help Cicero.

'So, it is a good name, Cicero. A good strong name to have.'

'Why not more people have it?'

'I do not know.'

There was an awkward pause.

'What it is you do here?'

'I study the stars.'

'Truly? Seem a lot to learn.'

'Yes. It is a lot to learn.'

'Well, I must be getting back inside,' said Goodricke.

'Hole up, now mon. I wan' ask you someting,' said Cicero.

'Yes?'

'You cannot hear, but you unnerstan me anyway. How you can do this?'

'I can tell by the movement of your lips when you speak.'

'Even with me accent?'

'Even with your accent.'

'Can such a thing be done?'

'Well, I am doing it. It does take a lot of practice.'

A breeze came up bringing a slight chill with it. Goodricke looked up into a clear night sky. There was Antares, shining red in Scorpio. *It was there yesterday and it will be there tomorrow,* he thought, *whatever else happens on this miserable planet.*

'Cicero, may I ask *you* something?'

Cicero was not sure what to say. No one had ever asked his permission for anything.

Goodricke continued.

'I cannot choose to hear. If my hearing returned I am not sure if I would regard this as a complete blessing. Of course, I would want to hear, but I wonder if I sometimes would wish *not* to hear. But you have this choice. You should speak to others.'

'Why?'

'Why not?'

'No one listen.'

Goodricke thought for a moment and realised to whom he was speaking. He was probably made aware from an early age that nothing he ever said counted for anything. He lived in the servant's quarters and did not sit with them at the evening meal. Was he still a slave? Goodricke was afraid to ask. This was just one more experience that sharpened the distinction between the unpleasantness of life on the ground, as he thought of it, and the sense of purity and peace the stars provided.

'Cicero, from what you say you do not speak because no one listens. I understand that. But Mrs Dalrymple, cares. She is not your enemy, Cicero. You should talk to her.'

'What good it is to say what me think? Instead I work. The plants give me peace. You unnerstan?'

'Yes, Cicero. Yes, I do. But promise me you will try and speak with her sometime.'

'Maybe. Sometime. But will we speak again?'

'Of course. Of course, we will.'

'Thanks, mon.'

'Well, good evening, Cicero.'

Cicero had almost asked whether Goodricke might want to see his drawings. After all, what was the point if no one ever saw them? But felt he could only reveal them to a friend. Perhaps another time.

17

Proof the Earth Rotates

Eleanor lit a few more candles when Goodricke arrived. She had thought it might make it easier for him to see others as they spoke. He would not suspect that was why she was doing it, would he?

'Good evening, Master Goodricke.'

'Mrs Dalrymple. I thought you might wish to know I was in the back garden earlier chatting with Cicero.'

Eleanor did not quite know what to say. Before she could reply Goodricke spoke again.

'Is he free to come and go?'

'Of course, he is. Why ever not?'

'Nothing. I just wondered.'

'I know what you are thinking. It is true he came from an unfortunate circumstance, but he is not a slave. Not now, anyway. Surely you have noticed?'

'I had never thought on it. I just assumed he was not.'

Goodricke was relieved, at least somewhat.

'You missed your morning meal.'

'Yes. Sorry. I did not retire until near dawn.'

'I see. You were watching the stars again,' she said with a playful smile. 'But do they not continue to appear the same from one night to the next?'

'It might seem so. A few stars may change their appearance and I am beginning to think it is worth the time to properly explore this.'

'As well you should! There are so many! Please excuse me, I'll just see to Cook and the meal,' said Eleanor, who had no real idea what he was talking about.

Pomeroy and Guthrie arrived. They looked at each other when they saw Goodricke.

'Ah, Goodricke. Pomeroy and I have a question for you, do we not Pomeroy?' said Guthrie.

'Yes. We have been saving it for you. We could not think of anyone else to ask.'

Goodricke regarded them with a small measure of suspicion.

Eleanor returned with the housemaid who placed a platter of beef and vegetables on the table.

'Yes, well,' said Guthrie, 'of course our...'

'Mr Guthrie?'

'Yes, Mrs Dalrymple.'

'Would you do us the honour of saying grace this evening?'

Guthrie nodded, but thought it best to not try to match Goodricke's earlier eloquence.

Pomeroy had started to serve himself.

'Grace, Mr Pomeroy,' said Eleanor.

Pomeroy held the meat in mid-air unsure of whether to put it back on the platter or on his plate.

After his perfunctory prayer Guthrie collected himself as if he was trying to remember a script.

'As I was saying, we know our planet rotates. I mean to say, that is the current state of affairs, is it not?'

'Yes, Mr Guthrie,' said Goodricke. 'What, pray, can I help you with?'

'Well, the question is this. Is there any *proof* the Earth rotates? Is there not some observation or experiment that can only be explained by an Earth that spins? Mind you, we accept it rotates nonetheless.'

'Indeed, we *do*, sir,' said Pomeroy.

'But we were wondering if it is more than mere belief.'

Eleanor thought this a good question herself and wondered at the answer.

'Not that I know of,' said Goodricke.

'No? I would have thought there was *something*,' said Guthrie.

'There is not. Sorry to disappoint.'

'There is no observation, or…or some type of experiment whose result proves that our planet spins about? What do you say to that, Pomeroy?' asked Guthrie.

Pomeroy was not listening. He regarded Goodricke as if he were following a conjurer's sleight of hand. *How does he know what we are saying?* he wondered.

'What do I say about what?' asked Pomeroy.

'Return to your parsnips, sir,' said Guthrie.

The conversation drifted through more mundane topics. But while Pomeroy chewed his beef and Eleanor offered pudding Goodricke was still digesting Guthrie's question. Why *would* anyone search for some observational proof? After all, the Earth's rotation was an accepted fact. But he felt that was not how natural philosophy should be practiced.

Later that evening Goodricke found he could not shake the question. He looked at the globe his father had bought for him in Groningen so long ago and prodded it into motion. He became determined, there and then, to find observational proof the large globe beneath him behaved like the smaller one now slowly spinning before him.

*

The next afternoon Goodricke sought out Pigott at his observatory. He found him seated in his usual spot at the base of the observatory wall, head leaned back, eyes closed and sunning himself.

'Ah, John. And how is your good self this day? I was going to stop by later. Would you care for some cider?' he asked, slowly raising the jug.

'No, thank you Edward. Listen, I have been thinking on a new problem.'

'Have you indeed. It is a fine day for it.'

'It is nothing we have yet discussed. Most perplexing. It emerged during the evening meal with the other lodgers at the Treasurer's House. One of them asked if there was any experiment whose outcome could only be explained by a rotating Earth.'

'I see. One of them just thought up that question on the spot? I do not believe that for an instant. He planned it and was trying to catch you out.'

'I suspected as much afterwards, but thought it an interesting question all the same.'

'Well, no matter. You cannot know of any such experiment because there is none. My thought is they already knew as much, although how is a wonder.'

'Perhaps so, but I am still grateful.'

'And why is that, pray?'

'Because it pointed me to a very interesting problem, vexing as it is.'

'You mean you wish to now prove the Earth rotates?'

'It is a goal I have, yes.'

'Why on Earth, if you will pardon the term, do you wish this on yourself? We know it rotates. If you are wanting something to fill your time, I can easily provide you with other problems more workable.'

'I am sure. But this is a niggling problem. Do you not agree?'

'I have never thought on it. Why should I? Why should anyone? To solve it will not advance our knowledge one jot.'

'Why must you assume so? The method by which it is solved could itself lead to some other insight or conclusion.'

'If you say so, John.'

'Edward, I intend to think on it in my free time, unless there is some objection.'

'John, there is no need to make this so warm a dispute. I was thinking of all those before us who searched and failed to find any proof of the Earth's rotation - Copernicus, Kepler, Descartes, Galileo, even Newton himself. I do not wish to sound harsh, but do you believe you can succeed where the likes of these have failed?'

Goodricke sighed.

'Edward, what is most important in life?'

Here we go again, thought Piggott, bringing his fist to his forehead. Goodricke dripped with idealism, a quality acceptable in a callow youth, but one he himself was long past. His attitude seemed a bit too solemn, if not downright pompous, characteristics he could not abide. Poor Goodricke needed to relax a little.

'I'm afraid you are a bit ahead of me now.'

'It is a simple enough question. What is it that makes life truly satisfying? Warmth and comfort? A full belly? Income? Love? I say it is none of these.'

'O Lord. I fear an aphorism approaches.'

Goodricke ignored his comment and continued.

'What is most important is simply this; having a problem worth solving. That is the top need.'

Pigott was poised to reply, but could not think of anything clever to say. Goodricke had caught him off guard. He had to think for a minute.

'John, even should I agree, are there not other problems in astronomy more worthy of your time? That is my point.'

Goodricke simply shrugged.

'Well, fine. Think on it if you must, but take care this does not distract from the real problems in astronomy.'

'It *is* a real problem in astronomy, Edward.'

'Not quite. But look at yourself. You seem tired and I daresay you must be hungry. Do you not wish to tend to those needs as well?'

'Edward, surely you have had that special moment when a problem was solved, that shock of recognition that accompanies an insight? Something wonderful happens. There is special feeling at the moment when the solution to a problem is seen. It is not only understood, it is felt. It does not even matter if another has solved it beforehand. This is when I am most alive, experiencing that sharp moment of clarity. It makes one feel like, I do not know, somehow complete, real. Nothing else compares. I quite pity anyone who has never had the experience.'

'You are a strange fellow indeed, John Goodricke and no mistake,' said Pigott. 'Well, if that is what you believe then that is what you believe. I have not the language to counter it. But there is one thing I am curious on.'

He pauses.

'And that is?'

'Suppose these fools had asked instead what proof have we the Earth orbits the Sun? Then what would your reply have been?'

With this Goodricke knew their disagreement was over, if not resolved. Edward was testing him on basic astronomy, a favourite activity. It was a part of their conversations he had come to expect and enjoy.

'Ah. That is a different question altogether, is it not? Let me think on it.'

'Do not take too long.'

They were silent for a moment. The Sun's visibility low in the sky foretold of a clear night for observing. Pigott could sense Goodricke's mind at work.

'Come, come. This you should know.'

'This answer is a tad more complicated as there are two possible answers. Well, one really.'

'And what are these?'

'Stellar parallax and stellar aberration, of course.'

'How do they differ?'

'The chief distinction is that parallax depends on the Earth's position in her orbit whilst aberration depends on motion.'

'A sound reply, but why is parallax not proof the Earth moves in her orbit?'

'We have not the capacity to observe it. The fixed stars, because of their immense distance, have no sensible parallax. It may be argued those nearest have a large parallax, but is yet so small we have not the power of detection.'

'And what of aberration?'

'That was explained by James Bradley some years ago now. It is, in short, the displacement of stellar positions due to the Earth's orbital motion. This we have observed and I believe the more complete term is annual aberration. Edward, must you keep testing me?'

Pigott ignored this. He knew Goodricke enjoyed being challenged, but he was finding it harder to think of new questions.

'As we are on the subject of stellar motion what is proper motion?'

'That is the real motion of the star through space.'

'Can you say more?'

'Right. It is the apparent angular motion of a star on the celestial sphere across our line of sight.'

'Why can we detect this but not parallax?'

'Easy. A star exhibiting proper motion will move uniformly in one direction across the sky such that its change in position accumulates. A star displaying parallax, however, will return to its original position after one year.'

'One more question.'

'Edward, please.'

'What is improper motion?'

'Edward, you know as well as I there is no such thing. Enough of this jousting.'

'Correct! You are ready to receive your parchment.'

'From what? The Edward Pigott College of Natural Philosophy?'

'That would be as good as any.'

'It probably would, but there is something I have been wanting to ask. What can one do without a telescope that is worth doing?'

'Oh, that depends.'

'On what?'

'On what you wish to observe, of course. A glass is useful for studying the Moon or the discovery of a new comet. But as for stars it adds little beyond measuring their position or counting their number. It does not make them appear larger. It does not add any new information about the star itself that can be seen with the unaided eye. Anyway, you do not need one for what I have in mind for you.'

'You have something in mind for me?'

'Yes. Why do you seem surprised?'

'When were you going to tell me?'

'When you were ready.'

'You mean when you were.'

'Fair enough.'

'Right then, what is it you have in mind for me?'

'You should consider a search for stars of inconstant brightness. This is a study that has languished and is something easily done from your window.'

'I have been wondering whether it is a study of much importance.'

'I believe it to be. Mind you, one must first capture the change in brightness and then, in an exercise requiring infinite patience, detect whether this change has some regularity. You yourself have already spotted a star you thought to be a variable whilst at Castle Howard, did you not?'

'Yes, in Perseus. I believe it was Algol.'

'Ah, the eye of the Medusa. Good on you, sir. He is already suspected to be a variable, but is he periodic?'

'Is that of any real value?'

'If I may quote someone not too far from me, it may lead to some other insight or conclusion. I believe those were your words? We cannot know in advance what may be of most consequence to our understanding of the heavens.'

'Right then. I shall continue thinking on the problem of the Earth's rotation.'

'As you wish, John, but I shall wager ten guineas that it will be Algol that will first bear fruit.'

18

The Royal Society, Spring 1782

Joseph Banks bore a comportment only the French word *formidable* could quite capture. 'He is the only person I know,' a wag once remarked, 'who can strut while sitting.' Once he became President of the Royal Society his ability as a shrewd operator became all the more visible. He would never repeat Martin Folkes' habit, a predecessor, of dozing during meetings. The era of unremarkable Fellows was over and he would see to it, by God, that the Society would never again have a lacklustre reputation.

Banks sailed with James Cook's expeditionary voyage to the South Pacific thirteen years earlier. Its primary purpose was to study the transit of Venus, or when Venus could be seen passing in front of the disc of the Sun, a rare event. The transit was observed and exquisitely timed, making it possible to work out a much more exact Earth-Sun distance, a fundamental parameter necessary for the determination of the data found in the *Nautical Almanac*.

But Banks was not there for Venus. He was a botanist who manoeuvred himself aboard by personally bearing the £10,000 expense for his staff of eight and all their equipment, including his own massive desk. In the end, more botanical research was performed than astronomical. He and his assistants conducted studies and collected specimens on every island the *Endeavour* reached.

The voyage lasted three years and the *Endeavour* was feared by some to have been lost at sea or, worse yet, taken by the French. When it finally did return it was not Cook who received public accolades so much as Banks. His detailed drawings, plant specimens and seeds made him famous for it was not botanical knowledge he advanced but *British* botanical knowledge. The significance of the transit of Venus may not have been so easy to grasp, but that of over one-thousand four hundred new plant species was. Banks botanised Britain. He became a favourite of King George who appointed him to develop the new gardens at Kew. This success was followed by his installation, at the young age of thirty-five, as the President of the Royal Society. Banks' stated goal was to ensure that for the first time in its history the 'royal' in the Society's name had meaning in every sense of the word.

Not all members were loyal. An autocratic leadership style inevitably led to conflict: Banks and his allies against the Astronomer Royal Nevil Maskelyne and his supporters, who held that Banks' regime represented a monopoly in favour of botany and other 'trivial sciences'. The opposition was strengthened by Maskelyne's popularity and by the simple fact that he was the only paid permanent scientific officer of The Crown.

This day's meeting of the Royal Society would likely add to the acrimony. On the agenda were deliberations over the recipient of the Copley Medal, awarded for the year's most significant scientific paper. William Herschel was under consideration for his discovery of a new planet. Maskelyne, who had been the first to receive news of this from Herschel, thought it was indeed a seventh planet. Herschel, however, did not commit to this and his paper on the matter, read at a previous meeting, was simply entitled 'Account of a Comet'.

Maskelyne expected to hear some bleating, inasmuch as Banks believed the quality of Herschel's paper not very satisfactory. Herschel may have been good at astronomy, but

Maskelyne had to agree his paper was not well written. It was almost as if he could not be bothered and wished to return full attention to his star survey. Herschel may have not been a vocal member of the opposition to Banks, but he was an astronomer nonetheless. Maskelyne expected Banksians amongst the membership would soon be voicing their opposition, as instructed. It could go either way.

Herschel may not have argued that 34 Tauri was a new planet, but his announcement did stir the astronomical community into action. In the months following it was lost in the glare of the Sun, or 'out' during daylight hours. It reappeared in the autumn night sky and a change in position was confirmed. It was not the motion of a comet. It was a new planet.

Since Herschel did not originally appear to make this claim forcefully enough, some argued he did not deserve the Copley. On the other hand, those that did confirm the planetary orbit did not make the initial discovery of the anomalous motion that brought about their observations in the first instance. Maskelyne thought, on that basis, Herschel would ultimately receive the award. He also knew that Banks felt that if any astronomer had to receive the Copley, it should be Herschel, arguably the most productive and authoritative astronomer of his day.

The meeting was held in the society's new quarters at Somerset House, a decided improvement over those at cramped Crane Court. The new larger meeting room allowed for the pomp Banks wanted for a gathering of the membership, seated in terraced rows facing a long central open area. Chandeliers laden with candles provided illumination while portraits of past Society presidents oversaw the proceedings. Banks sat on a small dais at the far end, the Society's hefty mace on the table between him and the assembly, its presence signifying a formal meeting. Made of silver, a harp, thistles and fleur-de-lis were embossed on the upper end, a richly gilt club.

After preliminary comments Fellows who wished to speak were called upon.

'Fellow Thomas Hornsby is recognised.'

'President and Fellows,' began Hornsby, 'the matter before us is whether Mr Herschel is deserving of this award. Might I remind you there would be no precedent in awarding it to him, since not all past recipients have been deserving of it either!'

There was a smattering of nervous laughter at this odd logic. Banks scowled.

Hornsby continued.

'Should Mr Herschel be graced with this signal honour, it should not be considered as a lapse in our judgement as his work meets any new standard we have adopted for its receipt. It would therefore be most inconstant to deny him while we yet agree his work superior to that of past awardees.'

Hornsby took his seat. He was a Council member whom Maskelyne knew and respected. He was also the Director of the Oxford Observatory and a supporter of Herschel, but he was also neutral in the Society's squabble. *A clever non-committal speech that said little.*

'Fellow Percival Slee is recognised.'

Now this one is a true Banksian toady, thought Maskelyne. Slee had sailed with Banks on the *Endeavour* as a young assistant and never looked back. Or, as others believed, never looked forward. His one guiding principle was whatever pleased Banks. Maskelyne knew he aspired to a seat on the Council. *Not if I can help it.*

'Mr President, Council Members and Fellows', began Slee, one hand grasping his lapel, the other sweeping the air.

'Gentlemen, we swim in murky waters. Mr Herschel is a skilled astronomer, but there are those who say the award should go to the individual who first established the orbital path of this object as planetary. Who might that be? We have learned that the able French astronomer Monsieur Messier had suggested it was indeed unlike any comet he had ever seen. Indeed, the French may have surpassed us as both Monsieur LaPlace and Monsieur Lalande have argued it a new planet. Which of these gentlemen is deserving? Do you not see the confusion here?'

Maskelyne knew there was no way on God's green Earth the award would go to a Frenchman.

'It therefore appears this honour properly belongs to Mr Herschel. Some of you here, I know, believe the award should only go to a true Englishman, but let me remind you that it is the achievement, and not the man we award.'

'*What?*' thought Maskelyne. '*Is Slee supporting Herschel?*'

Slee had paused just long enough to allow Maskelyne time to stand.

'The Reverend Nevil Maskelyne is recognised.'

Maskelyne looked first at Banks and then at Slee. He had not expected this support from Slee and had to reconsider his position.

'Gentlemen, I find myself in agreement with Mr Slee. May I remind you that we have awarded the Copley to an American, Mr Benjamin Franklin. It would not therefore break with any precedent to so recognise Mr Herschel. Is it not true that for ages this object had been observed and catalogued as an ordinary star? Indeed, gentlemen, it is so recorded in Flamsteed's stellar atlas. It is only because of Mr Herschel's diligent and persistent eye it was shown to be otherwise. This was no accident, gentlemen, but due to devotion to his task, something in itself laudable. He has stimulated the research of others and the advancement of astronomy. After determining this not a star he generously shared this information with others. His work deserves credit for it lead us to the discovery of a seventh planet.'

All heads now swivelled towards Slee. Harold Warrilow tugged his elbow. Slee bent down as Warrilow whispered advice and then stood erect.

'One final comment. Perhaps ours may be considered the age of comets. Perhaps it is true that new comets are discovered almost fortnightly. Perhaps we may not award the Copley to someone who thought it a comet? But remember that Mr Herschel did suggest it might be otherwise. Is that not so, Reverend Maskelyne?'

Somehow Slee knew the details of his correspondence with Herschel. He could only reply that that was indeed so. He found himself supporting the position Banks appeared to have all along. A plan was in play.

'Indeed, sir. I have received correspondence from him wherein he states this may possibly be a planet. He only wished to have others examine it themselves, a laudable and most noteworthy act.'

After the meeting Maskelyne approached Banks who was downing his second sherry. He was sure Banks held some ulterior motive in supporting Herschel.

'Well, Sir Joseph, it appears Mr Herschel will now succeed.'

'Indeed sir, and so he shall.'

Maskelyne had an inspired thought.

'Sir Joseph, has this new planet yet been named?'

'Have you not heard? Georgium Sidus, or simply 'George' after King George,' replied Banks with an expression somewhere between a smile and a smirk.

Of course, thought Maskelyne. This name would only have come as a 'suggestion' to Herschel who did not seem to care whether it was a planet in the first instance. It would certainly strengthen Banks' support from the King, as if he did not already have enough of it.

Maskelyne reflected on Banks' posturing during the meeting. He had likened him to a helmsman, deftly steering his ship through the shoals. He had the depressing thought that Banks would use the mace to knock the next astronomer rowing towards the Copley into a reef.

19

Georgium Sidus

'Goodricke, I bring news.'

'Edward. And what news is this?'

Pigott had unexpectedly arrived at the Treasurer's House.

'Why don't we repair to The Grouse? I will tell you all about it and then we can also discuss this new clock of yours,' added Pigott, as an incentive.

'The Grouse?'

'A coffee house. Surely you have had coffee.'

'I have never had coffee.'

'What? You never.'

'True.'

'Then I shall buy you the best York has to offer.'

'I hear coffee tastes like mud.'

'Trust me, you shall enjoy it.'

'If you say so.'

'I do John. I do.'

*

The Grouse was busy, but then, it often was. If one wanted any news this was the place to be, where pamphlets, newsletters and broadsides were available. The coffee was almost an afterthought.

They entered a large rectangular low-ceilinged room, suffused with the scents of coffee, tobacco and wood smoke, the atmosphere more subdued than that of an alehouse.

Pigott walked over to the empty end of one of the communal tables and gestured for two coffees.

'It is not quite the same as an alehouse, is it?' asked Goodricke.

'You are a keen observer, Mr Goodricke.'

'It is easy enough to see, but why?'

'Men do not come for the coffee itself. They are here to discuss matters of finance, make deals and talk politics. And it is only men, of course. No respectable woman would set foot in a coffee house.'

'Why not?'

'Well, in a coffeehouse anyone may approach anyone else and start up a conversation, or an argument, familiar behaviour no lady would tolerate.'

'If you say so.'

'John, must you always say that? I am not the last word.'

'If you...sorry.'

'Right. And there is a good reason to offer them your custom. It is really the only place to properly discuss matters of commerce, politics, even philosophy or scientific discourse if you can find such a debate. A public house would not serve any of these quite as well.'

'Why ever not?'

'Have you not yet noticed that half the population of York is permanently in some stage of intoxication? For thirst one drinks ale, or gin more likely, not the water that comes from the stinking Ouse.'

Goodricke recalled the stench at the King's Staith.

Pigott continued.

'One cannot soundly transact, or keep to their wits, if impaired. Why allow weakness or embarrassment?'

'What about the water used for the coffee?'

'An excellent question. This establishment claims to bring it in barrels from springs elsewhere.' He looked around and leaned forward.

'And there is another benefit to coming here.'

'Which is?'

'Coffee is expensive, my dear fellow. Costs more than a pint! Keeps out the riff-raff,' said Pigott, leaning back with a sweep of his arm.

'Perhaps, but I'll wager they do not have many here who deliberate over matters astronomical.'

Pigott laughed. 'No, although *I'll* wager there have been a few tongues wagging over that subject at Button's in London of late.'

Goodricke gave him a quizzical look.

'Button's, a coffee house near the Royal Society.'

'All well and good, but you started to speak of something,' said Goodricke.

Their coffee was brought over. Goodricke took a tentative, inaugural sip.

'Well?' asked Pigott.

'I may keep to tea.'

'Fine. Keep to tea. Anyway, as I was saying, it seems that Mr William Herschel has discovered a new planet. Well, that is what some believe, anyway. I have just learned this from Father.'

'Are you sure about that?'

'He was observing 34 Tauri with his supposedly superb optics sometime early last spring and apparently detected movement. You mean to say you have not heard about this?'

Goodricke's brow furrowed.

'I may have read something about it in a letter. 34 Tauri is shown as an ordinary star in Flamsteed, is it not?'

'Are you falling behind in your correspondence, John? Anyway, you are right, it was *thought* to be a star. Just barely visible to the naked eye under the absolute best of conditions. No longer. It is Herschel who is now the star.'

'Are you not happy for him?'

'I am not unhappy, but there are any number of others I would rather see receive the laurels that shall now come his way, not to mention the Copley medal.'

'And what is that?'

'An award, no *the* award, presented annually by the Royal Society for the most important scientific paper submitted in the past year. I have acquired a draft copy of the announcement that states Herschel received it for the discovery of this new and singular object – and please do not ask how I obtained it.'

He reached into his frock coat and unfolded a sheet of paper.

'Let me see. Ah, *William Herschel* etcetera, etcetera … *a discovery which does him particular honour, as, in all probability, this star has been for many years, perhaps ages, lay within the bounds of astronomic vision, and yet till now, eluded the most diligent researches of other observers.* Etcetera, etcetera,' said Pigott, finishing with a flourishing wave.

'Impressive. But I asked if you think him not worthy? My understanding is that he is a reasonable enough fellow, from what little I know.'

'Well, whether he is worthy or whether he is poor company are two different things. It is just that he can sometimes irritate.'

'I would rather we discuss my clock.'

'John, this is the discovery of a seventh planet. Do you not wish to learn more of it?'

'The discovery yes, but it appears you wish to talk more about him.'

'Perhaps, but allow me this point. I do not dislike him entire, but he is rather taken with himself. Astronomy is to be taken seriously, but one should not take oneself too seriously in its practice. No, that is not quite right.'

'Edward, what exactly is troubling you?'

Edward paused, thought a moment, and continued.

'Do you recall our conversation in The Swan?'

'We have had many. To what do you refer?'

'Our first where I believe I judged the emptiness of space.'

'It is not empty, Edward. It is filled with stars.'

'All right then. I was referring to the feeling of emptiness within oneself the infinite cosmos can instil.'

'I remember something of the kind and I believe I did not agree, as you may recall, but really what does any of this have do with Herschel?'

'Vanity, John. The immensity of this universe renders one's acts utterly meaningless. One must be vain indeed to remain ignorant of this simple truth. But the more he stares into the vastness of space, the more he is enamoured of his own achievement, not less.'

'Edward, I am not sure of your reasoning here. He does good work.'

'As do you. As do we all. But we do not use that to inflate our own egos. To do so, in my view, only reveals some degree of self-doubt.'

'Then let us have a difference of opinion on the matter. It is not his astronomy you do not care for. It is him. Fine. At least be pleased for astronomy.'

'True enough. Do not misunderstand. We are not enemies so much as we are not friends - and we do share a correspondence.'

'Edward, all this is a subject for another time. The matter at hand is more important than the man's nature. Is this object a new planet or not?'

'Oh, it is a new planet, all right. It recently has re-entered the night sky and one or two continental observers have confirmed the orbit. I believe the Astronomer Royal has done so as well.'

'Does it have a name?'

'Georgium Sidus, if you can believe it.'

'What?'

'Gee-orgi-um Sidus.'

'Ah, Latin.'

'Yes, the Georgian Star - after King George, of course. I suspect the French are none too pleased.'

Goodricke looked into his coffee and then spoke.

'Edward, should we not now have an eight-day week?'

'I do not know, John. Should we?'

'Well, why are there seven days in the week?'

Pigott had never given it much thought. Had anyone? It appeared Goodricke had.

'I imagine it has something to do with scripture. Our Lord created the heavens and planets and on the seventh day He rested. Something like that. Anyway, we also work six days but keep the Sabbath holy and refrain from toil.'

Goodricke gave him a reproachful stare.

'Edward, surely you must know it has everything to do with the seven objects in the sky that move with predictable regularity. Well, at least the seven before this new planet came along.'

'I may have read something like that, but it is not exactly a deep thought, is it?'

'I only call upon it to play a little game with this new planet. Indulge my own poor attempt at sarcasm, something you seem to enjoy on occasion.'

Pigott sighed and nodded.

'Right. The question on the floor is this - does not the addition of this new planet require we change to an eight-day week and, moreover, each day in this new week be named Georgium Sidus?'

'Now you are talking rot,' said Pigott.

'I am not, sir. We simply extend the reasoning behind the origins of the present seven-day week and how they acquired their names. It began with the twenty-four-hour day the Romans borrowed from the Egyptians. Or was it the Babylonians? No matter. Not hours as we now use them, but days of twenty-four equal divisions. Each hour, according to astrology, was assigned a different deity, deities named after each object that moves in the sky. Do you follow?'

'Not yet.'

'Well, first think of the objects that move and arrange them in order of decreasing distance as measured from the Earth. In other words, assume that the Earth is the centre of the solar system. So, in terms of this decreasing distance we have Saturn the furthest out, then Jupiter, then Mars, the Sun, Venus, Mercury and the Moon. These are the seven objects that move.'

'But the ancients did not know the distances to these objects, so how were they ranked according to distance from the Earth as you say?'

'They were not ranked by distances as we now know them, but by the speed of their motion through the heavens, or from slow to fast. Anyway, don't let's quibble. May I continue?'

'If you must.'

'Thank you. The first hour of each day is the regent hour. Each day is named after the object assigned to this regent hour. I say 'object', but to the Romans it was a deity. Saturn, the slowest object that moves, is assigned to the first hour of the first day or from midnight to one o'clock. So that day becomes Saturday. The following six hours in that day are then assigned Jupiter, Mars, the Sun, Venus, Mercury and the Moon. But the *day* is named after the object assigned to this first hour. That is the important bit. Do you follow now?'

'Keep talking.'

'Right. The eighth hour of this first day begins the sequence anew with Saturn, Jupiter, Mars, the Sun, Venus, Mercury, and the Moon assigned to the next seven hours. After this *second* repetition you begin the third, but there are only three hours remaining. The twenty-fifth hour of the first day would have been assigned to the Sun.'

'But there is no twenty fifth-hour.'

'Now you have it. The Sun is assigned to the first hour of the *next* day and the remainder of the sequence continues with Venus, Mercury and the Moon. Then the cycle begins anew. The next seven hours are again assigned a deity in this same manner and then the next seven again. This leaves the Moon to be assigned to the twenty-fifth hour of the second day, but again there is no twenty-fifth hour and so it is assigned to the first hour of the *third* day.'

'I see that well enough, but how does this end up being seven days? When does this sequence stop?'

'Simple. It lasts one-hundred and sixty-eight hours, or the common product of seven and twenty-four. An easier way to think of it is that the complete cycle ends when each of these seven objects has been assigned to the first hour of a day – seven days. The point is that the controller of the first hour of each day, the regent hour, dominates that day and that is why it is named after the deity of that hour. Now do you follow?'

'So, that is how we have come to have Saturn's day, the Sun's day, the Moon's day - Saturday, Sunday, Monday. I say, where does Tuesday come in?'

'It is not all that smooth. Others have mucked in. I am sure you know of the Nordic origins for some of these names, do you not?'

'Do I?'

'I should hope so. Tuesday was named after the Norse god Tyr. The Romans had named this day after their war-god Mars or *dies Martis*. Wednesday was named to honour Wodan, so it became Wodan's day, but the Romans called it *dies Mercuri*, after Mercury. The French names continue the original ones; *Mardi* for Tuesday and *Mercredi* for Wednesday.'

'All of this assigning of deities to hours bears the odour of astrology. You are not a follower, I trust?'

'Lord, no, but its computational efforts have borne fruit for the rest of us. Anyway, that is how the days acquired their names and why we have seven. At least pretty nearly.'

'How are you to know of this anyway? I mean to say, it was not a subject at, where was it - Warrington?'

'Father has books. A library actually.'

198

'Of course. Now what of King George's Star, or 34 Tauri or whatever the bloody hell it is? Then we would have for the second day Sun, Venus…wait that's not right.'

Goodricke smiled.

'Why bother? We now have eight moving objects and eight goes neatly into twenty-four three times with no remaining bit so that means the first hour of every day of the new eight-day week, using this method, would be named King George's Day!' said Goodricke excitedly, drawing the attention of one or two others who peered above lowered broadsheets.

Pigott motioned for him to lower his voice. He decided not to press the question of why eight days, it was a joke after all. And one made by Goodricke! Why spoil the mood? He replied with an inspired comment.

'Would that not lead to much confusion? Good sir, can you accommodate me on George's Day? No? Then what about George's Day? George's Day? Why yes, that suits. I am free on George's Day, but not George's Day. George's Day, it is then!'

They laughed and Pigott wished they had been drinking ale instead.

Their laughter subsided and Goodricke spoke.

'Now, what about my clock?'

'You and your bloody clock. Are we now being serious?'

'Edward.'

'Seems odd, *me* asking *you* to be serious. However, do we understand the function of an astronomical clock?'

'Yes, Edward. It must be for both timekeeping and time measurement, but not, in my case, to keep sidereal time.'

'Clever aren't we. Tell me why not.'

'Sidereal time is necessary to locate the position of a star not visible without a glass.'

'How does it do this?'

'The purpose of any clock is to represent the heavens. An ordinary clock times the position of the Sun but a sidereal clock indicates where to find stars by locating the vernal equinox. Also, astronomers use sidereal time because in doing so they need not concern themselves with where the Earth is in her orbit.'

Goodricke raised his palms as if to ask *anything else?*

'Can you say more about the vernal equinox?'

'It is the point where the Sun crosses the celestial equator. Also, it used as a zero point for a stellar coordinate known as right ascension measured eastward along the celestial equator to any star's hour circle. The sidereal time is the hour angle of the vernal equinox. So, local sidereal time will equal the hour angle of any star plus its right ascension. If you have the sidereal time and know a star's right ascension, you know its hour angle or, in other words, where to look for it.'

Pigott looked into his empty mug and put it back on the table. *He knows his astronomy, right enough. It is now time.*

'What of your programme?' he asked.

'What about it?'

'One doesn't observe willy-nilly, as I believe you have once remarked. Not if one is serious. You must have some observing objective, a plan.'

'What might you advise?'

'There is one area I have mentioned or have you forgotten it?'

'A search for stars of variable brightness.'

'Not quite. More to find the *period* of variability of one. Many stars have unfortunately been incorrectly marked as variable because of thin cloud or some other misinterpretation. It is, as I have said, an area of study that has been at a standstill for several decades and needs someone who has the patience and stamina to observe and to record at a consistently high level. And you do not need a telescope for this.'

'No, but I require a clock.'

'Indeed, you do. Right, then. Let us to Mr Hartley straight away and order this blasted clock.'

20

The Clock, Summer

'Right, squire, that was a job shifting this lot. Is this the right spot?'

One of Hartley's delivery men had spoken.

'Perfect. Thank you'

The other mover began to unwrap the weights and pendulum.

'I will install those myself, please,' said Goodricke.

'Right you are, then. Shall we set the time for thee? Only a guess mind you.'

'No, no, I shall attend to that as well. Thank you.'

Goodricke gave them each a coin and showed them out. He stood before his new clock in rich anticipation. It was a scientific instrument, *his* scientific instrument. Its true purpose was not to tell the time, but to *measure* it. Devoid of all ornamentation, it had no spandrels or lacquered case, no veneers, fan emblems or marquetry. The dial face was a clean white with black hour and minute hands, thin and pointed. Below the centre of the larger dial face was a separate dial marking the seconds only. The case was solid oak. Not only was this less expensive than some exotic wood, such as Spanish mahogany, but its density also reduced vibrations that might upset the clock's goings. He knew he would have to also fasten it to the wall to dampen any movement. If it rocked even the slightest bit the weights, once they descended to the length of the pendulum, could begin to swing in sympathy with it and abstract its energy.

What Goodricke saved on cosmetics he spent on installing everything that could be added to regulate the clock's goings - a deadbeat escapement to eliminate recoil in the gear train, a pendulum rod with a mercury bubble installed to compensate for any expansion in warm weather that might affect the amplitude, and the 'endless rope arrangement' to prevent the clock from slowing whilst a weight was being wound up. The crucial step now was to set it to the correct time, but how?

The average person did not need to know the time to the nearest second. The nearest minute would certainly do, or even the nearest quarter hour. But astronomers required accuracy. It was this need that drove the development of the mechanical clock as a precision timekeeper. The real link between astronomy and timekeeping was made with the conversion of angular measurement in degrees to one of a measurement in time, the 'hour angle' of a star. This enabled the determination of longitude and the drawing of accurate maps and charts. It was the accuracy required by astronomers that raised the standards by which all the best clocks were made.

He had briefly thought a sundial might be used to set his clock. The clock could be set to noon when the sundial showed noon. This could work in principle, but there was no sundial anywhere on the grounds. One could be acquired easily enough and installed on the forecourt below. Cicero could alert him the moment that the dial indicated the sun was at upper culmination or high noon. But his clock had to be accurate. This sundial method would only work if the time interval between each successive solar meridian crossing was the same from one day to the next. It was not because the Earth's orbit was not perfectly circular. Any astronomer knew that the speed of the Earth varied as it moved through an elliptical orbit causing the moment of noon measurement to vary slightly throughout the year.

The best plan was to set his clock against that of another accurately set by using stars – the clock in Pigott's observatory. But how could he synchronise his clock with another, hundreds of yards away?

Goodricke stopped pacing and walked over to the window. There was the Minster and in it, Great Peter. In that instant, it all came together. He grabbed his cloak and hat, and bounded down the stairs.

*

'Mrs Dalrymple? I am looking for Cicero.'

'I believe he is in the back garden, his usual spot.'

'Thank you.'

'John, before you go I would like to ask something.'

'Yes, Mrs Dalrymple?'

'On second thought, it is nothing really. I'll see you at the evening meal.'

'Of course.'

Goodricke fairly ran out the door.

Eleanor had wanted to ask him about Cicero, but sensed it was best to just let him speak when he was ready.

Cicero was picking out weeds from the herb garden as Goodricke approached.

'Cicero.'

Cicero returned a brief nod.

'I need your help with something.'

'What can me do to help you?'

'I am wondering if you might come to my room tomorrow near to noon. Will that be all right for you?'

'No problem, mon, but how me know when it near noon?'

'Of course. I'll have a pretty good idea. I will come and collect you. Will that be all right?

'Yeah, mon. But why?'

203

'I need to borrow your ears,' said Goodricke slapping his own and smiling as he left.

*

Goodricke walked along Bootham Road with a skip in his step. He went straight into the back garden expecting to find Edward sitting against the wall, jug in hand.

No Edward. He entered the observatory.

'Hello, Edward, are you here?'

He called up to the observatory's second level. Edward poked his head into the opening.

'Goodricke, good sir. What brings you here in bloody broad daylight?'

Goodricke went up to join him and saw he was making an adjustment to the transit. *Good, everything will be just perfect.*

'I have it.'

'Have what? Ah, your clock. It arrived in one piece I trust?'

'It is all fine. I came to explain how we might set it.'

He was not in the least surprised to learn Goodricke had arrived at a solution.

'I have wondered about that, but could not think how it might be done myself. So, what is this method?'

Pigott folded his arms, sat on a stool and gave Goodricke an expectant look.

'It is all rather simple. I set my clock using yours. You set it using known transit times of selected stars. Is that not so?'

'As I have already said.'

'Right. So now the key to setting my clock is Great Peter.'

'Now you have lost me. Who is Peter and what has he to do with this?'

'Great Peter, Edward. In the Minster.'

'The bell, Great Peter. What of it, or him?'

'I expect you can hear it ring from here?'

'You can hear it from anywhere.'

'Good. So, at the exact moment he makes the stroke of twelve you shall note the time of your clock to the second.'

'But Great Peter's own timing is likely inaccurate. You cannot use it to set your clock.'

Goodricke impatiently waved him off.

'Do you not see? That is of no matter. You will note on your clock the time it strikes twelve and I shall do the same using *my* clock. The difference in the times between our clocks is the error in my clock. Simple, is it not?'

Pigott thought it hardly bore mentioning, but felt he had no choice.

'Yes, but John, you cannot hear Great Peter.'

'Cicero can.'

Pigott thought for a moment. It was a brilliant plan, except for one small problem.

'John, if you want a truly accurate clock you must take into account the time it takes sound to travel. The sound of each ring will reach me *after* reaching you. We shall not hear it ring simultaneously.'

'I have already thought of that. A reasonable estimate of the distance of this observatory from Great Peter places it about fifteen hundred feet further than my window. Now, as the speed of sound is about eleven hundred feet per second, I feel subtracting one second from your time will sufficiently compensate. What do you think?'

Pigott wondered why he had not thought of any of this. After all, he heard Great Peter enough times. Perhaps it was because he heard, but never really listened.

'John, one more question. How do you know of Great Peter's ringing at all? Did you just assume?'

'Ah, it was when I was at the Minster, in the Lantern Tower. Great Peter rang and I felt its pulsations through the stone.'

Pigott paused to process this and came back to the moment.

'Right. Of course. Well, when would you like to do this?'

'I assume it rings the noon hour?'

'It does. Not that it matters, but I believe the north-west tower holds six clock bells as well. They ring every quarter of an hour during the daytime and precede Great Peter's striking the hour. This could alert Cicero when it is about to ring and we could both take note of the twelfth peal. When do we do this?'

'Why not tomorrow? My clock has been installed, the weights are wound and the pendulum now swings at the second interval. We can then record and share our separate times of Great Peter's action.'

'I must congratulate you on your solution, John. Your plan has a sound ring to it.'

'Yes, and needless to say I shall require this adjustment from time to time.'

Goodricke reminded Pigott that he too once had his enthusiasm.

*

'Well, Cicero - any questions? All you need do is drop your arm as you hear Great Peter strike the hour. I can look at both my clock and you if you stand well next to it. When you drop your arm for the twelfth peal, I shall note the time shown on my clock. But please move your arm as it rings, not after. You will have to catch the rhythm. Can you do this? It is important to be accurate.'

'No problem, mon. I got it.'

Cicero could not help but notice Goodricke's rooms were not much more furnished than his own on the ground floor. He moved to his designated position and stood at the ready, his arm upraised. Not that it would be any more accurate to do so, but he extended his forefinger as well.

Goodricke positioned his chair so that he could keep one eye on the second hand while watching Cicero's arm mark the sound of Great Peter, inked quill at the ready.

The sound of his own breathing and the ticking clock was all Cicero could hear. He was surprised at how nervous he was. It was a simple enough task, but he did not want to disappoint.

Over at the Minster six bell ringers arranged themselves in a circle in the northwest tower's ringing chamber and prepared to announce the coming of the noon hour. At 'catch hold!' they began ringing through the sequence of changes familiar to all of York. As they neared the end, another of their number began to haul on the tufted tail of the rope leading up to Great Peter. Ten tons of brass lumbered to life, the huge clapper swinging closer and closer to the trailing side sound bow. The bell ringer, slowly lifted from the floor with each oscillation, could not know he was also advancing the cause of science.

Great Peter struck the noon hour sending its richly resonant E flat sound wave out to Cicero, spurring him into motion. His dipping arm matched its cadence while Goodricke's head bobbed in sympathy. The critical time was recorded just as it struck twelve. Goodricke imagined Pigott doing the same a second later. He now had the data needed to accurately set his clock.

Cicero could not help but notice Goodricke's expression. *Why all the excitement?* he thought. *It is just a clock, after all.*

21

Visions of Nature

Cicero looked through Goodricke's open doorway.
'Master Goodricke? It is I, Cicero, come to visit.'

It was a late afternoon in July. Goodricke had invited Cicero because he enjoyed his company. And, since the clock would need frequent resetting, he thought he might be interested in how he planned to use it.

He motioned for Cicero to enter

'Please, have a seat.'

Cicero had brought a small sheaf of papers bound in gardening twine.

'What have you there?'

'I want to show you me drawings, me water colour.'

'Drawings of what, Cicero?'

'Flowers. Paintings of flowers.'

'I had no idea. When did you begin this?'

'Since I come here, mostly. I work some in Jamaica, but no water colour there.'

'May I see?'

Cicero placed the small stack of drawings on the table. He rubbed his hands on his breeches before untying the twine and left Goodricke to look through the paintings himself.

'Cicero! These are wonderful!'

There was one magnificent watercolour after another; rich illustrations of orchids, perennials and primula, bulbs, large and small, flowering shrubs, a lily spotted with shades of orange and recurving petals, digitalis with tubular white flowers. Everything about them was exquisite; the colours, composition and clarity, the work of a natural talent

'These are very good Cicero, very good indeed.'

Cicero started breathing again.

'You like them?'

'Yes, Cicero. Very much.'

'But why you like them?'

Goodricke realised that Cicero might think he was just being polite. A truthful answer was expected and he carefully considered his reply.

'What you are asking, I think, is what makes a good drawing, or watercolour as you have here.'

'I suppose.'

'I would say that what you are trying to do is capture some truth. Your watercolours do not necessarily have to be perfect reproductions, but they must somehow stimulate that same response that looking at the real thing produces. For you to be able to do this must mean that you understand what it is you are looking at. Does that make any sense?'

'I not sure what you say.'

Goodricke sighed and thought he may well have been talking rubbish.

'Actually, I am not sure either, but I will say the one thing I know to be true.'

'What that?'

'Well, if a drawing is good, I will want to go back and look at it a second time – as I have just done now, with your watercolours.

'Yeah mon, that make sense.'

'Where did you learn to do this?'

'I jus' teach meself. It ease me up.'

'How do you do it?'

'I jus' draw what me see.'

'But not all these are in our garden.'

Cicero shrugged.

'I find them. It is what me do in me own time.'

Goodricke suspected the grounds of the Treasurer's House would inevitably become too confining for Cicero, if they were not already.

'Have you shown these to anyone else?'

'No one. Me mother know of it, but no other person.'

'I am honoured you show them to me, Cicero.'

'No problem.'

'Perhaps Mrs Dalrymple might wish to see them as well?'

No reply.

'She does care for you, you know.'

Goodricke thought for a moment and simply nodded. After all, Cicero wouldn't even speak to her. He was still not sure why it was he spoke to him, let alone show him his drawings. There was a bottled-up anger, but these drawings showed another side altogether. He hoped, in time, it would win out.

'What this?' asked Cicero who changed the subject by pointing to a sheet of paper tacked to the wall. On it, in large florid script, was written *Non est ad astra mollis e terris via.*

'This? It is Latin for there is no easy way from the Earth to the stars.'

'Soun' like you wan go there.'

'You know, Cicero, sometimes I believe I do. What it means, though, is that any understanding of the stars only comes after very hard work. Perhaps you might have more of an idea of what I am doing if I show you my astronomical journal.'

The journal, a large leather-bound volume, contained the fruit of all his efforts. He was not sure what to show Cicero, but felt he must make a reciprocal act of disclosure.

He selected a rare page that had drawings on it, as well as columns of figures.

'Here for instance is the path of a comet I recorded over a period of a few weeks.'

Goodricke pointed to crudely sketched depictions of Cygnus, Vulpecula, Sagitta and Aquila vertically stacked in a large rectangle graduated in degrees and right ascension. Above it he had written:

> *The following is a draught of the track of the Comet from Nov 15th to Nov 22nd. Its place on the 15th and 17th were observed by Mr E. Pigott - the rest by myself. The figure and the stars were taken from Adam's Celestial Globe 18-inch radius, in which all the stars of Hamstead's catalogue are set.*

'What these here? Them look like animals.'

'Those are constellations the comet passed through. The top one is the Swan, followed by the Fox, the Archer and then the Eagle.'

Goodricke was embarrassed to now see how poor his drawing skills were, when compared to Cicero's. He continued.

'This line here is the path of the comet over time. Do you see?'

'But this comet business, what it is?'

'Well, it is something that moves quite rapidly, is in our solar system, and obeys Newton's Law of Gravity.'

'Yes, but what it is?'

'I have no idea.'

'Who know what it is?'

'No one I know.'

Goodricke changed the subject.

'Here is something else that might be of interest.'

He turned to another page, skipping past text and columns of figures.

'What that?'

'A drawing of a spot on the Sun.'

'But how you look at it? It not too bright?'

'Well, one way is to use these cards here.'

Goodricke reached over to his little bookshelf and drew out two pieces of heavy stock paper. One of them had a tiny round hole in the centre. He held the card with the pinhole in the foreground and the other behind it.

'Keep your eye on this card here.'

He aligned the cards and slowly separated them.

'Do you see?'

An image of the solar disc appeared on the rear card.

'Them little black bits, are them sunspot?'

'Yes. Those are sunspots. A telescope is better of course, but it must have a filter. Mr Pigott has one for his telescope, and that is how I made this drawing.'

Cicero looked again at the drawing of the sunspot, showing an inner dark area ringed by an outer lighter pattern.

'This one of them spots?'

'Yes.'

'But what make them? What it is?'

'No one knows. One idea is that they might be a type of volcano on the Sun, but I do not think so.'

'So how you know them spots are on the Sun and not like a cloud?'

'A very good question Cicero. We know they are *on* the Sun and not above it because of the manner in which they disappear from view as they approach the Sun's limb. From this we have learned the Sun spins upon his axis and takes about twenty-five days to make one rotation. We know this by timing the spots as they disappear from view and return again.'

'But still, what is this sunspot? What make it?'

'No one knows.'

'Like the comet.'

Well, yes, like the comet.'

Cicero thought for a minute and asked, 'You look at stars too?'

'Yes, that is what I do the most.'

'But what you can know?'

'Another good question. Sometimes I wonder about that myself. Well, it is not the case that all stars are of a constant brightness. Some, it seems, change their brightness.'

'You mean they do not keep to the same brightness? I never know.'

'A few, yes.'

'Do you know any stars do this?'

'Well, Mira is one, and a few others.'

'How you find them?'

'You compare them to other stars nearby that we know do not change their brightness.'

'So, if you find one like this what then you do?'

'Well, you make certain it is changing and then you tell others.'

'But what you learn besides some star twinkling more than others?'

'Well, suppose I find that one of the stars twinkles as you say but does so in a regular manner. That would be of some interest.'

'Can you do this?'

'I hope so.'

Goodricke was slightly unsettled at how Cicero's questions made it so easy to question the worthwhileness of all his efforts. He thought a moment and reached for his Flamsteed star atlas.

'Have a look at this.' He pointed to a figure drawn in over the stars with winged sandals and sword held aloft.

'This is Perseus from Greek mythology. His image is revealed when you connect the stars like dots. Well, sort of anyway. That is why this group of stars is so named.'

'What he is holding?'

'That is the head of Medusa. She was killed by Perseus, at least in Greek mythology she was.'

'Seem a bit rough.'

'Well, the Greeks were not squeamish with their myths, but look here.'

He stabbed the page with a forefinger.

'This is the star I shall study next.'

Cicero leaned over for a closer look.

'Why that?'

'It has been identified as variable in the past. Also, nearby stars are believed to be of constant brightness and have a range of brightness between them. That helps.'

'It have a name?'

'Algol.'

'Funny name.'

'Yes, I suppose it is.'

'So it change?'

'Well, I think it does, but I want to know if it does so in a regular manner. That is why I need the clock. I shall use it to measure exactly how long these changes last and how often they take place.'

'But it like the comet and spot on the Sun, don't it? No one unnerstan' what really happen? So why you trouble with all this? You never unnerstan' what you see.'

Goodricke thought about this for a moment. True enough, perhaps, but it would not stop him.

'This is how science works, Cicero, how it moves forward. We must not keep from something because we do not fully understand it. We can never completely know what our discoveries will mean to those who come after us. Newton perhaps said it best. He wrote that if he saw further than others it was only because he stood on the shoulders of giants. I do not consider myself a giant, but one day, all the same, someone may stand on my shoulders and see a little further. Sorry, I did not mean to make a speech.'

'Not to worry. You have good knowledge.'

Maybe, thought Goodricke, *and maybe it is all just so much blather. Is Cicero better at understanding his plants than I am at understanding stars? I have never come this close to art before and now I know how bad I am at making even a simple drawing. Is discovering something in astronomy as creative as painting in watercolours? Is it creative? Who is more creative? Handel or Herschel? Does Cicero simply draw what he sees? No. He discovers meaning in what he sees and then draws that. What am I looking for but data? Is that creative? Perhaps not in the same way, but for either of us to do what we do it's not what we look at that matters, but what we see.*

Cicero regarded the clock.

'So why you buy this, then?'

'I shall need it to measure the amount of time a star's changes in brightness last. That is the idea, anyway.'

'I never know. I think you use a clock only to know the time it is.'

'Oh no, Cicero. It is not just to know the time of day so precisely. What would be the need?'

22

Algol, Winter 1782-83

The setting sun shone through clear, still air. A tranquil scene to some, but to others the coming darkness discharged demons. Daytime's din dwindled to the sound of the last thrown bolt as residents retreated to the safety of the hearth. York even had its own evil spirit, the Barguest, a monstrous black dog with huge teeth and claws. The sounds of scuttling rodents, little noticed at midday, became the Barguest at night.

Not everyone believed that phantoms sailed through York's dark, empty streets. Such threats appeared in polite culture only in literature or on the stage. Thieves and murderers, on the other hand, were another matter. A shape in the shadows could be an innocent shrub or a creeping cutthroat.

Goodricke's attitude towards nightfall was free of all suspicion. For him the darker and longer the night, the better. It was irksome that true darkness was all too brief in mid-summer, but with winter approaching, it lasted much longer. Night time was also when his vision was at its most acute. On a clear, moonless night, he could find the dimmest of stars as well as detect subtle differences in their colours. The yellowish white of Procyon was not the same as the bluish white of Vega. The orange of Arcturus was distinguishable from the yellowish red of Antares. No one knew why stars had different colours or why they had colours at all. It was not something he would ever think about.

Someone with average eyesight might well distinguish Alcor and Mizar, the double star in the handle of Ursa Major separated by only two-tenths of one degree of an arc. Goodricke, however, could detect objects separated by half this amount. He could also bring to bear his excellent peripheral field of vision. If he stared directly at a faint star it would sometimes fade. But by shifting his gaze ever so slightly off to one side, he could have it reappear.

The brightness scale of stars was established by the ancient Greek astronomer Hipparchus. The twenty brightest stars were designated as 1st magnitude whilst those at the limits of visibility under perfect conditions were set at 6th magnitude. A star's magnitude number, therefore, was a measure of its brightness - the lower the magnitude, the brighter the star. A brightness difference of one magnitude meant that one star was approximately two and a half times brighter, or fainter, than another. Stars were later ranked by letters of the Greek alphabet. The brightest star in any constellation was generally known as alpha followed by the Latin genitive of the constellation's name. The brightest star in Lyra became alpha Lyrae, the second brightest, beta Lyrae and so on. Eventually, the brightest stars also acquired proper names such as Antares or Regulus. The second brightest star in the constellation Perseus, beta Persei, was also known as Algol.

When observed from York's latitude, Perseus circled the North star without ever setting. Now, as winter approached, it sat high in the sky directly above Taurus and to the west of Auriga. It came into view shortly after seven, crossed the meridian about midnight and would remain visible until dawn.

Goodricke knew that Edward's encouragement to search for variable stars was not simply an offhand suggestion on what he might study. Whatever Edward's true commitment to astronomy, he did have a fertile mind. This was a neglected area of study and he had earned Edward's trust to explore it. It was not something he would have been offered that first day at The Swan. But now, after proving himself, he had risen not only in Edward's estimation, but also his own.

In previous months, his journal noted observations of a 'Nebula in Vulpecula', 'Herschel's Planet', 'Sun's Spots' and similar objects. All well and good, but he would now spend more time searching for variables.

But how? What, exactly should he search for? Should he simply confirm that those few stars previously marked as variables were, in fact, variable? That hardly seemed significant. No, the real challenge would be to find one whose variability was *periodic*. Now *that* would be a finding!

Algol had been suspected to be a variable for over one hundred years, but little was known beyond this. Was it ever mistakenly so designated because of high clouds or poor eyesight? Goodricke made no assumptions. It was easy to observe and it was well above the horizon, thereby minimising extinction by the Earth's atmosphere, the star's light having to travel through less of it to reach the eye. Another benefit to observing Algol was that nearby stars were known to be of constant brightness, making it easier to gauge any change in Algol's. If its brightness fell between that of two nearby comparison stars he could estimate to within a quarter of a magnitude where it lay between them. A telescope actually would do more harm than good. It would not make Algol any larger and also narrowed the field of view, restricting observations of comparison stars. This was to be a naked eye study.

Algol was first mentioned in his journal in early November by noting its historical background. Earlier astronomers had recorded it at 2nd magnitude and others at 3rd. Were they all accurate recordings of a true variable?

He wrapped himself in his cloak, positioned his chair before the open window and looked out beyond the silhouette of the Lantern Tower. The constellations began to appear, patterns that demarcated their location between one another and the positions of stars within them. This was a new kind of observing altogether, not the tracking of a comet or sketching of a sunspot. He was striking out on his own.

The magnitudes of all the stars near Algol had to be memorised. He could scribble something in the darkness, but he could not read in it. Dark-adapted eyesight would be ruined in an instant by the light from even one lit candle and then take nearly another half hour to again reach maximum sensitivity.

He visually stepped from Orion to Taurus to Auriga and over to Perseus. Mirfak, its brightest star, was easy enough to spot, but where was Algol? His eyes slid past it because it was *not* at its usual 2nd magnitude. And, if its magnitude of record was correct, this change was *real*. It had dimmed by two magnitudes *When do you return?* he wondered. *And will you become dimmer still?*

There were no immediate answers, but it was a beginning. There were no high, thin clouds - it *was* variable. He now only had to keep his eye on it, night after night after night. Well, Pigott did advise that observing variables required patience and stamina.

The hours passed. He looked at Algol and then at selected comparison stars. Aldebaran, no change. Capella, no change. Mirfak, no change. His mind wandered. His thought of his Warrington tutor, who convinced him this was not only something he could do, but do well. He wondered whether, if he had not lost his hearing, he would be sitting here at all. He was likely headed for the pursuits expected of an heir. But his loss of hearing kept him from the complex and elaborate world of London society. It was a loss he did not mind.

'...Knowledge of the stars cannot be found in noise and restlessness. Only in silence can one be intimate with them.'

The subtle shade of the coming dawn announced the end of the night's observations. Algol faded and he drifted off to sleep, still in his chair.

An hour later he awoke from the chill and closed the casement. Hopefully the coming night would again be clear. Scuttling cumuli clouds suggested as much. Was the ewer empty? Thankfully, it wasn't. He poured water into the basin and splashed it on his face, soaked a flannel and placed it on the back of his neck. A night in his chair had left him stiff, tired and cold. He wound his clock and, after using the chamber pot, built a fire in the grate. It would take a while to do any good.

It was only one night of observing. There would be many more as long as the weather participated. His thoughts drifted to Cicero and Jamaica. That would be a place to observe from! Warm and clear, night after night, but it too far south to observe Algol - Perseus could not be seen at all below thirty-five degrees of latitude. At least there would not be this constant chill. He wrapped his cloak about him, pulled the blankets up and slept the day away.

*

'Master Goodricke, you are just in time for the evening meal.'

'Mrs Dalrymple.'

Eleanor knew in an instant he was not his usual self. He seemed lost in thought, distracted.

'Soup? Pass your bowl, please. Mr Guthrie will you please get Master Goodricke's attention?'

Guthrie gently tapped Goodricke on the shoulder and motioned towards Eleanor.

'What? Oh, soup. Yes, that would be - that would be fine. Thank you.'

He kept his head down so as not to invite any interrogation by Guthrie or Pomeroy.

Do all stars change brightness?

Does this star come closer and then recede?
'What is that to anyone?'
'A strange avocation you have there, sir, and no mistake.'
He was in no mood for such questions.

The coming night promised excellent seeing. He finished his meal, thanked Eleanor and excused himself. She watched him leave. *At least he has eaten something.*

He returned to his rooms and eagerly prepared for the night's observations. The ink pot and quill were placed in easy reach. Scribbled notes would later be expanded into more complete journal entries.

Pigott had suggested other candidate variables. Delta Ursae Majoris and alpha Draconis were also observed, but they had not shown him anything. It was Algol he was after.

He began his observations just after seven. Unlit coal lay in the grate, his cloak had to provide whatever comfort it could against the cold. A few breaths warmed his fingers and little else. Algol was still at 4th magnitude, but only just.

Can it possibly be becoming brighter? he wondered. After twenty minutes or so he could allow himself to believe that it *was* becoming brighter. A check of nearby comparison stars confirmed this. They kept to their known magnitudes, so it could not be due to thin clouds. This was *something Algol was doing* right before his very eyes.

He likened it to watching the minute hand of a clock. You can't quite see it move, but move it does. Algol gradually surpassed nearby comparison stars in brightness. It returned to its recorded second magnitude a little after nine and settled at second. This was exactly what he had hoped to see. If it took over three hours to brighten, it should take the same amount of time to dim, should it not? But how long would it *remain* at this maximum brightness before again dimming? What was the overall period of this change? Still, it was progress. *Now, I've got you*, he thought.

Later that morning he wrote in his journal.

> *...I hardly believed that it changed its brightness because I never heard of any star varying so quick in its brightness - I thought it might be perhaps owing to an optical illusion or defect in my eyes or bad air but the sequel will show that its change is true and that I was not mistaken.*

He finished the journal entry, sprinkled powder from the pounce pot over the glistening ink and blew across the page. There was no doubting what was observed. Over the course of just a few hours Algol increased in brightness by two whole magnitudes. Not only had he confirmed its variability, he had discovered something extremely rare if not wholly unique - a rapid change in a star's brightness – a change that *must* be cyclical. He knew enough of the recording of a new star or 'nova' by a Danish astronomer to realise this was something altogether different. He had used the words 'nova' and 'variable' more or less interchangeably in his journal, but no longer.

Several questions remained. How long did it remain at its dimmest? How long did it remain at its brightest? Once brightened, or dimmed, how long did in remain in these states? In short, what was the exact period of this variability? He could not wait to tell Edward. He splashed water on his face and bounded down the stairs for a quick breakfast.

*

Goodricke had to catch his breath as he arrived at Edward's home

'Hello Phillipa. Edward is in, I trust?'

'In the drawing room, sir. Shall I take you through?'

Edward was stretched out on a settee, arms folded, sound asleep. She looked over at Goodricke with a shrug.

'Mr Pigott? A gentleman is here to see you.'

Pigott stirred, unshaven and unkempt. An eye opened.

'John. I was just dozing here. A good night for observing was it not?' he said, propping himself up on an elbow.

'Thank you, Phillipa,' he added.

'Shall I bring some tea for you and your guest, sir?'

'Yes. Excellent. Thank you,' said Edward.

She backed out with a little bow.

'You seem a bit animated this morning, John.'

'I have news,' said Goodricke as he took a seat by the warming fire.

'What news to awaken me? Has the King passed? No, that would not be enough. Have you breakfasted by the way?'

'No and yes. Edward, please.'

'I'm all ears John. Ah, sorry.'

Goodricke waved him off.

'It is Algol, Edward. He is a variable, definitely a variable.'

'But we knew that did we not? Montanari found this to be the case a century ago. And that other fellow, Ma-something or other.'

'Maraldi.'

'Right.'

'Yes, but they did not find what I have found.'

'And what exactly is that, pray?'

'I have seen it increase in brightness over a period of about three and one-half hours. It must be confirmed, of course.'

'And you are certain?'

'I am. When I began it was at magnitude four, but then to my amazement it increased to magnitude two, or the value of record. I am sure it will take the same amount of time to return to this lower brightness. Do you not see? I chanced on it at the point whence it began increasing in brightness. So, the next question is to determine how long it remained at its dimmest, but given the timing of all the changes I have observed, I believe it to be a brief period indeed. Then of course we must determine the time it remains at its brightest. Once the duration of each of these stages is known, we will have the complete period of its variability.'

'Are you certain?' Pigott was now sitting up.

'Edward, you have already asked me that. Yes, I am certain.'

'And how often does this occur? Do you know the frequency?'

'Edward, please pay attention. That is the next step. This is *short* period behaviour, quite unlike that of other variables such as Mira. Well, what do you think?'

'What do I think? It is truly novel, John. I never quite expected - when I suggested you undertake the study of variables - I never expected something quite so dramatic.'

Goodricke began to get an inkling of the significance of what he had done, but more work was needed.

'I thought we might observe this together to make certain? From your observatory, of course.'

'Of course, but there is one more thing.'

'Yes?'

'You ought to begin preparing a paper to be read at the Royal Society.'

*

Goodricke's last journal entry in 1782 read:

> *At half ten, bright as on the 28th at half eight and half twelve. The Singular Phenomenon of Algol's variation on the 28th instance and on the 12th of November last, I think, can't be accounted for in any other manner than that of supposing it to have suffered an Eclipse (if I may say so) by the interposition of a planet revolving around it. Mr. E. Pigott having sent me a note to desire an extract of my observations on the 12th of Nov.*

> *last gives the same opinion and thinks the*
> *imagined planet must be about half the size Algol*
> *at least. Future observations will set this*
> *phenomenon in a clearer light. If the period of*
> *Algol's change is regular this will prove that it has*
> *a planet revolving around him.*

He committed the beginning weeks of 1783 almost completely to Algol. A routine series of observations had become something much more significant. What was needed was more magnitude checks and the time of the observations. When he had enough data, he could calculate the complete period.

In February, he entered the following:

> *…Mr. E. Pigott also observed it but not so late.*
> *His last obsv. was at 2 o'clock, when he judged*
> *that Algol was nearly equal to ζ Persei but rather*
> *brighter. – Comparing my observations on the 28th*
> *of Dec. & 14th of this month with this appears*
> *its period is 17± Days.*

It was not long, however, before he determined this could not be correct. Discouraging at first, but it only spurred him on to undertake more observations, however many it took before the data would reveal Algol's true pattern. By May, he found it.

Algol, Spring 1783

Goodricke sat at his writing table, quill in hand. He had double-checked Algol's position in Flamsteed and reviewed his notes. There was no doubt the brightness changes were correct. He confirmed that it dimmed over a three and a half-hour period, finally determined it held steady for two hours at the minimum brightness and then returned to maximum brightness. This had been relatively straightforward. The next question had been how often did this change occur? That took many more months of observing and where his computational skills came into play. He found eleven dates where it was at or near its least brightness and the times they occurred. After making some allowance for missed nights due to cloud, he finally computed the common factor between the times of these minima. He regarded this for a moment after carefully, almost ceremoniously, entering it in his journal. This, finally, was the period for one complete cycle of Algol's variability, what this work had all been about.

> *Comparing all of my observations on Algol it appears that it changes from the 2nd to the 4th magnitude in about three hours and a half & from thence to 2nd again in the same space of time, so that whole duration of this remarkable*

> *variation is 7 hours and this variation recurs*
> *regularly and periodically every two days and*
> *twenty hours and three quarters.*

He had it all except for one thing - an explanation. Goodricke thought of himself as more of an observer than a theoretician and was prepared to leave any speculation on the cause of this to others. Still, he had to suggest *something*, and was sure Edward would be only too happy to discuss it with him

*

Algol's variability was the subject of conversation at The Grouse.

'Edward, we *know* the Sun has spots so why not other stars? Cannot Algol display spots? Then, as he rotates, his light would dim as he presented that side bearing the spot towards us. We do not know that any other star has planets. We do know a star can have spots. I had considered an orbiting companion, but is not the spot hypothesis more likely?'

'This is what troubles me with the spot hypothesis, John. Firstly, the spots on our sun are small and we do not detect any real diminishment of his brightness when they are prominent. Therefore, Algol's spot, or spots must be much larger than those on our Sun to cause his significant diminishment. If you are to accept this spot hypothesis then you must accept it wholly and not construct some new class of these objects that behave in a way hitherto unobserved. We *do* know spots on the Sun are not regular in their number and placement. They come and go. So why must we assume this an operation unique to our Sun? Why would not spots elsewhere behave in an irregular fashion as well? If they do, they would not likely present the periodic change you have determined. No, I think you are too quick to dismiss your earlier hypothesis, that he has a planet himself that orbits.

227

This provides the regular changes we have seen together. Is there any physical law preventing other stars from having planets? How is it different from other moons orbiting Jupiter as ours orbits us? Indeed, the universality of Newton's Law of Gravity allows for this. Or better still, why not have two stars orbiting one another? Would that not produce your observations?'

'Edward, now you are talking tripe'

'No, John, I merely speculate. A companion object is the most viable of explanations.'

Later that evening Goodricke reflected on Edward's suggestion. He dipped his quill and wrote the close of his paper.

> *If it were not perhaps too early to hazard even a conjecture on the cause of this variation, I should imagine it could hardly be accounted for otherwise than either by the interposition of a large body revolving around Algol, or some kind of motion of its own, whereby part of its body, covered with spots or such like matter, is periodically turned towards the earth. But the intention of this paper is to communicate facts, not conjectures; I flatter myself that the former are remarkable enough to deserve the attention and further the investigations of astronomers.*

He replaced his quill and sat back. *This is a happy compromise*, he thought. *I do not commit myself, but yet raise the possibility of this star having an orbiting companion.*

*

A fortnight later Goodricke slept through another breakfast while Herschel and Caroline were having theirs.

'What have you there Wilhelm?'

'A letter from Joseph Banks, President of the Royal Society.'

'Ah, him.'

'You do not approve?'

'He once ignored me.'

Herschel thought for a moment. 'I believe you refer to that meeting in the lobby of a London theatre a year ago or so.'

'Yes. A round little man, like those bulbs he so much likes.'

'Caroline.'

She shrugged.

'What? I am only making an observation. It is what I do.'

Herschel looked up from the letter with a sigh.

'You have made the most remarkable progress with your English.'

He finished reading and speared a slice of bread with his knife.

'Wilhelm, do you see how sunny it is this day?'

'Yes, it seems it will be especially fine. Let us hope it lasts through the coming night.'

'And we are inside.'

'Of course. It is too cold to sit outside.'

'Ah, too cold to sit, but never too cold to observe. Is that what you say?'

'Caroline, it is colder when one just sits. When we observe, we move.'

'But not so much. We have no choice but to observe outside, but we can also sit outside, or at least not sit inside.'

'Now you have confused me.'

'I would like a conservatory in the back. Glass everywhere with plants. If we had one now we could be sitting with plants and not inside this little room that is not all so warm anyway.'

Herschel was about to toast his buttered bread over the fire and hesitated, bread in mid-air.

'But the back garden is rather small. Where would this conservatory sit?' he asked while waving the bread about.

'It would join with the house and we could enter from the workshop could we not?'

He was silent for a moment. He wasn't thinking about whether it might be a good idea so much as how to explain why it was a bad one.

'The garden is small and that is where we observe from. A conservatory would reduce the space that already limits the size of new telescopes I plan to construct. Also, it would mean that access to the conservatory would only be through the workshop, not an ideal design.'

Caroline knew there would never be a conservatory. Her brother would surely one day build a larger telescope that could not possibly fit anywhere at New King Street. It was only a matter of time before they moved again.

'Of course, you are right. It was only a thought.'

Herschel resumed toasting his bread.

'What does he write?'

'Banks?'

'No, the man on the moon.'

'I shall read it to you,' he said while placing his half-toasted bread on the table and cleared his throat.

> *Dear Sir, I learnt at the Royal Society that the periodical occultation of the light of Algol happened last night at about 12 o'clock; the period is said to be 2 days, 21 hours, and the discovery is now said to have been made by a deaf and dumb man, the grandson of John Goodricke, who has for some years amused himself with astronomy. This is all I have yet made out; you may depend on any intelligence which I think likely either to amuse you or instruct you.*
>
> *Your faithful servant Joseph Banks.*

'Why would he send this to you? You have not done so much this kind of astronomy, have you?' she asked.

'No, not so much, but this is the second time he has written about Algol. In his other letter, he mentioned it may have been Pigott who made the discovery and not Goodricke. Maskelyne made mention of this work in a recent letter as well. It is the talk of our little community, I think. '

'So, Banks then, he is wanting you to observe this?'

'It seems so, yes. But this type of observation has no real use for the quality of my optics, if I may say so.'

'Still we might look at it. It would make a change from your monotone survey,' she said with a wry expression.

'Monotonous. Yes, if you like. Let us look at Algol as it appears Mr Banks seems to desire it, although I cannot imagine why.'

'As you say, Wilhelm. And I did mean monotone.'

24

Hershel's Algol

'Edward, I have stopped by to inform you I have received correspondence from Reverend Shepherd at Cambridge. I am sure you might wish to know of this.'

'Excellent! So, it is all going forward, then.'

'Apparently. He writes that he is only too pleased to read my paper on Algol a week Friday at the Royal Society. This will mark its formal acceptance, as I understand it,' said Goodricke, allowing himself a little excitement.

Goodricke and Pigott were in the parlour at Booth Street, sharing the unspoken hope the weather would clear to allow observing in the coming night.

'I must add that it will be interesting to learn of the reaction,' said Edward.

'Why do you say that?'

'You are an unknown, but not for much longer. And it is just as well your paper will be read by another astronomer and not some blasted botanist.'

'That was never going to happen, was it?'

'Of course not. Still, the friction between the mathematicians and the flower pots at the Society is warming, or so Father indicates, but that should concern us.'

Goodricke thought for a moment. 'Why did you suggest the Reverend Anthony Shepherd again?'

'He is the Plumian Professor at Cambridge, but more importantly he is a good speaker, given to a bit of drama. Also, he does not appear to be too connected with the Society's current conflict.'

'You say this conflict is not a problem, but you have now mentioned it twice.'

There were sounds of someone arriving at the front entrance. Nathaniel Pigott entered, hung his damp cloak by the door and stood before the fire, warming his hands. Looking over his shoulder, he spoke.

'Ah, John. It is good that you are here.'

'And how was your journey Father?'

'How is any journey to or from London? A test of one's endurance, but let us leave that aside. I have something important to relate. Please stay John as this matter concerns you. Just let me place a flannel on my face. Arrange for some tea, will you? I shall be back directly.'

Nathaniel stepped out, after introducing an uneasy atmosphere.

'Right,' said Edward who followed him out in search of Phillipa. Goodricke was left to sit alone, his earlier good mood ebbing.

Edward returned after a few minutes and sat next to Goodricke. He shrugged as if to say he had no idea what his father was on about.

Nathaniel soon followed, wiping a cloth across his forehead. He sat across from John and Edward, wearing the expression of a judge about to deliver a harsh sentence.

'Foul weather,' he muttered. 'Right. Edward, who has been informed of your observations of Algol with John here?'

Edward had a sense of foreboding.

'Who has not been informed amongst our small community is perhaps more the question. Letters have been sent to the Reverend Maskelyne and it was suggested that he might pass on this information to Mr Herschel. The star's unusual behaviour is not exactly secret.'

'No, but you will both be interested, actually *more* than interested, when I tell you that Mr Herschel has already submitted a paper to the effect that *he* is the discoverer of this star's novel behaviour, as you say.'

'What do you mean by 'submitted'? When? To whom?' asked Edward, his voice rising.

Goodricke looked at Edward and then back at Nathaniel, but said nothing.

'I was not there myself, but his paper was apparently presented in a rather unusual circumstance, although seemingly no less official for all that. It was read at the *Crown and Anchor*. You must know it Edward, the ale house near the Society's quarters. *That* was where Herschel's findings were revealed. More to the point, his work was read to the small assembly by none other than Banks himself, as an indication, I suspect, of his imprimatur.'

'At an ale house?' said Edward, leaning forward, fists on the table. 'Was this a formal presentation to the Society or was it not? And when was this again?', he asked, anger building.

'Thursday last.'

'And with John's paper scheduled Friday next,' said Edward.

No one spoke. Edward stood and paced. Nathaniel could only look down, as if this was somehow all his fault.

'This will not stand. I shall write to Herschel straightaway and make it known he has well and truly transgressed,' said Edward suggesting he had already formulated its content.

'I feel there might be more to this than bad timing,' said Nathaniel.

'Why? What do you mean?' asked Edward.

'It appears there was some desire Herschel pip John at the post.'

Edward stopped pacing.

'Who was so desirous? Banks? You did say it was he who read Herschel's paper there at the *Crown and Anchor*.'

'That is my understanding, yes.'

'But why? To what end? To award Herschel another Copley medal?'

Nathaniel stiffened.

'Perhaps, but I suspect it was done not so much to recognise Herschel, but to avoid having to recognise John here.'

Nathaniel pointed at Goodricke while looking at his son. He continued.

'What this young man has done, what he has discovered is truly remarkable. My personal feeling is that this is obvious to all and sundry. Or will shortly become so. There was the chance that it could have lead, a chance mind you, to the Copley. His work is that good.'

'*Was* the chance?' said a now steaming Edward, his anger mixed with sorrow for John. He worried this was the rude awakening to the politics of the Royal Society that had to happen, sooner or later. He sighed and sat again.

Goodricke wore a puzzled look. It was clear to Nathaniel and Edward that Goodricke did not, even now, fully appreciate how important his work was.

'This Copley Medal - how is the person who receives it chosen?' asked Goodricke.

Nathaniel replied, 'It is all straightforward enough. Nominations are reviewed and assessed by a committee who will then pass on their recommendation to the governing Council, stuffed with Banks' supporters I might add. Still, your discovery is most significant and worthy. Not like that of some past recipients, such as that trivial account of the value of Greek and Roman money.'

Edward looked at his father.

'What *are* you saying?'

Nathaniel sighed and wished Goodricke was not there to learn this. He looked at John and then at his son.

'Well?' said Edward.

'It is merely supposition on my part.'

'Are you saying they would rather ascribe this work to Herschel - that they would deny it to John because of his - because of some *affliction?*'

'I do not know the details or Banks' true motivation on the matter. This may not be anything personal mind you. It may be that some believe the Society has only recently attained, or re-attained, some respectable measure of status, especially where our French counterparts are concerned. It may be that, some, some would rather...'

Goodricke finally spoke as Nathaniel groped for the right words.

'...that some would rather not recognise my work because I am deaf and probably dumb as well. Because of this they believe the work is not mine but Edward's. Is this not the case?'

Nathaniel squirmed in his seat before replying.

'Not entirely, John, not entirely. It also has something to do with this conflict between Banks and others in the Society. If another astronomer were to receive the Copley so soon after Herschel then, in some quarters at least, they would just as soon it be him rather than John here.'

'You mean rather than a deaf mute,' said Edward.

'Well, no, not necessarily. Perhaps 'an unknown' is more accurate.'

'Tommy-rot,' said Edward. 'All those at the Crown and Anchor were likely in their cups. I tell you this will not stand.'

He turned to face Goodricke.

'I repeat. This will not stand. I shall communicate my rich displeasure on the matter to Herschel. I shall demand he retract his paper or at least see that it not be published in the *Transactions*. The Reverend Shepherd will read John's paper as planned. This matter is *not* settled.'

'You have spoken of him before. He seemed decent enough,' said Goodricke.

'The man is cold yet burns with ambition, not to mention that wraith of a sister,' said Edward.

'Now Edward,' said Nathaniel.

'What?' he replied. 'This is only one example of his not being able to give credit to others where it is due. And there is something else, Father, that adds to the injury. This is an insult to *me*. I mean to say, it is not a secret that I have been assisting - no, working - with John here these past two years and this is therefore some reflection on the quality of my tutelage.'

'Edward, perhaps this is not quite so calculated as all that.'

'No? By all the gods, I shall see John put right.'

'Mind how you go Edward. The Royal Society has a long memory.'

'Mind how I go? I have no desire to become an actor on that stage. It is just one pathetic little drama after another.'

Goodricke looked down at the table and then over at Edward. He did not know what he felt. This was his first paper. He wondered how typical this was of the whole business. Astronomy was an escape from all the muzzy thinking and vulgar ambitions found at ground level. Now it did not seem to be the unsullied activity he had hoped it would be.

Phillipa entered carrying a tray of tea and toast. It all remained untouched.

Calculators

'What are the plans for this evening to observe, Wilhelm?'

'They do not include Algol, I shall tell you that much.'

It was mid-afternoon. Caroline had just awoken after a long night of observing with her brother. Wondering whether he ever slept at all, she joined him and poured herself some tea.

'You are upset Wilhelm.'

'*This* arrived from York this morning,' he said, holding up the letter, the blue wax seal catching her eye.

'It is some problem?'

'I have been all but accused of attempting to steal the credit for discovery of Algol's periodic changes.'

'Who does this?'

'Mr Edward Pigott. It all has to do with my recent trip to London when I met with a few members of the Royal Society.'

'So?'

'I was asked what I had been working on, and I mentioned Algol and that I had written a brief account of my observations.'

'About what we observed? Yes, I remember, but all you did was to confirm this, no?'

'Banks had my letter with him. It made no mention of Mr Pigott or Mr Goodricke, for that matter. He was all too eager to read it before the assembled group. And, as it was the first paper on the matter presented before the Society, well…'

'I do not follow.'

'Do you still not see? This has been taken as my *official* word on the subject. It implies I am the first to observe and note the peculiar changes of this star.'

'But you were, were you not?'

'No, I was not, but that is not the point. The point is I was the first to formally present the work to the Society, in a manner of speaking. But I now suspect I was used by Banks. He did seem rather impatient to have it read, even if it was in a bloody ale house.'

'Wilhelm.'

'Sorry, but do you not see? He wished *me* to work on this particular star so that someone *else* would not receive the credit for its discovery as a true variable. And, what is worse, he planned the whole episode as my paper's formal presentation to the Society.'

'The man is gillful.'

'Guileful. Yes. I believe, Caroline, this is not worth the friction it causes or, more importantly, any damage to my reputation. I shall not be used by Mr Banks in this fashion. I shall reply to Mr Pigott and to Mr Banks. I shall apologise to the one and shall make clear to the other that my paper shall *not* go into the *Philosophical Transactions*. I… *we*, have enough to do and I think it best to now stay well clear of the matter.'

'Of course, *Mein bruder*. There is more to do than wait for one star to change its brightness, is that not so?'

'Yes, that is so, Caroline. That is indeed so.'

*

Banks tugged on an eyebrow while reading Herschel's letter. When finished. he sent for Slee and Warrilow.

They arrived as scheduled. Banks was staring into the courtyard of Somerset House as they entered.

'Gentlemen. It appears that Herr Herschel shall not be publishing, or claiming, any work on Algol,' said Banks, nodding to the letter on his desk.

'Is that a problem?' asked Slee. 'There are other candidates for the Copley, surely.'

'I concur,' added Warrilow.

'You always concur, Harold,' muttered Slee.

Banks, hands now clasped behind his back, rocked on his heels with a restless energy. It was not a pleasure to be in his company when things were not going his way.

'I have struggled to restore this Society not only to its former eminence, such as it was, but to surpass it. Look at the French, for God's sake. They are streets ahead of us. We have not had the likes of a Lavoisier since, well, Newton. And everyone knows, at the end of the day, he was as mad as a hatter.'

'If I may, sir, I would not be so casual with comments about Newton. It will only further antagonise the mathematicals amongst us,' said Slee as if they were an infestation.

'But what is the difficulty here?' asked Warrilow.

Banks groaned inwardly.

'Allow me to explain. Unfortunately, this year we have a dearth of candidates for the Copley. The next closest to Goodricke would be that fellow who determined the temperature for the congelation of mercury.'

'Hutchins,' offered Slee.

'Yes, Hutchins. But this work by Goodricke, well, *supposedly* by him, is well superior. The problem is, I seriously doubt he actually performed it. In fact, I suspect Mr Pigott is its true agent and has, for whatever reason, decided to allow it to be presented as Goodricke's, who apparently is as deaf as a post and likely just as dumb. Oh, he is a rascal that Edward Pigott, never fear.'

'But what of his father, Nathaniel is it? What does *he* say on the matter?' asked Warrilow.

'Ah, Nathaniel. He has been strangely silent. I do not wish to provoke his displeasure as he has not as yet openly sided with the opposition,' said Banks.

He took a pace or two, thinking.

'If the award goes to another there will be no speculation. But to this Goodricke? And as far as this Hutchins is concerned, I am sure he is a decent enough sort, hard worker etcetera, etcetera. But is this really a major discovery? I mean to say, mercury must have had *some* temperature of congelation. We just did not know what it was. On the other hand, we had, or rather our astronomers had, no idea at all that any variable star behaved in such a clockwork fashion. It does instigate more study, something good for science, I must confess. But why does it have to be this Goodricke fellow?' said Banks.

'Forgive me sir, but you seem to be in a bit of muddle,' said Slee

Banks only glared.

Warrilow spoke. 'By the way, what was it?'

Slee closed his eyes.

'What was what?' asked Banks.

'The freezing point of mercury.'

'I do not recall, nor really care.'

'Minus thirty-nine degrees on the Fahrenheit scale, for what that is worth,' offered Slee.

'Well, I am sure it was not an easy thing to determine. I mean to say; how did he *know* it was minus thirty-nine degrees? And in any case, that seems awfully bloody cold!' said Warrilow with a chuckle.

'Is that clear enough for you Mr Warrilow?' said Banks.

Warrilow straightened himself. 'Oh, indeed it is, sir, thirty-nine degrees. Or rather, minus thirty-nine.'

'No indeed, sir! I mean do you see why awarding the Copley to Mr Goodricke does little to promote the Society?' said an agitated Banks.

'Yes, I suppose that might be said.'

Good Lord, thought Banks, *Warrilow hunts rabbits with a dead ferret.* He sighed and resumed pacing while tugging on his eyebrow.

'The Maskelyne side will certainly support him and, I suspect, so will others. Still, the vote comes down to Council members only. On the other hand…'

He paused and Slee spoke.

'What might you have in mind, sir? Since the removal of the mutinous mathematicals most if not all of the Council membership now support you.'

With hands on his hips and leaning slightly forward Banks looked at Slee and then at Warrilow.

'Gentlemen, do you not understand? I wish to leave nothing to chance.'

*

Nevil Maskelyne stood on the roof above the Octagon Room at the Royal Greenwich Observatory to assess the coming night's observing conditions Fifty years of age, he was a man long shaped by a calm, calculating prudence.

Before him lay a magnificent panorama of the Thames and London beyond. The cerulean blue of the western sky had given way to a vivid rose-pink. He estimated the Sun was now about six degrees below the horizon as the brightest stars began to appear. To some this was poetry, but not to him. If this scene gave him any pleasure at all it was because it looked to be a cloudless night. He took one last look around before heading down to the transit telescope manned by one of his assistants, George Gilpin.

The work supervised by Maskelyne was distinct from that performed at any other observatory. The main objective was the annual, repetitive production of the astronomical data required by British mariners to determine their position at sea, a key mission of the only state-supported observatory. For centuries, the estimation of the longitude from a ship's rolling deck was considered solvable only through astronomy. The state's interest was therefore not an investment in science for its own sake, but in its potential to aid in the navigation required for imperial expansion, not to mention staying clear of reefs.

Furthering Maskelyne's status was that he too was a Copley Medal recipient for his experimental confirmation of Newton's Law of Gravity. This was done through a clever measurement of the deviation from the vertical of a plumb bob placed in the vicinity of Mt Schiehallion in Scotland. A fellow member of the Royal Society, Charles Hutton, used his results to determine the density of the Earth.

None of this, however, impressed Banks, who was ruthless in the consolidation of his authority. Hutton's removal from his position as the Society's Foreign Secretary compelled the resignations of several other members. Maskelyne survived but was removed from his seat on the Council. He and his followers opposed what they considered the gentlemanly dilettantism of those in Banks' circle who did not display any commitment to a continued line of research.

Another irritation to Banks was Maskelyne's overbearing religiosity. The elaborate Banks thought it excessive even for a Doctor of Divinity. Only Maskelyne's position as the Royal Astronomer goaded Banks' into a grudging deference. But once Banks became the President of the Royal Society, Maskelyne became accountable to him. He was the one person on whom Maskelyne had to call on for funds for new instruments and to whom he had to submit copies of his observations. Their smouldering enmity flared at the time Goodricke was first thought of as a potential Copley candidate.

'How are you this good night Gilpin?' asked Maskelyne as he entered the transit room where his assistant worked.

'Well enough, Reverend.'

'You are well prepared for this night's observations?'

'Indeed I am.'

Scheduled for the evening was the determination of the transit times of several astronomical objects - data gathering required for the publication of the next issue of the *Almanac*.

'I shall not be here this night, but I do wish to inspect our new clock just received from Coombe and introduce you to its workings. I am attending a talk at the Society on the morrow by Shepherd, from Cambridge, and wish to retire at a reasonable hour.'

'Is this new clock the interval timer you spoke of earlier, Reverend?'

'Yes, Gilpin, and much smaller than a long case clock. It is designed to beat thirty-six thousand times per hour. Coombe has indeed surpassed himself. It should work well to improve our measurements of transit times.'

Gilpin thought for a moment.

'Thirty-six thousand times per hour? That means it can measure to within one-tenth of a second.'

'Precisely, Gilpin, precisely.

26

The Variation of the Light of the Bright Star in the Head of Medusa, Called Algol, Spring 1784

The Royal Society's prefect called for order. An air of anticipation filled the room as the Reverend Anthony Shepherd, Plumian Professor at Cambridge, approached the lectern. The sweet scent of fattened lilac panicles wafted through open windows and the unusually warm, sunny weather elevated the mood of a membership already stimulated by the gossip and controversy prefacing this particular paper. Would it contend for the Copley Medal? Did not Herschel already announce something on Algol? Shepherd's baritone began to read Goodricke's letter to an expectant audience.

> *'I take the liberty to transmit to you the following account of a very singular variation in Algol otherwise known as β Persei, which you will oblige me by presenting to the Royal Society, if you think it deserving that notice. All that has been hitherto known concerning the variation of this star, as far as I can find after the most diligent researches, is comprised in the following passage in Du Hamel's Historia Regiae Scientiarum Academiae, liber IV, Sect. 6, caput VIII de rebus Astronomicis, ann 1695, p. 362. Id qouque testator D.*

245

> *Montanari stellam lucidiorem Medusae diversis*
> *annis, variae esse magitudinis: nullam pene in ea*
> *mutationem potuit advertere D. Maraldi annis*
> *1692 et 1693; fed anno 1694 aucta est imminuta*
> *insigniter, modo quarti, modo tertii, modi secundi*
> *ordinis stella apparuit. This, however curious, is*
> *only very vague and general information; but the*
> *following observations, lately made, exhibit a*
> *regular and periodical variation in that star, of a*
> *nature hitherto, I believe, unnoticed.'*

Warrilow pushed out his lower lip. He leaned over and whispered to Slee.

'My Latin is a bit rusty old boy.'

Slee looked over and replied, 'Just the build-up. He is only explaining previous work on the star.'

Shepherd continued reading Goodricke's account.

> *'The first time I saw it was on the 12th of*
> *November 1782, between eight and nine o'clock*
> *at night when it appeared of about the fourth*
> *magnitude; but the next day it was of the second*
> *magnitude, which is its usual appearance.*
> *The subsequent observations which I have made on*
> *this star are very particular; and I think it will be*
> *best to give a brief extract of them in their order*
> *from my journal; but it is necessary I should first*
> *specify the usual and greatest magnitude of Algol.*
> *Also, the relative brightness and magnitude of*
> *those stars, to which I compared it during the*
> *progress of its variation.'*

Shepherd knew which passages to dramatise. He cleared his throat and looked around before continuing at a slower pace.

The usual and greatest magnitude of Algol is this; of the second magnitude, and much less bright than alpha Persei, and not so much as gamma Andromedae; brighter than alpha Cassiopeae and beta Arietis, and nearly the same as, if not brighter than alpha Pegasi and beta Cassiopeae; not quite so bright as gamma Cassiopeae, and much brighter than epsilon Persei and beta Trianguli.'

He paused. Goodricke had compared Algol at only *one* stage of its brightness to that of *nine* other stars of known constant magnitude. This clearly showed how accurately Algol's own magnitude had been estimated. What followed was an account of the painstaking observations of all the stages noted, the time these lasted and the brightness of the comparison stars used. Goodricke had explained how night after night he gathered raw data, all the estimated magnitudes from maximum to minimum. The point of the whole exercise was to determine the period of variability, the number of days and hours between successive minima of brightness. Once this observational data was presented, Goodricke's computational skills were next revealed. His objective was a common factor, the number which most exactly divided into the times of minima – a main point of the paper. Shepherd concluded.

'...Hence the period of Algol's variation is 2 days, 20 hours, 49 minutes and 15 seconds...If it were not perhaps too early to hazard even a conjecture of the cause of this variation, I should imagine it could hardly be accounted for otherwise than either by the interpretation of a large body revolving around Algol or some kind of motion of its own, whereby part of its body, covered with spots or such like matter, is periodically turned towards the earth. But the intention of this paper is to communicate facts, not conjectures; I flatter myself that the former are

remarkable enough to deserve the attention of the
investigation of astronomers. I am etcetera.'

Shepherd made a little bow and stepped away from the podium. Questions were solicited, but silence ensued. Was this because the audience thought the work insignificant or because they were overwhelmed? A hand was raised.

'Mr Aubrey is recognised.'

'Sir, does he mean to say this timing of Algol's cycle was found to the second?'

'Indeed, sir. I believe it to be a mean value, but that is the time of its variability or pretty nearly.'

'Is that accuracy acceptable? Is it possible to determine the variability to such an exactitude?'

'Well, sir, you, or anyone else here present, are most welcome to perform their own observations in confirmation.'

Those who had been in attendance at the Crown and Anchor and knew of Herschel's paper now could not help but notice Goodricke's work to be far superior. Banks, in pushing the exposure of Herschel's observations, had inadvertently provided a means to measure the value of Goodricke's observations. Someone clapped. Then another and eventually, the whole assembly was standing and applauding. Maskelyne noticed that Banks remained still. *You now have a job on to prevent this one from receiving the award*, he thought.

27

Hannah Upton

Sir Thomas Upton took pride in his new Cavendish Square home. Portman Square may have been more prestigious, but this location equally suited his position in the office of Chancellor of the Exchequer. Outside, dust mixed with manure in the summer heat, but inside the mahogany gleamed.

The vast estates north and west of London had been transformed by land owners only too happy to make a profit converting farmland into commercial property. The small village of Marylebone had, over the last half century, expanded to merge with the city proper and add a new district with Portman, Manchester and Cavendish Squares the result.

Upton was an ally of the new Prime Minister, William Pitt the Younger. Pitt was also the Chancellor of the Exchequer and, as such, the dispenser of royal patronage. It was the older more experienced Upton who influenced Pitt in the execution of this office. He was not someone to be trifled with and, by all accounts, a hard man. If he had one soft spot, it was for his only child, Hannah. He was waiting to be called by his wife who was helping her prepare for this special day out. She entered his study without knocking.

'Come along Thomas, Hannah is most eager to receive your approval,' said Caroline as she beckoned sharply.

He walked through to the parlour and felt a surge of pride when he beheld his daughter. Hannah was wearing her new chemise dress bought for this occasion - a simple cylinder of cream-coloured muslin gathered at the neck by a drawstring and at the waist by a wide bright blue sash that matched her eyes. It was a daring style only recently introduced. Tall for her age, she was stunning in her beauty.

'Hannah, you are … my lovely daughter.'

Caroline and Hannah were taken by this rare display of emotion. He had watched her grow into a beautiful, intelligent young woman who amply demonstrated she was bright and literate. She was, like any young lady her age, full of life. He had doubts that day when he left her at Braidwood's academy, but there was nothing to lose and a world for her to gain. He bitterly recalled those who suggested he lock her away, as if she were a blight on the family name. It was his undying belief in his daughter's true ability that led him to Braidwood, who watered her native intelligence bringing it to flower.

Any lingering sadness he felt, though, was not because she was deaf. He had long come to terms with that and he communicated with his daughter as well as any parent, perhaps even better. This languishing anguish was because he had witnessed more than one young man's ardour quickly subside once he heard her laboured speech. Upton worried whether there would ever be anyone prepared to marry and care for her and, if it came to that, provide him with a grandchild.

'Thomas, wait until you see the bonnet as well,' said Caroline. 'Let me help you.'

She positioned a large straw bonnet on her daughter and adjusted the blonde curls flowing beneath it. Hannah twirled and gave her father a mock bow.

He collected himself. 'You look a picture my dear.'

'Thank you, papa.'

He placed his hands on her shoulders and smiled.

'Are you looking forward to today?'

'Oh yes, papa, Pwiscilla is ah-whiving soon,' said an excited Hannah.

Priscilla Winthrop was a year older and her own stay at Braidwood's academy had overlapped with Hannah's. Upton had arranged for a carriage to collect Priscilla and from there they would travel to a tea garden. It was a bit unusual for two young women to go out unchaperoned, deaf or not. Their parents, however, believed the more they went out into the world and interacted with it, the better.

A maid entered.

'There is a young lady here sir. Says she has come to collect Miss Hannah.'

Hannah fairly leaped through the door to greet her friend. Upton and his wife looked at each other. Caroline sighed as they followed her out.

'Hello Priscilla. Lovely to see you. As you can see, our Hannah is ready,' said Caroline.

'Hannah! Your dress! I feel so old fashioned!' said Priscilla.

Hannah and Priscilla began to communicate in signs, a skill Sir Thomas had not acquired.

Priscilla then focused and said, 'Sir Thomas, Mrs Upton. A lovely day is it not? We are going to have such a splendid time!'

Thomas Upton secretly wished his daughter could speak as clearly as Priscilla.

'The driver has been instructed to take you to the Adam and Eve Tea Garden. Your mother does not think they do a good enough job keeping out persons of low character - so they should let you two in all right,' said Upton.

Laughter all around as Caroline rolled her eyes in mild reproach.

'I have instructed him to collect you at Marylebone Road entrance at five o'clock. So, do not keep the poor fellow waiting!'

Hannah and Priscilla departed, white gloves waving as they turned into Oxford Street. The heavy wheels rolled through puddles spattering passers-by while their own stockings and brushed shoes remained dry. They giggled as the coach bounced them about.

London's parks provided respite from the chaos and clamour of a congested London, a retreat from noisome streets. Pleasure gardens, however, provided much more. They answered the public's longing for relief from the boredom of daily life. The Adam and Eve Tea Garden located at the upper end of Tottenham Court Road, like its many counterparts on that sunny Saturday, enveloped its visitors in the thick perfume of flowers, exotic displays and stimulating exhibitions – a dream world constructed for a vibrant, vivid and memorable experience.

At the main entrance Hannah and Priscilla jumped from the carriage with giddy enthusiasm and skipped into a promenade shimmering with leisurely strollers, a motley mix of both sexes, people of all ranks and conditions, a non-stop parade that was itself an entertainment.

As they strolled arm in arm into the heart of the gardens they caught sight of an odd-looking character wearing a mask and an eye-catching coat and jacket made of a patchwork of colourful diamonds, a harlequin, hired to entertain. He was unlike anything either of them had ever seen. Upon approaching Hannah and Priscilla, he made an impossibly low bow. A flower for each magically appeared as he rose.

Hannah, too surprised to speak, signed 'thank you'. They were both startled when the harlequin unexpectedly signed 'you are welcome' in return before skipping off into the crowd.

'What just happened?' asked Priscilla.

Hannah could only laugh and shook her head.

They came to an outdoor café and took a small table. It took a moment before they realised a waiter had arrived. Priscilla had lost her hearing at a later age and offered to order for them both. She signed to Hannah and asked what she would like.

'Cheesecake - the biggest piece that they have! And their tallest glass of syllabub!'

Priscilla laughed and asked for two orders. The waiter departed, wondering what all that hand waving was about.

'Hannah, I really do believe they only have one size for everything here.'

Priscilla could speak well enough for Hannah to lip-read, but was always eager to practise her signing and chose to communicate in that way.

'Have you learned our Mr Braidwood is now here in London?'

Hannah signed, 'Oh yes. My papa had something to do with that,' followed by an expression of mock imperiousness.

'How so?'

'He was telling me and mama that he mentioned to King George how successful he was in teaching us. So, the King decides he wants a school for the deaf in London. What the King wants the King must have!'

They laugh.

'He offered Mr Braidwood one hundred guineas if he would but move his academy here. Can you imagine? Apparently, he accepted because he is now here with his family. I believe they settled in Hackney.'

'It is very nice there,' signed Priscilla. 'A lot of trees.'

'You know Hannah, we should visit him.'

'Yes!' signed Hannah. 'Maybe even a surprise visit!'

'That would be lovely!'

Priscilla wore a more thoughtful expression.

'We owe him so much.'

Hannah became thoughtful as well.

'I shall never forget my first day there. Do you know what I am most grateful for?' signed Hannah.

Priscilla briefly waggled an extended forefinger.

'What?'

Hannah signed, 'He was a good teacher, but he was more. He taught us how to live as deaf people. He prepared us for those who do not wish us in their company. I once was at a dinner party where a joke was told about a deaf farmer and his deaf cow.'

'That is so terrible!' signed Priscilla with emphatic sharp gestures.

'But that is not what was terrible. When this brute learned that I was deaf he did not care a fig! He was not embarrassed! Mr Braidwood knew these moments would come and he prepared us for them. He made us believe we should never be ashamed.'

Hannah reached over to Priscilla and wiped a tear away. She sat back and signed.

'I am sorry. I have made you upset.'

'No, please, it is all right. Do you know what bothers me the most now about being deaf? It has to do with Father. Mother as well, but more Father'

'Surely you are well treated?' signed Hannah.

'Of course! You know that already. Father thinks I do not know, but I believe he is worried that no man will have me. That I will become a spinster, unhappy and alone.'

Hannah signed that she suspected her own father held similar thoughts. Ever the romantic, she saw a bright side.

'But Priscilla, that is why we are here now,' she slowly signed.

'I do not understand.'

'The more we go out into the world like everyone else, out like this…,' She gestured to their surroundings, '…the more likely we shall both encounter the right gentleman who shall love and care for us, I am sure of it. But let us not dwell further on such melancholic thoughts. It is a lovely day and we have much time here yet.'

Their refreshments arrived and Hannah paid. She took a sip of her syllabub, leaned back and smiled as the warmth of the wine and sun took their effect. She opened her eyes and was about to sign to Priscilla when she spotted someone sitting nearby saying *Goodricke*, or so she thought. Probably some other Goodricke.

'Hannah, do you know what happened here last week?'

'No, I am sure I do not.'

'A balloon came down on these very grounds.'

'A what?'

Priscilla finger-spelled 'balloon'.

'A balloon that carried a man, an Italian I believe - a Mr Lunardi. It was a giant balloon filled with hot air that can float above the trees! Anyway, something happened and the balloon with poor Mr Lunardi in it landed here instead of wherever it was supposed to go. How does one steer them about? Can you imagine riding in one? I should love to try it. Do you think it would be possible to ask him for a ride in his balloon? Would that not be the most exciting thing ever? I believe he is very dashing as well. Hannah? Are you paying attention?'

Hannah was not. She was certain the two gentlemen sitting nearby were speaking about the very same Goodricke she had known in Edinburgh.

'Lovely weather. Should have brought our wives.'

'Think for a moment, Warrilow,' said Slee. 'We came to chart our strategy to insure this Goodricke fellow does not receive the Copley Medal. And an inn or coffee house would not do where we might be interrupted. Here we are not at all likely to be overheard by a wife or maid.'

'But why this place?'

Slee sighed. 'Because I live nearby and wish to be incommoded as little as possible.'

'Slee, what exactly does Banks have against this Goodricke fellow?'

'Well may you ask. As I see it, there are two reasons. In the first instance, he is not convinced the work is all down to Goodricke, who, as Banks has said, is as deaf as a post. I myself doubt he performed the work Shepherd read. It is not clear he can even write, at least not that well.'

'Well, it must be somebody's work.'

'Banks suspects that it is the work of Edward Pigott.'

'He has said as much. But if so, why would he not choose to claim it as his own?'

'A good question, Warrilow. Apparently, the relations between Nathaniel and Edward are rather strained. Banks believes that Edward would avoid any credit simply to spite his father.'

'A tangled web,' said Warrilow.

'Apparently so, but the other reason Banks is not eager to see the Copley awarded to Goodricke is that he simply wishes to avoid an association between Goodricke and the Royal Society. He is afraid that too many will ask why the achievement of the year is awarded to someone who cannot even speak. Warrilow, are you not listening? What are you staring at?'

'Those two, just there, do you see them? I must say, they have been performing the oddest of gesticulations.'

Slee looked over.

'Speak of the deaf. I believe that to be some type of deaf communication, after a fashion.'

'Really? It looks more like they are playing pat-a-cake. It is enough to make a dog laugh. I say, one of them is now staring. Most discomfiting.'

'Take no notice.'

'Indeed. They probably do not even know their own names.'

'May we return to the matter at hand Warrilow? I have written out a list of all the Council members and have marked those who might need a little reminder of their vote and the consequences of not allowing the Society president his due.'

He unfolded a sheet of paper and pressed it out on the table.

'These consequences are what?' asked Warrilow.

'Loss of their Council seat for one. I mean to say, if Maskelyne can be removed, anyone can. The rest is best left to the imagination, but you can assume their scientific career, such as it may be, shall proceed no further.'

'Hannah, stop staring! It is not polite.'

Hannah finger spelled 'Goodricke'.

'Do you remember him?' she asked.

'Who?'

'John Goodricke. He was with us at the academy.'

'I think so. He was a quiet young man if you know what I mean, but what is this about?'

'Those two at the table just there speak ill of him and have insulted us as well.'

'Who?'

'I am going over to them.'

'What? Must you? Is that wise?'

Hannah raised her palm as a gesture for Priscilla to stop signing and stood. She could not believe she was going to do this, but either Braidwood's belief in her meant something or it did not. Still, this was a bit more 'going out into the world' than she bargained for.

Slee and Warrilow sensed her approach and looked at each other bemusedly. This tall blue-eyed beauty became a larger distraction with each approaching step.

Hannah gathered herself and took a breath. She knew it made no sense to sign as she spoke, but her blood was pumping and she could not contain a building anger.

'I *do* know my own name.'

As she spoke her primary hand was held in a fist with an extended thumb as the hand moved towards her forehead in a vigorous arc.

'I am Han - Hannah. *Hannah Upton.*'

The index and middle finger of her primary hand were now extended. Her fingers then moved from her head downward in a gesture made with more than its usual energy.

'Well, jolly japes for you,' said Warrilow with a grin.

Slee smirked.

She continued, undeterred. There was a strength and pride never before felt.

'I know your names too, Warrilow and Slee. And I have another name for you - my fa-father's. Thomas — Sir Thomas Upton.'

She stopped to take a breath. Their changed expressions made it clear they began to reconsider their situation.

Slee lost his smile first. He could not stop himself from following her signing, a mesmerizing complexity of gestures. Warrilow noted Slee's concerned look and the smile fell from his face as well.

'I understood every word you have said about me and my friend.'

She turned and gestured over to Priscilla.

'And here is another name for you. John Goodricke. I know him and I have understood everything you have said about him.'

Slee and Warrilow looked at each other as the implications of what she said finally sank in.

Hannah stared a moment longer. They remained speechless. She gave a little shrug as if to say, 'That's it then' and walked back to a wide-eyed Priscilla.

'Slee, what the bloody hell just happened?' whispered Warrilow.

'Bloody Christ!' spat Slee. 'We're for it! That's what just happened.'

Warrilow sat back and stiffened. 'Well, don't look at me! It was not I who chose this place!'

Slee looked over at Hannah who returned a haughty glare while raising her glass in a mock toast.

'I do not believe it. That was Sir Thomas Upton's daughter, Banks will be none too pleased,' said Slee, rubbing his forehead.

'Well, bugger it. Let's not tell him.'

'Oh, no need my friend. I am sure Upton will do that for us.'

28

The Copley Medal

'I am working on my correspondence, Molyneaux. You know when so engaged I wish no interruption.'

'Sorry sir, but he is rather insistent.'

Joseph Banks stopped writing and looked up over his spectacles. Slee and Warrilow were not scheduled until much later. So, who was this? He looked over at his clock and then slowly returned his stare to Molyneaux.

'Who is insistent? I have no morning appointment.'

'His card, sir.'

Molyneaux reached across the same massive desk that sailed on the *Endeavour*, placed the card down and stepped back.

Banks squinted through his spectacles.

'Sir Thomas Upton? Here?' His mind raced. 'Perhaps you had better let him through.'

'Sir.'

Molyneaux backed out. Banks heard a muffled 'He will see you now, sir', followed by 'Too bloody right he will.'

Banks' pulse went up a tick. He was not easily intimidated, but it did not bode well for someone like Upton to arrive unannounced in a black mood.

He began to rise as Upton entered.

'Sir Thomas. I am heartily glad…'

'*You* sir, shall remain seated and listen.'

Banks' instincts told him to avoid belligerency. He sat back down and said nothing. No one had treated him so brusquely since Captain Cook on the *Endeavour* those many years ago.

Upton had cooled since learning of Hannah's tea garden encounter, but was still molten beneath. His white shirt, carefully knotted white silk cravat and white cuffs were immaculate - a sign of wealth. From his expensive wig with side curls to his blue frock coat with its bright brass buttons to the buckles on his shoes he was an imposing figure. He seated himself across from Banks, carefully placed his tri-cornered cocked hat on the desk and rested his hands on his walking stick. He stared at Banks without blinking as if there was not a moment to be wasted in getting the measure of the man.

'Banks, what opinion do you hold of the deaf?'

'Sir? I do not understand your question.'

'Come now, Banks. It is simple enough. How do you regard those who suffer from this unfortunate malady?'

'Sir, you mock me. With all due respect, I do not understand the purpose of your visit or your question.'

'Then, allow me to explain. Two of your instruments insulted my daughter as well as conspired against Mr John Goodricke.'

'To whom do you refer, sir?'

'A Mr Slee and a Mr Warrilow.'

'They are members here, yes, but I am not yet sure of what they have done, if anything.'

'Then you shall learn of that, sir. What makes their behaviour, and yours, particularly iniquitous is the low regard it belies for those who suffer this malady.'

Banks realised he had been slowly spinning his quill pen between a now ink-stained thumb and forefinger. He slowly replaced it in the inkstand and briefly attempted to rub the stains away. This was no administrative matter. It was personal. For once he was caught flat footed. *Slee and Warrilow will pay, whatever they have done.*

'Sir Thomas, I am afraid I do not quite follow. If this is about Mr Goodricke I can assure you he is being given every consideration.'

'Banks, are you aware that both he and my daughter attended the same academy for the deaf in Edinburgh? And at *my* behest King George has seen to it that this academy is now in London, such was his regard for the good works of the owner? You are aware of these facts and yet cultivate a contemptible prejudice against the deaf?'

'Indeed not, sir, I was not so aware,' said a now barely audible Banks, with 'King' ringing in his ears.

'So again, sir I ask - what is your opinion of the deaf?'

'Well, sir, they... deserve no less than any of us.'

Upton stood and collected his hat.

'I expect Messrs Slee and Warrilow shall apprise you of the details of this sordid episode. Furthermore, they shall sign a joint letter of apology to my daughter Hannah for their wretched behaviour. Whatever her condition she is a lady of standing and deserves to be treated with the respect and deference due any other. As for this Mr Goodricke, I confess I am not *au fait* with the gentleman's work. However, as you should be aware, there are those within these walls with whom I share a confidence. If there is the merest penumbra of suspicion he be wrongly denied his due, I shall learn of it. Is any of this unclear?'

Banks knew full well Upton was not someone one wanted as an enemy. His imminent capitulation, however, was made tolerable for even now he could think of a way to award Goodricke the Copley yet diminish its import.

'It is all absolutely clear, Sir Thomas.'

'Then, by your leave, sir.'

'Your servant, sir.'

*

Nathaniel Pigott ran the two hundred yards to his observatory, no small feat for him. Every step along the rain soaked path squished or squirted, but the news could not wait. He came to the entrance, hurriedly scraped what little mud he could off his soles and entered.

'Edward!'

Edward's head appeared in the opening to the upper level.

'Yes, Father, I can hear you. No need to bloody shout. I am checking the equipment for damp after last night's rain. Give us a moment, would you?'

'I have news!' said Nathaniel, pulling a letter from his waistcoat. He took a seat and read it again with a smile and shake of his head as if he still could not believe it.

Edward descended while holding a rag. He wiped his hands, tossed it aside and leaned against the steep stairway to the upper level, arms folded.

'It would appear you have brought news,' said Edward with a trace of sarcasm while nodding to the paper his father was holding.

'News indeed!' said a still breathless Nathaniel, while holding up the letter.

'This happens to be from Shepherd, you know, the Cambridge Shepherd.'

'I know who he is, Father.'

'The Council has just voted.'

Edward leaned forward.

'On what, pray?'

'Our Mr Goodricke has been awarded the Copley medal!'

Edward stood erect to speak, but fell back against the steps. He thought this might happen, but the reality was more impactful than imagined.

'When did they vote?'

'Tuesday last. Well, what do you think of that, eh?'

Edward knew the work was worthy, but given the current climate at the Royal Society it had to be very good indeed.

'There's a bit more to this, however. Something of an, um, addendum.'

'More?'

'Yes.'

Nathaniel pursed his lips and continued.

'It was a double award. They also gave a medal to Hutchins.'

'Who?'

'Thomas Hutchins, for his determination of the freezing point of mercury. '

'The planet?'

'Edward.'

'Sorry, but why two *this* particular year…is there any precedent?'

'Yes. Actually, more than a precedent, as it were. Three were awarded in '66, I believe. There was Cavendish, DeLaval and, um…'

'Never mind who else! Why two awards *this* year of all years?'

'Shepherd copied Banks' own remarks on the matter into his letter, or at least his forthcoming remarks. It is a draft, mind you, but I doubt it will change much.'

'How did he ever come by that?'

'We have our sources.'

Nathaniel put on his spectacles and cleared his throat.

> *Gentlemen, Your Council having observed with pleasure that the series of papers read before you in the course of the last year have been more interesting than usual and that in years less fertile Godfrey Copley's medal had remain unadjudged. They have seized the opportunity which presents itself of paying a debt partly due to this liberal institution by dispensing of one unadjudged medal. They have therefore directed me to present two of our worthy contestants in the pursuit of knowledge this year with that honourable mark of the Royal*

Society's approbation. Mr. Goodricke is awarded for his discovery of the period at which the light of Algol suffers a diminution, and Mr Hutchins for his investigation and determination of the point at which mercury held in fusion by the ordinary temperature of our atmosphere is fixed by cold into a malleable metal.

'There it is. What are your thoughts?'

'He has a way with words.'

'You might say that.'

'The bit I find suspect is where he says - what was that? – 'They have therefore directed me…' I think he meant I have therefore directed *them*. So, the question still stands.'

'Well, there are some things we are simply not privy to. But I believe Goodricke is to be congratulated nonetheless. The Copley to someone so young and his first paper at that. The lad has a remarkable career ahead of him.'

Unlike me, thought Edward.

'Of course, much of the credit is due to you,' added Nathaniel, as if he could read his son's mind.

'No, Father. All I did was point him in the right direction. I have done very little. John is largely self-taught when it comes to his astronomy.'

'Surely you had some hand in this?'

'Father, you are not suggesting that any of this is my work? I can assure you…'

Nathaniel waved him off.

'No, no. Of course not. I meant in his *training*, in what you have taught him. That is all.'

'Let me speak. plain. Did either of us believe someone so afflicted was capable of executing such a work? Not at first, let us be honest. We shared an underestimation of his capacity. He truly is a rare individual. I can go so far as to say there is nothing more I can teach him.'

'Do you really think that?'

Edward shrugged.

'Perhaps I can suggest a few more candidate stars to study as variables, but as to his own observing skills and strategy, there is nothing useful I can add. There is, however perhaps something I might subtract. Something I may not wish to.'

'I don't quite follow.'

'I think you do. The lad fairly drips with idealism. Sometimes his approach to astronomy might be a little too fervent.'

'And you wish to awaken him from his…dream?'

'Can you think of anyone better suited?'

'No. But perhaps I was hoping this association might restore some of your own faith.'

'Is that why you had me tutor him and not yourself?'

Nathaniel's initial good cheer was now deflated. He was not expecting the conversation to take this turn.

'Edward, I only thought you would do a better job. I was not wrong. You deserve much of the credit for this work, whether you wish it or not. And you, more than anyone, know his work to be genuine. Others doubt this. Believe me, I know. You have been his friend and defender in so many ways. That is to your credit. It is a quality you cannot deny; however miserable you pretend to be. I believe he has changed *you*, not the other way around.'

They are both silent for a moment.

'Fair enough. So, let us return to the subject at hand, eh?' said Edward, finally.

'Yes, let us. Well, um, perhaps it is possible that the awards are based purely on merit, that the Council simply could not decide between the two?' posited Nathaniel.

'I doubt it. Banks does everything for reasons of strategy. Do you not recall that episode at the Crown and Anchor? What was all that about? All that business with Herschel? Perhaps it was not meant to set the award to Herschel. More likely it was meant to undercut John's originality. We were both pretty certain Banks was against

Goodricke from the outset so something or someone caused him to change his mind, or rather his strategy.'

Nathaniel nodded. 'Perhaps you are right in this. I do know one thing though, this is still no guarantee of Goodricke's complete acceptance, despite any accolades that may now come his way,'

'What are you saying?'

'Think for a minute. He is *still* not a member. It is, obviously, possible to receive the Copley without being a Fellow of the Royal Society. So, let us see how long that takes, eh? Oddly enough, that may be a little more difficult than achieving this award.'

'I hadn't quite thought of that. In any case, I wish to give John this news as I doubt he has yet heard. Or should we wait for something official to reach him?' asked Edward.

'Oh, bugger Banks. You go ahead and tell him. I believe he would rather the news came from you most of all.'

*

'Mrs Dalrymple is in the dining room, sir. It is the evening meal, you see,' said Emeline.

'I shan't be long. I am here to see Mr Goodricke.'

'Just this way, sir.'

Edward followed her to the dining room. Mrs Dalrymple was present as well as two other gentlemen, but no Goodricke.

'Mr Pigott ma'am,' said Emeline.

'Mr Pigott! This is a lovely surprise. Won't you join us? We have only just begun.'

'No, thank you ma'am. I am here for John.'

'I see. Emeline, tell Master Goodricke he has a visitor. Now, Edward, are you sure you shall not join us?'

Pigott surveyed the table. He had never met the other residents but quickly surmised one of them had sandbagged Goodricke with that premeditated question on the Earth's rotation.

'On second thought, it will be a pleasure to join you, Mrs Dalrymple.'

Pigott took a seat and smiled at Guthrie as Pomeroy reached for a second helping.

'Edward Pigott.'

'I am Guthrie and this one here is Pomeroy.'

'Mr Pomeroy,' said Pigott as he nodded in his direction. He was hoping he did not reply with a mouthful of food. He knew in an instant it was Guthrie.

Eleanor, who had been to the kitchen to instruct Cook, returned to the table.

'So, Mr Pigott, to what do we owe this distinct pleasure?' she asked.

'I have some news for John.'

'Not bad news I hope.'

'Oh, to the contrary, ma'am, to the contrary.'

'Can you not you tell us?'

'John should be present.'

'Of course.'

'By the way, where is he?'

'Well, he is often late and sometimes does not sit with us. Sometimes he does not come at all. Really, I do not know how he survives.'

'What is it you do Mr Pigott?' asked Guthrie

'I work with Mr Goodricke.'

Pomeroy looked up from his plate at Pigott as if he finally noticed he was there.

'So, like him, you sleep in the day and stare at the stars at night?' asked Guthrie.

'You could put it like that.'

Eleanor began to sense that Guthrie, without knowing it, was out of his depth.

'It seems a rather cockeyed way of living.'

'Perhaps. But it can only properly be pursued by those who can afford to do so.'

Guthrie knew this to be a deliberate slap. It was a way of saying that astronomy was the leisure pursuit of a gentleman, of someone independently wealthy, neither of which he was.

Eleanor failed to contain her smile. He would never learn.

'Ask *him* about that bright star. He should know,' said Pomeroy while elbowing Guthrie and pointing his fork at Pigott.

Guthrie's irritated expression suggested the question was to have been saved for Goodricke.

'What star is that, pray?' asked Pigott with a silky smile.

'That bright one in the east, just after sunset. We are not sure if it may be a planet. I say it is Venus, but Pomeroy thought it Jupiter.'

'Pomeroy is correct.'

Pomeroy wiped his chin and smiled at Guthrie.

'Surely not, I mean to say, it is too bright to be Jupiter.'

'It cannot be Venus,' said Pigott while nodding a thanks to Emeline who placed a plate in front of him.

'Please help yourself, Mr Pigott,' said Eleanor.

'Why not Venus?'

'Mr Gusty, permit me to explain.'

'Guthrie.'

'Yes, Guthrie. Venus can never be more than forty-five degrees from the Sun.'

'Degrees? Is not distance measured in miles?'

'Perhaps I should put it another way,' said Pigott, demonstrating with outstretched arms.

'Point towards Venus with one hand and then point towards the Sun with the other. The angle formed thus between your arms can never be more than forty-five degrees. So, if you see something bright in the eastern sky at sunset, it can never be Venus, whatever else it may be.'

'I do not quite follow,' said a now frustrated Guthrie.

'I can only explain it to you, sir. I cannot comprehend it for you as well.'

Eleanor's laugh was cut short as Goodricke arrived.

'Master Goodricke! Where *have* you been? And us with company this evening.'

It took Goodricke a second to notice the additional person at the table was Pigott.

'Edward! What has brought you here? Has your father finally given you the shove?'

'Not just yet. Soon perhaps. I have some news for you John. Wonderful news.'

Goodricke gave him a quizzical look as he shook out his serviette.

'You really have no idea, do you?' he said.

Goodricke shook his head.

Pigott could contain himself no longer. His voice went up a register. He was glad there was an audience.

'The Royal Society, in London of course, has seen fit to award our Mr John Goodricke here the Copley medal for his work in astronomy.'

'That is wonderful, John!' said Eleanor, despite not having the slightest idea what the Copley medal was. Guthrie and Pomeroy looked at each other. Goodricke was expressionless.

'Don't you have anything to say, John?' asked Pigott.

'I think I may have had some help.'

'No, John, this is all your work. Truly,' replied Pigott, not realising Goodricke was thinking of Hannah, not him.

'I am so glad for you John, you have worked very hard,' said Eleanor

Goodricke seemed uncomfortable.

'You are too modest by half,' said Pigott. 'Let us finish up here and go out for a pint to celebrate.'

A muted Guthrie excused himself with a quick nod to Goodricke, and Pomeroy soon followed. Eleanor was interested to learn more, but Goodricke remained stubbornly modest. After the meal, they all rose from the table and she gave Goodricke a silent hug as he and Pigott departed.

Goodricke and Pigott stopped at the stairs. Pigott could sense he was somehow distracted. He did not seem to wish to commemorate the news, but why ever not?

'What a pair. That Guthrie is the sort that pisses more than he drinks. I put him to rights, though and that other gundiguts,' said Edward.

'Oh, Pomeroy? He is harmless.'

'If you say so. Nevertheless, that Guthrie fellow was well and truly beaten from the field. He shall not trouble you again. But never mind him. Surely you have no plans for the evening?' said Pigott with a clap of his hands. 'I do believe this news deserves to be properly celebrated.'

'I-I was planning on observing.'

'Oh, no, my son. Surely that can wait?'

'Perhaps. Then again one might say it is the sort of commitment that made the Copley possible in the first instance.'

Pigott smiled and placed his hand on his friend's shoulder.

'Well, if that is what you wish. Let us merely postpone it then. Perhaps my father shall join us. I'll call in the next few days.'

'Fine. See you then.'

'One more thing, John. No rush mind you, but a trip to London must be planned.'

'Right. Good-night, Edward.'

'Good-night.'

John could have shown a bit more enthusiasm on learning the news. *Something isn't right*, he thought.

Goodricke slowly ascended to his room. It was not observing he wished to return to, but to finish writing to Hannah. Her recent letter had been a complete surprise and generated much thought. He had to strain a bit to remember her - their shared time with Braidwood was brief. She would now be what, eighteen? She had written that she would like very much to see him should he ever come to London. Her description of the tea garden episode and her father's reaction, however, suggested that the award of the Copley relied on manoeuvring as much as merit. Perhaps his work was worthy, but he would just as soon not have had this sideshow intimate otherwise.

After responding to Hannah, he realised there was another letter he had to write.

*

Henry Goodricke had returned to his home on the Noorderhaven Canal to find Levina waiting for him.

'This arrived for you, today.'

'Oh?'

One look at the seal told him it was from John. The arrival of a letter always brought with it a certain moment; it may be pleasant, it may be bad news. It was the only way personal information moved.

He read it as Levina anxiously looked on.

'Is our son all right, Henry?'

He had to collect himself before replying.

'Sorry, my dear. Oh, yes. He is well. Apparently, his work in astronomy has been most highly regarded by the Royal Society. He has been awarded the Copley Medal.'

'And what is that?'

'I have heard of it. I believe it is the highest honour they can bestow on one's work.'

Levina, let out a sigh of relief and sat on the settee. He looked at the letter and then at her. It was the first time she had ever seen him shed tears and she reached for his hand.

29

London 1784

Edward Pigott, after three years, knew Goodricke's typical twenty-four-hour cycle. If the night sky was free of cloud, he would observe until first light. He might or might not have breakfast, sleep until early afternoon, perhaps have some bread and jam from a sympathetic Mrs Dalrymple, have his evening meal and begin observing again. Late afternoon was the best time to arrive unannounced.

The door was open. It was just as cold inside as out. Goodricke was writing in his astronomical journal. Pigott moved around to catch his attention.

'Hello John.'

Goodricke held up a finger to say *Let me finish this. I'll be with you in a moment.*

Pigott surveyed the still sparse accommodation. A full coal scuttle sat next to a cold hearth. The little library of astronomy texts, at least, had grown. He stepped forward and read over Goodricke's shoulder.

> *At 7h 1/2 hours in the morning the thermometer was at 12° 1/2 - This morning is the coldest day next to Decr 31 1783 and Jany 25th last. The thermometer was at a southern exposure on all these days.*

Goodricke placed his quill aside and stretched.

'John, you have let the fire expire.'

'I never actually lit it. At least not this past night.'

'Why ever not? It does get rather cold here on a winter's night, does it not?'

'A bit. But do you keep a fire in your observatory?'

'You know we do not. Rising heat affects the seeing.'

'There you are then. This is my observatory, so, no fire. At least not in the night.'

'But it is winter and it is bloody cold.'

'Edward, stop fussing. Anyway, it is not so cold as to freeze mercury.'

This deft allusion to Hutchins was not lost on Pigott and a signal to change the subject.

'That is what I have come to discuss. Not Hutchins of course, but the matter of our London journey. Why don't we go over to The Swan for a pint and a meal? Better than the food in this place, eh?'

'The problem is not the food here, the problem, at least according to Eleanor, is that I do not partake of it enough. I am afraid that I have never really explained to her that I do not prefer common meals.'

'Why not, after all this time?'

'Edward, you have not come to discuss my dining habits, have you?

'No, of course not. So, lets away, shall we? At least the company will be better, if not the kitchen.'

'Ah, the company. I understand Mr Guthrie is soon to move on. So, I shall have a new dining companion.'

'Thank heavens for that. I thought the man a prig.'

'Perhaps. But he did set me on an excellent question.'

'We're not *still* on about *that,* are we? Can you not just accept the Earth rotates and move on to another problem? Lord knows there are enough of them.'

'You have made your point, Edward. A time waster to you, but not to me. Sometimes I believe I see a solution only to have it slip out of focus.'

'All right, all right. Let's not dawdle, then. A full tankard might help you think on it.'

*

At The Swan sipping their ales, Pigott gave plump Cassie, all bosom and lace, a friendly pat as she left with their food order.

'She's a smart girl, eh?'

'Perhaps you might marry her,' said Goodricke.

Pigott wondered if this was meant in jest.

'Sorry. Did I speak out of turn?' asked Goodricke. 'I thought it a mere pleasantry.'

'Perhaps as I am seriously thinking on it I did not see the humour.'

'What? You never.'

'Why not? She is a lovely lass is she not?'

Pigott then broke into his sly smile to indicate he was not at all serious.

Goodricke knew his friend kept his own counsel. He could tell a lot about a person by what they thought was humorous, but this was not quite so easy with Edward.

Pigott waved his hand.

'Are you still with us?'

'Sorry. Just musing.'

'Apparently. Are you prepared for a trip to London?'

Cassie returned with a loaf and cutlery. Pigott was distracted by her ample cleavage as Goodricke answered.

'How much preparation is required?'

'As far as the medal presentation goes, not so much. Neither you nor Mr Hutchins will have to speak. I doubt they will want to make too pompous an event of it in any case. Or rather Banks will not. The value of the event will be to meet others. You have not yet met Herschel, for instance. I know that his paper on Algol may have been an unpleasant episode, but I now believe it was purely due to the plan of another.'

'Fair enough. If he were to walk in here now I would not know him,' said Goodricke as he tore at the loaf.

'I would bet that you would. Anyway, what else do you have planned? You will certainly wish to meet with Maskelyne for one and not just at the meeting, but at the Royal Observatory. I should think you would find it most illuminating.'

'How so?'

'It is not quite the sort of astronomy we do and is perhaps best understood by actually going there.'

'Can I invite myself?'

'Need you ask?'

'Right then, I shall contact him and also Thomas Wright and Alexander Aubert, as I hope to meet with them as well.'

'Excellent. It would do you well to have read Wright's well-known work entitled *An Original Theory or New Hypothesis of the Universe* beforehand.'

'It's just there now on my shelf,' said Goodricke.

'On your shelf yes, but have you read it?'

'The major claim he vouchsafes is that the Milky Way is an optical effect maintained by our position in a layer of stars. I would say he is correct. What do you think?'

'Yes. Well…'

'Aha! You have not read it yourself!'

'I was waiting for you so that we may discuss it.'

'Rubbish.'

Goodricke paused.

'Edward, there is someone else I hope to see as well.'

'And who is that?' asked Pigott as he waved his empty tankard at Cassie who walked over with smile.

'Two more please. There's a love.'

Goodricke had decided he could now mention Hannah. By now Pigott would not suspect any connection to the circumstances of the Copley award. How could he?

'Edward, there is also a young lady I have not seen for many years I wish to call upon when in London. Her name is Hannah Upton. We shared some time together at Mr Braidwood's academy.'

Pigott paused in mid sip.

'That place in Edinburgh where you were first schooled.'

'Just so.'

'How well do you know this Miss Upton?'

'Not well at all. I have not seen her these past ten years.'

'She is not by any remote chance related to a Sir Thomas Upton, is she?'

'He is her father.'

'Well, good luck there then!' said Pigott.

'Edward, it is just a reunion. Nothing more.'

'That is what you say now.'

Perhaps Goodricke might not be so monastic after all. thought Pigott. He sensed it was best not to press the subject and would let Goodricke say more when he wanted to.

'So, your London sojourn will not be all astronomy. Excellent. But never mind that for now. We need to discuss practicalities.'

'Such as?'

'How we shall reach London, for one thing.'

'By coach I assume, how else?'

'There is a little more to it than that.'

'What else is there?'

'Which coach and where we sit.'

'Does all that really matter?'

'Indeed, it does. We take the mail coach. We can choose to sit inside or outside. It is three pounds to sit inside and one pound five shillings to sit outside. I prefer the outside myself. The journey takes five days.'

'But surely you can afford to ride on the inside? So can I, for that matter.'

'Yes, but inside you are all rather jammed against one another. Would you prefer to sit hard by someone with bad breath who sweats and stinks, or farts or vomits or all of these? Even worse, they may wish to chat. That would not do well for you I should think. It can all become rather tiresome after twenty-four hours of grinding together in close quarters, I can say.'

'Ah.'

'Besides, from up top you can see the stars - at least when the night is without cloud.'

'We travel at night?'

'The mail coach runs at night to make better time, as there is less congestion at the stops, that's the theory anyway. So, it won't be any real change for us, sleeping by day and travelling during the night.'

'The outside it is.'

'That's sorted then. I'll make the arrangements.'

'Just one more thing, though,' said Goodricke.

'And what is that?'

'Can we wait until it gets a bit warmer?'

They shared a good laugh as their ales arrive.

*

Six weeks later, Goodricke and Pigott sat atop the York to London mail coach. They were seated slightly above and behind the driver. Behind them, facing to the rear, a guard held a cocked blunderbuss. Goodricke worried that a proper bounce would catapult him clear into the night and he kept a tight hold on the iron handle by his side. Their five-day journey was nearly at an end as they neared London in the coming dawn. The road improved, but the air did not.

Goodricke, lulled to dozing by their rhythmic trot of the four-horse team, was brought fully awake by a growing odour and jostled Pigott.

'What is that almighty stink?'

'Oh, that. London.'

'But how far is it?'

Pigott looked for a landmark.

277

'About five miles, perhaps less. We should be passing a milepost soon.'

'It can smell that bad at this distance?'

'The wind carries it. It is much worse in the city proper. You might wish you had lost your sense of smell as well, I'll be bound.'

'What is the cause?'

"Name it. Cheap coal, the stinking Thames, mountains of manure not to mention the smell of thousands of wet horses when it rains, which it often does and countless chamber pots emptied daily into the street. Then there are all the wastes and poisons used in manufacture such as tanneries and putrefying animal carcasses, and rotting corpses.'

'*What?*'

'Common graves with bodies stacked in them remain open until full. You'll get used to it all soon enough.'

Pigott wore his mischievous grin while holding on to his tri-corner. Goodricke wasn't sure that he would ever get used to it. He could not help but notice a hovering haze as they approached. By the time they rolled into the journey's terminus at Charing Cross they were beneath a mantle of smoke.

Stiff from the cold and damp they climbed down and stretched as the guard lowered their bags. As the other passengers exited Goodricke was amazed how the odour spilling from its interior managed to briefly overpower the stink of the street. It had been good advice to sit up top.

'Where do we go from here?' he asked.

'Our accommodation. I don't know about you, but I could use a bit of a wash up and a lie down. I have booked us into the Evans at Covent Garden.'

'Are we walking?'

'It is just nearby. Or we could acquire a hackney carriage if you prefer.'

'No, no we can walk. Is your father staying there as well?'

'Good Lord, no. He prefers the Freemason's Tavern over at Great Queen's Street. We'll meet up at the Royal Society tomorrow.'

'I cannot wait.'

Pigott was not quite sure how to take this.

*

Samuel Johnson walked along the Strand to the weekly meeting of his literary club at The Turk's Head tavern, swinging his walking stick as a warning that he was not about to move out of anyone's way. Most of those he brushed aside were familiar with his moody antics.

Men tended to dress according to their rank and profession, but not Samuel Johnson. Physicians and notaries wore black. A barrister dressed in black over which he would add a gown. Everyone knew the difference between the wig of a lawyer and that of a physician. Johnson, however, never considered himself above the social standing of a tradesman and today wore his usual outfit in shades of brown, a full-bottomed wig, metal buttons, buckled shoes and ruffles of lace.

His lifelong battles against lethargy and idleness had intensified. He had not mellowed with age. Perhaps this came from an increasing sense of mortality and he required of himself that he reject morbid thoughts, rise earlier, read more, and move closer to the consolations of religion and industry. He had numerous physical ailments, but the most debilitating was mental. His battle with melancholia was known to many. A brisk walk to the convivial atmosphere of his club was the day's high point.

Goodricke sensed something familiar about the approaching figure. He and Pigott were walking along the Strand towards Somerset House, the home of the Royal Society. Their footpath was lined with bollards to prevent coaches from encroaching on pedestrians and the tall gentleman coming towards them methodically tapped each one with his walking stick. He gave a brief nod as he passed and Goodricke remembered.

He stopped and touched Pigott on the shoulder as the tapping receded.

'I know him.'

'Who?'

'That fellow who just passed.'

'That odd sort?'

'Yes.'

'So, who was he then?'

'Samuel Johnson.'

'Surely not.'

'Samuel Johnson, the author of the English dictionary, if I am not mistaken.'

'Are you certain? How would you come to know him?'

Goodricke briefly explained the visit to Braidwood's academy as they resumed walking. It was only for one morning and many years ago, but it was him.

'Well, if that was Johnson, I should write and ask if it might be possible to visit him.'

'Are you certain? Can I just do that?'

'Of course! And why not? You have a connection. I should think any amount of time conversing with him might have you soon forget his appearance, and the odour, if I am not mistaken. From what little I know of him he would not be someone at a loss for words.'

'But where does he live?'

'John, sometimes you disappoint. Simply address your query 'Samuel Johnson, London' and have him reply to our lodgings.'

'I am not sure if he would wish to see me.'

'Up to you. But remember, you are in London. There are opportunities here that York does not provide. Or anywhere else for that matter. I plan on attending a Handel oratorio myself. You could do worse than meet up with him. Mind you, I doubt he knows much astronomy, but I am sure there are other matters you might discuss.'

'Come to think of it, there might be something.'

'There you are then. So, add him to your list.'

'You know, I think I shall.'

'Well done.'

Pigott regretted mentioning Handel. They had become so good at communicating it was easy to forget Goodricke could not hear.

They arrived at Somerset House and stopped before the entrance, where Nathaniel Pigott waited.

'Greetings, John, Edward. Well, this is a smart day, eh?'

'Good day, Father. Yes, but John may be tad nervous.'

'Nothing to be nervous about. Banks will give a little speech. Well, little for him. You approach, accept the medal and return to your seat. Simple. As I say, they do not wish to turn this into too much of a fuss. The award speaks for itself and I suspect that this is one Banks would just as soon forget in any case.'

'Father.'

'Of course, in no way do I diminish the significance of this day. John here is certainly worthy, despite what some of these blossom brains might have preferred. There are many others who are rightly impressed and hoping to meet him. Shall we go up?'

They entered the Society's main meeting room as members mingled and enjoyed informal conversation. Goodricke suspected it was the largest room he had ever been in. Nathaniel, who took it upon himself to be his *de facto* escort, looked at Goodricke and spoke.

'Come this way, there is someone you should meet.'

He guided him over to an unassuming man whose dress and manner suggested he was not of the upper class. Goodricke guessed his age as about forty or so, old enough to be his father.

'John, this is Thomas Hutchins. Mr Hutchins this is John Goodricke.'

Hutchins extended his hand.

'Ah, Mr Goodricke, my congratulations to you, sir.'

'And my congratulations to you as well, sir.'

'Mr Hutchins, have you come all the way from Canada?' asked Nathaniel.

'Indeed not, sir. I live here in London now, but am still with the Hudson Bay Company.'

'I see. And do the properties of matter remain your interest?'

'I prefer to think of myself as a naturalist. Chemistry is but a side line.'

'But you have won the Copley for your work in that discipline, have you not?'

'Indeed, I have, sir. I must say I was rather surprised at that myself.'

That boor Banks, thought Nathaniel who wasn't sure Goodricke captured all their conversation, but perhaps it was just as well.

The sergeant-at-arms announced the meeting was about to begin. Nathaniel motioned to Goodricke to take his seat and sat next to him to let him know when he should rise to receive the award. The room quieted and the meeting commenced.

'Who is that seated next to Hutchins?' asked Warrilow.

Slee stared for a moment and then realised who it was.

'*That* is John Goodricke.'

'Our quarry? A mere stripling?' said an incredulous Warrilow.

'Nineteen years, I believe.'

'Good Lord. Has anyone younger been awarded the Copley?'

'I do not believe so. What is more, I do not believe anyone younger ever will.'

'I say, but that is odd.'

'What is?'

'He doesn't *look* deaf, does he?'

Slee shook his head and turned his attention elsewhere. They had been verbally scourged by Banks and written their letter of apology, but there was not much to be done after that, except that neither of them could ever expect to be appointed to the Council. Banks would see to that even though it might benefit his opponents.

Nathaniel was right, thought Goodricke. The award ceremony was perfunctory. Due in part to the regard for modesty this presentation was without pomp, any reluctance to recognise Goodricke notwithstanding. He did, however, catch a few members saying, 'that is him' or 'a mere boy' as he approached to accept his award. To his credit Banks seemed to exhibit no ill will and warmly shook his hand. Banks was momentarily taken aback when he heard Goodricke clearly speak and say, 'Thank you for this honour sir.' He briefly looked around as if for confirmation that this was the real John Goodricke and not some impostor.

After the brief ceremony, members stood around in little knots drinking sherry served by strolling waiters. Goodricke was standing with Nathaniel and Edward as member after member came by to shake his hand and offer a 'well done'. A tall gentleman approached wearing an expression between condescension and curiosity. Goodricke instinctively knew who it was.

Nathaniel gestured towards the approaching figure with his glass of sherry.

'John, I present Mr William Herschel.'

Herschel stood a head taller than Goodricke and was twenty-seven years his senior. He found it difficult to reconcile the Algol paper with the boy now before him.

He looked briefly at Nathaniel as if to ask whether Goodricke will understand if he spoke.

Nathaniel made a gesture to the effect that he may proceed.

'It was a great good fortune that you happened upon a variable with such a peculiar property. I trust that you accept that any effort to secure the same result on my own was only to confirm your work.'

Good Lord. That's right to the point, thought Nathaniel.

Herschel noticed Goodricke's gaze switch from his eyes to his lips and back again. Goodricke's reply was clear and distinctive.

'A simple misunderstanding, I am sure. But Algol is not that *rara avis* you seem to think. It was patient diligence that made this discovery, not good fortune. I am sure there are other stars possessing the same property not yet discovered. Of the multitude of stars available to study I doubt that I happened upon the only one such object. I am also certain there are others beyond the range of the unaided eye that shall bear the same result if such a thing be of any interest.'

Herschel was not sure if this was all meant as a rebuke or honest advice. He was caught off guard by the intelligent and confident air that did not match his youth or deafness.

'Of course, you must be right. A pleasure to make this acquaintance. I am sure there are others here who wish to do so, as well. Perhaps we might correspond?'

'I am hopeful that we shall,' replied Goodricke.

Nathaniel and Edward said nothing as Herschel nodded and stepped away. Edward lifted another glass of sherry from a passing tray.

Goodricke noticed another member sidling over, distinctive and dour in clerical dress. He looked at Nathaniel to make the introduction.

'John, I have the pleasure of introducing the Astronomer Royal, Nevil Maskelyne. Reverend, this is John Goodricke.'

Maskelyne had already been briefed that Goodricke could carry on a conversation if spoken to directly.

'Master Goodricke. It is a signal honour to meet the someone so young to receive this recognition. My congratulations.'

He performed a deep bow and Goodricke was quietly bemused by his display.

'An honour to meet you as well, Reverend.'

'I understand that we can expect a visit from you in due course?'

'Yes, tomorrow if that suits?'

'It will. Nathaniel. Edward.'

Maskelyne departed.

'A man of few words is he not?' said Edward.

'Indeed,' replied Nathaniel, who wondered what Goodricke would make of the Royal Observatory and Nevil Maskelyne.

30

The Royal Observatory

The letter was simply addressed 'Samuel Johnson, Esq, London' It took a moment to recall its sender. It had been eleven years since his visit to Braidwood's academy, but Goodricke had left a lasting impression. Johnson allowed himself a small smile as he began reading. He held a candle closer to the page, its flame singeing his wig.

*

Goodricke was wearing his new frock coat, acquired especially for London, when he met Pigott for breakfast at the Evans.

'You're looking rather smart today. Is there someone at the Royal Observatory you are trying to impress?' asked Pigott.

He immediately saw his remark was hurtful and backtracked.

'Sorry old fellow, I should have understood this to be a special occasion.'

Goodricke returned a reprimanding look.

'It is.'

He chose not to add that he had really acquired it for his reunion with Hannah later in the week.

'Right. Let us be off,' said a now chastened Pigott.

Goodricke was unsure how far the Royal Observatory was from Covent Garden or even in which direction. Pigott explained that a hackney carriage was out of the question. They would instead hire a boat to take them down the Thames to the Royal Hospital for Seamen located in Greenwich. From there it would be an easy walk to the observatory. Besides, Pigott explained, hackneys charged a shilling for a mile and a half, but on the river the fare was only sixpence for any reasonable distance.

They made their way back along the Strand towards Somerset House. The overnight rain had ceased and clouds broke as they descended the Somerset Stairs to the river. Goodricke noticed the long riverside extent of a massive building to his right. He had seen many London structures in a parlous state, but nothing quite as large.

'The old Savoy,' said Pigott. 'Use to be a palace. Belonged to the Earl of Savoy I believe, became a hospital under Henry the Seventh and is now God knows what. A warehouse mostly, or places of business to various and sundry,' he said as he waved his tri-corner at a passing tilt boat, a kind of river omnibus.

The wind picked up and Goodricke held on to his hat as he stood on the small dock.

'Once a palace and now a warehouse?'

'I know, eh? A change typical of London all the same. Ah, we have a boat.'

Pigott announced their destination and paid the boatman. They clambered aboard, greeted the other passengers and sat under the awning meant as protection from the weather as well as detritus dropped from bridges by mischievous young louts. Pigott had Goodricke sit on the outside to better take in the sights. From this perspective, the Thames appeared much broader, the opposite shore more distant. They occupied a four-man boat and Goodricke quickly came to admire the oarsmen's skill at steering them through the heavy river traffic. He could only imagine their rhythmic grunts with each hard pull.

Pigott nudged Goodricke to get his attention.

'We are moving into the outgoing high tide.'

'Is that a problem?'

'Well, things can get a bit dodgy near London Bridge.'

'Why?'

'Swift waters. Can you swim?'

Goodricke was not sure if this was meant as a joke.

'I do not know. I have never tried. Do you mean to say that it is high tide now?'

'You are asking me? And you an astronomer? The problem is not that it is high tide. The problem is that high tide has just peaked.'

Pigott checked the conditions ahead and even from a distance he could see the river roiling against the arches of London Bridge. He decided not to mention it further.

The Thames was London's major thoroughfare. They moved among oyster boats, colliers, fishing-smacks, barques, sloop-rigged barges, pilot boats, the occasional wherry and other tilt-boats. As they glided beneath Blackfriars Bridge someone above vomited and the awning did its job.

London Bridge loomed, each rowers tightening his grip as they approached. First one made a quick glance over his shoulder and then another, as they struggled to manoeuvre the boat, the oars now used more for steering than propulsion. As they neared, Goodricke understood the problem - the current was forced through narrow gaps between the arches where it was turbulent and swirling.

The rowers struggled to keep the boat on a line. If it spun it truly would become a tilt boat and toss its occupants into the maelstrom. They finally shot through the wider central arch without colliding with a buttress or another boat. Goodricke knew anyone dumped into these waters would not last long, least of all him.

The river calmed, London Bridge receded as the dome of St Paul's came into view. He made a mental note to explore it as they floated past. The White Tower just ahead, made ominous through its luminous Caen stone, was not something, on the other hand, he ever wanted to see the inside of.

Downstream from London Bridge a multitude of tall-masted vessels made it a different river. Some unloaded in mid-stream, causing the tilt boat to weave through attending barges and lighters. Pigott pointed out a man-o'-war at anchor bearing two gun decks, the name on the stern, *Agamemnon*, gleamed in gilt. It fairly dwarfed the merchant vessel, *Aurora*, lying at anchor next to it.

Tar caked wharves along the Wapping shoreline came into view. A closer look revealed a somewhat dispiriting sight, prompting Goodricke to get Pigott's attention.

'What is that business just there? They look to be children swarming about like, like…'

'Rats?' offered Pigott. 'Those are mudlarks - a recent addition to London's lovely scenery.'

'But what are they doing?'

'They scavenge the riverbank for anything of value. They might be looking for stray lumps of coal or whatever else they can pull from the mud or floats by. On a good day, they might pilfer a corpse. They perform a good many other ill acts, I shouldn't wonder. There will likely be more at low tide.'

The mudlarks clambered about barges and prowled the mud before the Wapping Stairs. They slowly walked along the shoreline heads down, scanning this way and that. Some carried a staff to probe the brown, sticky substance. Occasionally one of them would give a start over the discovery of something of value. Goodricke realised how meagre their income must be, dressed in rags as they were. One of them, clearly bowlegged, suspended his scratchings to return Goodricke's stare until the boat made the bend towards Greenwich.

They reached the landing at the Royal Hospital, the threshold to the sublime architectural composition ahead. They disembarked and Pigott paused to let his companion take in the ensemble of four separate quadrants composed of architecture rich in detail and imposing grandeur. Two symmetrically placed domes echoed St Paul's English baroque style. Colonnaded porticos framed the long central axis leading to the Queen's House ahead, a magnificent visual stop.

'Edward, this all has the look of St Paul's, does it not?'

'Well spotted.'

'So, this is Wren as well?'

'None other. Except for the former royal residence ahead. I believe all this was designed so as not to block Her Majesty's view of the Thames.'

'I had always thought Wren an astronomer.'

'It is true that he was the Savilian Professor of Astronomy at Oxford, but he dabbled in architecture as well.'

'He did more than dabble.'

'I was being a bit sarcastic.'

'Indeed. But what is the purpose of this complex?'

'Well, all this is a home for sailors either retired or permanently injured.'

'I had no idea.'

'Wait until you see what Maskelyne does for our sea faring enterprise.'

'And what is that?'

'You'll see, soon enough.'

They neared the former royal residence.

'Who did design the Queen's House?'

'Inigo Jones. He also designed Covent Garden near to where we are stopping. You know, John, it would not lower your rank to acquaint yourself a little more with architecture, not to mention art. Just to the right here is Thornhill's Painted Hall that is certainly worth a visit.'

'Another time. I am anxious to visit the observatory.'

'If you say so, but you're really missing something.'

No reply.

'Right then. You can see the observatory just there,' said Pigott while pointing to the structure perched on the edge of a small plateau on Greenwich Hill.

Goodricke felt a *frisson* of excitement.

'That main observatory building you see was also designed by Wren although one might not imagine him its author. Now, one more thing. I am going to leave you here. There is an ale house in the village I wish to visit. You go on ahead. I shall catch you up.'

'You do not wish to attend?'

'The conversation should be between you and Maskelyne. You go on alone. I shall come along to extract you when it is nearer our time to return.'

'Well, if you are sure.'

'I am.'

'Right then. See you after.'

Goodricke continued up the path on Greenwich Hill as Pigott peeled off with a little wave.

As he approached, Goodricke could see Pigott was right. The observatory did not appear to have any design elements suggestive of Wren, so far as he knew. Neither did it look at all like an observatory.

He reached the top and turned to take in the prospect before him. There was the Royal Hospital below, the ribbon of the Thames and countless spires beyond, with the dome of St Paul's the most prominent feature. He now understood the observatory's location. It was perfectly situated on high ground and away from the smoke of the city. He continued along the eastern edge of the complex and entered the forecourt. Nevil Maskelyne, robed in his black clerical garb, waited at the main entry.

'Master Goodricke. Welcome. You were espied coming up the path from the hospital.'

He looked past Goodricke to see whether anyone else had joined him.

'Are you alone?'

'Mr Pigott accompanied me along the river. He, ah, he had some business in the village and says he will join us later.'

'Nathaniel or Edward?'

'Edward.'

'Of course. No matter. It is your company I wish to receive. Come inside, take some refreshment and I shall show you about, although I fear there is not all that much to see.'

Goodricke was led to the ground-floor apartments. They walked through to a small dining room and Maskelyne gestured toward a seat. A dish of cold meats and bread was waiting. A woman entered with a pot of tea. Goodricke started to rise, but Maskelyne raised his hand. After she left Maskelyne spoke.

'She is but the housekeeper and not Madam Maskelyne as you may have thought. There has not been a Mrs Maskelyne here for twenty years. However, I shall soon marry Miss Sophia Rose of Northamptonshire. Do you know the family?'

Goodricke shook his head.

'No matter.'

He was mouthing his words.

'Reverend, I appreciate your kindness, but it is not necessary to speak as if I had little facility with the English tongue. Should you speak in a normal manner I assure you I shall understand. Or pretty nearly.'

Maskelyne was taken aback by this slight stricture.

'Master Goodricke, let me say how pleased I was for you, and for astronomy. This was a difficult year for an astronomer to be selected.'

'Why so?'

Goodricke suspected he already knew the answer, but wanted Maskelyne's version.

Maskelyne regretted bringing up the subject.

'Perhaps, this may not be the time to review the Society's politics. I shall say, however, that you now have supporters where you had none before.'

'I am thankful to learn of this but what the Royal Society thinks shall not influence the direction of my work.'

'Well said and true enough, but one or two more papers such as already produced will surely lead to your admittance as a Fellow.'

Goodricke was uneasy. He was not one who worried about how to improve his standing.

'Thank you, again, Reverend, but I have come to learn of the work done here.'

'Of course, of course. But first I wish to hear a little of the observing methods leading to your discovery.'

Goodricke wanted to say that it would all be there in the *Philosophical Transactions. Does Maskelyne wonder whether I actually did this work?*

'I shall be happy to do so.'

He then described how he discovered Algol's periodicity and added, in detail, the stepwise determination of what that was. His casual facility with the entire process convinced Maskelyne.

'That is all really. Might you have any question I may address?'

'No indeed, none. I presume that now you have developed this method you are eager to apply it to other suspect stars?'

'Of course.'

Goodricke paused. After recent events, he was reluctant to disclose which ones he had in mind and changed the subject.

'And now may I learn something of your work here?'

'What do you know of it?'

Goodricke sipped tea while neglecting the meat. He studied Maskelyne for a moment. It was difficult to imagine him smiling. His single-minded erudition seemed to permeate the entire atmosphere of the place.

'I am not familiar with the particulars, but surmise that most of it, at least, to be in the service of His Majesty.'

'Ah, not His Majesty but His Majesty's *navy*,' replied Maskelyne, a hand emerging from beneath his clerical garb, the forefinger extended.

'The primary task here is to aid navigation?'

'Our primary task is the preservation and extension of the Empire.'

Goodricke could only think of what that had meant to Cicero. But it might be imprudent to point out that said Empire did not bring good things to all its subjects.

'How is this aid to navigation performed? I assume this refers to what has been known as the longitude problem?'

'This should go some way in answering your question.'

Maskelyne reached over to the sideboard for a small book.

'You may keep this copy as a gift.'

Goodricke read the title page.

NAUTICAL ALMANAC
and
ASTRONOMICAL EPHEMERIS
for the year 1784

So, this is the famous Almanac I have heard so much of. He turned to a random page.

Configurations of the Satellites of Jupiter at 2 o'clock in the morning for August 1784.

On other pages:

Sun's Longitude,
Sun's Right Ascension in Time,
Sun's Declination North,
Equation of Time for September 1784,
The Moon's Passage over the Meridian at Noon,

The Moon's Right Ascension at Noon for November 1784.

Every line of data on every page would have required a prodigious amount of calculation, something impossible for Maskelyne to have accomplished alone. He thumbed through it to discover there were twelve pages for each month. One hundred and forty-four pages of a painstaking distillation of data. This small volume gave a ship's captain several options to determine the longitude at sea using basic astronomical observations alone.

'Reverend Maskelyne, I was of course aware of this work but not the prodigious amount of computation involved - how is it all produced? I mean to say - it is a task far beyond what any one man can accomplish.'

'You are correct. Each copy of the *Nautical Almanac* contains one-thousand three hundred and sixty-five entries. These include such as the timings of the positions of the satellites of Jupiter, the Sun's longitude, the positions of the planets, the position of the Moon for every day of the month and the distance of the Moon from the Sun and certain stars for every three hours of every day. Needless to say, *all* of these calculations are for observations made from *here* at Greenwich. I trust I need not explain how the timings recorded therein make it possible for a ship at sea to know her true location?'

'I believe I understand this. When a ship is at some position to the west or to the east of Greenwich there shall be some discrepancy between the positions recorded here and those observed at sea. The amount of this discrepancy will depend on the number of degrees distant from the Prime Meridian.'

'You are correct.'

'But again, this must require countless calculations. How are they performed?'

'It is simple enough in principle. I have developed a system, a procedure, to ensure that everyone works in the same manner to the same level of accuracy. It is all explained at the end of the copy you are holding. Page one hundred forty-five.'

Goodricke turned to it and read the first paragraph.

> *It may be proper first to premise, that all the Calculations of the Ephemeris are made according to apparent Time by the Meridian of the Royal Observatory at Greenwich: And the Sun's, Planets', and Moon's Places, with the Particulars depending on them in the 2nd, 4th, 5th, 6th, and 7th Pages of each Month, are computed to the Instant of Apparent Noon, or that of the Sun's Center passing the Meridian of Greenwich.*

He closed it and looked earnestly at Maskelyne.

'You said everyone works in the same manner. But who is everyone?'

'My computers.'

'Computers?'

'That is the term.'

'Where are they? Here?'

'No, indeed not. They are scattered about. Most are in or near London. There is one working here at the moment whom you shall meet. When you are finished with your tea I shall show you the library, then the Octagon Room above us and finally to the assistant, or computer, now working in another building.'

'I am ready now.'

'Excellent. Come along then.'

Goodricke followed him up a narrow staircase leading to a library across from the Octagon Room.

'This is where we collect all works on astronomy published here or abroad.'

Goodricke could not help but reflect on his own small shelf back in York. He walked over to a row of volumes for a closer inspection. A title caught his eye.

'May I?'

'Of course.'

He removed it and read the title page:

A
Proposal to Determine our
LONGITUDE
by
JANE SQUIRE

'I had no idea,' said Goodricke.

'In what way?' replied Maskelyne. 'That it was a woman who made a proposal to the Board of Longitude? There were many proposals, and this one was far from being the poorest. It remains, nonetheless, a good example of bad science. It is based on, as I recall, an elaborate but non-mathematical correspondence between the geometries of the celestial sphere and that of our 'terraqueous globe' as she called it. It may pique one's curiosity, but is most impractical. Still, I do not believe it failed simply because she was a woman. It would be churlish to place her below other proposals that were the height of folly themselves.'

'You have my interest, sir. Can you provide an example?'

'The one that most easily comes to mind was by a Mr Digby who proposed a wounded dog be placed on each ship. The knife associated *with* the wound was to remain here at Greenwich. At noon, in Greenwich, it was to be plunged into something termed the Powder of Sympathy. This action was to cause the dog at sea to yelp in pain, thereby providing a sort of canine time signal from which longitude might be determined.'

'Just the one dog?' Goodricke had an image of dozens of dogs at sea, all yelping simultaneously.

'Surely this was meant as a parody. A satire?'

'I do not believe so. But there were so many others beyond reason, it was difficult to distinguish the serious from the silly.'

'Were there any that *were* reasonable, at least in principle?' asked Goodricke as he returned Jane Squire back to the shelf.

'Oh, yes, yes. The Reverend Whiston, who succeeded Newton as the Lucasian Professor of Mathematics, proposed a scheme relying on the variation of the dipping of the magnetic needle in a compass. Mr Edmund Halley determined that the magnetism across our globe is not uniform in its power and the degree of dipping is dependent upon the location of the compass. But this would require a much more detailed mapping of the magnetic variation and also some technique, never truly provided, to accurately calibrate and read this dipping.'

'I see. And what of Mr Harrison's clocks?'

Maskelyne immediately wondered whether this was the question Goodricke had been working up to all along.

'Ah. Harrison. You have heard of him.'

'Of course.'

'Most persistent,' said Maskelyne, the forefinger reappearing.

'Let me at once say I support the role of horology in astronomy. Anyone holding the title of Astronomer Royal will know that accurate timekeeping is critical to the execution of his duties. Nonetheless, any successful method of finding the longitude at sea must not only be correct, it must also be practical. His Majesty's navy currently consists of some two hundred ships of the line. And then there are the even more numerous merchant class vessels. Are we to put such a clock as Harrison's on board each? And, if we are to be prudent, should we not put two clocks on each vessel, lest one becomes faulty or damaged? This means hundreds of clocks of a quality and reliability that hardly anyone is capable of constructing, not to mention the cost. Indeed, Mr Harrison himself produced only very few clocks over the years. And now he has passed. Perhaps one day this will happen, but for now we must rely on such as this volume I have presented.'

The forefinger disappeared and Goodricke sensed that the subject was now closed.

'Let us proceed to the Octagon Room also known as the Great Room.'

They moved across into a magnificent space that was true to its name. The ceiling was close to fifteen feet in height. On six of the eight half-panelled walls were tall, elegant leaded windows. They could, in Goodricke's quick estimation, provide an astronomer a clear view of the Sun, Moon and planets, but there was only one telescope present and it was not fixed. It may have been gleaming brass and well made, but it seemed more of an affectation than a professionally used instrument. Moreover, this 'Great Room' did not have any purpose-built openings for a telescope. Goodricke did not have his compass with him, but was almost certain not one of these windows was south-facing.

'Reverend, this may seem an impertinent question, but what type of astronomy is this room used for?'

'At the moment, very little.'

'Was this not built for Flamsteed who performed meridian observations year after year? For that a south-facing window is necessary, yet this room does not appear to have one.'

'You are correct. It was constructed over the old foundations of Greenwich Castle as a needed cost saving. However, as you can see, the requirements of the practice of astronomy were not uppermost in the mind of its designer.'

'But was not Wren himself an astronomer?'

'Yes, but he was also an architect, and in the case of this building I believe it was the architect that spoke. How this building would be apprehended from below was perhaps a factor in its execution. It looks upon a complex with royal associations. It would not do well to then look up from there and see this building turned to one side, something it would have had to do to accommodate the purpose of a true observatory. Instead, it sits dutifully on this hill, showing its best face to the Queen's residence. I am not able to say this was indeed Wren's true purpose. I merely speculate.'

Goodricke recalled the view of the observatory on his approach. Perhaps it did have a certain correspondence with Queen Anne's former residence. Still, Flamsteed had to have worked from somewhere.

'But Flamsteed yet produced his magnificent atlas. His primary instrument, the transit, required an *exact* north-south alignment. The principal axis of this room does not possess such a condition. So, was not all this therefore useless to him?' said Goodricke, waving his hand about.

'You are correct. Flamsteed never worked from here. He was forced to set up his transit elsewhere, in hardly the best of conditions in a temporary structure no longer used. This room has played only a small role in the practice of astronomy, but a large one in the presenting its image. Perhaps that too is important.'

Goodricke had not expected any of this.

'Is this Mr Pigott who advances?' asked Maskelyne, looking out of one of the tall, narrow windows.

A lone figure was striding up the hill. His hat covered his face, but Goodricke would recognise that jaunty step anywhere.

'Let us go to greet him,' said Maskelyne.

They stepped into the forecourt as Pigott arrived.

'You were espied coming up the hill,' said Goodricke.

Pigott gave him a look as if to say, '*I was what?*'

Maskelyne looked askance at Goodricke and then spoke.

'Welcome Edward. And how does your Father, sir?'

'He is well, thank you. I trust my arrival is not inopportune?'

'No, indeed. I was just about to introduce Master Goodricke here to the working part of the observatory. You shall join us of course?'

'An honour, Reverend,' said Pigott, who began to think he may have arrived too early.

'Then come just this way across the forecourt. This was added by my predecessor, Mr Bradley,' said Maskelyne while gesturing at the building ahead.

Goodricke easily saw that its principal axis lay along a strict east-west line. Symmetrical in design, it had a two-storey central section with a single-storey wing on either side. Maskelyne led them to a central doorway leading into a corridor running the length of the building. To the left was the transit, to the right the quadrant room and directly ahead his assistant's working space. Before knocking, Maskelyne explained what they were about to see as if he was a sculptor unveiling a new work.

'Here you shall have some idea as to how the *Almanac* is produced. As I mentioned earlier to Master Goodricke, all required calculations are performed by a small group of assistants. But the initial data they work on must all flow from here. Come and meet the computer today in residence, Mr Charles Barton.'

Maskelyne gave the door a soft knock. Barton opened it and his hand reflexively went to his collar. He had removed his frock coat and cravat.

'Reverend! I was not expecting…'

'It is quite all right Barton. This is Mr Goodricke and Mr Pigott who hail from York and have come to visit.'

'Goodness. You have come a very long way indeed,' said Barton.

'Indeed, they have and they are most interested to learn of our work in producing the *Ephemeris*. Perhaps you could say a few words about what you are now working on?'

'Of course. Come in, gentlemen,' said Barton, his mind racing. Bloodshot eyes accentuated an ashen pallor. Ink stained cuffs and fingers gave the look of a drudge,

He hurriedly donned his frock coat, collected himself, looked around and gestured them towards a table piled with papers. Goodricke could not help but notice that on some of the pages there was no room left to add a single digit more. On the bookshelf were tables of logarithms, trigonometric functions and others all in the aid of mensuration. There were no general astronomy texts. A narrow stairway presumably led to sleeping quarters above. It was a small, self-contained world.

'Now, ah, let me see,' said Barton, groping for where to begin.

'Um, yes here. Now, yes, at the moment I am working on these lunar tables here for September of the coming year. We, myself and others, in a prescribed stepwise manner, compute the tables you see in the *Nautical Almanac and Ephemeris*. The numerous calculations required are made less arduous by using 'table look-ups', as they are referred to. The use of logarithmic tables of course means that we can avoid multiplication or division. My work for any one entry of a lunar distance in the *Almanac* shall use ten or more of these table-look ups and many more sexagesimal operations. We do not work in decimal notation. Now, yes, let me take you along the aforesaid stepwise path that results in the production of just one number for the lunar tables.'

Goodricke could not help but think the man an automaton. Pigott stifled a yawn.

Barton's explanation was long and leaden. At selected points in his narrative, he held up a page dense with figures in an attempt at some clarification. He was proud to conclude that all the calculations necessary to produce one number took only a few hours. Pigott tried, and failed, to hide his complete disinterest. Goodricke spotted a mouse run under the door to the quarters above. He imagined it to be Barton's sole companion, occasionally sallying forth towards dropped supper crumbs.

Maskelyne knew the prescribed algorithm by heart, inasmuch as he wrote it. His only real interest was to see whether Barton had assiduously followed it.

'Thank you indeed, Barton, and well said,' pronounced Maskelyne as the signal for departure. Goodricke gave a slight wave as the door closed and Barton disappeared to return to his calculations. *So*, thought Goodricke, *the main purpose of the Royal Observatory is the production of columns of figures, not astronomy as I practise it.*

'Let us now to the transit, just along here,' said Maskelyne.

Goodricke had seen transits before but was just as interested in the building, clearly purpose-built for the protection and use of this instrument.

'This instrument has been replaced since Bradley's time, but sits on the original blocks and is, of course, precisely aligned along the meridian,' offered Maskelyne, while giving it a loving tap.

'The Prime Meridian itself,' said Goodricke.

'Not to the French!' added Pigott.

'You are correct, Master Goodricke,' said Maskelyne, ignoring Pigott's comment. 'I trust you are aware of how a transit is employed?'

'Let me think,' said Goodricke. 'Well, first you note an object's height above the celestial equator at the time it is on the meridian. From this you note its right ascension and from there, one can then reduce the observations into data useful to others. Am I not correct?'

Pigott suppressed a smile on hearing his friend appropriate Maskelyne's signature phrase.

'Yes, you are...correct'

'But, of course, you understand why I cannot use such an instrument,' added Goodricke.

'Why ever not?'

'Its initial purpose is to mark the time an object crosses the meridian. In order to do this the observer notes the time on his clock to the second, but must then look away from it to reacquire the object in the transit eyepiece, all the while counting out the remaining seconds by listening to the ticking clock until the moment of transit. I am therefore unable to use one in the traditional manner.'

Pigott wondered whether this comment was really necessary.

'Of course, Master Goodricke. My apologies, sir.'

'Oh, not necessary.'

Pigott tried to soften the atmosphere.

'I should like to see Graham's mural quadrant, if I may.'

'Of course. Just here at the other end of the building.'

The quadrant was so-called because it was designed as one-quarter of a circle. The outer arc was finely graduated in degrees and its purpose was to measure the altitude of an astronomical object. Originally, mural quadrants were painted on the wall, hence the name. This one, however, had a graduated brass arc attached to the stone surface.

'The quadrant is perfectly aligned to its meridian plane?' asked Goodricke.

'Of course.'

'And its accuracy?'

'One second of arc.'

'This is a Bird quadrant is it not?'

'Correct.'

He stepped forward for a closer inspection of the degree marks.

'Ah, I see. The object's zenith distance is what is obtained and from there the declination can be found.'

Pigott stepped around to the opposite side of the pier to view another quadrant.

'This was Halley's quadrant, was it not?''

'Indeed, sir, it was.'

Pigott and Goodricke shared an awareness that what began as a scientific instrument was now a memorial.

After a moment, Pigott spoke.

'Between these two it must be possible to observe just about everything from here.'

'You are correct.'

He then noticed the nearby clock.

'That clock there,' said Pigott.

'Yes?'

'Who is the author?'

'That is the work of a local clockmaker, John Arnold. Do you know of him?'

'Of course.'

'Yes, his clocks are exceedingly accurate.'

'I believe Arnold has also made a copy of Harrison's number four?' asked Pigott.

'You are well informed. He did so as a result of my solicitation.'

Maskelyne may not be so narrow minded as some assume, thought Pigott. He clearly kept himself at the forefront of horology. He squared up and looked over at John.

'Well, if that clock is accurate I am afraid we must take our leave. The return journey will take some time and there may be a wait for a boat. I hope you do not take offence.'

'No, indeed, sir. Master Goodricke, it has indeed been a pleasure and again my congratulations.'

'Thank you, Reverend. You have been most kind. I trust we shall correspond?'

'I am sure of it, Master Goodricke.'

A few more pleasantries were made and Maskelyne stood by to watch them leave until they were out of view.

They walked down Greenwich Hill in silence. Finally, Pigott spoke.

'What is it you have there?'

'Ah, he gave me a copy of the *Almanac.*'

'Well, that about sums it up. What are your thoughts?'

'He is, well, different somehow, an odd mixture.'

'John, you may not recall, but in our first conversation I made it clear how astronomy can require drudgery.'

'I do so recall.'

'Take Barton. Good Lord, the poor wretch is working himself into a mere shadow. The hard truth is, though, the *Nautical Almanac* has likely prevented many a vessel from foundering.'

'I am sure any ship's captain would rather have it than not.'

'What else did you two discuss?'

'Harrison. He said something about his clock being too expensive a proposition.'

'But, as you have just seen, our Astronomer Royal does not entirely run anti-clockwise.'

'Very clever, Edward.'

'Were you at all disappointed?'

'Why would I be?'

'The word 'Royal' in its title does not necessarily make it the best equipped observatory in the land. I have not seen it myself, but I have heard the Earl of Macclesfield's observatory is the best equipped. And there is Hornsby's in Oxford, and Aubert's just nearby and of course our own in York. There is precious little that can be done from here that we cannot do. No, the Royal Observatory's real achievement is the *Nautical Almanac,* the result of Maskelyne's most diligent stewardship. But it is not too exciting in itself, is it?'

'No, I imagine not.'

Goodricke paused.

'You knew, didn't you?' he added.

'Knew what?'

'That I might be disappointed?'

'Let us just say I thought you might find it less interesting than expected because you practice an astronomy not quite so content to wallow in the tried and true.'

'Perhaps.'

'I do have one question.'

'Yes?'

'What was all that about when you made sure he understood you knew how a transit was used, but that you could not so employ it?'

'Oh, that.'

'Yes, that.'

'I am not sure, to be honest. Perhaps I felt he did not accept me as fully as a hearing person.'

'I understand what you are saying. At least I think I do, but John, never lose sight of one important fact.'

'And what is that, pray?'

'Maskelyne is on your side,' said Pigott as he hailed a boat heading upriver.

'I hope the tide is now well out,' said Goodricke.

The Dome and Dr Johnson

After another fortnight in London Goodricke became impatient to return home to York. He slept only fitfully. Even were he to remain awake to observe, the seeing conditions were impossible from Covent Garden. He knew they were better at Greenwich and likely from Aubert's observatory as well. He briefly considered asking permission to use either of them while in London, but thought to do so might be something of an imposition.

Goodricke read through Aubert's paper, *A New Method of Finding Time by Equal Altitudes*, before his visit so that he might ask an intelligent question or two. The man was no fool, and had more of a passing interest in exploring the occupants of the night sky. His observatory, with its typical Bird and Dollond instruments, was at least the equal of the Royal Observatory. Pigott was right about that. Perhaps its location on Loampit Hill just southwest of Greenwich Hill provided as many clear nights as he had in York. After visits to the observatories of others, he began to consider the possibility of having his own one day, but where?

London's attractions held little interest for him. There was much that he could not consider as entertainment in any case. The crowds that apparently gathered for public executions both puzzled and disturbed him. It also did not help when Pigott offered to loan him his copy of the *New Atlantis*, a guidebook to London prostitutes with addresses, physical characteristics and specialities. It was bothersome to learn how London sharpened their differences. Perhaps his coming visit with Samuel Johnson would improve his mood. But the desire to return home was there and he decided to do so after he met with Hannah and her parents. Even his enthusiasm for that was fading.

He had left his door open and Pigott appeared.

'Morning, squire.'

'Edward.'

Pigott stepped in and took a seat, hat in hand.

'So, what have we in store for today?'

'I have been meaning to visit St Paul's, so I shall do that this morning. Afterwards, I shall look to Mr Johnson. He is expecting me.'

'Of course. Forgot about that. You lucky devil. Should be interesting.'

'Which?'

'Either. They are both old and hard, full of mystery and meaning.'

'You are welcome to join me, you know.'

'Oh no, old boy. He is all yours. Besides, I have an appointment with some young ladies.'

'It seems you are the lucky devil.'

'Well, there's many who would drop the adjective. But there is a Handel Festival taking place and we shall take in this evening's performance at the Haymarket, with a fancy meal afterwards.'

'And who is the young lady? Or did you say ladies?'

'I did indeed! Sisters, actually. The daughters of Viscount Melville.'

'I do not know of him.'

'He allies with Pitt the Younger and is the Member of Parliament for Edinburgh.'

'It should be a lovely evening for you.'

'But my last here, I am afraid. I plan to return to York on tomorrow evening's mail coach. Pressing matters. Am I right in assuming you shall soon follow?'

Goodricke was not surprised to learn Pigott had decided to head off on his own. It was just his way. And Pigott was right about his own desire to return.

'Perceptive as usual, my friend. Yes, I shall soon follow. I just have one or two more visits to make.'

*

Later that morning Goodricke hired a sedan chair as Pigott had advised and made his way to St Paul's. The four bearers stepped in unison to minimise any rocking motion whilst shouting at others to 'make way, make way'. The sedan chair was a convenient way of traveling through London. He could not imagine how a woman wearing a corked rump or high coiffure could fit, or sit, in one.

They reached the front steps and a bearer smartly opened the small door. Immediately he stepped out he leaned back to absorb the height and breadth of the façade. He asked the bearers to wait while staring up at the Classical portico surmounted by a colonnade and above that, a pediment holding the sculpted relief of the conversion of St Paul, two hundred eighty feet above. All of this, framed by two towers, implied a massive structure beyond. The immensity he beheld upon entering induced deference unlike York Minster's liberating spirituality. It was a masterpiece of Wren's creative power.

He walked along the nave until directly beneath the dome. Apparently, there was a walkway around its base indicated by a few faces looking down at him. A small sign by a doorway indicated the way above and, after one hundred and sixty-four spiralling stone steps, he emerged at the base of the dome. From this perspective, the eight murals depicting the spiritual journey of St Paul decorating the dome interior came into sharp clarity. He looked down at the starburst mosaic on the cathedral floor and realised its extent was best appreciated from this vantage point. A bench ran along the base of the dome wall. He sat there for a while, contemplated its structure and came to a conclusion as to its design.

A mother and young daughter, smiling and slightly out of breath, entered and joined him on the walkway.

'Good day, sir,' said the woman in acknowledgement.

'It is magnificent, is it not?' she said, unable to take her eyes away from the dome's murals.

'I believe it has the profile of a cubical catenoid,' said Goodricke, eager to share his small discovery.

She returned a puzzled look.

'I am not sure of your meaning, sir, but it is beautiful all the same.'

She then leaned down, cupped her hands over her daughter's ear and spoke. Immediately the child excitedly ran halfway around the base of the dome, stopped and waved with enthusiasm, barely visible behind the protective railing. Her mother then turned and spoke, her face just inches from the dome wall. Goodricke could not quite make out what she was saying, but thought the last word might have been 'arms'. She then turned to look across at her daughter who had by now stood on the stone bench and raised her arms well up. She then turned to the wall to whisper her own instructions, prompting her mother to wave her arms as well.

What just happened? He then understood. The circular base of the dome was so carefully constructed a whisper made against its walls could be heard from the side opposite. This rare acoustic quirk would be a pleasant discovery for anyone, but not for him. It produced an unexpected and newly experienced distress over his deafness. He returned to the cathedral floor and briskly walked the length of the nave to the waiting sedan chair.

*

A short time later he arrived at number 8 Bolt Court just off Fleet Street, paid the bearers and, hoping he had the right address, knocked. An elegantly dressed young Negro answered.

'I am John Goodricke come for Mr Johnson.'

'Yes, John. I am Francis Barber and attend to Mr Johnson. Welcome.'

Goodricke thought it unusual for a servant to give their name.

Barber stepped aside and motioned for Goodricke to enter.

'Please come through.'

He led Goodricke into a nearby parlour.

'Mr Johnson has already explained that you cannot hear, but are yet able to speak.'

'Um, yes. That is so. For the most part.'

'Please, take a seat here. Mr Johnson shall be with you directly.'

As he began to leave he turned back to Goodricke.

'I thought you might wish to know you occupy a seat of some privilege.'

Goodricke returned a puzzled look.

'I do not take your meaning, sir.' He realised he had added 'sir' while addressing a servant, but this one somehow compelled it.

'Mr Johnson rarely has visitors, his abode now more of a sanctuary than ever.'

'Mr Goodricke.'

Samuel Johnson stood in the doorway, his bollard-tapping stick in hand.

'Some tea to the study if you will, Barber.'

'As you wish.'

Goodricke cleared his throat and spoke.

'Dr Johnson it is an honour and a pleasure to see you again. I thank you for accepting my request for an audience.'

'Indeed so, and it is good to see you as well, young Goodricke, but I am not a king and this is not my court.'

Goodricke was tongue-tied and said the first thing that came to mind.

'Your manservant is rather unusual.'

'In manner or appearance?'

'Perhaps more in manner, sir.'

'Francis is not a manservant as such. Perhaps that explains his manner and his appearance.'

Goodricke thought of Cicero and wondered whether Barber had trod a similar path.

Johnson had not aged well. One eye was almost closed and the other rheumy. There was a laboured breathing and the right side of his wig, oddly enough, appeared to have been burnt. He seemed more ragged, more tired than the man he had met all those years ago.

'It is good to see you again, sir.'

Johnson waved him off and stood.

'We shall not get very far if you keep repeating yourself. How long has it been? Ten years? Eleven? You have done well I understand.'

'Sir?'

'The Copley medal, lad.'

'Yes sir, thank you.'

Am I now famous? wondered Goodricke.

'Mr Braidwood must be proud.'

'Yes, sir, I expect so,' said Goodricke, wondering whether Braidwood knew. He realised, at that moment, he had likely underestimated the award's significance.

'It was my great good fortune to have been his student, but you helped as well.'

'I?'

'Your dictionary - the one you had sent to the academy. I read it no end.'

'Did you now? Hmm. Let us go to my study and have a proper discussion.'

Goodricke wondered whether he was up to whatever it was Johnson meant by this.

As they entered Johnson pointed to a chair with his walking stick. The bookshelves could not accept a single volume more. Papers were piled everywhere. It was a place of work.

Has this all been ill-planned? He had not thought through what to discuss with someone who was clearly an intellectual superior. Perhaps not in astronomy, but certainly in matters of the world, of life.

'I do not recall all the other students of that day, but I do remember you. Tell me about yourself Goodricke. How have you been faring?'

'Well, as I mentioned in my letter, I have been working on some problems in astronomy.'

'Stop,' said Johnson, waving his stick as if he were knocking disagreeable words out of the air.

'Not really interested in astronomy today. Nor tomorrow. I want to know how *you* have been getting on.'

'I am well, sir.'

Johnson simply stared. Goodricke imagined gears spinning in his brain.

'You are well you say? How can you be well, for I fear you spend a great deal of time goggling at the stars and little else? Hmm?'

Goodricke had not expected a sudden inquisition. Damn Pigott for saying this would be a good idea.

'Sir, I assure you…'

'Assure me? There is very little you can assure *me* of, young man.' Johnson's impatience had grown with age and, on days like today, it was worse when his gout flared.

Goodricke struggled to interpret Johnson's mood. This was not someone given to idle chat. He was asking why he had become who he had become. He was interested in his thoughts of the world he had grown up in. He would not the least bit interested in Algol, but perhaps astronomy might be a starting point?

'I can tell you how I have been if you will permit me to tell you why I take to the study of the stars.'

'It may be a start, but remember that half the truth is often a whole lie.'

314

'There are two reasons. First it is because I am deaf. The lack of hearing does little to slow my study of the heavens. I am sure there are other pursuits where it is an encumbrance, but I see it an asset in those astronomical.'

'Hmm. And your second reason?'

Goodricke hesitated and chose his words carefully, but not carefully enough.

'It is, I confess, a welcome distraction from what I have experienced of the world. I am not given to conflict or harsh words, but there is much that is disheartening. I do not possess the position or the ability to declare meaningful opposition. So, astronomy is, as I say, a distraction from the sufferings of the lower orders.'

'Lower orders? Lower than whom? But never mind that. What interests me is that you said distraction when I believe you meant diversion.'

'Sir?'

'Do you not see the distinction? The former is an activity that turns your attention away from something you wish to study whilst a diversion channels your attention to something else you may well prefer to concentrate on. They are not the same. Do you follow? You hesitate, young Goodricke. Let me place my query in other terms. Does your astronomy divert your attention from the conditions of society or does it distract you from them?'

'I am not sure of the distinction, as you say, sir.'

Johnson sighed and renewed his explanation.

'It is simple enough. As a distraction, the stars turn the mind from the *intended* concern but as a diversion they steer you to another path not wholly undesirable. I do not believe you wish to attend to the problems of society. Rather, as you confess, you seek the stars to avoid them. It is your diversion, not your distraction. Or am I in error?'

Goodricke wondered whether there was indeed a meaningful distinction. He had the disturbing thought that his confusion lay in the fact that what was once a distraction had *become* a diversion. He had developed a tough outer shell, like an insect's carapace.

He lowered his head and then looked back at Johnson. First, there was that episode in St Paul's, and now this. It was not a good day.

'Permit my ignorance, but it sounds like you lead a solitary life.'

Goodricke felt this needed defending.

'My work, sir, if properly pursued, fairly demands it.'

'No, no, you need not protest. I see in you a proper circumstance.'

'Sir?'

'If one is idle, be not solitary. If one is solitary, be not idle. You are the latter, are you not? And that is all to the good.'

'Sir, I have not thought on it.'

Johnson saw his guest's discomfort.

'Young Goodricke, you are little different from any young man all at sea in society and whose ideals are dashed on its dreaded rocks. You may be unique in your ability to flee to the domain of the stars, but are learning that you must remain, despite this, a passenger on our little planet as she whirls about. Take care, though, that you do not become the cynick. Therein lies the greater load.'

'I do not follow, sir.'

Goodricke was beginning to think he could not keep up with this man.

'Cynick. Did you not capture that word?'

'I did, sir.'

'I thought you read my dictionary. The word is there.'

'Indeed, sir! I did not read it from A to Z of course, but found it most useful in my training by Mr Braidwood. I wish I had the volume to hand now.'

Johnson smiled for the first time since he had arrived.

'There is one just there,' he said, pointing with his stick.

Goodricke stepped over to the dictionary laying on a lectern, being much too massive to hold. The rich brown leather and heavy cream-coloured paper brought back moments at the academy. He turned the pages to 'cynick' and read aloud.

> *'Cynick. Noun. Singular. From the Greek κύνικοσ. A philosopher of the snarling or currish sort; a flower of Diogenes; a rude man; a snarler; a misanthrope.'*

Goodricke instantly thought not of himself, but of Pigott. Was any of this his friend?

'There are several possible applications here, sir. All seem clear save one.'

He returned to his seat.

'Their application to what? Or should I say to whom?'

Goodricke had never met anyone with quite this level of mental acuity. He may have looked a heap, but his mind was formidable.

'Perhaps we might expand on the meaning of a flower of Diogenes. I do not follow this inclusion.'

'You are familiar with Diogenes?'

'He was a Greek of the fourth or fifth century BC who was the author of this school of thought, was he not?'

'The fourth. And what are its core values?'

'I, ah prefer to hear these from you.'

This was all the stimulation Johnson needed.

'To a cynick, happiness depends utterly on being self-sufficient. This means an opposition to all convention. It is a mental attitude. The adherent will disassociate himself from any influence that may fetter in any way the expression of his individual freedom.'

Johnson paused to see whether he was understood and raised an eyebrow.

'I follow, sir. So far.'

'Some think, mistakenly so, that the cynick has an indifference to wealth or success. It is not enough to say he is untroubled by the gaining or the losing of these. He bears them an uncompromising hostility.'

'The cynick therefore cares not for awards, or accolades?'

'No, indeed! The cynick wants *nothing* to do with inherited status, class, rank, honours, reputation. It is life stripped of all convention. His happiness derives from the mastery and kingdom of his own will and mind. Is this you? Is this your aspiration?'

'No sir. At least I do not believe so.'

'Hmm.'

'Is not then a cynick but a simple hermit, an ascetic?'

'No, he is not. That is a facile interpretation. The cynick lives fully within the culture he condemns. He uses confrontations with it to sharpen his philosophy and also to live as an exemplar. His philosophy cannot be taught in any conventional school and therefore he must live as an example to others.'

'Do you know of any?'

Johnson gave a wry smile.

'Well, some might have said it of *me*, but this is untrue. It can be said of cynicks they are characterised by a fearless freedom of speech marked by a mordant wit and repartee. *That* surely has been said of me, but, no, I have not been without a desire to succeed.'

'Do you regret this?'

'I do not.'

'But why, sir?'

'Surely you see the layers of impoverishment in our society are not to be removed by the dogma of the cynick.'

'But do they not reject the pursuit of rewards that when vigorously pursued by others results in conditions leading to the poverty of many?'

'True. But in and of itself their philosophy is not enough. It is too self-contained, They, like the rich, can pursue their aims whilst also ignoring the plight of the poor.'

'Can one be a cynick and not know of it?'

'I am doubtful. A true cynick will want to evangelise.'

Well, whatever Pigott is, he is no cynick, thought Goodricke. And, for that matter, neither was he. Nonetheless, it did bother him that he had to stop and think about it.

'So, my young man, what is most important to you, hmm? I mean to ask, what have you come to determine is the most import thing in this life?'

Goodricke could hardly believe he had heard this. He remembered how easy it was to declare what this was to Pigott. Why was it so hard to do so now?

'I think it is to have a problem to work on - something to occupy one's mind to the fullest.'

Johnson stared and, after an unbearable silence, spoke.

'I believe you are right in that. I believe you are right, indeed, although I have said it differently.'

'Sir?'

'To strive with difficulties and to conquer them is the highest human felicity.'

'Yes, sir.'

There was a knock and Barber entered with a tray.

'Tea, sir. Will there be anything else?'

'No, not until we dine. Thank you, Francis.'

'Very good, Mr Johnson.'

'He intrigues you, does he not?'

'I confess he does. Would it be too bold of me to ask how he arrived?'

'Francis is from Jamaica. He was the son of a house slave. My friend who aided in his arrival would say I had need of one even less than Diogenes. He was brought to me to compensate at least one man for the injustice of slavery. But never mind all this. Please explain the work you have done leading to this Copley award.'

*

Edward Pigott was in a good mood. He had the company of two handsome women and was looking forward to the performance. He wasn't necessarily a fan of cantatas or even Handel, for that matter, but *Ode for St. Cecilia's Day*, celebrating the role of music in the creation of the universe, had some appeal. And, as an evening's entertainment, it was as good as any.

Herschel was spotted almost immediately on entering the theatre lobby.

'William. It is Edward. Edward Pigott.'

'Of course.'

Herschel was immediately reminded of Pigott's letter, but the cheerful greeting suggested no ill will remained.

'May I introduce Hermione and her sister Hyacinth, daughters of Viscount Melville. This is Mr William Herschel. Composer and astronomer.'

'A composer of astronomy? That sounds most interesting, sir,' said the more flirtatious Hermione. No one bothered to correct her and Pigott did not think it all that far off in any case.

'And permit me to introduce my sister Caroline and Lady Pitt,' said Herschel.

Edward acknowledged them with a smile.

'So, William, I understand that you have left Bath and located to Datchet. All is well I trust?'

'Indeed, sir. I am now working on a new telescope. It…'

Edward interrupted.

'And Caroline, are you well?'

'I am, sir.'

Pigott could barely hear her.

'And have you continued performing? I am sure you can produce an aria that is the equal of anything we are about to enjoy.'

Caroline could only look at the floor.

Lady Pitt placed the tip of her fan on her chin, stared at Pigott and then Herschel.

'Come, William, or we shall be late for the performance.'

The little assembly broke up, the touching of a fan to the chin the code to end conversation.

Pigott and his companions entered the theatre and were escorted to their seats. The audience sat in relative darkness while the orchestra's area was illuminated by the new Argand burners arranged along the front of the stage to better illuminate sheet music.

Handel's music gradually pulled him in. The third aria, tender and poignant, filled the firmament with a meaning he never thought it to have.

Vigorous syncopated orchestral and choral textures followed, tendrils of sound winding out into the dim distance, an accompaniment to some endless yearning. He thought of his friend for whom such an experience was never possible and hoped he'd had as good a day, in his own way.

32

Vauxhall Gardens

'Cicero, do you have a moment?'

Eleanor Dalrymple stood in the doorway to the back garden.

'A letter has arrived from Master Goodricke,' she said.

She stepped into the garden and sat at the edge of a bench. Cicero sat at the other end.

'He sends his regards to us both. He also asks something of you, Cicero. Would you please prepare two or three detailed drawings of some plants? What does he mean by this? Do you draw, Cicero?'

She paused, hoping against hope.

'He is well?'

Eleanor, moved beyond measure, could barely choke out a reply.

'Yes, Cicero. He is well.'

He tried not to notice as she blinked away her tears.

*

'I am nervous, papa.'

'But why should you be, my dear? You hardly know the fellow,' replied Thomas Upton.

He felt there was no need for anxiety. Goodricke could not possibly be the sort to reject her company out of hand merely because she was deaf, was he?

A casual evening had been planned at Vauxhall Gardens. Sir Thomas and his wife Caroline would accompany them. They shared a small unspoken hope that this might possibly be someone who could care for Hannah.

A maid entered.

'A gentleman has arrived for Miss Hannah, your grace.'

Upton had explained once before that he was not 'your grace', but now was not the time for a correction.

'Show him in.'

Goodricke slowly stepped in. Caroline and Hannah were seated with Sir Thomas standing by them.

He extended his hand.

'Sir Thomas.'

'Well, John Goodricke. It is indeed a pleasure and an honour to have you here. This is my wife Caroline - and I believe you already know Hannah.'

'Lady Upton, a pleasure. How are you, Hannah?'

Goodricke nervously fingered the brim of his cocked hat as he took in her beauty. This was a young woman before him, not the child he knew in Edinburgh.

Hannah thought Goodricke displayed a curious mixture of compassion and coolness.

'John, how good it is to see you again, after all this time,' said Hannah as she extended her gloved hand, palm down.

Goodricke missed half her words. He took her hand with a brief nod.

The maid returned as if on cue with a tray of sherry. Upton passed the glasses around.

'I believe a toast is appropriate, but am not sure to whom or to what,' he said in a jocular manner.

'Mr Bwaidwood?' said Hannah.

'Excellent choice, Hannah. To Mr Braidwood, then.' said Sir Thomas.

They drain their glasses.

'Have you been enjoying your stay in London?' asked Caroline.

'I have met some interesting people at the Royal Society, but on the whole, London is rather overwhelming, is it not?'

'Samuel Johnson has written a rather clever line that says when a man is tired of London he is tired of life,' said Sir Thomas.

'Had I known I would have asked him about that sentiment. I am not sure I would agree.'

'I do not quite follow,' said Sir Thomas.

'I called on him at his home in Bolt Court just yesterday. A most interesting and intriguing fellow, I must say.'

Sir Thomas and Caroline exchanged glances.

'Indeed?' said Caroline.

'Yes. We shared a rewarding discussion. He is of a superior intellect, but unfamiliar with matters scientific.'

Sir Thomas was at a loss for words.

This lad's youthful appearance makes him easy to underestimate, he thought.

Caroline smiled broadly.

'Hannah may recall he visited when we were with Mr Braidwood,' added Goodricke.

'Is that right Hannah?' asked her mother.

Hannah's eyes widened.

'Oh yes! The dictionawy man!'

'So, my own daughter has met him as well?' asked Sir Thomas, looking at Hannah.

'He came to visit Mr Bwaidwood shortly after I ahwived. A most odd fellow.'

More polite discussion followed when Sir Thomas decided it was time to leave them alone for a while, as he and his wife had planned.

'Well, John, Caroline and I shall let you two, um, fill in the last years. Hannah will let us know when we can all leave, but not too late mind. It promises to be a lovely evening.'

'Thank you, papa,' Hannah said.

He escorted Caroline out and Goodricke wondered whether he was now part of some plan regarding Hannah. He chose a chair, rather than share the settee.

'John, can you understand me when I speak?'

While she could understand him easily enough, he had to admit it would help if she signed as well. He thought it ironic that the inability to understand another deaf person pushed him deeper into his own deafness.

'It has been some time since I have used signing. But I am sure I can recall it well enough with your help.'

'I can speak, sign and fingerspell as well. Between them I hope to be understood,' she said

'You need not speak. I can understand your signing. I still remember how to use it.'

'Thank you, I shall speak as well to keep in practice.'

'Of course.'

'It has been a long time has it not?' signed Hannah.

'Ten years?'

'Odd, though.'

'What is odd, Hannah?'

'The manner by which we meet again.'

'I do not understand.'

'It was through that chance encounter at the tea garden with those two men. I am not sure, to be honest, I would have ever written you had that not happened, but I thought you ought to know about it.'

'But how did you know where I was?'

'Oh, that was no problem. Papa found out easily enough.'

'It must have been awful for you.'

'What was?'

'That experience in the tea garden.'

'At first. But I feel better for it.'

'How so?'

'Stronger. I feel stronger,' signed Hannah, with a bit more vigour.

'I am glad of it, Hannah.'

Goodricke was conflicted about asking for more details, but had to ask.

'What was your father's reaction?'

'He was furious when I told him what happened. He met with that fellow Banks, but I really do not know much more. Nor do I wish to. It is all done with now.'

They both sensed talk of that episode was not enough to fill ten years of separation.

'I remember you, you know. But you took little notice of me,' said Hannah.

Goodricke looked down, an admission.

'I understand you are doing well. Papa mentioned something about this medal. I do not understand it, but it does sound rather important.'

'Not without your assistance.'

The allusion did not go unnoticed.

'I am sure you did not need my help.'

'How have you been getting on yourself?' he asked.

'I am blessed to have caring parents and for knowing Mr Braidwood as well,' she signed.

'That seems so long ago, now.'

'Yes, but unforgettable all the same. It changed all of us. Do you not agree?'

'Of course.'

She wore a mischievous expression.

'John do you remember Rose Ballantyne?' she said, fingerspelling the name.

'She was one of the students with me who addressed Mr Johnson, as I recall.'

'Was she not more than that?'

'What do you mean?'

'It was known by all you fancied her.'

Hannah had prodded a distant memory of how he once regarded Rose from afar. It was, at the time, a new emotion carrying him to some unknown destination. In the end, he did little and said less.

'I was young, Hannah. We were all young. And we lived closely together,' as if some excuse was needed.

'John, I am only teasing, please do not be upset, but I am glad you did not end up marrying her.'

'We were but children, Hannah, why ever would you say that?'

Hannah just smiled and shrugged and Goodricke realised he was being a little too prickly.

'What has become of Mr Braidwood? Do you know anything?'

'Oh yes! He has moved his academy here, to London. Did you not know?'

'I did not, but am glad to learn that others continue to benefit from his work.'

'I am sure of it. Priscilla and I were thinking of going to visit. You remember her do you not? Or maybe she arrived after you left. She was with me in the tea garden that day and we talked of going to Hackney where he now is. It would be lovely if you would join us.'

'Perhaps someday, but I wish to return to York soon.'

'Of course,' signed Hannah after some hesitation.

'Tell me, what is your life like there? How do you spend the day?'

'I sleep, most of the time.'

Hannah returned a quizzical look.

'You sleep? But that is of little achievement. Are you unwell?'

'No, no. I am often awake until the dawn as is anyone who studies the stars.'

'Is that important to you?'

Goodricke often wondered why the lure and wonder of the night sky needed explaining.

'It is to me. And to others.'

An awkward pause.

'But what else?'

'I am not sure that I follow you.'

'I mean besides your star-gazing,' she signed with a smile.

'Very little. There is not the time.'

He changed the subject.

'Hannah, what is it like for you?'

'What is what like, John?'

'To be deaf.'

She returned a puzzled look.

'But you know. Why do you ask?'

'I was wondering if it was the same for you. That is all.'

She reflected for a moment.

'I have often likened it to being in a glass jar. The world outside is visible and beautiful, at times. You can see it clearly but cannot completely connect with it. Sometimes I forget this glass wall is there. But then I come up against it and remember. People on the outside often do not see me. To them the jar is empty. Do you not feel the same?'

Goodricke had never thought of his own deafness in quite that way. He doubted that she had ever accepted deafness as an advantage as he had.

'No, I do not. I must confess that sometimes I believe I am glad I cannot hear. No, that is not true. I mean to say that let us suppose I was able to hear. I should think there would be times that I would wish for the ability to shut out all sound. Just as you can close your eyes and be blind I might wish there to be some way to shut out all sound when I wanted to.'

'That is a strange thing to say, but what of the opposite that is the actual case?'

'I do not follow.'

'In your current state has there not been any moment, any one single moment, when you wished you could hear some sound, any sound? Never once?'

He thought of his experience at St Paul's, but the revelation it brought was too new, too raw. He was not sure exactly why he had reacted the way he did, but he knew something had changed, a new secret to be kept.

'I study the stars. I need not have my ears for that.'

'If you do nothing else then yes, perhaps you need not hear. But…'

She paused in her signing.

'But what?'

'I wonder whether you might be unhappy.'

This was no longer teasing and her comment jarred. Conversing with Samuel Johnson had been easier.

'I do not know that I am.'

'It is enough that one is unhappy, but worse when one does not know it.'

'Hannah, why do say this? You hardly know me.'

'Please forgive me. But you seem to prefer York, so you resist change. You seem to try too hard in your work and I see that you are proud. These things are barriers to happiness, are they not?'

Goodricke had not known what to expect from seeing Hannah again, but this was all too personal, too soon.

'What about you Hannah? Are you happy?'

Hannah suddenly stood and took a step or two.

'I am sorry not so much for myself but for my parents, for papa.'

Goodricke glanced out of a window and saw her parents walking in the garden.

'Why?'

'He is worried that no man will take me as a wife because of my deafness.'

Goodricke thought of their meeting just now. Had her father seemed overly solicitous?

'I am sorry, Hannah.'

'There are times I think a solution would be to marry another also deaf. But then who would teach our children how to speak? My thoughts go all a-swirl and I become confused and tired.'

'Hannah, I do not know what to say.'

'I have strayed too far beyond mere pleasantries. But then, I think neither of us has the time for those.'

'Perhaps not.'

'Anyway, it is a lovely day and I do look forward to Vauxhall Gardens. Have you been?'

Goodricke brightened somewhat.

'No, no. I have not.'

'Have you seen *any* pleasure garden here in London?'

'No.'

'Oh, but you must! There is all manner of unusual sights!'

'Well then, let us go.'

*

They were all silent as the landau carried them towards the Thames. The view was not especially compelling along Great Swallow Street but improved as they rolled through St. James' Park. With its magnificent specimen trees and a great pond stocked with pelicans and other waterfowl, it provided a brief moment when they could believe they were passing through a countryside estate.

A boat awaited at the bottom of Whitehall Stairs. *Of course*, thought Goodricke. *Sir Thomas would never chance a tilt boat.* They sat in cushioned seats and were rowed upstream to Vauxhall Stairs on the south bank. As they disembarked Goodricke detected a new odour mixing with the others comprising London's feculence.

At the top of the stairs he saw why - Fasset & Burnett's Vinegar Manufactory was just nearby. It triggered a memory of his illness with scarlet fever. He hoped this tea garden visit would erase this sudden recollection.

They came to the grand entrance of the Vauxhall Pleasure Garden, London's largest and most popular. The landscape was unlike anything else Goodricke had seen or could even imagine. They entered into a lively, frolicsome atmosphere. It did not take long to see that social codes dictating whom one could mix with were suspended once one stepped inside it. It was an experience of mass entertainment.

'Let us proceed a little further along to sample the sights and later we shall return to the supper-box we have reserved.'

'What is a supper-box?' asked Goodricke.

'Places to dine John. Do you see them just there? They are outside, but private spaces all the same,' said Caroline.

She gestured ahead towards the boxes situated along a sinuous colonnade lining the walkway on either side.

She continued.

'They are also places to see and be seen, rather like a theatre box. I do believe see Samuel Johnson attends on occasion. He used to come, anyway. The boxes do not open until nine when the gardens become dark enough to become illuminated. It is all quite a spectacle, I must say.'

As they moved further into the grounds they passed pavilions in classical, gothic and *chinoiserie* styles. Exotic plants included Gingko trees, chusan palms and bamboo. Interplay between the built and the planted was styled to immerse visitors in a dreamlike, other worldly space.

One of these novel structures reminded Goodricke of the Pigott's observatory when he saw, on closer inspection, that it was an octagonal bandstand. He then spotted a statue of Handel at what appeared to be the centre of the gardens and realised that music must be at the at the very heart of its entertainments. It had not escaped him how Sir Thomas and his wife were subtly steering them away from one musical attraction after another as they walked along. *This must be quite an experience with sound*, a thought he kept to himself.

They stopped and gathered to study an elaborately painted sign; *de Loutherbourg's Amazing Eidophusikon* imploring one and all to enter and witness the wreck of the *Halswell*.

'The sign says the next show will soon start. Shall we chance it?' asked Sir Thomas.

No one had any idea what an *Eidophusikon* was, but 'why not?' became the general consensus. It did not seem to entirely rely on the ability to hear.

They entered a semi-darkened theatre space that soon filled. The curtains opened to reveal a stage far too small for any kind of live performance. Goodricke thought it seemed a lot of fuss for a poorly lit painting until he realised the image before them held real three-dimensionality, an ocean scene with rolling waves. It was an automated miniature theatre complete with special effects.

Gradually the sky somehow darkened and the sea became more animated. From behind the rocks at the left the *Halswell* appeared in full sail under painted stars. The whole scenario was uncannily realistic. About two-thirds of the way across the *Halswell* foundered and sank from view accompanied by gasps from a startled audience. Goodricke suspected there was very likely some auditory accompaniment. He could not help but think this was yet another experience diminished by his lack of hearing.

After they stepped back outside they all agreed it was quite unlike anything they had ever seen.

'What did you think of that then?' signed Hannah.

'It was interesting on the whole, but the stars were all wrong.'

'John! Is there not one ounce of poetry in you?'

'Well, they were.'

'Perhaps you might write a letter of complaint to Mr Loutherbourg.'

'Perhaps I shall.'

Hannah noticed her parents a few steps ahead, placed her hand on his arm and stopped.

'John, forget Mr Loutherbourg, or whatever his name is. Write to *me*. Will you promise me that?'

Her signing was now slower, emotional.

'Of course. Of course, I will.'

She paused and looked around for a moment as if making a decision.

'You might not be able to read my lips that well, John, but surely you can feel them.'

Hannah kissed him briefly so as not to attract attention, but long enough, nonetheless. He felt as if everyone was staring. It was as if he had become, in that instant, Vauxhall's newest attraction. He was about to summon something to say when she placed her fingers on his lips and a forefinger to her own.

Hannah's mother had turned at the precise moment to see her daughter's display of affection. She did not point it out to Sir Thomas.

'Dusk approaches, shall we proceed to our supper box?' she said.

Sir Thomas spoke Shortly after they were seated.

'Ah, the whistle has sounded.'

'The what?'

'The whistle, John. It is to announce that the lamps are about to be lit.'

The first whistle was the signal for lamp-lighters to hurry to their allotted stations. At the second whistle, they lit pre-set cotton-wool fuses to guide the flame from one oil-lamp to another and another. Fifteen thousand lamps simultaneously burst into flame. The effect was staggering. Goodricke thought, at that moment, Vauxhall Gardens could well compete with his stars as a diversion.

33

Return

'Master Goodricke! You have returned!'

'Mrs Dalrymple.'

Goodricke had not quite reached the stairs before Eleanor had spotted him. She surveyed him up and down, hands on hips.

'Did they not feed you in London? You are all anatomy, I am sure. And how is it you arrive in the morning?'

She always had a way of making him feel caught out.

'I travelled on the overnight mail coach. A bit tiring.'

'I shouldn't wonder!'

'Well, lovely to see you, Mrs Dalrymple, but I must to my bed now.'

'No, no. Leave your bags. I shall have Emeline take the clothing for a proper clean first. I'll have her carry them up later.'

Goodricke had one foot on a step, but paused.

'How has Cicero been keeping?'

'He is well. He is, we, were a bit curious about that mention of drawings in your letter.'

'Oh, yes. An inspired thought. There is no urgency.'

'He did ask after you.'

It took Goodricke a moment to understand the implications of what was said.

'That...that is most extraordinary Mrs Dalrymple. Indeed. Most extraordinary, but please excuse me now.'

Eleanor called up after him as he ascended, a fruitless action.

'We shall see you for the evening meal shall we not? I shall instruct Cook to prepare something special.'

Later that afternoon, Emeline carried his clothes upstairs. The door was open and she peeked in. Goodricke was fast asleep. She placed them at the foot of the bed and reflexively tiptoed out. Goodricke slept through the evening meal-time and all through the night.

The next morning, he suffered Eleanor's stares. She did not have to say anything, but his hearty appetite for breakfast eased her concern.

'Is Cicero about?' he asked as he pushed away a bowl scoured free of porridge.

'In the back garden, I believe. You must see what he has accomplished!'

'And what is that then?'

'He has begun to restore the small greenhouse that was in some disrepair. He says he wants to grow orchids. Wait here and I shall fetch him.'

Goodricke suspected Cicero would grow orchids in order to draw them.

Eleanor returned with a somewhat bewildered Cicero.

'Cicero, why don't you join Master Goodricke and I shall brew up some tea. Help yourself to bread and jam on the table.'

Cicero looked back at Eleanor for confirmation.

'Go on, Cicero, sit.'

The other residents had left for the day. He wondered if she would have invited him in had they still been there.

'Master Goodricke. You are well? Missus say you wan' see me?'

'It is good to see you, Cicero, but I would think that it would be *you* who wanted to speak with *me*, Cicero.'

'Why that?'

'Because of my request for drawings from you - that I would like some fine drawings of plants. The best you can do.'

'I remember, but why I never know. You wan' dem for your room?'

'No, no, not for me. Let us just say for now I have a good reason. I know that you have drawings, but I was thinking of something new - in your best watercolours.'

'Dem finish.'

'I can easily supply you with more. So, will you do this for me?'

'No problem, mon.'

Eleanor returned with a fresh pot of tea and left them to speak.

Goodricke leaned forward.

'I understand something has changed since I have been away has it not? Why, Cicero?'

'I no know. She always kind, and anyway, being angry all the time, it just make me tired.'

'Yes, Cicero, I believe it would.'

'But why you want me drawings?'

'I have good reason, but would rather not say at the moment. You will learn it soon enough.'

'All secret then? Sure. I will do some more watercolour. Maybe I do one of an orchid, but must it soon come?'

'No, not soon. An orchid would be perfect. One more thing, Cicero.'

'What that?'

'My clock needs to be set again. Can you help me with that?'

'Yeah, mon.'

'Well, that is all settled then. Let us enjoy some of this lovely jam.'

*

A few days after returning Goodricke began to feel the comfort of his old routine. He was just stepping out to visit Edward when Emeline met him at the bottom of the stairs.

'Post for you Master Goodricke. Just arrived.'

'Thank you, Emeline.'

'No trouble, sir.'

He took the unopened letter with him. He had not yet seen Edward since his return and wanted to discuss ideas for observations. Edward may not have fully shared his passion for astronomy, but he nonetheless had more observing ideas than the time to pursue them. The high cirrus clouds suggested a clear night of observing ahead.

'It looks like things are getting back to normal', he thought, with a skip in his step.

'Good afternoon, Phillipa. Is Edward about?'

'Master Goodricke. I believe he is in his usual spot, and welcome back, sir.'

'Thank you, Phillipa.'

He detected the scent of Bayberry. The rebellion in the Colonies was officially over with the signing of the Treaty of Paris ten months earlier and Anna had wasted no time in replenishing her stock of candles.

He found Pigott sitting, as usual, against the wall of the observatory, enjoying his cider. It was that time of day.

'Goodricke, good sir. When did you return?'

He held up the jug and Goodricke waved it off.

'Two days. It has taken some time to reacquaint myself with York.'

'I think you mean to become reacquainted with yourself in York.'

Goodricke had to take a moment to process the distinction.

'Yes, you may be right there.'

'Of course, I am right. How was the rest of your stay?'

'Well, if we are to keep to your point of view, then you should be asking whether I liked myself in London. Not the same thing as liking London.'

'*Exactement,* as our French cousins say. But seriously, did you not like London?'

'Pleasant enough, but a bit of a madhouse is it not? I am not sure I should like to repeat the experience.'

'I am certain you have not enjoyed all that can be offered there. Well, no matter. I thought you at least acquitted yourself quite well at the Royal Society. Father has so remarked.'

'Thank you for that, but I did not do all that much.'

'You did not shrink from conversation with others as difficult as it must have been. You must know that some of those who were present presume their discourse to be beyond the reach of their company, but not you. You engaged with equanimity and received respect in return.'

'Whatever you say, Edward.'

He remembered the letter he had stuffed into his waistcoat

'What have you there?'

'A letter that has only just come.'

It was from his sister Helen.

Dearest Brother,

It pains me no end to have to tell you of the passing of our dear Father…

Goodricke stopped reading to stare at the sky and catch his breath.

'John?'

'Father has died.'

Pigott immediately stood.

'What? John, I am very sorry to learn of it.'

'I owe him everything, Edward, everything.'

'Does it say anything of the circumstance?'

Goodricke returned to the letter.

'A chest complaint with fever. She does not say more. I had no idea he was even ill. I should have been told.'

'But was he not back in Holland? Do not berate yourself, or your sister. There was nothing to be done.'

'Perhaps. Yes, you are right. But I must now prepare to leave as soon as possible for home. The funeral and what not.'

'Of course. I am sure that Father and I will wish to assist in any way possible. We can take you there. It is Ribston, is it not?'

'Yes, sorry. I seem to be in a bit of a muddle just now.'

'Well, let us go in and see him now. He is working on his correspondence and should have this news.'

They were both silent as they slowly walked back to the house.

*

Funerals were observed by as much pomp as family resources permitted. Henry Goodricke's cortège made no small impact as it made its way from Ribston Hall to the nearby church. Black horses with black plumes pulling a funeral carriage in a pall of black velvet all clashing with sun-lit shades of green.

After the service, the family arrayed itself around the gravesite, a shadowy circle, solemn and silent. Goodricke looked across at his grandfather, now even more dour, if that was possible. Like all members of polite society, the Goodrickes were expected to behave in a calm and restrained manner, suppressing any expression of feelings in public, especially at funerals. His sisters wore hard faces, his mother was expressionless. It seemed she had, after all, adapted to the British way of life. As for his grandfather, his typically dispassionate bearing, for once, seemed appropriate. But Goodricke knew better. He would be no replacement for a caring father.

He reflected on how utterly fortunate he had been to have a father who refused to accept his deafness as a drawback. When younger, he simply assumed that all deaf children were seen to as he had been. Now he knew better. Was there anything of his father in him? Did this have anything to do with why he believed he must somehow help Cicero? In the way one thought drifts to into another he recalled what his Roman namesake, Marcus Tullius Cicero, wrote about the dead; *their life continues in the memory of the living.*

He vowed to keep his father's memory alive. But for now, he only wanted all this to be over with and return to the simple life enjoyed before ever leaving for London.

34

Changes

Summer ended, longer nights returned and more of Goodricke's time was taken up by astronomy. He had acquired a small achromatic telescope by Dollond that widened observing options. Correspondence now included Herschel, Maskelyne, Aubert and others. The new season may have brought clear skies, but the death of his father remained as a small cloud.

He brooded over whether he had made it clear just how grateful he truly was. They may not have had much time together of late, but it was enough to receive the occasional letter, it was enough to know he was in the world. Reunions in that strange world of dreams, were all that remained.

'Why does it need to be so tall?'

'…because the pendulum inside must be very long. The longer the pendulum, the more time it takes to swing from one side to the other. The shorter the pendulum, the faster it swings. So, you see there is one length where it takes exactly one second to swing from one side to the other. And that is the length you see before you.'

'If it is longer still, it moves slower and slower, is that not correct? And longer still?'

The dream ended and he awoke with the nagging thought he was about to discover something important, but he knew not what.

The loss of his father was not the only thing that dampened his spirit. When he first began his astronomical studies life was blessedly uncomplicated, his deafness easy to live with. But this had become increasingly difficult to do, causing him, ironically enough, to work all the more. Astronomy may have remained an easy diversion from the world's imperfections, but not from his own. His Warrington tutor may have been right; nature was best studied in silence, but that was the silence of the external world. An inner voice had a growing insistence he could not shut out.

How did drying leaves sound when they rustled in the autumn wind? Might this be a small sign of a summer's passing? What of that grouse he startled? How did it sound as it burst from the brush? He had once read that their cry was like a warning to walkers - *g'back, g'back, g'back!* He could not recall the song of any bird.

It was more than just the loss of audible nature. Any incidental sound could mark a moment or colour an experience. How would he have been different if he could hear? How could he ever know? Astronomy had been his one truth, but it was no longer the complete fulfilment it first was.

He had begun his work in astronomy by perpetuating the ancient Greeks who believed there was a difference between the realm of the heavens and existence on Earth. Planets were simply shaped bodies that moved in perfectly circular paths. Stars never changed in appearance or position. The sublunar world of mortals, however, was disorderly and impure. But the dichotomies of the terrestrial and heavenly worlds were becoming less clear. And, as the heavens were beginning to show deviations from perfection, it had also been a profound mistake to assume that the only real value of the Earth was that it provided a platform for viewing the stars.

He was, finally, beginning to admit there was more to life - even that brief visit to the strange world of Vauxhall Gardens taught him as much. And there was Hannah. He could no longer deny that her correspondence kept him from the vulgar and tawdry as much as did the stars. Maybe more.

Her letters lay in a small pile. He was at first unsure of what he wanted to say in his replies, but finally admitted that in their brief time together a connection had been established. She had grown impatient with the lack, or quality, of London suitors and made it clear she preferred his company. Her comment about his happiness still stung, but it somehow made her more appealing, not less.

Nonetheless, his work in astronomy hadn't wavered. Herschel had submitted a paper to the Royal Society on the proper motion of the Sun - an account of the direction in which it was moving as it coursed through the heavens. Goodricke wrote to Herschel saying how his conclusion *'perfectly coincides with my sentiments'*, but went on to point out that some stellar positions recorded by early astronomers and used by Herschel were in error. Herschel's denial prompted Goodricke to respond, in part, *'you seem not to have perfectly understood the meaning of my letter...'* Herschel may have been the senior of the two on a number of counts, but Goodricke knew when he was right.

*

Searching for another variable was now priority. Before beginning his observing on one September night, he returned to the introduction in the book Pigott had given him.

> '...*And as among the Sciences there are none which Astronomy comes behind on Account of its Antiquity, and the Pleasure that attends the Study of it, so it will yield to none of them on the Account of its Usefulness, and the Advantages it affords to human Life. By it we discover the wonderful Harmony of Nature, wherewith the Frame and Structure of all created Beings are*

> *linked and knit together, to constitute the great*
> *Machine of the Universe.'*

Keill may be just a bit windy, he thought, but he felt he needed some inspiration to help push all other thoughts aside before returning to his observing.

He blew the candle out, opened the casement, positioned his chair and began scanning. It was a clear calm night and the seeing excellent. Over a thousand stars spangled the sky as they rolled westward. One of them, somewhere, would have an anomalous brightness. The imaginary ecliptic running through Orion's belt made a handy referent. He first examined those stars nearest the western horizon. Nothing. He moved eastward and up from Lyra, Cygnus, through Pegasus, Andromeda, Perseus, Auriga, down to Orion and back again. Nothing.

He began his third scan and was panning away from Lyra when he sensed its pattern just did not look right. *Yes.* The second brightest star in that constellation, beta Lyrae, was *not* the second brightest star as it should have been. He was sure of it and did not wait until dawn to write in his journal. Squinting in the dim light, he wrote.

> *September 10. I thought that β Lyrae was much*
> *less than usual. It was much less than γ Lyrae &*
> *was less than a star of the fourth magnitude…*

This was what he was looking for. He could now investigate whether beta Lyra, like Algol, was a short period variable. He had his next star.

*

Three months later Pigott and Goodricke were sitting in The Grouse. The fire emitted a loud crackle and spat sparks, awakening a customer dozing at the next table. Goodricke sipped his coffee as Pigott looked up from his reading.

'How close are we to finishing beta Lyrae?' asked Edward.

'It is well finished. I thought you knew. I shall soon send the paper on it and it will be read early in the new year, I should think.'

'Who is reading it for you?'

'Sir Henry Englefield.'

'Ah, the very same Sir Henry who read my paper last week. Did you know John, we have become known as the York astronomers?'

'Have we indeed?'

'Father has related that this is so and, as he is one himself, I do not suppose he much minds.'

'What are we known for?'

'Our industry on variables mostly. What did you think? We have generated quite a bit of talk amongst the membership.'

'Banks as well?'

'Oh, forget him and his fawning foot lickers. No, I mean by the mathematical astronomers in the membership.'

'I have only written on Algol, Edward.'

'Do you still not understand? You discovered a variable with a shortened period, the first ever, and now you are about to introduce another. That these are the only two in all the heavens would seem an unlikely prospect, would it not? '

'I never thought otherwise.'

'But you do not press the issue of the cause.'

'To what end? Perhaps they are spotted and rotate like our Sun. Or perhaps they are orbited by a sister star. We shall not have the answer in our lifetime.'

'Perhaps, but that is no reason not to think on it.'

'If I am to speculate, I prefer to do so on another problem.'

'Yes, well, the less said about that the better.'

'Mock me if you must but believe I shall one day prove our little happy home to be spinning.'

'It is a little home, is it not? Have you ever wondered on the true extent of the heavens? Is every fixed star at the centre of its own system of planets every bit as full and large as our own? Is our Sun and her orbiting acolytes but an inconsiderable part? I forget myself. You do not speculate.'

'Again, to what end? Our abode may well be a tiny corner. But I tell you, sir, I would not esteem myself one whit less. Would you?'

'I do not esteem myself in the first instance,' replied Pigott, who was impatient to change the subject.

'John, I wish to propose a research problem we might share, but first I have a bit of news that I am not sure you will wish to receive.'

'That is all I need.'

'It may not be as bad as all that. Father has begun to discuss our return to France. If I know the man at all he has lit a long fuse. But not to worry. It will be months yet before there is a bang of activity.'

'You are right. This is not good news.'

'I thought I should mention it so that you do not come to visit one day and find only cobwebs.'

'There is no humour to be found in this, Edward. And why leave? I had the impression York was a place to settle, the final stop of the Pigott family pilgrimage.'

'A fair point. On the other hand, the Pigott family has spent as much time in France as here, more, now that I think on it. Anyway, I thought it best to mention it.'

They were both silent for a moment. Goodricke sighed and spoke.

'All right then. What is this research you began to mention?'

'Ah, yes. You wish to prove our planet turns on its axis. For what I propose we must assume it does so, so that should appeal.'

'And?'

'But does it do so with an equal motion? Why should we assume this? Now *that* would be something worth investigating would it not?'

'I suppose it would.'

'Would you be willing to be in aid of this?'

'What did you have in mind?'

'The idea is to determine whether the Earth turns on its axis with an equal motion.'

'How do you propose we proceed?'

'Equal motion would be the case where its velocity in the first three to six to nine to twelve hours is equal to the following three to six to nine to twelve hours. Would you agree to this definition?'

'Yes, sorry. Continue.'

'First, you will have to get as many of the best clocks by Mudge, Cummings, Arnold, etcetera, observe by them all the times of those stars which pass twice on the meridian in twenty-four hours. Do you follow?'

'So far.'

'Of course, you do. Their rate of going being known by the whole revolution of the fixed stars. Then see if this agrees with the half revolution. If they disagree then, maybe some difference will be found, especially when the Moon is in a special position. Well?'

'But if the Earth does not rotate this shall be a complete waste of time.'

'Sometimes I am close to throttling you,' said Pigott.

'Sorry. Still, though.'

'John, there are more important problems to work on.'

'Such as?'

'Such as I have just described, for one.'

'You are right. I shall assist of course. Your definition of the experiment seems sound enough. Mind you, I have no transit.'

'I know of one not too far from here.'

They return to their coffee, each musing. Pigott returned to his broadsheet.

'What have you there?'

'*The London Chronicle.*'

'I have never read it.'

'You ought to read more.'

'I do read.'

'Yes, well.'

'I do, Edward,' replied Goodricke while glaring at the table.

'Right then. What have you last read?'

'A paper from the *Philosophical Transactions* that...'

'My point exactly.'

'*The London Chronicle* is not exactly high literature.'

'What of it? In any case, our prejudices must come from someplace, must they not? And, as far as literature is concerned, I have just completed *Les Liaisons Dangereuses.*'

'Could you say that again, please?'

'Sorry. *Dangerous Liaisons* by de Laclos.'

'I did not know you read French.'

Pigott lowered the paper.

'John, my mother is French. I grew up in France.'

'Of course.'

Pigott returned to reading and snapped the paper forward with a start.

'Uh-oh. Here is some news you will not wish to receive.'

'What do you mean?'

'It seems your Dr Johnson has fallen off his perch.'

'What? When was this?'

Pigott looked at the date.

'Over a fortnight since.'

'May I read it?'

Pigott handed him the paper.

> *Last night between seven and eight o'clock, dies, in his 76th year, at his house in Bolt-Court, Fleet street, Dr Samuel Johnson, so universally known*

*and celebrated in the learned world, that nothing
we can say on that head can add to his fame.*

Goodricke quickly looked through the pages for more information.

'I believe this is just a first, brief notice. There is bound to be more in a later issue,' said Pigott.

Goodricke found a more recent edition on the rack. On the front page was more news as Pigott had predicted. He could not believe what he read, Johnson had left his complete estate to his Negro manservant, Francis Barber.

Pigott saw his friend was in some discomfort.

'It wasn't as if you knew him all that well.'

'Perhaps, but there was much to learn from him. He may have displayed an intemperate coolness, but he was warm at his core. I know that many thought him at odds with society. There again, there is much to be at odds with.'

'I expect that is indeed true.'

'You say that, but I do not see it in your conduct.'

'Nor I in yours, John. Do not assume those who are aware of inequity, but do nothing, are somehow more exemplary than those not so aware.'

Goodricke knew he was right and wondered why he had criticised his friend for doing as little as he had himself.

'Of course, Edward, apologies. It is just that I wish the same good fortune for others as I have enjoyed.'

'One is simply born to good fortune, John, and there's an end to it. Perhaps I do not dwell on the imperfections in our society, but this would only serve to make me melancholy. I simply choose not to be so, otherwise I should make a miserable companion.'

No, my friend is not a cynick, thought Goodricke. *He is simply detached in his own Pigott way.*

'Well, Edward, I thank the Lord for that. Let us remove these thoughts and find an alehouse. Are we in agreement on this, at least?'

'I would say that is the best idea you have ever had.'

'I will be glad when this day is over. I will be glad when this *year* is over.' said Goodricke as they got up to leave.

Father's passing, Pigott departing and now this news of Johnson.

'I am reluctant to consider what the new year shall carry forward, Edward.'

'Life, John. A mere series of events. It will not do to refine upon its nature.'

The customer at the next table had resumed dozing.

35

Beta Lyra and Delta Cephei, 1785

Joseph Banks became uneasy when the letter from John Goodricke arrived. It wouldn't have anything to do with Herschel's Algol paper or that tea garden debacle, would it? It was a while ago, after all. He was relieved to learn it had nothing to do with either. Goodricke had written on behalf of someone named Cicero Samms, excellent at illustration, and would he be so kind as to enquire of William Aiton, the Director of Kew Gardens, whether there might be a position that could make use of his talent? Goodricke was aware, apparently, of Banks' role in the creation of Kew and adroitly assumed this young man's chances would be improved were the introduction to come by way of him.

The letter also explained he was sending drawings to convince him that his representation would not be an embarrassment. *So that what must be in that tube that has also arrived.* He opened it to find magnificent illustrations of *Digitalis purpurea* and *Ilex verticillata*. The orchid was especially exquisite.

He thought for a moment and decided, why not? If word of his involvement on behalf of an acquaintance of Goodricke's became known, and he would see to it that it did, what harm could it do? It should, at the least, promote an image of even-handedness, of someone free of all

351

prejudice. Whether it was actually true was another matter entirely. He reached for his quill.

*

Attendance was high at the Royal Society meeting, despite the winter weather. Word had spread that another paper by that young York astronomer was to be read. Sir Henry Charles Englefield was introduced and began reading Goodricke's paper before the membership.

> *Dear Sir. The account that has been lately given of the regular variation of Algol's light, and the notice astronomers have been pleased to take of it, are well known. It is natural to therefore suppose, that the relation of other similar phænomena may also meet with the same favourable perception. Of this kind is the following, which I beg the favour of you to present to the Royal Society.*

He looked up to see he had everyone's attention, and continued.

> *On the 10th of September 1784, whilst my attention was directed towards that part of the heavens where β Lyræ was situated, I was surprised to find this star much less bright than usual, whereupon I suspected that it might be a variable star: my suspicions are afterwards confirmed by a series of observations, which have been regularly continued since that time, and which will presently follow in their proper place. At first I thought the light of this star subject to a periodical variation of nearly six days and nine hours, though the degree of its diminution did not then appear to be constant; but now, upon a more close examination of the observations themselves,*

> *I am inclined to think, that the extent of its*
> *variation is twelve days and nineteen hours, during*
> *which time it undergoes the following changes.*

Englefield paused briefly for dramatic effect and continued.

> *1. It is of the third magnitude for about two*
> *days.*
> *2. It diminishes in about one day and a quarter.*
> *3. It is between the fifth and fourth magnitude for*
> *less than a day.*
> *4. It increases in about two days.*
> *5. It is of third magnitude for about three days.*
> *6. It diminishes in about one day.*
> *7. It is something larger than a star of the fourth*
> *magnitude for little less than a day.*
> *8. It increases in about one day and three*
> *quarters to the first point to complete the whole*
> *period.*

A more detailed list of observations made over sixty-eight separate nights followed. A single cycle of the brightness variations took twelve days and nineteen hours. Like Algol, it too was a short period variable, but, unlike Algol, the magnitude changes varied continuously. In Algol, the brightest magnitudes held steady before dimming to minimum magnitude, but in beta Lyrae the brightness changes were continuous throughout the entire cycle. Also, there were two minimum magnitudes, with one a whole half magnitude dimmer than the other. Goodricke's only reference made to the cause of these variations was that they might be due to 'spots upon the surface of a rotating star'.

Maskelyne listened intently and at the conclusion of the reading was convinced Goodricke had discovered yet another short period variable. He knew the diligence necessary to accurately measure the brightness of beta Lyrae to nearby comparison stars. It was exceptional work. Still, knowing the political climate, he preferred just one more such example before he would begin in earnest to campaign for Goodricke's inclusion as a Fellow. That would make it just about impossible for anyone to deny his acceptance. He departed without speaking to anyone.

*

News of the positive reception of the beta Lyrae paper gradually reached Goodricke. He had to admit to himself that it did matter, after all, what others thought of his work. Well, a certain few anyway. When he first began observing, he looked at everything - comets, sunspots, the Moon. But he now largely devoted his time to variables. Delta Cephei was his next target.

The winter of 1785 was particularly unfavourable and robbed him of weeks of observing, but by March the weather cleared and he returned to the delayed study of this star in earnest, another short period variable. From his earlier observations reaching back to October through to June, he managed to observe it over ninety nights, using his well-honed method of comparing its brightness to that of nearby stars. When he was finished, he knew he had a correct result. Delta Cephei was a variable star with a period of five days, eight hours and thirty-seven and a half minutes. He addressed his letter on this discovery to Nevil Maskelyne that concluded by asking *If you think this account worthy of notice, I beg you will be so kind as to communicate it to the Royal Society.*

Again, he was not inclined to commit to a cause of variability, especially since this star's brightness changes were different still – they were far from symmetrical. The interval from maximum to minimum brightness was over five times that of minimum to maximum. He would leave it to others to attempt to explain the cause of *that*. It was only important they understood his observations were correct.

Maskelyne indeed thought it all correct and read Goodricke's paper on delta Cephei to the Royal Society that autumn. At its conclusion, he was asked a question by William Wales, an astronomer who had sailed on Cook's second voyage to observe the transit of Venus.

'Thank you, Reverend Maskelyne for your presentation of this excellent work. I wish, however to ask for a point of clarification, if I may, sir.'

'You may proceed.'

'At the end of Mr Goodricke's account - he has written that the cyclic period of the variability of delta Cephei is five days, eight hours, and thirty-seven and one-half minutes?'

'Yes, that is what was so determined.'

'And this was all done with the unaided eye?'

'Of course.'

'Thank you, sir. I wish to impress upon all assembled here how difficult this must be. I daresay, it is an accuracy achievable only through deep commitment. Mr Goodricke has indeed provided us with another remarkable result.'

And, thought Maskelyne, *he shall be rewarded accordingly.* He now began to plan for Goodricke's admittance as a Fellow.

36

Kew Gardens, Summer

How are you keeping Cicero?'
'Well, sir. Me well.'

Goodricke had sought out Cicero in the greenhouse.

'You have planted a lot of new things in here.'

No reply.

'Cicero, you enjoy working with plants, do you not?'

'Yeah mon, but you know it now.'

'But are you not even better at drawing them?'

'Maybe. I no know.'

'How would you like to spend more time drawing them and get paid for it as well?'

Goodricke was eager to tell Cicero that he had received a letter from no less than William Aiton, the director of Kew Gardens. He had the answer he had hoped for. A position for an illustrator was now available and would this Mr Samms be interested?

'I have just received a letter from William Aiton.'

'Who that is?'

'William Aiton is the Director of Kew Gardens in London, well, in Richmond, nearby. Do you remember those drawings I asked for?'

'Yes, but it is some time now. What is this Kew Garden?'

'The formal name is the Royal Botanic Gardens at Kew and they want to know if you would like to work for them as an illustrator.'

'How this happen?'

Goodricke placed his hand on Cicero's shoulder.

'I had those drawings sent on to Kew and asked if they might take you on as an illustrator. They like your work Cicero. Do you understand? They want to know if you might be interested in going there to work for them.'

'You joke me a joke.'

'No, Cicero, no joke.'

Cicero walked over to a bench and sat.

'I did not want you to be disappointed. That is why I never said anything. You do not have to do this. You can stay on here and there is an end to it. But think on it.'

'But what Mrs Dalrymple say?'

'I am sure she will be happy for you. I know this is all quite sudden, but you have to ask yourself if you want to spend the rest of your days here in this garden.'

Cicero shrugged. 'I no know. You want to stay and keep looking from your window?'

Goodricke was caught off balance. He sat next to Cicero and tried to think of the right answer.

'Cicero, the stars are the same no matter where I view them from. But this, this is different. You will be moving to a whole new world.'

'Let me think 'bout it, like you say. I have time?'

'Of course. You have time.'

They sat there for a moment while neither of them spoke. They both knew that the offer would be accepted, and that Cicero would be leaving

'You know, some nights me can't sleep so I come out and look at dem stars meself.'

'Be careful of the Barguest,' said Goodricke with a smile 'What that?'

'A large dog that walks about in the night - an evil spirit.'

'Sound like Jamaican Duppy.'

'I imagine so. I suppose every place has its evil spirits.'

'Truly. Anyway, I come out in the night. When I look up I can see you sit in your window sometime. You work long nights, don't it?'

'Yes, yes, I do, maybe too much. Anyway, that was all I had to say. Please think on it, but do not leave here before helping to set the clock! It will have to be timed with Mr Pigott's again soon. And one more thing.'

'What it is?'

'I shall miss you, Cicero. I truly will.'

*

Later that autumn Joseph Banks was sitting in his club sipping his postprandial port when William Aiton appropriated the next seat.

'Joseph! Fare thee well?'

'Oh, Aiton. Well enough.'

A waiter approached.

'Sir?'

'I'll have another. Will you join me?'

'Most kind, Joseph. I believe I shall.'

'Very good, sir,' said the waiter.

'So, how are things keeping at Kew?'

'Fair to middling. Fair to middling.'

'I am sure they are better than that,'

'Well, we have taken on a new illustrator.'

'Is that so noteworthy?'

'Do you not remember? You recommended him.'

Banks had to stop and think.

'Oh that. Yes. I never heard anything and had forgotten about it altogether. So, you took the fellow on?'

'We had to consider our economies for one thing. And there was the other matter to consider.'

'What other matter?'

'Joseph, Joseph, Joseph. No need to pretend old boy - the fact that is he is a Negro, well, a mulatto, but the same thing. Still, though, he is very skilled and the public need not interact.'

Their port arrived, but Banks was now thoroughly distracted.

'Sir?' said Hightower when Banks did not lift his glass from the tray.

'Yes, yes, thank you,' said Banks. He took his glass and handed Aiton the other.

'What do you mean - a Negro?'

'Just that,' said Aiton as he sipped. 'You know, Joseph, I did not have you down as one of these anti-slavery types. Was it not you who was instrumental in having breadfruit introduced into the West Indies from Tahiti to feed the slaves and keep them productive. Or am I mistaken?'

Banks' flushed. Whatever his personal feelings regarding slavery they could never take precedent over the requirements for stewardship of the Royal Society. It would be unwise to take a position in opposition to the Society's benefactors and supporters. This was not what he had done, of course, but it did put out the scent of where his true sympathies might lie. When it came to slavery he was ambivalent at best. He, like many others, believed it should simply be left to die a natural death as society developed. He regained his footing.

'No, you are not mistaken, Aiton, and anyway, what of it? The young man is talented as you say so we should both feel this a demonstration of our, our impartiality and fairness. Would you not agree?'

'Of course, of course. Just having a little fun Joseph. No harm done, eh?'

'Indeed.'

'On another matter, the newly appointed Governor of the Bank of England, George Peters…'

'Yes, yes. I have received an invitation to his event as well,' said Banks, with a hint of impatience.

'Excellent. See you there, Joseph,' said Aiton as he downed his drink and departed.

Oh, Goodricke - you clever, clever lad, thought Banks as he drained his own glass and called for another.

37

Letters, Autumn

Goodricke again arrived late for the evening meal, a habit he had long acquired. The other residents had already departed, and he and Eleanor were alone.

'More tea? Anything else?'

'Thank you, no. The meal was very enjoyable.'

'John, may I ask you something?'

'Of course.'

'Do you recall, some time ago now, when Mr Guthrie enquired whether the Earth rotated?'

'Yes, Mrs Dalrymple, but he was asking if there was any proof of this. We know she rotates.'

'Of course, but his question has held my interest, and apparently yours as well. I was just wondering whether you have secured a solution. That is all.'

'Many would know of it if I had. But no, no solution as yet.'

'Does this take you to much distraction?'

'Do I appear distracted?'

'I must confess it does appear so, at times. Is there something else that occupies your mind of late?'

'No, ma'am.'

'May I ask another question?'

Uh oh, he thought, *she has been working up to something*.

'Of course.'

'It is absolutely none of my business, but who is Hannah Upton?'

She caught his startled expression.

'John, there are few secrets here. It has been easy to see who has been sending you these many letters.'

Emeline, thought Goodricke.

'She is a friend. We were at Mr Braidwood's together.'

'And her home is in London?'

'Yes.'

He did not like where this was going.

'But has it not been some time since you were there? When do you plan to return?'

'I have no such plans, not at the moment anyway.'

'Do you not care for her?'

'I…yes. Yes, I do.'

'Well then.'

'I am not sure what to say, Mrs Dalrymple.'

He had surprised himself with this disclosure.

'I am sorry to cause discomfort, but feel I must speak plain.'

Eleanor's remonstrations were usually tinged with humour. Not this time.

'There are times when I feel I have come to know you, John, and other times when you are a complete mystery. What I do know, what I believe, is that there is one way in which we are all the same. We all want love, whether we wish to admit this or not. For some it is easy to find, others find it hard. But it is always easy to lose. Do you understand what I am trying to say?'

'No, ma'am.'

'John, I fear you may find fault with a fat goose.'

'I do not understand.'

'Yes, you do, John. Her letters have been arriving for some time, yet you remain in place.'

'Mrs Dalrymple…'

'John, hear me out. Everyone has but one true love in life. As for myself, I doubt I shall ever find another. I shall say his name and see his face when I die. What shall you take with you? Life is brief, John. Take care that the one hoped to meet does not become the one you cannot forget.'

Goodricke had never heard Eleanor refer to her husband or speak in such a personal manner. He attempted to change the subject.

'Shakespeare, was it not?'

Eleanor rose and placed her hand on his shoulder.

'No, John. That was me,' and she stepped away.

A perceptive woman, is our Mrs Dalrymple, he thought. He had tried to return to his simple life, but thoughts about Hannah would never allow it. Mrs Dalrymple was right. How much longer would he remain sitting by his window? Was he looking at the stars or now hiding amongst them? Was this what Samuel Johnson sensed? His mind raced as he trudged up the stairs to his room.

*

Later that evening, Goodricke found he could not shake off Eleanor's counsel. He reached for his quill, thought for a moment, and wrote.

9 October 1785

Miss Hannah Upton
Cavendish Square
London

Dearest Hannah,

I pray this shall find you and your parents in continued good health and spirits. I have been well myself, although too often tired. I put that down to not only observing during the nights but sleeping less during the days. What a fix this is!

It has now been a year and more since we shared the experience of Vauxhall Gardens. That day combined the pleasure of not only your company, but also a magical part of London not ordinarily encountered. I see now I was too eager to return to my pattern here.

I shall not blame you should you assume this to be yet another missive relating more of my unremarkable days in a dull province or simply another accounting of my work with the stars. I fear that I have too often failed to distinguish a page in my journal from a letter to you. Unfortunately, there is more to recount of my nights than of my days, and would not blame should you be a little jealous of Andromeda.

I have often thought on a return to London, but only with the intimation that our reunion was but ancillary to some wider purpose. Your company would simply be incidental to matters related more to my alleged profession. This has not happened because it bears no inspection for honesty. It would be an odious perjury. I do not understand why I have not journeyed simply to see you, and there's an end to it.

I have demurred at allowing you to believe the sole purpose for any return was to have your company. My desire to do so may be a reluctant admission that my little life here, begun in hope and optimism, may have run its course and it is now time to depart. It is, however, difficult to do so before I can more fully understand the next chapter. Permit me, though, to now freely admit that a visit requires no justification beyond the solace of your companionship. If there is to be anything beyond that it can only be learned in your presence and not through these miserable scratchings alone.

Yours most sincerely and respectfully,

John Goodricke

Hannah Upton read, and reread, his letter. She was not quite sure what to conclude. Was he asking whether he might come to London with the express purpose of seeing her? He did not seem to half dance around the subject. She concluded though he was confessing that he was finding it more and more difficult to predicate a return to London on professional priorities alone. The truth was that the desire to see her again had overtaken them. She collected her thoughts and replied.

A C Theokas

26 October 1785

John Goodricke, Esq.
The Treasurer's House,
York

Dearest John,

I am well, as are my parents who offer their own warm regards in return. Thank you indeed for your concern as to their situation.

I must write that yours of 9 October provoked much thought. It was not dressed in the usual borrowed robes of rhetoric but came more from your heart, a most welcome departure.

Please forgive my admonition, Sir, but you have been a tad slow off the mark! I rejoice in that you appear to have moved from it at long last.

Your company would be, as it has always been thought to be, most assuredly welcome. We here are all pleased no end you solicit a return to Cavendish Square, if indeed that was what you were asking!

I fear, Sir, you do berate yourself unnecessarily when you say your prose has suffered from an imbalance of topic. Any words from you are a pleasure. When we correspond, our mutual affliction is lain all aside and we communicate with unburdened facility. Do you not see this? It is where we can be the most direct and the least misunderstood. I must hasten to add this does not mean that your company would not be a welcome substitute to the page.

Priscilla and I have continued to visit tea and pleasure gardens. There are so many here! The latest visit has been to Ranelagh Gardens. The main attraction is the Rotunda. It is a huge space some liken to the Pantheon in Rome, although I have never seen that. It is quite spectacular with all manner of exquisite displays of paintings, gildings and a thousand lamps that imitate the performance of a noonday Sun. One can easily see how this attraction seeks only to secure the company of those of an elevated station. It was all occupied by the great and the gay wearing cloths of gold and glittering with precious stones. We also saw a firework display upon our exit. They had something called Fruiloni Wheels, I believe. Have you ever seen such a thing? They are

*quite large and fire shoots off as they madly spin about. The Sky
Rockets were perhaps the most to exhilarate, soaring quite high up
whence they explode producing a rain of stars most colourful! Of
course, one cannot hear them, but it must be an almighty bang as I
could feel their concussion.*

I pray I do not I prattle on.

*I shall conclude. But let me state that I now look forward to your
next visit. Will you let me drag you about to such scenes?*

Yours most affectionately,

Hannah

*

Goodricke reflected on a '*rain of stars most colourful.* and
thought of his own stars as dead and cold by comparison.
The night was free of cloud, the stars sharp and clear, but
he went to an early bed and was soon asleep.

38

Edward, Winter 1786

Goodricke believed that Cicero would have eventually moved on, with or without his help. But Cicero's question why *he* remained lingered. Then there was Mrs Dalrymple, saying in her own way, that he might want to think of moving to London before it was too late. And now Pigott had asked they meet. He suspected that he wanted to announce his own departure. That was bad enough, but he sensed that Pigott would also ask why he remained. *What do they all see that I cannot? How has my once simple life become so complicated?*

Edward arrived.

'Fancy a walk, old fellow? It is a splendid day and I thought we might secure a meal afterwards. Pay Cassie a visit. I'm sure she would love our company.'

'I'll just get my hat and cloak. I should inform Mrs Dalrymple I shall not be here for the evening meal.'

'Right enough. I'll wait for you outside.'

Shortly afterwards, Goodricke joined Pigott in the forecourt.

'What did you have in mind?'

'I thought a stroll along the New Walk first would be pleasurable. What do you say?'

'Fine,' replied Goodricke, now certain Pigott wanted more than just a stroll.

They walked in silence to the beginning of the New Walk at Skeldergate Bridge. A popular attraction, it stretched for over a mile to where the River Foss joined the Ouse. In keeping with a preference for order and formality, hedges were planted to separate the gentrified walk from the surrounding 'natural' and wilder landscape. They walked under elms that provided the leafy avenue with shade and dappled sunlight.

'Have you heard anything from your former groundskeeper?'

'Cicero?'

'Yes. Seemed a nice enough fellow, although we never actually spoke.'

'I have had the one letter. It seems he has settled in well at Kew.'

'Yes, I know all about what you did.'

'What did I do?'

'John, really. Father said Aiton had a chuckle over that one. Who would have thought – Joseph Banks given a tumble by the likes of you when so many others tried and failed. I say, sir.'

'I was not trying to give him a tumble.'

'If you say so.'

'Honestly, I was not. I was just trying to help Cicero.'

'Well, *I'll* believe you, but thousands won't. Who now attends the gardens there?'

'No replacement as such. Eleanor's relation sends over someone from time to time to keep things in order. It is his property, after all.'

'Do you miss him?'

'Cicero was not easy to get to know. Perhaps I am not either, for that matter. But, in the end, we had a true friendship. And do not forget, he did help me set my clock.'

'Yes, well, how will you set it without me? Without the Pigott observatory?'

Goodricke stopped walking and squared up to Pigott.

'What?'

'It's done, John. We are leaving. Pulling up stakes and returning to France.'

'So, what are saying? That you are leaving York for good?'

'There are no plans to return so, yes, likely for good.'

'When?'

'A few weeks. I depart first and then father and mother follow in the spring.'

Up until this point Goodricke had never really imagined what life would be like in York on his own. The heyday of their friendship was over and a feeling of impending loneliness struck.

'Where will you go?'

'Louvain.'

'But why leave at all?'

'I could simply say it is our itinerant way. But you have to understand that we have already spent a great deal of time in France. My mother misses it. I was educated there. Father's professional reputation was made there. The coming transit of Mercury is best seen from there. It is more like a return home than the leaving of one. And you must admit that York is a bloody bore.'

Goodricke had to agree. Whether York offered more than an open window and a clear view of the stars was of little concern when he first arrived, but no longer.

'Cicero has left and now you. How shall I ever set my clock?'

'Well, as I say, Father does not leave until spring. I am sure he will be happy to offer any assistance you may require.'

'I know you have mentioned leaving, but it does seem rather sudden all the same.'

'I am sorry for it, but it has been on the cards that we would again move on, it was just a matter of when.'

'What about our collaboration to study the Earth - to learn whether she spins with constant speed?'

'I am afraid that will have to wait a bit longer. Gives you more time to learn whether she spins at all.'

'Edward, I never suggested that.'

'No, of course not. Sorry to jest. You shall, I am certain, one day announce a proof of this.'

'Perhaps.'

'But what about you, John?'

Here it comes.

'What about me?'

'How much longer shall you remain here?'

'I am not sure. Why should I leave?'

'Why do you want to remain is the question Why not remove to London?'

'You may be right.'

'Of course, I am right. Go to London. Enjoy life more.'

'I shall miss working with you, Edward.'

'We can correspond.'

'Then I shall miss your company.'

'And I yours as well. But do not change the subject. Is it not well past time you returned to London to pay her a visit? Besides, you have outgrown York, have you not?'

'Edward, have you entered into some sort of conspiracy with Mrs Dalrymple?'

'What? Good Lord, no. Why ever ask? Ah, I see. She has suggested much the same, has she not? Well, it must be good advice then.'

How is it we became friends? thought Goodricke. He was boringly bookish while Pigott was reckless and self-indulgent, but their shared humour and moody moments meshed as gears in a clock's train, each prodding the other into motion. In the end, though, it was astronomy itself that was the bond.

'Yes, Edward. It may well be time to move on myself.'

'That's settled then. Cassie awaits.'

39

April 1786

Spring came after a winter of too many drab days and starless nights. It offered the promise of little more than warmer weather. His solitude may have felt good, but it no longer felt right. Perhaps an acceptance into the Royal Society as a Fellow might be the final push needed to move to London? It would certainly erase any lingering doubts that his work on variables was his own. But what would Hannah think? What did he hope she would think? He was discovering that the rules of logic that held him in good stead with his astronomy had limited application to life itself.

After picking over his evening meal Goodricke rose to return to his rooms for a night of observing.

'But you have eaten little,' said Eleanor.

'Sorry. Not much of an appetite of late.'

'Well, perhaps you might have something later.'

'Thank you, Mrs Dalrymple.'

By the time he completed the climb to his rooms he felt a new shortness of breath accompanied by a pain in his chest with each inhalation. Nonetheless, he set about another night's observing and any terrestrial trials were soon forgotten as he reached for the stars and their perfect light.

*

Nevil Maskelyne began the meeting of the Council in a confident mood. The three candidates to be voted on for admittance as Fellows included Goodricke. There were twenty-one members, but the attendance was always less. A casual count showed the majority were 'mathematical astronomers', three of which, including himself, had read Goodricke's papers at the Society's meetings. Even a few of Banks' so-called followers would support him, he suspected. No real advantage would come from his chairing the meeting, but it did add extra pleasure.

After the usual preamble, the vote began on Goodricke.

'Mr Nathaniel Pigott.'

'Aye.'

'Reverend Andrew Shepherd.'

'Aye.'

'"Mr William Wales.'

'Aye.'

After the eighth 'aye' was heard Maskelyne let out a small sigh of relief, an emotional display for him.

Before passing around the prepared document for their signatures, he read it aloud.

> *John Goodricke, Esq. of York, a gentleman well versed in various branches of Mathematics, particularly Astronomy, and well known to this Society, on account of several valuable Papers, which he has communicated, being very desirous of becoming a member thereof: we whose names are subscribed, do of our own personal knowledge, certify that he is very deserving of the honour he solicits, and likely to become a valuable and useful Member.'*

Nathaniel Pigott thought he detected a slight tremolo from the usually sonorous Maskelyne.

*

'A letter has arrived, ma'am. For Master Goodricke.'

'Who is it from?'

Emeline squinted at the address.

'A Nevil Something from The Royal Society, ma'am.'

Eleanor told herself she wasn't being nosy, but she did wonder whether it had been from a Miss Hannah Upton of Cavendish Square.

'Why don't you take it up to him then?'

'Yes, ma'am.'

Eleanor returned to the kitchen. After a few minutes, Emeline stood in the doorway, kneading her hands.

'He is not well ma'am. Best come quick.'

Eleanor raced up the two flights of stairs, outpacing the younger Emeline. Goodricke lay in twisted sweat soaked sheets. He turned his head slightly at Eleanor's touch.

'Oh Lord, he is much with fever.'

'Sorry,' said Goodricke, barely audible.

'Emeline! Dr Marlowe! Fetch Dr Marlow - the one just down Bootham Road. Emeline!'

Eleanor now noticed the wide-open window.

'And shut that bloody window!'

Emeline broke free from her trance.

'Yes, ma'am!'

Eleanor dipped a cloth in the basin and wiped his forehead. Without his wig he looked more youthful, exposed. Goodricke tried to focus his eyes.

'Sorry.'

'Stop saying that!'

She hastily added another blanket. It seemed an hour, but it was only a few more minutes before she heard a commotion on the stairwell.

Marlowe entered carrying a small bag. Eleanor thought it was only for appearance sake, since there wasn't all that much he could ever do anyway. She thought him old and ineffectual, but it was needs must.

'Mrs Dalrymple. Now what seems to be the urgency? Your maid here could hardly construct a declarative sentence.'

Eleanor stood aside and gestured at Goodricke.

'I see. Now, young fellow, let's see what this is all about, shall we?'

Eleanor finally noticed the cold grate.

'Emeline, make a fire and keep it going.'

She turned back to the physician who had begun his perfunctory exam. His expression grew graver by the minute and then he stood to face her.

'This is as bad as it can be, I am afraid. He has fever, rapid breathing and his pulse is serrated. He also suffers a sharp pain in his side just here.'

The blanket had been pulled back and he applied a slight pressure to Goodricke's side causing him, and then Eleanor, to wince.

'Is it the pneumonia?'

'I am afraid that it is. How long has he been like this?'

She could not recall. Did he attend yesterday's evening meal or was it the day before?

'A day, possibly two,' she said, her voice beginning to break.

'So, this is likely a rapid onset. The disease is now virulent within. How old is the lad?'

'How old? Um, he is just twenty-two. No, twenty-one.'

'He seems a bit slight.'

'Is that a problem?' asked Eleanor.

'Youth can help if it comes with vigour.'

'Can anything be done for him?'

'Some are bled but I must confess I am not in support of this approach. Others recommend the bowels be opened with a clyster but again I am not in favour…'

'Oh, for God's *sake*! What *are* you in favour of?'

'Yes. Of course. Cold compresses, China tea if you have any. A warm poultice of mustard, chalybeate waters to purge…'

373

Eleanor could barely listen. Her heart sank. She could not blame the physician for his lack of a cure. There was none. Either Goodricke would survive this or he would not.

'Let me consult with a colleague. I shall return this afternoon. In the meantime, just keep him comfortable. But I must warn you of the seriousness of this. Any relatives should be contacted.'

He turned to leave just as a breathless Emeline entered, carrying a bucket of coal.

'Right. You tend to the fire and I will see about some clean bed linens,' said Eleanor.

She looked about his room. Nevil Maskelyne's letter lay on the table, unopened as Emeline furiously built a fire in the grate. Why had this happened? A lack of warmth and food is what brought this about, all too late now. She felt an irrational hatred for the stars.

'Emeline, stay here while I sort the linens and tea. Keep this cold compress on his forehead. Did he say China tea? Yes, I think I have that…but we will not purge him or bleed him or anything. Let him be at peace.'

'Yes ma'am,' said Emeline, now fighting back tears.

As Eleanor left she thought she must inform someone, but whom? The Pigotts have left and Goodricke's family were not nearby. *We are his family now*, she thought.

*

Dr Marlowe did not return until the early evening. Goodricke lay in clean linens and was wiped free of sweat. Nonetheless, his laboured breathing had worsened.

'I have spoken with a colleague who confirms my diagnosis. I fear this to be at an advanced stage.'

Goodricke sensed the presence of others, but could not keep his eyes open and did not have the energy for speech. Despite the fever, his mind remained clear. He thought of his father. He could hear *him* speak, at least.

'Why does it need to be so tall?'

'The pendulum must be very long. The longer the pendulum the more time it takes to swing from one side to the other. The shorter the pendulum the faster it swings. So, you see, there is one length where it takes exactly one second to swing from one side to the other. And that is the length you see here.'

'But what if it were longer…'

'It would take longer to complete one swing'

'And what if it were even longer still? What if it were very long?'

'Why then, slower still.'

Suddenly, he is back in the dome at St Paul's. The little girl is still there, standing on the side opposite. She waves at Goodricke to get his attention. What does she want? She vigorously points upward. He looks up into the top of the dome to see a cord hanging from the centre, slowly moving. He follows it downwards. A pendulum bob is on the other end, moving through its long slow arc, inches from the cathedral floor. He looks back at her. She has her palms held up as if to ask, 'Can you not see what is happening?'

He looks again. The pendulum bob now swings in a different direction as if its plane of motion has twisted in space. But how can this be? It cannot. It is the entire cathedral itself that has moved.

I understand! The only force acting on the pendulum is gravity and gravity acts only downwards. It therefore cannot cause any twisting of the pendulum's plane of motion. There is simply no other force present to cause this. Therefore, the only other explanation for the apparent rotation of the pendulum's plane of motion is that it is not the pendulum that is moving, it is the Earth and the cathedral along with it. Gradually, the floor, the walls, the entire cathedral shall appear to rotate about the pendulum. This, at last, is experimental proof the Earth rotates. How simple!

Goodricke gasped, opened his eyes and tried to speak.

'What is he saying?'

Marlowe leaned in closer to his weak whisper.

'I can prove it. Please. I can prove it.'

'What is he *saying*?' pleaded Eleanor.

Marlowe looked up and shook his head.

'I am afraid he has become delirious.'

I understand it now. I have solved the problem.

The pendulum slows. Slower still. It comes to a dead stop.

Marlowe searched for a pulse and found none. He looked up at Emeline and then over to Eleanor.

'I am afraid the young lad has had his time.'

'What does he mean ma'am?' pleaded Emeline.

'He has passed Emeline, he has passed.'

Eleanor managed to control herself, but Emeline was lost to tears.

Marlowe was now all business.

'I shall assist in any way I can to help with the arrangements, of course. I am sorry, Mrs Dalrymple. Is there anything else I can do to assist?'

'No, nothing,' whispered Eleanor, now gripped by grief. She looked about for some task to steady herself, something to keep from fainting dead away.

'I shall see to his things.'

*

Later that week Eleanor returned to Goodricke's rooms with a heavy step. She had promised to have his possessions sent on, but it was a closure difficult to accept.

His writing table had remained just as he had left it. The correspondence stacked in one corner reminded her of the unpleasant task ahead to inform others. Besides Edward, Hannah, and Cicero she thought to add the Astronomer Royal who would likely pass on the news to others in his professional circle.

She saw the globe on his table and gave it a little spin. Had he solved that problem? He would have told her if he had.

What should happen to his little library? Perhaps Mr Pigott could advise.

One title caught her eye, Samuel Johnson's *A Journey to the Western Islands of Scotland*, a travelogue of a journey taken some years earlier. It gave her a small start to see it was signed by Johnson himself. Master Goodricke could still surprise. She turned to a bookmarked page and read the underlined text:

> *'It was pleasing to see one of the most desperate of human calamities capable of so much help; whatever enlarges hope, will exalt courage; after having seen the deaf taught arithmetick, who would be afraid to cultivate the Hebrides?'*

She carefully slipped the book back into its spot and looked about. There was not all that much to pack away, not much to show for five years. His rooms had to be prepared for a new occupant, but her heart was no longer in it.

Epilogue

London, Louvain, Liverpool

Nevil Maskelyne did not have to venture out to the offices of the Royal Society, but Eleanor's unexpected news compelled him to do so, despite the weather. Wind and rain whipped through the forecourt at Somerset House as he arrived. He proceeded to the records room and retrieved the official declaration of Goodricke's election as a Fellow. He found a desk, borrowed a quill and added a simple statement:

> *Mr Goodricke never was admitted. He died soon after his election.*

A few acquaintances, surprised to see him, received only a brief nod as he returned to his waiting boat.

*

Hannah Upton was inconsolable. Sir Thomas returned home to find his daughter on the settee, eyes red and glistening. Caroline, holding her in a gentle grip, looked forlornly at her husband and then nodded to the letter lying on the carpet before them. Upton read it, looked at his daughter and was at a total loss for words.

Hannah could barely speak through fresh tears.

'He is gone, papa. I shall never see him again.'

Sir Thomas Upton sighed, walked to the window and stared out at a rain swept Cavendish Square.

*

A day later Cicero Samms was detailing a water colour as a young lad approached.

'Cicero Samms?'

'Yes?'

'I was asked to bring this to you. A letter from York.'

He said it as if it came from the moon.

'Thank you.'

Cicero was pleasantly surprised to see it was from Eleanor. After reading it he folded and refolded the paper as if he could somehow squeeze it out of existence. He carefully cleaned and replaced his brushes and told others he needed a brief walk. Not sure at first where to head, he made for the Chinese Pagoda and its contemplative atmosphere. He had often thought of Goodricke. Why had he helped him? He wished he had got to know him better, but his presence at Kew told him enough.

*

Edward Pigott sat on the sun-lit terrace of his new residence in Louvain, a bottle of Bordeaux nearby, the letter from Eleanor next to it. He wanted a glass or two in him before he opened it. It would not be about the weather in York. He read it and then reread it as if somehow the words might have changed or that he misread it. He put his head back and thought of his friend, of the many conversations they shared. He had underestimated how much he missed his companionship and any thoughts of it resuming were now forever put to rest. He returned inside to locate a paper about to be submitted to the Royal Society: *The Latitude and Longitude of York Determined from a Variety of Astronomical*

Observations. He picked up his quill and edited the last page.

> *I have again marked with an asterisk the observations made by Mr Goodricke, who desired me to communicate them. This worthy young man exists no more; he is not only regretted by many friends, but will prove a loss to astronomy, as the discoveries he so rapidly made sufficiently evince: also his quickness in the study of mathematics was well known to several eminent persons in that line.*

He returned to the terrace and refilled his glass.

*

The *Aurora* gently rocked at her berth in Liverpool. She had arrived from London to collect passengers and speciality cargo for the Atlantic crossing to Boston.

Captain Joshua Taylor, anxious to sail, oversaw preparations to weigh anchor. He watched a crewmember ascend the mainmast ratlines to negotiate the difficult transfer to the futtock shrouds reaching outwards and upwards. When he did not drop to the deck Taylor returned his full attention to the purser.

'Are all the passengers aboard, Mr Hawley?'

'All but one, sir.'

'And who is that, pray?'

Hawley ran his finger down the manifest.

'A Mrs Eleanor Dalrymple.'

'A married woman? Alone?'

'Not quite, Captain. I understand her to be a widow of some standing.'

Taylor stepped to the gunwale, looked at the waiting horizon and then turned to his purser.

'Why was I not informed of this? Nothing untoward shall be tolerated. Spread the word, Hawley.'

'Yes, Captain. Um, there is another matter, sir.'

'What other matter?'

'I have been informed one of our passengers may be attempting to pay off his debts with our topsail.'

'Is he indeed?'

Taylor knew this could mean delay. He did not know whether it was even true and made a quick decision.

'Perhaps we do England a service by removing a swindler to the Colonies. That should be sentence enough.'

'I agree, sir. Except they are no longer the Colonies.'

Taylor frowned.

'Sir? I believe this may be her now.'

Eleanor Dalrymple was hastening up the gangway, carrying a hat box and portmanteau. A bearer followed, dragging a large trunk. Hawley rushed over to assist and received a breathless 'Thank you, sir.'

Captain Taylor approached as she stepped aboard.

'Mrs Dalrymple, I trust? I am Captain Taylor and this is our ship's purser, Mr Hawley.'

'Yes, Captain. Apologies for my late arrival.'

'Nonsense, not at all. We welcome you aboard the *Aurora*. I trust you will find your accommodation sufficient and we shall endeavour to make your voyage as pleasant as possible,' said Taylor with a slight bow.

'Now, if you shall permit me, ma'am, I must see to our departure.'

'Of course. Thank you, Captain.'

Taylor found her dark beauty intriguing. *Why is this woman undertaking such an arduous crossing alone? Perhaps she will agree to dine with me one evening.*

'Mr Hawley, - escort her to her quarters.'

Eleanor took one last look around before stepping below. Well-meaning friends had questioned this journey, but she was determined. She would sail to Boston, find her husband's grave, and lay a flower upon it.

Author's Note

Goodricke's Time is not an alternate history. The major characters, Johnson, Braidwood, Enfield, the Pigotts, Herschel, Banks, and Maskelyne, all lived and interacted with Goodricke. An attempt was made to convey the customs and conditions of eighteenth century England with realistic detail and fidelity to historical fact. In that spirit, words and expressions peculiar to that time are frequently used and I make no apology for this. All text that is both indented *and* italicised are verbatim extracts. This includes material from Goodricke's own astronomical journal, letters published in the *Philosophical Transactions,* Banks' announcement on the awarding of the Copley, the addendums regarding Goodricke's passing written by Maskelyne and Pigott and direct quotes from several books.

Fictional characters such as Eleanor Dalrymple, Cicero Samms, Hannah Upton, and Percival Slee are introduced to augment, not alter, the orbit within which John Goodricke moved. History provided events and a timeline that needed little alteration.

Léon Foucault, in 1851, was the first to demonstrate that a pendulum's 'twisting' plane of motion was the long sought experimental proof the Earth rotates. While there is no evidence that Goodricke ever actually thought on this problem, it is indicative of his dogged determination.

Today, we have a Big Bang of books on the conditions of the early universe, the end of physics or the beginning of time. Amidst this popularisation of astrophysics, it is all too easy to regard Goodricke's own work in classical astronomy as prosaic, even rudimentary.

The practice of classical astronomy, however, still requires specialist, long-established skills. Just ask any keen amateur. They will tell you it would not be a trivial task to locate the constellation Perseus, identify Algol and, using only the naked eye, paper, pencil and simple pocket watch, accurately determine its period of variability to within a few seconds.

Goodricke could not have imagined his legacy. The most important physical property of a star is its mass. It is this that determines the radiative energy it will produce and for how long. The majority of stellar mass determinations have been made from the analysis of eclipsing binary systems, such as Algol. He could never have known for certain its variation was due to a sequence of eclipses, a conclusion that had to await confirmation in the spectroscopic era. But he made that all-important first step.

Astronomers cannot perform experiments using stars, but if they could, one would surely be to place one star near another to see what happens as their separation is varied. Stars, however, perform this experiment for us. We now know that some evolve to become red giants - they bloat as they evolve. If they orbit a nearby companion star, and are near enough, then some of this expanding stellar material will fall into the gravitation well of the companion. It was Goodricke who first discovered the complex light changes such a system produces when he observed beta Lyrae.

He never concluded all short-period variability was due to an eclipse. His historic timings of the brightness changes of delta Cephei showed them to be highly asymmetrical, unlike Algol. This was not the type of variability expected from two objects orbiting, and periodically eclipsing, one another. Later spectroscopic analysis revealed this star was indeed not a binary, but a single star that brightened and dimmed as a result of its own contraction and expansion. This discovery led to the creation of a new class of stars, Cepheid variables. One hundred and twenty-five years after Goodricke the periodicity of this pulsation was discovered to be dependent on their luminosity or their actual energy output. If you know how bright a Cepheid, or any star, appears and you know its luminosity, its distance can then be determined in a straightforward manner. In this way, Cepheids became the first rung in the ladder of galactic and extra-galactic distance scales.

It is impossible to know how deeply deafness affected Goodricke's view of life. What we can be sure of is that he was very bright and certainly dedicated. For him to overcome deafness in that era was an accomplishment in itself, achievements in astronomy notwithstanding. Historians of science typically only briefly allude to this disability before turning to his astronomy. The world of the deaf Goodricke occupied deserved more of a telling.

Astronomers in the late eighteenth century shared a common ideal of intense, even reckless, professional commitment. They often endured, as a result, prolonged exposure to hard winter nights and many, such as Flamsteed, presumably took ill because of this. We cannot know whether such an exacting regimen directly lead to Goodricke's own poor health, but it does provide poignant meaning to a passing that eclipsed the lifetime of work he had ahead of him.

A.C. Theokas

Made in the
USA
Middletown, DE